BEYOND THE LIMIT

CINDY DEES

Published by Sourcebooks Casablanca, an imprint of Sourcebooks
P.O. Box 4410, Naperville, Illinois 60567-4410
(630) 961-3900
sourcebooks.com

Printed and bound in Canada.
MBP 10 9 8 7 6 5 4 3 2 1

Chapter 1

GRIFFIN CALDWELL GROANED AS HIS BUDDY—HIS exceedingly shitfaced buddy—Axel Adams stood up, waving a flimsy plastic champagne glass in his meaty fist and slurred, "A toast. To the groom. The greatest guy ever to shove a grenade up a camel's—"

Griffin leaped up and slapped a hand over Axel's mouth in the nick of time. But the sudden movement made his own shitfaced head spin and his stomach alarmingly threaten revolt. "*Sit. Down*," he hissed to Axel.

On Axel's other side, Trevor Westbrook yanked on Axel's massive arm. Between Trev and himself, they managed to wrestle the mountain of a SEAL back down to his seat.

Axel grinned lopsidedly at him. "You look like a"—he let out a yeasty belch that made Grif rock back in his seat, grimacing—"like a jackass in that clown suit."

Grif grinned down at his powder-blue tuxedo, complete with a chest full of blue-edged ruffles. His baby-blue bow tie hadn't survived much past the wedding ceremony and hung untied around his neck. He would've tossed the stupid thing entirely, but they had to return the rented tuxes tomorrow and he wanted his deposit back. It had been a joke for them all to show up at their teammate Leo Lipinski's wedding wearing the ghastly things.

Janine, the bride, had been annoying bordering on bridezilla about the whole shindig, and they hadn't been able to resist an urge to poke that beast. She'd been anal-retentive about planning the wedding down to the last detail. Well, not the very last detail. She'd forgotten to tell the groom's brothers on SEAL Team Reaper to behave themselves.

Wait till she climbed in Leo's car and got a whiff of the vanilla extract they'd poured into the car's air-conditioning system. Every time the car ran for the next month or so, it would smell overwhelmingly like chocolate chip cookies. Or till she got her groom naked later and discovered that, after he'd passed out at his bachelor party, they'd doused his entire body with blue shoe dye. Only his face and hands had been spared. Poor bastard looked like a Smurf and would for a couple of weeks.

Chuckling, Grif raised his champagne glass to Leo, who scowled back from the head table, obviously worried at what else they had in store for him. Smart man.

A vibration in Griffin's pants pocket made him rock his front chair legs down to the floor and dig out his cell phone. His *work* cell phone. The other guys at the table were abruptly reaching for phones, too.

Crap. They were supposed to be off duty tonight.

He looked at the caller ID. Their boss, Commander Calvin Kettering.

Either the old man was doing Leo a solid and pulling them out of the wedding reception before they could raise more hell, or the world was coming to an end. Off-duty SEALs were, well, *off* duty, except in the direst of emergencies.

"Aww, man," Ken Singleton complained from across the table. "I was just about ready to bust out with a new song."

Ken was a wannabe country singer-songwriter and actually had a decent voice. But the guy's talent for lyrics, that was another matter. Griffin grinned. "Let's hear the chorus."

Kenny drummed a snappy rhythm on the table and sang, "Run, Leo, run. Look what you have done. Don't mean to be rude, but dude, you're screwed. Janine's knocked up, and her daddy's got a shotgun."

The team's baby, Sam Dorsey—barely into his twenties and straight off the gullible boat—gasped. "Is that why Leo married Janine?"

Grif guffawed, registering with amusement the glares from guests around them. His cell phone vibrated again. Insistently.

"Party pooper," Axel complained, glaring at his own phone, housed in a black leather case with a chrome skull mounted on it. "Reaper Team's on leave."

Griffin stood up, hauling on the larger man's arm. "C'mon, big guy. We gotta go." There were two kinds of SEALs: the lean, fast ones, of which he was one, and the slower, strong-as-an-ox ones, of which Axel was the poster child. The guy wore a long beard and a leather vest, and he rode a chopper when he was off duty or not wearing a blue tuxedo at his teammate's wedding.

"Don' wanna go…"

Trevor picked up an unopened bottle of champagne. "C'mon, gents. We'll take the party with us."

Griffin nodded gravely. "Now you're talking. This is why you're my favorite redcoat wanker." Trevor was a crossover guy from the British SAS, handsome, elegant in bearing, and a hell of a fine operator.

Joaquin "Jojo" Romero staggered to his feet, causing

Griffin to do a double take. Jojo was a freaking incredible athlete—hell, he'd been drafted by the NFL—and was never clumsy. Although, come to think of it, Griffin couldn't remember ever seeing the guy drink before, either.

With his free hand, Griffin snagged the open bottle of whiskey Kenny had smuggled in earlier. Ken was the team's ALPO—alcoholic libations procurement officer—and damned good at his job.

In a gaggle of baby blue, they piled out of the officers' club and into the crew bus the text had said would be waiting for them outside. Passing around the bottle, they polished off the whiskey while the bus drove them to an airplane hangar on the Naval Air Station Whidbey Island flight line. It was raining tonight in northwest Washington State, and headlights and taillights sparkled outside like white and red jewels. Or maybe Grif was just drunker than he'd realized.

With a start, he realized this wasn't just a ploy by Kettering to get them out of Leo's wedding. A crew chief waved them over to a sleek Learjet parked near the hangar entrance. It was hooked up to a ground power unit, and the interior and exterior lights were on.

WTF? They were going somewhere tonight?

But…their kits…a mission briefing…their support team… Crap, he was confused. And his head was starting to pound. He needed more hair of the dog.

"Welcome aboard, gentlemen," an Air Force pilot who looked about twelve years old boomed.

"Hush. Not so loud." Trevor enunciated with breathy care. "We're all very drunk."

The copilot grinned. "So I gather. Technically, it's

illegal for you to bring that liquor aboard a military aircraft."

Griffin winked at the kid. "If you don't tell, we won't have to kill you."

The copilot's smile widened. "We'll turn the heat up back here so it's nice and warm for you guys. You'll have a few hours to sleep it off before we get to our final destination."

Grif jumped on that. "Which is where?"

"Classified."

The copilot paused in the act of pulling the accordion-fold door across the cockpit entrance and bellowed, "Sweet dreams, ladies."

Somebody launched a plastic champagne glass in the kid's direction, and he retreated, laughing.

The engines wound up, their high-pitched scream splitting Grif's *effing* skull in two. A collective groan went up around him.

"More champagne, gentlemen. That'll fix what ails us," Trevor announced.

The jet taxied out for takeoff, and they passed around the bottle, taking turns chugging from it. As the plane lifted off the ground, climbing into the night, Griffin closed his eyes and passed out.

Sherri Tate looked around the WWII–era army base and artillery range. It had long ago fallen into disrepair and was well on its way to derelict. Better this, though, than endless rounds of press conferences and cocktail parties with handsy senior officers and drunken congressional staffers pawing at her.

When Calvin Kettering had approached her a few months back and asked if she would consider trying out for the SEALs, she'd been all over any assignment that would get her out of Washington D.C., out of nylons and high heels, and out of range of men who assumed that because she was attractive she was also stupid.

She was stoked to finally experience the real military. She wanted sweat and dust, bugs and sunburns, honest physical exertion. Maybe here at this secret training facility she would finally get a chance to be more than just a pretty face.

Two insanely fit-looking women came out of the rusted Quonset hut before her, wearing tank tops, shorts, and athletic shoes. One was tiny, blond, and shaped like a gymnast. The other was of medium height, brunette—maybe of South Asian–Indian heritage—and ripped like a bodybuilder.

"Ladies," Commander Kettering said briskly, "this is our newest trainee."

The two women stopped in their tracks and jumped to attention as soon as Kettering spoke.

He continued. "This is Sherri Tate. Sherri, these are Lily VanDyke and Anna Marlow. They'll show you the ropes."

No ranks. Interesting. She got that rank didn't much matter in the SEALs, but she was startled—and secretly pleased—that he'd ignored military protocol completely. Without another word, Kettering turned, climbed back into the Hummer, and drove out of sight. Only a trail of dust marked his passing.

"Welcome to the weirdness, Sherri," Lily said

brightly. Even in combat boots, the woman barely came up to Sherri's chin.

Anna added in a husky voice that would be sexy as hell if Sherri rolled that way, "Is that your only bag?"

Sherri glanced down at her duffel. "Commander Kettering told me to pack light." Truth be told, he'd emailed her a packing list so detailed he'd even told her how many sports bras to bring and had specified no thongs.

"Did he forget to tell you to pack tampons, too?" Anna asked laughingly.

Sherri rolled her eyes. "Do either of you know what he has against thongs?"

The brunette grinned widely in response. "Did you pack some anyway?"

"Of course. Out of general principle," Sherri retorted.

Laughing and joking about male fixations on female undergarments, they stepped into the Quonset hut. The back half of the space was stuffed with stacked, rusted metal bed frames, wooden desks, and office chairs straight out of the 1940s, their vinyl seats shredded with mildewed stuffing hanging out.

The front half of the space was appointed like a typical military barracks, the walls lined with single beds, a footlocker at the bottom of each, and a center aisle down the middle. Six beds were neatly made up.

"Are there other women here?" Sherri asked, looking around for more candidates to fill the beds.

"Nope. Just Anna and me," Lily answered. "Our guess is Kettering plans to end up with a half-dozen women here."

As she claimed a bed and footlocker, into which she

transferred her uniforms, plus plenty of workout gear, Sherri asked, "What did Commander Kettering tell you about this program? I know practically nothing except the Navy wants to train women SEALs."

Anna replied, "Lily has the dirt on that."

Sherri looked expectantly at the petite blond, who said shyly, "My brother works in the office of the Joint Chiefs of Staff. He heard a rumor that the new Secretary of Defense, Rita Chilvers, ordered the Navy to graduate a woman from BUD/S and put her into the SEALs. Apparently, she declared it past time to tear down the last male bastion."

"The SEALs can't be happy about that," Sherri replied.

Lily snickered. "Oh, they're livid. If they got their way, they would never let a woman play in their sandbox."

Sherri privately disagreed with Lily. If a woman was strong enough, fit enough, and mentally tough enough to play with the big boys, there wasn't much the SEALs could do to keep a woman out of their hallowed ranks… except kill her.

Which she might not put past the SEALs to do, if push came to shove.

"Personally," Anna added, "I don't mind getting paid to run around in the woods for a few months. I was already training for the CrossFit games. Now I'm getting paid to do it full-time, and with a bunch of hot guys thrown in. Win-win for me."

"What hot guys?" Sherri asked with interest.

"Kettering says a SEAL team is going to help train us."

"As in they're going to run us through BUD/S here?" Sherri asked, startled. Basic Underwater Demolition/SEAL training was *only* taught at Naval Base Coronado in San Diego.

"That's what I hear." Anna's dark eyes sparkled as she flipped back her luxurious black hair. "Most of the SEALs I've seen are *hawt*."

Lily leaned forward. "What are they like? We don't get them on army posts I mean, we have Rangers. And they're all gung ho about blowing stuff up. But I hear SEALs are even tougher."

Sherri sighed. She'd met plenty of Special Forces types. Or at least wannabe special operators. They bathed in testosterone and actively worked at being arrogant jerks.

Anna replied, "I hear SEALs don't talk much and can go all night." She waggled her eyebrows suggestively.

Sherri grinned. "In other words, they're perfect one-night stands."

Fair-skinned Lily blushed, which made Sherri and Anna laugh.

Lily lowered her voice. "Cone of silence?"

Sherri and Anna nodded and leaned in close to her. Lily murmured, "My brother overheard the Chief of Naval Ops say the fix is on. They've decided to graduate one woman from BUD/S regardless of how she does, just to shut up the Secretary of Defense. They're going to create a recruiting poster for publicity purposes and never use the woman as a real SEAL. Then they'll wash out all the other women who try for the teams."

Lily might as well have kicked Sherri in the gut.

Nausea rolled through her as Kettering's plan became crystal clear.

Sherri had been a pageant queen. She was willowy, blond, blue-eyed, and beautiful. Furthermore, she was a public affairs officer, accustomed to speaking to the press. She could deflect the hard questions and diplomatically redirect the rest. Heck, she was even training for the Olympics in heptathlon and was in ridiculously great physical condition. Of *course* Kettering had chosen her to be a fake SEAL and silence the powers that be.

Great.

Just great.

Calvin Kettering didn't intend to let her—or any other woman—be a *real* SEAL. Was she never going to shed the plastic beauty-queen image?

Scholarships from the pageants had paid for a college education she could never have afforded on her own. But no one had warned her she would never live down being a beauty queen. Pageant promoters might call them "talent" contests or scholarship competitions, but to most people they were still about hot babes in bikinis.

She asked, "If they're not going to let any of us be actual SEALs, why did Kettering bother hauling us to some secret facility to train? Why not just toss us in the regular SEAL training pipeline and let us go down in flames?"

Lily shrugged. "No idea."

Sherri sniffed a mystery.

Anna said seriously, "Lily and I have a pact. Regardless of who's chosen to make it through, and regardless of how they try to pit us against one another, we're going to remain sisters and refuse to backstab each other."

Thank God. "I'm in," Sherri declared. "We stick together no matter what."

The three of them traded fist bumps to seal the deal.

Anna added, "Speaking of which, there's a decently equipped gym down the street. Lily and I have been working out around the clock in anticipation of the SEALs kicking our butts when they get here. We were just heading over there. Wanna come?"

Sherri grinned. "Hell yes."

Griffin was the first to wake up. The pressure change of the descent had crammed ice picks in his ears, and he cleared them quickly. He shoved up the window shade, and a shaft of brilliant sunlight blinded him. He slammed the shade back down. Crap on a cracker, he felt like death.

More prudently, he eased the shade up an inch to peek outside. Sunlight glittered off patches of water winding through forest below. *Da hell?*

He kicked Trevor's foot and reached over the headrest in front of him to tap Axel on the side of the head. "Rise and shine, kids. We're getting ready to land," he announced.

The others roused, Axel slower than the rest, but then he'd been drunker than the rest. Griffin still didn't feel entirely sober, but he could fake it if he had to.

Kenny groaned. "Remind me never to mix whiskey and champagne again. I feel like my ex ran me over with a truck and backed up to make sure she killed me."

Griffin snorted. Kenny's ex-girlfriends were exactly the type to do that. The man liked his women wild.

His watch said it was 5:00 a.m. That would be West Coast time. Given that the sun was up, they'd obviously flown east through the night. But to where? And why?

He waited impatiently while the jet completed its descent and landed. He didn't see a single building outside. Just trees and more trees. He felt naked going into an unknown situation without at least a sidearm—but Janine had insisted: no guns at her wedding. And Leo had reluctantly backed up his bride.

The interior of the jet went silent, abruptly watchful, as the aircraft pulled to a stop. No one moved as the smart-ass copilot opened the hatch, lowered the steps, and announced sarcastically, "We're here. You can go now."

What the hell? Today is as good as any to die. Griffin scowled and, hunching over in the low-ceilinged aisle, made his way to the exit. The bright morning light was excruciating, but that wasn't what made him squint in deep displeasure.

Nope. That honor was reserved for his boss and the trio of women standing with him on the tarmac, all of them smartly turned out in uniforms—one in navy whites, one in marine beige, and one in army green—all spit-polished and standing tall.

The other guys piled out behind him in a disorderly jumble, and he was suddenly acutely aware of what a disheveled mob they made, slouching in rumpled lounge-lizard tuxes, all of them in need of a shave and a shower, smelling like booze and stale sweat, cringing away from the sun and their hangovers.

As one, the women burst into gales of laughter.

They were laughing at him and his guys.

Laughing.

He was a United States Navy fucking SEAL, for crying out loud. The pride of the American armed forces. The best of the best. Embarrassment started a slow burn in his gut.

The smoking-hot blond on the end who honest-to-God looked like Malibu Navy Barbie gasped at Calvin Kettering. "Good one, Commander. Where'd you scrape up these losers to masquerade as SEALs? You really had us going there…" She dissolved into another fit of laughter.

Griffin indignantly straightened to his full six-foot-plus height, but he supposed it was hard to take a guy seriously when he looked like a bad impersonation of Dean Martin and smelled like a sewer.

Kettering looked even grimmer than usual. "It's not a joke. These…degenerates…are SEAL Team Reaper. The hand-picked team I've chosen to turn you ladies into the first female Navy SEALs."

A bucket of ice water couldn't have sobered up Griffin faster. *Female SEALs?*

Female.

SEALs.

"Come again, sir?" he choked out.

"Welcome to Operation Valkyrie, gentlemen."

Sherri slid behind the wheel of the topless Jeep, slipped on mirrored sunglasses, and peered sidelong at the dark-haired hunk shrugging out of his baby-blue tuxedo jacket to reveal a ruffled white shirt clinging to acres of muscles. He was six-feet-two of rugged deliciousness as he tossed the stained jacket in the back of the Jeep and swung into the seat beside her.

Kettering had briskly introduced him as Reaper platoon leader Griffin Caldwell, who had the good grace to look chagrined as the commander declared the men unfit to drive and ordered her to take the wheel of the Jeep.

She steered the Jeep behind Kettering's Hummer, which everybody else had piled into. The vehicles drove away from the asphalt runway in the middle of Nowhere, USA and headed deeper into nowhere.

Her passenger filled more than just the seat beside her. His masculine presence filled the whole Jeep. He smelled like whiskey and the clean sweat of someone who worked out a lot. It was actually a whole lot sexier than she'd like to admit.

She'd met SEALs at various formal events in DC, but they'd always been buttoned into starched uniforms, tugging at their shirt collars and looking intensely uncomfortable in the limelight. This was the first time she'd ever seen a SEAL in his native environment, bumping down a dirt road, his gaze on a swivel, headed into an op—that ridiculous baby-blue tuxedo notwithstanding.

She stifled a smile as she eyed her passenger discreetly.

Serious confidence poured off the guy. Not in an aggressive way, rather in a quietly self-assured way. Nope, this was no scrawny desk jockey. Griffin Caldwell was a warrior in prime fighting trim. He seemed at ease in his body. She wished she could say the same.

It wasn't that she didn't like herself. She just wished sometimes that she was less...conspicuous. Heads turned everywhere she went. Maybe that explained her longing to wallow in mud. It might hide her looks.

"Where are we?" Griffin asked in a sandpaper-rough voice that made her toes curl into tight little knots of pleasure. Muscles rippled along his jaw when he spoke through a feral stubble of beard.

"Camp Jarvis," she answered, surprised that he didn't know.

"What state are we in?" he blurted out.

"I'm in a state of rest and general well-being, looking forward to starting training. You look like you're in a state of acute life-choices regret."

"You're hilarious," he grumbled. "Seriously. What state in the United States are we in?"

"North Carolina. South of Cape Fear near the Atlantic coast. Camp Jarvis was an Army base in World War II. Decommissioned after the war. Marines from Camp Lejeune use parts of it to practice blowing stuff up. A piece of it has been cordoned off for us to train in."

"Train for what?" he asked sharply.

She blinked. What part of the phrase *female SEALs* didn't he understand? She answered smoothly, in her best public affairs officer voice, "Commander Kettering will fill you in on the details."

Caldwell swore under his breath, obviously deeply displeased by this whole adventure and by her evasion.

Tough. She wasn't about to be the one to torque off this big guy. Not in the confines of a small vehicle, and not while he was scowling like he seriously wanted to strangle someone.

He yanked the baby-blue tie from around his collar. The cheap satin slithered across the tanned, corded tendons of his neck and had her swallowing hard. He tossed it over his shoulder into the back seat.

Keep your composure, Sherri. If you're going to be working with these men, you have to get used to all that…testosterone.

Her public affairs training kicked in again. Make conversation. Keep it light. Casual. Distract him from why he's here.

"Wedding?" she asked sympathetically. She had her fair share of butt-ugly bridesmaid dresses lurking in the back of her closet. But she'd never been forced to wear anything to compare with the sheer hideousness of his schlocky tuxedo.

She swerved a little as Griffin pulled the blue cummerbund from around his narrow, hard-looking waist. He twisted to the left and leaned toward her to pull the thing from behind his back, and his face came within about a foot of hers.

She made the mistake of glancing over at him. Good Lord above. That man's eyes were as blue as sapphires. And glittering as brightly with irritation. Except, when her gaze met his, his expression changed in an instant, heating into blue flame. He assessed her with a thoroughness that stole the oxygen from her lungs.

"You're a beautiful woman."

"Thank you," she said automatically.

"No. I mean it. You're *really* beautiful."

"I am aware that some people think so," she replied dryly.

He settled back into his seat, facing forward. She risked a single sidelong peek, and was relieved to see him staring ahead stonily.

Belatedly, he gave the cummerbund a flip into the back seat.

"What is a woman like you doing out here?" he demanded without warning.

"Driving?"

"Why won't you give me a straight answer?"

She shot back, "Because they're not my answers to give. Why won't you just be patient and wait for Commander Kettering to explain everything?"

"Because I got hauled out of my buddy's wedding and flown across the entire country while I'm supposed to be on leave after a long-ass deployment in a twice-filled shithole. Kettering's explanation had better be good."

She had no idea if helping train the first female SEAL would constitute "good" in his world. Somehow she thought not, and opted not to answer.

His big, tanned fingers moved down his front nimbly enough to make her gulp as he unbuttoned the ruffled shirt and shrugged out of it. As the wrinkled cotton peeled away from his body, she practically drove into the ditch. *Kowabunga*.

She'd expected these SEALs to be built, but not like *that*. Griffin's skintight white T-shirt could have been painted onto a set of washboard abs straight off the pages of a porn magazine. Not that she had the time or inclination to look at such things. Well, not often, and not sober. Initiated by her girlfriends, of course.

A thick vein ran the length of his impressively bulging left biceps. She took advantage of him looking off to his right to sneak a full-on gawk, and all of his muscles were sharply defined, ripped, and real. *Hell-ooo, sailor*.

She was running out of mental superlatives to describe the man.

The Hummer ahead turned onto the unmarked dirt road that led to their classified training area, and she followed. They bumped past an electrified steel fence marked with big red signs ordering everyone to stay out. She parked beside Kettering's Hummer and jumped out as the other five men and her teammates piled out of the larger vehicle. Her legs actually felt wobbly.

Griffin came around the back of the Jeep to join her, his gaze sliding down the length of her body and back up. Slowly. Thoroughly. Taking in the length of her legs, the slim fit of her white slacks, the fill of her tailored white uniform blouse. That gaze missed nothing. And made her tingle in places she didn't often *tingle*.

"My, my, my," he murmured softly, for her ears only. "The scenery out here is spectacular."

Spectacular, huh?

Pot, meet kettle.

Anna must be having mental orgasms. All of the other men were, in their own ways, as hot as Griffin Caldwell. There would be no shortage of eye candy around here when the other guys lost those dopey tuxedos.

Kettering pointed at the buildings, starting with the Quonset hut on his left. "Instructors' racks. Your kits are in there, gentlemen. I had your go-bags and the other gear you'll need sent ahead. Weapons lockup is next door. That warehouse on the end is outfitted as an urban assault training facility."

He pointed at the row of buildings across the dirt road, starting with the big one on the far end. "Gym. Cafeteria, infirmary, common area, and my office.

Swimming pool is behind the gym. Quonset hut opposite yours is the trainee bunkhouse."

He pointed at the last prominent feature of their miniature facility. "And that is the bell. I assume it needs no explanation."

Everyone who'd ever considered being a SEAL knew about the brass bell mounted in the middle of the BUD/S training facility. Anyone who rang it was out. Done with training. Done ever trying to be a SEAL. Sherri would *die* before she touched it.

Kettering barked, "Tate, Caldwell. You're swim buddies."

She gulped and glanced at Griffin, who was still frowning as if he'd missed some important piece of information.

Kettering paired up tiny Lily with a mountain of a guy called Axe, which Sherri sincerely hoped was a nickname. Axe sported a bushy beard over craggy features and struck her as the sort who either ate rusty nails for breakfast or was actually a total teddy bear under that gruff exterior.

Anna was paired up with a guy Kettering called Trevor. He was the only SEAL who didn't look like he was on the losing side of a bad hangover this morning. In fact, he managed to look halfway dapper in his obnoxious blue tuxedo.

The other three men—introduced as Kenny, Sam, and Jojo—looked smug at not being assigned to a woman.

Then Kettering snapped, "What are you all standing around for? PT gear. Back here in five minutes. Move!"

Sherri made it back outside in three, which was why she was present when Griffin strode over to Kettering and asked softly, "What are we doing, here, Cal?"

"You heard me. We're training these women to be SEALs."

"No woman has made it through pre-pre-BUD/S at the Naval Surface Warfare School so far, and that's nowhere close to the actual BUD/S course in difficulty."

Sherri's eyes narrowed. The way she heard it, several women had met the fitness standards of the pre-BUDS program, but they'd been drummed out for other totally BS reasons.

Kettering shrugged. "We're going to train this bunch until they can hack BUD/S."

Griffin snorted. "How long are you planning to keep us out here? Forever?"

Kettering's voice was implacable. "As long as it takes."

Griffin shook his head in disgust as Lily and Anna came outside. "You've had some crazy ideas in your day, boss, but this one takes the cake."

She barely caught Kettering's muttered retort. "Who said this was my idea?"

Griffin flung her a derisive look as he headed for her side. He'd grasped Kettering's meaning instantly and wasn't about to take her seriously.

She sighed. It would have been hard enough in the best of circumstances to get these men to accept her and the other women as fellow operators. But it would be darned near impossible without Kettering's unqualified support.

The other men strolled out of their building, wearing black T-shirts bearing an image of the Grim Reaper carrying a giant scythe on the front. *Right. Team Reaper.* She'd heard of them. She'd given a few press briefings about their exploits tracking down and capturing high-profile terrorists.

Everyone fell into formation, women in the front row, men slouching in the rear...and making no secret of ogling the ladies' rears.

Sherri ignored Caldwell's stare burning a hole in her running shorts. She hoped he enjoyed the view. It was as close as he'd ever come to getting inside her britches. Anna made a point of grinning over her shoulder at the guys, while Lily looked mortified.

Kettering spoke to the group. "Welcome to Operation Valkyrie. As I've already told Grif, I brought you men here to train the first female SEALs. We won't be running this like the formal BUD/S course in California. But we will simulate BUD/S conditions and training requirements."

"Hooyah," one of the men muttered from behind her.

Kettering continued grimly. "One more thing. Only one of these women will go to the BUD/S facility in Coronado. She will be the public face of women in the SEALs. The other two candidates will stay here and complete their spec ops training away from the prying eyes of the press. Assuming they can survive the course."

Sherri's stomach dropped to her feet. The last thing she wanted was to be thrown into competition against her fellow trainees.

"Whoa, whoa, whoa," Anna blurted out. "Are you saying that one of us will be a sacrificial lamb, thrown into the spotlight and not a real operator, while the others get to be actual operational SEALs?"

"That's correct," Kettering replied.

Well, that sucked. Particularly since Sherri knew which one of those Kettering thought she would end up being. Anna and Lily were plenty attractive and could certainly be made camera-ready. But she was the one with years of experience under her belt dealing with the media and with military politics.

Kettering gave the men a long, hard stare and then said sternly, "We're all professionals here, and we have a job to do. Let's get to it."

Faint grumbling was audible out of the back row.

Kettering turned the formation ninety degrees, which put Griffin beside Sherri at the front of the pack. They took off running while Kettering turned and walked toward his office.

Griffin made a point of letting her set the pace. Eyes narrowed, she started her wrist stopwatch and stretched out into a 10K racing stride. Might as well start earning these guys' respect right away. She knew from running with Anna and Lily that both of them could handle this brisk clip. She also happened to know this pace would meet the pre-BUD/S run-time requirement for a 10K distance.

"You think you can hack the big leagues, Blondie?" Griffin—Grif—she would just stick with Caldwell—drawled at her as they headed down the road.

"I do."

"Care to place a small wager on whether or not you'll last a week out here?" he shot back.

Something about his tone just irritated her—like a grain of sand in her eye, or a pebble in her shoe. Maybe it was the smug way he looked at her. Or the patent disbelief in his dark, dark blue eyes that a woman would dare to breach the sacred male fortress of the SEALs. Or maybe it just pissed her off that any one man could be so damned attractive.

"Name your bet," she snapped.

"Loser buys a bottle of whiskey for the winner."

"I'll do you one better," she challenged. "Loser buys a limited edition hogshead of Glengoyne single-malt aged scotch for the winner."

Trevor whistled from behind them and commented in his crisp British accent. "The lady knows her fine spirits."

"You're turning me on, talking dirty like that, Tate." Griffin flashed her a grin so hot it made her miss a step.

The man. Had. Dimples. Tactical nuclear dimples.

Damn, damn, damn. She was a total sucker for them.

She barely righted herself in time to avoid face-planting on the gravel path.

Returning his insolent smile, she let her gaze slide down his magnificent body and back up to his face, where his grin faded, replaced by a smoking-hot stare that would have incinerated a lesser woman.

Her right eyebrow arched. "You think you're man enough to keep up with me, Caldwell?"

Chapter 2

Griffin was here to hate these women. Hell, to break them. Kettering had made that clear without saying it in so many words. Grif had no time for reluctant admiration. But the oh-so-hot Miss Tate had guts to challenge him openly like that.

He drawled, "Darlin', I know I'm more man than you can handle. So, are you gonna take the bet or not?"

"You're on," she ground out. "And don't call me 'darling.'"

He laughed quietly at her elbow. "Oh, this is going to be fun."

Griffin had to give it to Blondie. She ran like a SEAL. Her stride was long and steady and relaxed. But then, the woman was built like a freaking cheetah, all long limbs and lean, slinky body, and she moved with the grace of one. She looked like she could keep up this blistering pace all day long. Her breathing was deep and easy. Nice control she had. Not many amateur athletes had it. Must have had some marathon training.

The three stooges—Kenny, Sam, and Jojo—kept up a running commentary in the back of the formation.

"Nice view out here, man."

"Trees are skinnier than I expected."

"That's not bad in my book."

"I dunno. I like a bit of trunk on a tree, as long as the bark is smooth."

Anna finally commented from behind Griffin. "I had no idea SEALs were so dumb."

Lily jumped in with, "Maybe it's just the fact that women are so much smarter that makes guys seem dim-witted."

Kenny broke out in song, belting, "Call me dim, call me dumb, but baby, baby, throw me a crumb. Gimme a hug, gimme a kiss. I promise I'll make you groan like this." He then let out a protracted groan that simulated an orgasm.

Anna commented, "Lily, did you hear that? I think a cat just yowled and then barfed up a hair ball."

Lily's laughter chimed, and Sherri chuckled beside Griffin.

He smiled to himself. Kenny had walked right into that one. These women weren't likely to be dazzled by the mere fact of Ken being a good-looking SEAL who could sing and hence be dying to leap into bed with him.

Sam and Jojo had the good sense to fall silent in the back of the formation, at any rate. Both guys were in their early twenties—too young and horny to have figured out how to finesse a woman.

Trevor, on the other hand, had probably been born to charm the ladies. Griffin was convinced it was the upper-crust British accent that did the trick. And for some reason that eluded Griffin, women crawled all over Axel with his tough-guy biker vibe. It had something to do with leather and motorcycles, apparently.

Griffin was interested to note that Sherri didn't participate in the ribbing now flying back and forth between the other women and the boys. Did she consider herself above such things? If so, she was in for a rude shock when she hit the unfiltered locker-room humor of the SEAL teams. As it went, the Reapers were taking it easy on these women. Silently, he was proud of their gentlemanly restraint and made a mental note to thank them later.

By the time the formation turned around to head back to base, several miles down an abandoned road, he was startled to realize he was sucking a little wind. Of course, he was more hungover than a drunkard in a distillery.

Miss Priss looked cool as a cucumber beside him, completely unconcerned about the pace. Fine. So she could run. He would break her when it came time to survive hypothermia or make SEAL swim times. Or in the gym where no woman could match the upper-body strength of a hyperfit SEAL. Or just through the sheer mental and emotional pressure that broke even the toughest men.

"What does being swim buddies entail?" Sherri asked him, admirably not out of breath.

"We'll do everything together in training. It'll be my job to let someone know when you drown or otherwise die," he answered, startlingly huffing for breath.

"Gee. Thanks. I'll make sure to actually save you."

A crack of laughter escaped him. "You think you could save me from drowning?"

"I know I could. I just have to convince you."

He snorted. "Good luck with that."

She smiled slyly at him, and it was his turn to nearly fall on his face. Her sky-blue eyes practically glowed against her golden tan. Her lashes were long and luxurious as she gazed sidelong at him through them. The sculpted curve of her cheek caught his attention. The slender length of her neck. The satin perfection of her smooth skin—

Cripes.

How in the hell was he supposed to focus on his job when his "teammate" was so damned beautiful he couldn't take his eyes off her? She was stunning for real. As in mesmerizing.

He shook his head. No way could women work on the teams if they were this distracting. When the bullets started flying, his first impulse would be to throw himself on top of her to protect her.

The idea of her body beneath his, warm and sleek, her slender limbs wrapped around him, made him stumble yet again. *Whoa! Where did that come from?*

"You okay over there, Caldwell?" Sherri asked mildly. "You seem to be having trouble with your balance."

The woman was mocking him.

His mental balance was all kinds of messed up. But he damned well wasn't about to admit that to her. He scowled and paid closer attention to his footing, vowing *not* to look at her again.

Except, out of the corner of his eye, her ponytail was driving him a little bit crazy, swinging back and forth jauntily, all silky and blond and girlie. What the hell was something like that doing out here in the dust and heat with a bunch of SEALs? It didn't help that the ponytail's owner was every bit as perky, chatting about the history of the abandoned military base as they toured it.

Sherri Tate had a mean streak in her, all right. She knew he and his guys felt like death warmed over, and she was relishing bebopping along, all chipper and cheerful.

Give them one decent night's sleep to recover from

Leo's wedding, and he and his brothers would grind these wannabes into dust. It was all well and good for the girls to have one fast run in them, but they would never keep up with SEALs twenty-four seven.

That said, his skull was going to split in two if he didn't get some water soon. And some relief from the relentless sunlight reflecting off white sand. Only years of ingrained discipline, along with a crap-ton of experience with pushing through pain, kept him going. That and the stubborn refusal to be shown up by a girl.

He'd never been gladder to see anything than that decrepit cluster of buildings as it came into view ahead, marking the end of the run. He needed fluids, a hot shower, food, and sleep, in that order.

"That was the short route," Sherri announced brightly. "We've mapped out a 15K loop, too."

She sounded entirely too pleased with herself.

"Wanna show that to us after lunch?" Griffin asked casually.

"Sure. Sounds great."

Anna and Lily were equally enthusiastic about the idea. Meanwhile, his teammates threw him baleful glares behind the ladies' backs.

Well, hell. That had backfired spectacularly. He scowled as Sherri smirked knowingly at him. That smile of hers was a lethal weapon.

"Fall out," Kettering called from the front porch of his office as they came to a halt between the Quonset huts.

Griffin bit back a groan of relief as he took a liter of water from the cooler standing in front of the instructors' hut and slugged it down. "Where can a guy get a shower around here?" he asked no one in particular.

"Only showers are at the gym," Sherri answered, chiming in to laugh with the other women.

What was so blasted funny about that?

He tossed clean clothes, towel, shampoo, and a razor in a bag and headed for the gym. When he stepped through the men's locker room into the shower, he pulled up short. There was only one big room, with six showerheads. Down the middle was a freshly built wooden wall no more than five feet tall partitioning the space into three showers for the ladies and three for the men.

And all three women were already bathing on the other side…soapy and naked…

He averted his eyes quickly, catching only the barest glimpse of glistening skin, tanned arms, and sudsy hair.

"We won't look if you won't," Sherri called out as Axel plowed into Griffin from behind, obviously gobsmacked by their shower mates.

Griffin grunted. "Watch it, Axe."

"I am watching." Axel breathed in awe. "Day-umm. I'm gonna like having girls in the SEALs."

Using his open palm, Trevor smacked Axe on the back of the head. "Don't stare like an uncouth lout. Be a gentleman, for fuck's sake."

Griffin moved to the far showerhead and turned on the water. Right across that wall, Sherri Tate was buck naked, covered in slippery suds, with rivulets of water coursing down her body. What did her breasts look like, freed from a running bra mashing them down? He already knew her legs were a mile long, sleek and smooth. Did she have tan lines? If so, where?

It would be so easy to peek over that wall. Hell, to walk around it. To draw her slender body against his, loop her leg over his hip, and bury himself in her heat while the water pounded down on them—

Whoa there, soldier!

He was no fan of the idea of women SEALs, but he had to at least *try* to be professional about it. Which meant the hard-on throbbing painfully between his legs was probably not appropriate. At all.

If he'd had a shower stall to himself, he would have taken care of the problem. But no way was he jerking off in front of Axel and Trevor, let alone where Sherri could overhear him or, heaven forbid, watch him do it.

Crap. The idea of her watching him jerk off made him even harder.

"Do you guys have soap and razors over there?" Sherri called. "We'll share if you need some."

Oh, he needed some, all right. Griffin choked a little. "They're standard in our go-bags."

"That was a fun jog, wasn't it?" Sherri commented. "It felt good to get out and stretch my legs."

Lily and Anna agreed readily. The short, blond one, Lily, said, "After lunch, we should do some yoga. Limber up a little."

Aww, hell. Now he was picturing Sherri making like a pretzel. The kinky possibilities were endless. At the next showerhead, Trevor groaned under his breath. Griffin knew the feeling. At least he wasn't the only one struggling to keep his mind on business.

He tilted his head back to rinse the shampoo out of his hair, and the suds slipped down his body like Sherri's hands would, soft and quick. His erection leaped and throbbed, jutting out from his groin uncontrollably.

Fuckety fuck fuck.

He spun to face the wall lest his brothers spy his predicament and choose this place, in front of the ladies, with his boner swinging in the breeze, to rib him about it.

Teeth gritted, Griffin reached for the heat control on his shower and yanked it to full cold. The shock of the icy cascade wrung a gasp out of him as his entire body clenched painfully.

"You okay over there, Sparky?" Sherri asked.

Did she have to be so observant? Couldn't a guy freeze his pecker into submission in peace around here? He ground out, "I'm good, thanks. How about you? Need me to scrub your back, Tate?"

"Anna or Lily can get it for me, thanks," came her chirpy reply.

All three men groaned at that. No doubt his buddies were also envisioning the three naked women, only feet away, erotically washing each other. Both Trevor and Axel had their backs turned and seemed more tense than usual. Maybe he wasn't the only one having a hard time controlling his body's autonomic reactions to being naked and in close proximity to three smoking-hot women.

What the hell was this world coming to? He was in the freaking shower with *women*. Women who thought they were going to be SEALs.

Over his dead, shriveled...body.

Okay, so it was definitely weird showering with men. Sherri was relieved the guys had the decency to turn their backs. She didn't linger in the shower, for darned sure. She got clean and got out.

On her way back to the barracks, she grabbed a couple of sandwiches, an electrolyte drink, and an apple from the cafeteria. A local woman named Sue came in each morning and cooked for the day, leaving behind grab-and-go snacks and big kettles full of Cajun yumminess.

When she arrived in the Quonset hut, Lily and Anna already had their heads together. Anna said without preamble, "What do you think of this arrangement where only two of us get to be real SEALs?"

Sherri flopped onto her bed, leaned against the wall, and unwrapped the sandwich. "I think it's inevitable. The public's going to be ragingly curious about the first woman SEAL, and the military will channel and control that curiosity by feeding the press what they want it to know. If I were in Kettering's shoes, I would do the same thing."

Lily added, "Well, I think it stinks."

"Me too," Sherri replied glumly.

After inhaling her lunch, Sherri stretched out for a quick nap. Now that the SEALs were here, she suspected chances to rest were going to be few and far between.

It was midafternoon before Kettering poked his head in the door and told them to suit up in fatigues and combat boots.

As the heat of an Indian summer afternoon baked them, she fell in behind Caldwell. This time the men led the way. Apparently, Kettering had shown the guys the perimeter road around the artillery range, which measured a little over nine miles long.

The pace was slightly slower, *slightly* being the operative word. Given that she would have to sustain it longer, Sherri did her best to relax and conserve energy.

Except her gaze kept straying to Caldwell's broad shoulders, narrow waist, and the steady pumping of his muscular legs. And that caboose of his. *Wowsers.* It was high and tight, promising driving power and all-night stamina—*annnd* there went her pulse again. *Shoot.* She couldn't afford to hyperventilate every time she looked at her swim buddy's butt.

She tried to take interest in the towering cypress trees festooned with long ropes of Spanish moss. *Nope.* The moss swayed in perfect time with the deep, steady breaths he took. How about the clouds? Surely, they had interesting shapes today. Indeed, the building thunderheads reminded her of the way Griffin's hard muscles bunched and flexed across his arms and shoulders. *Well, fudge.*

She finally gave in and lost herself in fantasies of what it would be like to sleep with a man like Griffin Caldwell. If she couldn't fight her imagination, she might as well let it distract her. Not that she envisioned sleeping with him specifically, of course. Just someone vaguely similar in size, build, looks, and general smart-assery. It wasn't ideal for maintaining a steady running stride and slow, even breathing, but it was better than falling on her face.

"You okay in the rear?" Caldwell called out to the folks in the back of the formation.

Kenny yelled back, "Loving the rears, Grif!"

Sherri rolled her eyes. Men. They were all just overgrown adolescent hormone monsters.

Sam piped up, "Give us a song to run to, Kenny."

Lily jumped in immediately. "Please, no obscene marching songs about picking up women in bars."

Sherri shook her head. Lily was shouting into a hurricane to ask a bunch of SEALs to behave themselves and be tasteful.

Kenny belted out, “Came to town to run with girls. Worked ’em out until they hurled. Picked them up and ran again. Turned them into manly men.”

The guys laughed, and Sherri snorted. Never in her adult life had any man looked at her and seen a “manly” woman.

Anna sang out, “Came to town to train with SEALs. Got drunks instead, what is the deal? Asked the boss where is the beef? He looked at me in disbelief. These SEALs, I said, they aren’t real men. We’ll run their asses off again.”

Sherri burst out laughing, in spite of doubting it was a good idea to taunt their trainers. But even shy Lily laughed in delight.

No surprise, Griffin picked up the pace. Considerably.

Anna, ever the outgoing flirt, asked Trevor, “So how does a hot Brit end up running around with a bunch of SEALs?”

He responded, “I came on a training exchange with the Reapers, but I’ve applied to stay permanently with these reprobates. They couldn’t survive without me.”

Which, of course, prompted guffaws from the other men.

Sherri asked no one in particular, “What are your field handles?”

When no one answered right away, she said lightly, “If you won’t tell us yours, we ladies will give you our own handles.”

"Oh yeah?" Griffin challenged. "Like what?"

She considered his back as they ran. "I'd have to go with Sir Grumpy Pants for you."

He snorted. "I'll stick with Grif, thanks."

She tsked. "So unoriginal. I'll bet that handle doesn't last too long once we women come on board permanently." He glanced at her, and she didn't miss the way his jaw rippled. Clenching his teeth in disgust over that idea, was he?

"How about you, Axel?" Sherri asked. "What's your field handle?"

"Axe."

Lily piped up, declaring, "That's totally lame. We definitely need to replace that."

"Oh yeah?" the big biker demanded. "What would you call me?"

"Teddy Bear," Lily shot back without hesitation.

That caused a round of laughter and ribbing, with Axel threatening grievous bodily harm to anyone who called him that to his face.

"Jojo?" Sherri asked. "How about you?"

"Joaquin is my real name, but everyone has always called me Jojo. It became my field handle by default."

"Ladies?" Sherri asked. "Can we come up with something better?"

"Fabio," Anna replied immediately.

"No!" Jojo yelped.

Sherri bit back a giggle. Jojo's mane of hair, currently pulled back in a ponytail, was black, not blond, but he was a very pretty man. And big. Not as beefy as Axel, but he still looked like he could pick up a truck.

Griffin commented, "Jojo—correction, Fabio—is

from Hawaii and came to us by way of the National Football League."

"Griffff," Jojo growled.

Anna giggled. "Well, that explains a lot. All those hits to the head and all..."

"Hey!" Jojo protested. "I opted out after the draft. I was undersized to play in the NFL, and I wanted to do something meaningful with my life."

Sherri could actually respect that and relate to it. She nodded and murmured, "I know how you felt."

Again, Griffin glanced over his shoulder, his gaze far too observant for her taste.

"What about you, Sam?" Sherri asked quickly, hoping to distract Griffin from following up on her too-revealing comment.

"I don't have a field handle—" he started.

The men shouted him down. Kenny reported gleefully, "His field handle is Babycakes."

Sherri grinned. "Thank God that's already taken. I shudder to think of being stuck with that." She glanced back at the last guy on the team. "And you, Ken? What's your handle?"

"Alpo."

"Like the dog food?" she blurted out. "How'd you get that?"

"It stands for alcoholic libations procurement officer," he replied.

"And?" she prompted when he said no more.

"And," Griffin jumped in, "that man can sniff out booze anytime, anywhere. It's a gift. We'll be in a country where liquor is completely forbidden, and he'll still manage to find a case of beer or a fifth of whiskey."

Anna laughed. “That sounds like a heck of a useful field skill.”

“You have no idea, darlin’,” Kenny drawled at her. “I’m a man of many talents.”

Anna shot back, “Composing song lyrics *not* being one of them.”

He crooned, “You’ve done broke my heart with your cruel, cold words. I’m a man on the edge, and I’m sinking fast.”

The guy really did have a good voice, rich and soulful, perfect for country music.

Sherri asked, “Have you ever considered singing professionally, Ken? You have the voice for it.”

He shrugged. “Maybe someday when I’m done with this gig.”

Anna added, “Just promise you’ll hire a songwriter and not try to write your own.”

In a flash, Ken swerved and bumped into Anna, knocking her off balance.

Jojo jumped forward and caught Anna’s elbow, steadying her in a display of reflexes so fast Sherri wasn’t exactly sure what she’d seen. Dang, it was so easy to underestimate these men. They loped along, joking around like a bunch of goofballs, and then in the blink of an eye, they were stronger and faster than she could believe.

The pace Griffin set pushed her very close to her maximum speed. Unfortunately, she got the impression the guys had at least one more gear in them, if not several more. Her running watch said this pace also met the pre-BUD/S qualification time for a fifteen-kilometer run.

But the guys seemed unimpressed and plowed onward like they did this every day. She had a sneaking suspicion she, too, would be expected to do this daily from now on. *Yikes*.

Finally, a year or so after they left the compound, the white clapboard buildings and rusted Quonset huts came into sight. The men peeled off, running directly into their barracks, and the women jogged into theirs. As soon as their door closed, the women collapsed on their cots, panting.

Sherri didn't even have the energy to unlace her boots and kick them off.

Anna commented, "Am I the only one who had a hell of a time keeping my mind on running out there? Did you see Trevor's *ass*? My God. I have needs, and that man's accent makes me think dirty thoughts."

Lily laughed. "I don't know about an Englishman. I kind of like American guys who are big and cuddly."

Sherri rolled on her side to stare at the petite woman. "You don't seriously have a crush on Axel, do you? Or is Jojo the lucky guy?"

Lily answered indignantly, "I don't chase after men. And certainly not the ones I work with."

She made an excellent point, of course. It was a lousy idea to date coworkers and doubly fraught with problems in a military hierarchy. Still, Sherri couldn't help but enjoy the overall eye-candy factor.

Sherri laughed ruefully. "Well, at least now we know how they're going to get rid of us. They're going to flaunt their hot bodies and distract us until we can't function."

Anna sighed blissfully. "What a way to go."

Lily looked vaguely scandalized and began stripping off her boots and socks.

Sherri followed suit, commenting, "What do you want to bet they haul us over to the gym after supper just to make the point that they're bigger and badder than we are?"

The other women groaned.

Frankly, she could stop exercising for today and not be sorry. Her legs were tired, and she would be sore tomorrow after the back-to-back runs today. But she had a sneaking suspicion the pain was just getting started.

What had she gotten herself into? Throwing down against a SEAL platoon was far from the smartest thing she'd ever done.

But it wasn't as if she could turn down a challenge. Her family used to joke that *Competitive* was her middle name. What could be more challenging than becoming the one thing no woman on earth had ever managed to be?

Still. Maybe she'd bitten off more than she could chew this time.

Bah. Her mantra had always been *No risk, no reward*. And the corollary to that theory was *Never quit*.

She suspected her mantra was going to be put to the test out here. Big time. But she'd be twice damned before she let Griffin Caldwell get the best of her.

Sure enough, sunset found them sweating in the gym, pumping out push-ups, pull-ups, burpees, and whatever other forms of torture the guys could cook up. At least she was able to take some satisfaction from Griffin's poorly disguised surprise as she demonstrated upper-body strength most men would envy.

Kenny, Sam, and Jojo kept up a running commentary of double entendres that cracked the three guys up and might have annoyed Sherri had she not fully expected to be harassed for being a woman. She noted that Trevor stood back from the ribbing, preferring to ignore it all. Classy guy.

Jojo called, "Pump it out. Faster. Faster!"

Sam added, "Deeper, ladies. Deeper." That was in response to four-count lunges, a form of torture Sherri had never encountered before.

Jojo commented, "Man, I love wet T-shirts."

"Are we making you wet, yet?" Kenny teased the women.

That one got a reaction out of Griffin. He threw a silent, quelling stare at the trio, and they subsided instantly. Sherri would accuse them all of being psychic, but it probably just boiled down to the men knowing each other that well. Griffin could throw them a look, and the others knew exactly what he meant by it.

As for her, Griffin Caldwell was a mystery. He seemed by turns attracted to her and furious that she lived and breathed. He looked as if he couldn't make up his mind whether to be intrigued or appalled by her attempting to become a SEAL. She knew the feeling. She couldn't figure out whether to be attracted to or infuriated by him, or both.

When she caught him staring as she finished knocking out a set of pull-ups, she asked, "What? You didn't think women could have upper-body strength?"

He shrugged. "I'm not impressed, yet."

Liar. All three women were world-class athletes. Lily might be tiny, but she'd been a champion gymnast and had a ridiculous strength-to-weight ratio. Anna had been in the top ten female finishers at various international CrossFit games. As for herself, she held one of the top five scores in the world this year for women's heptathlon—seven track and field events run over two days—which made her a hella good all-around athlete.

She followed Griffin over to the weights, and he started loading metal disks onto a bar. He glanced up at her. "How much do you want to lift?"

"Are we going high rep-low weight, or high weight-low rep?"

He considered, then said, "Show me the max you can dead-lift."

"Load up three hundred, then."

"Three hundred pounds?" Griffin blurted out.

"Yes," she replied a little impatiently. "I didn't mean three hundred bags of marshmallows."

"Okay, then."

She helped him slide the last weights onto the bar and secure them.

Tugging her lifting gloves into place, she addressed the bar, spine straight and shoulder blades squeezed back for optimal leverage. Gathering herself, she gripped the bar and pulled for everything she was worth. Groaning with effort, she stood up straight, bringing the bar to her hips.

She dropped the bar with a clank of steel and a grunt of satisfaction. *Choke on that, Caldwell*.

She looked up to see all the men staring at her. She huffed. "Seriously? What did you guys expect when you heard women were training to be SEALs? A bunch of Girl Scouts singing 'Kumbaya' and doing camping crafts while applying their lipstick?"

"I don't know what I expected, but it wasn't that," Axel answered for all the men, lifting his bushy beard toward the bar at her feet. Lily swatted him on his upper arm, and he squawked in protest. The other pairs went back to working out.

"You wanna lift?" Sherri asked Griffin. "I'll spot for you."

"Let's take a walk."

She frowned, following him outside in the gathering dusk. The noise of crickets and frogs was deafening, and the last vestiges of color were draining from the sky into the west, leaving a vast, midnight expanse overhead. It reminded her of Griffin's eyes, deep blue and fathomless.

"What's up?" she asked as she fell in beside him.

"What are you really doing here?"

"We've been over this. I'm training to be a SEAL." She paused, and then added dryly, "With your help, of course."

"You do realize the men on the teams will never accept you, right? Even if you were to manage, by some miracle, to meet the physical standards."

"Why not?" She had a good idea of how he would answer that question if he were completely honest, but she wanted to hear him say it out loud.

He shoved a hand through his dark-brown hair. It was rather longer than Navy regulation, and its soft waves begged a woman to run her fingers through them.

A whole day of looking at him hadn't diminished

the pull she felt toward him. If anything, she was more tempted than ever. He struck her as the kind of man who, if she flirted with him, would jump at an invitation into her bed. Griffin Caldwell in her bed? He'd be tanned and hard—oh my. Now *there* was a mental picture—

Without warning, he turned to face her, gripped her shoulders, and backed her up against the clapboard wall of the cafeteria. She stared up at him, shocked at how her breathing accelerated and excitement tore through her veins. Griffin was powerful and dangerous, completely unlike any man she'd ever spent time around.

He stared at her, his chest rising and falling every bit as fast and hard as hers. He surprised her by releasing her shoulder to push a strand of hair back from her face, and she froze, fascinated and wary of where this was headed.

"Christ," he murmured. "I can't get enough of looking at you."

Her brow puckered a little. *Really? This is about my looks?* She sighed. Sometimes she got so sick of how hung up people were about how she looked. She'd won the genetic lottery. Folks could get over that already. She would love, just once, for a man to look at her and see her mind. Or her loyalty. Or her courage.

He muttered, "I want to understand you."

"What is there to understand?"

"Explain to me what a girl like you wants with becoming a Special Forces operator like me."

She chose to ignore the "girl like you" part of the question, focusing instead on what motivated her to be here. "I expect I want roughly the same thing you do. To serve my country and do something cool in the process."

"There's a hell of a lot more to being a SEAL than that."

"And that's what you're here to teach me."

"It's more than a skill set, or even a mindset. It takes…heart."

"Are you saying women don't have heart? That we aren't brave enough? Tough enough? Stubborn enough?"

His face was swathed in shadows, his jaw and nose mere outlines, his eyes unfathomable caverns of black. Still, she couldn't miss the frustration rolling off him. It was a living thing, twisting around them both, tightening like a noose pulling them together, yet holding them apart.

Their wills clashed as she stared back, challenging him to acknowledge that she had the mental and emotional wherewithal to match him step for step.

No way was she going to be the first to look away. She would stand here until her feet grew roots to make the point. She could, she *would*, go toe-to-toe with a SEAL…and not flinch.

He clearly was trying to measure her, maybe also to intimidate her.

Hah. As if! She'd stared down plenty of four-star generals and congressmen who thought they could bully her because she looked soft and feminine. Poor bastards had never bothered to see the steel underneath.

She continued to stare at Griffin, trying to make out details in his expression, vividly aware of how attracted she was to his lean cheeks, his strong profile, the absolute self-confidence that was an intrinsic part of him.

His frustration shifted. Changed. Morphed into

another kind of frustration altogether. She became even more vividly aware of the rise and fall of his chest, just inches away from hers. He leaned closer and braced his left hand against the wall beside her ear, his right hand moved to cup the back of her head. It was all so aggressively masculine. And sexy as heck.

In slow motion, he drew her face up to his.

And she didn't protest.

His body was hard and hot, scorching her like freshly forged steel. Her own private furnace.

She ought to complain. Insist that he treat her professionally. Not think of her as a woman at all. She was just another soldier. Another SEAL trainee…

Except she couldn't remember the last time she'd gotten up close and personal with a man who made her feel this way…

Who cared if it was just lust? It was still fantastic. This man was a fire sizzling through her veins, boiling her blood. She ought to pull away. Or at least look away.

I could lose myself in those eyes of his…

Her gaze dropped to his mouth, where she was immediately fascinated by the generous curve of his lips. His strong, straight teeth shining white in the starlight. The way he caught one side of his lower lip in said teeth. He was fighting a need to kiss her.

I want him to kiss me…

Maybe she should kiss him.

Must. Not.

She arched into him, pressing against him as night settled gently around them.

He started this. Why shouldn't I finish it?

Her stare locked with his as she lifted her chin the last

few millimeters into kissing range. His breath mingled with hers, light and hungry.

This is a terrible, terrible idea.

But she couldn't think of anything she would rather do in the whole wide world than be right here, right now, surrounded by this man, crushing her breasts against his chest, about to kiss him.

Her mouth opened slightly. She ran the tip of her tongue across her suddenly dry lips. Time stopped for a long moment as she fought a losing battle against the desire raging between them.

He tilted his head down in sudden decision, his mouth capturing hers in no uncertain terms. His dynamic presence exploded around her…or maybe that was erotic attraction exploding inside her.

Their kiss was hot and wet, a carnal thing complete with tongues and sucking and groans from deep in her throat that startled the hell out of her. This was no tentative hello, no cautious introduction. This was lust and raw, raging hunger. Apparently, Griffin was as direct about his desires as he was about his opinions.

It made him even more irresistible. He saw what he wanted and went after it. No hesitation, no doubts. It was so damned alpha of him.

She crawled all over him, turned on like mad, doing her best to suck his tonsils out of his throat. His left hand slid down her spine until he gripped her behind, pulling her snug against his groin, making no secret of how turned on he was by her.

She rubbed the junction of her thighs against that promise of sweet, sweet release, relishing the zinging pleasure ripping through her. She wanted sweat and the slap of thrusting bodies, to be filled by his hot flesh, to drive him out of his mind. She actually purred a little in the back of her throat at the thought of it—

Whoa. When did she turn into a cat in heat?

Apparently, when Griffin Caldwell kissed her.

Yeah, but what a kiss.

It was sexual and frank, and frankly fantastic.

And then, just like that, he tore his mouth away from hers. Stumbled back. He jammed his hands in his pockets, and she saw through the fabric they were balled in fists. His face abruptly looked carved from stone, his eyes glacially cold.

The cool night air swirled around her, damp and misty, chilling her to the bone.

"That's why women can't be in the SEALs," he rasped.

She registered shock first.

Then disappointment.

Dismay.

Rejection.

And then came outrage, flowing fast and hot through her veins.

Had that kiss been all about humiliating her? She'd been ready to leap into bed with him, damn him!

She glared furiously at his shadowed face and ground out, "You think because you deign to bestow a kiss upon me, I'm going to collapse at your feet, swooning? You think because I have sexual desires I can't be a soldier? You think because I find you moderately attractive I can't keep my mind on the job?" Her voice rose with each question. "Just how freaking shallow do you think I am?"

His mouth clamped shut, and she caught the ripple of muscles along his jaw.

"You're the one who kissed me," she flung at him. "How shallow does that make you?" As her fury gathered steam, she stepped forward and poked him in the chest. "I don't think women in the SEALs are the problem, Caldwell. I think misogynistic male chauvinist pigs in the SEALs are the problem."

"Sherri. Calm down."

"Don't tell me to calm down! You keep your hands, and your mouth, and…and"—she fluttered her hands at him—"all those muscles…to yourself, mister. I'm a professional soldier, and I'm here to do a job. You either get on board this train or stay out of my way. Got it?"

"No," he ground out. "I don't."

She glared at him, speechless with anger.

"No matter how fancy you slice it, Sherri, no woman has what it takes to be a SEAL. You'll never have what it takes. You have no place on the teams and never will."

There it was. The truth had finally been spoken aloud. The SEALs didn't want women and would do everything in their power to keep women out. And on a more personal note, *he* didn't want *her*.

Her anger drained away as quickly as it had flared, leaving behind only a dagger of hurt buried to the hilt in her heart.

She said soberly, "What are you going to do when I prove you wrong, Griffin?"

Frustration gleamed in his gaze as clear and bright as Venus hanging low on the horizon.

She continued implacably. "The day of the female SEAL is coming—soon. If not me, then some woman a lot like me is going to make it past all the obstacles you throw in her path. Where will that leave you? Will you be in…or out?"

He threw up his hands and turned away from her, but she continued battering at his ramrod-stiff back. "Where will that leave you, Griffin? Will you be part of the SEALs, or will you be obsolete? Are you going to let your prejudice and archaic attitude drive you off the teams?"

He whirled around so fast she lurched back from him reflexively. "My team is my family. My life, dammit."

He brushed past her, striding away into the darkness. She called after him as he practically ran from her. "Then you'd better get used to the idea of women. We're coming for you. *I'm* coming for you, Griffin Caldwell."

Chapter 3

GRIFFIN WAS SHAKEN LIKE HE HADN'T BEEN SHAKEN IN years. Rattled as hell.

He veered away from the instructors' bunkhouse and kept walking, following the dirt road into the trees. The night and the forest closed in around him, calming him enough that he could breathe semi-normally. This was his native environment where he felt most at home, most in control. Night was the time of the SEAL. They owned the darkness.

Was Sherri right? Were women SEALs inevitable? Worse, was he obsolete?

All SEALs came with an expiration date. Some of those dates were set by bad knees or a bum back or, for some unlucky bastards, by a bullet with their name on it. He generally avoided thinking about the end of his career, not only out of superstition, but also because he couldn't imagine not being on the teams. What would he do with himself if he wasn't running ops with his brothers, his hair on fire and balls to the wall?

An empty void was all that came to mind.

Normalcy.

Slow death by boredom.

His stride lengthened as sudden fury ripped through him. No woman, not even one who kissed like Sherri Tate, was chasing him off his team.

He broke into a run, speeding up until he was pumping

along in a full-out sprint. Sky-blue eyes chased him. A mysterious, sexy smile taunted him. Even Sherri's scent, soft and sweet, hounded him.

He ran until his lungs burned and his legs were on fire.

Finally, as the panic receded, his pace slowed. He fell into a walk, winded as hell. Weary, body and soul, he turned around to head back to camp.

A sick feeling in his gut told him Sherri was right about the future of the teams. He either accepted women into his band of brothers, or he was out. Finished.

SEALs were famous for their ability to adapt to any situation…but could he adapt to this? He truly didn't know if he could or not.

Only one way to find out.

Dammit.

He made it back to the barracks at about the same time the other guys piled into the Quonset hut after their workouts. Kenny opened a cooler where, for the past few hours, a case of beer had been icing.

"Beer?" Ken asked him, holding up a brown longneck.

"Nah." Griffin's hangover still clung to the edges of his brain, and a headache jackhammered at his eyeballs. It would have sidelined anyone with a lower pain tolerance than he had. He stretched out on his bed, arms folded behind his head, staring at the ceiling.

Trevor, who bunked beside him, sat down and asked quietly, "You okay?"

Sometimes it sucked having teammates who were so blasted perceptive. At least Trevor had cracked thirty years of age and achieved a modicum of wisdom in a decade of special operations for Great Britain. Griffin muttered for Trevor's ears alone, "These women. They're knocking me off my game."

"No kidding. I never thought I'd see the day when women could meet Special Forces standards. But here we are."

"What do you think of it?" Griffin asked him. "Would female operators fly in Europe?"

Trevor's intelligent gaze was troubled. "I honestly don't know. Politically, Europe is pretty liberal. But women in hard-core combat? That's a stretch. I'm going to take a wait-and-see attitude."

A smart approach. Too bad he, as the platoon leader, didn't have that luxury.

Trevor added, "If you want to talk it over or just vent, I won't carry any tales back to Kettering. I've got your back."

"Thanks, brother."

Trevor met his gaze candidly. His eyes telegraphed that times were changing around them both, and he, too, understood the stakes. Adapt or get out.

"Yeah. That." Griffin sighed in response to his teammate's silent message.

Axel declared loudly from across the room, "Never thought I'd see chicks do stuff like that. Did you see Lily banging out those pull-ups? Hell, she can do more than I can!"

Trevor laughed. "Yes, but you're a giant lump of meat. She's a tiny little thing with no weight to move."

Axel grunted. "I didn't see you beating Anna at push-ups. How many did she do? Six hundred, all told?"

Trev shrugged. "Something like that."

Griffin eyed the Brit closely. Trevor looked about evenly split between dismay and being wildly impressed by Anna's mad skills.

Kenny passed the Brit another beer. "You need this, bro. That Anna girl is totally into you."

Griffin was interested to see a certain desperation flash across Trev's face. Was the guy panicked at being pursued? Or maybe panicked at what he might *do* about being pursued? A person never could tell with those Brits. They held their emotions close to the vest. Either way, Griffin felt Trev's pain. What was a guy supposed to do when completely attracted to one's *female* future teammate?

Sam, usually slow to speak, weighed in. "Didn't think I'd ever see women that strong or that fast. I'm thinking these ladies may just have what it takes to make the teams."

"It takes more than strength or speed," Griffin snapped. "It takes courage. Smarts. Guts. Aggression. It takes… Hell, I don't know what it takes. More. It takes more."

Trevor replied thoughtfully, "Who's to say women—not all women, but some women—don't have that 'more' factor?"

"Have you ever met a woman who made you think, 'Damn, she'd make a great SEAL'?" Griffin snapped back.

Trevor grinned. "I've never met one who was allowed to try. Maybe if we let them give it a go, they'll prove themselves to us."

Griffin swore luridly. They were talking about women. Running on SEAL teams. In desperation, he tossed out, "Think about the missions we do. The conditions we live in. Do you guys seriously want women out there with us?"

Axel spoke slowly. "I wouldn't mind it if they could pull their weight. And it sure as hell would beat looking at your ugly mug all the time, Grif. That Sherri girl—she looks like a princess. Or a movie star."

Kenny emerged from his beer to comment, "Cal says Tate was a no-shit beauty queen. Finalist at the Miss America pageant a few years back."

Somehow, Griffin was not surprised. He'd seen some gorgeous women in his day, but Sherri Tate was a rare beauty.

Jojo spoke up. "Speaking of beauty queens, where'd you disappear to with Sherri, Grif? Is she as hot a lay as she looks like she'd be?"

Griffin jerked upright, his head pounding violently at the sudden movement. "She's a freaking naval officer. Watch your mouth, Jojo."

The room fell dead silent.

God *damn* it. The last thing he wanted to do was alienate his teammates over a woman. He sighed. "I'm sorry, man. I don't know what to make of these women. I tried to talk with Tate about why ladies want to be SEALs."

"And?" Trevor asked expectantly.

"She said she wants to serve her country and do cool stuff."

Axel responded, "Well, yeah. Isn't that why we all do this?"

Griffin's brows twitched together. Of all the guys, Axel was the one he would've least expected to be okay with women SEALs. Axe was a good ol' boy and prone to calling women things like *li'l ladies* and *fillies*.

Kenny shrugged. "This is all a waste of time. As soon as we push women to our fitness standards, they'll fold up and go home."

Trevor shot him another of those troubled looks that communicated louder than words: Yes, but what if the women made the standards and didn't go home? Then what? Grif had no blasted idea.

Sam, the newest to the team, commented, "I don't care if women make it as long as they can do the job. They sure as shootin' improve the scenery."

The kid was missing the point. Women might look good—hell, look great. But they *would* degrade the performance of the teams. Any unit was only as strong as its weakest member.

Sherri unsettled him like no person—male or female—had ever unsettled him. It wasn't just about how she looked. Or that he thought about hot, sweaty sex every time he got within eyeball distance of her. She had an elusive…*something* about her. Secrets. What were they? Where did they come from? It made him want to dig down in her psyche until he uncovered all of her darkest mysteries.

For surely a woman who had the motivation to try for the impossible was carrying around some deep emotional shit.

More irritated than he'd been in a long time, Griffin made an early night of it. Not only did he have a hangover to shake, but tomorrow would be an early morning. He planned to show Sherri Tate a thing or two about what it took to be a real SEAL.

He should have known it would happen.

She came to him in his dreams, a ghostly siren, so seductive and enthralling that he gladly gave himself over to her spell. Her slender, strong arms drew him against her full breasts, her kiss drew the breath from his lungs, and her white-hot desire drew the will to resist clean out of him.

He smelled her lust, sweet and musky, felt it in the way she surged against him. As much as she wanted him, he wanted her even more. His erection was painfully hard, sending driving need pounding through his belly, blanking all thought except burying himself inside her heat and sex until they both exploded in soul-rending orgasms.

Griffin woke with a lurch, drenched in sweat, as his watch vibrated. He fell back against the mattress, swearing silently.

Far more slowly than he willed it to, the dream retreated. Sherri's imaginary arms disengaged from around his body, and his brain only gradually came on line.

Four a.m. Time to go teach a princess a thing or two about what SEALs are made of. Except the bedsheet tented over his erection, and he rolled onto his side rather than advertise his predicament to his brothers.

The other guys were starting to rouse, and he lay there listening to them move around, reliving that vivid dream in his mind. Damn, that woman was stuck there but good. One thing he knew for sure: he had to get himself squared away with Sherri—and fast. Distractions of any kind—be they problems with wives or girlfriends, money woes, or anything that took a guy's mind off the job—were trouble.

He rolled out of the rack, pulled on pants, and tucked his problem child painfully behind his zipper. Yanking a black T-shirt down over his head, he stepped into boots and strapped on the worst attitude he could summon. At oh-dark-thirty and with him horny as hell, it was a freaking snotty attitude. Good. Now, he was ready to face Sherri.

At 4:05 a.m. sharp, he and the other SEALs barged into the girls' dorm, shouting, banging on trash cans, and tipping over furniture.

Sherri was first to catch the hint and leap out of bed, scrambling for clothes. Grif averted his gaze from those mile-long legs with sharply cut quads and well-defined calves. The dark-haired one, Anna, wasn't so spry and got dumped out of her cot onto the floor in an unceremonious heap.

By 4:10, Grinder PT was well underway, the ladies on the road in front of their hooch, knocking out burpees and sit-ups, doing wind sprints over to the pull-up bar beside the gym, and sprinting back to the Quonset huts to drop and give 'em twenty. Push-ups, that was.

All the while, the men hovered over them, shouting insults and criticizing everything from their technique to their hair color. This morning, the Reapers had shifted into full-on BUD/S mode. The sexual interplay from last night was gone, replaced by flat-out mental warfare aimed at shredding the trainees' confidence and determination.

Sherri ran over to Griffin's push-up station for the fifth time, looking ragged around the edges. She was sucking wind and looked to be in pain. *Welcome to the jungle, baby.*

"Drop and start pumping 'em out, Tate," he snapped. "Don't waste my time. I've got places to go and things to do."

She assumed a front leaning rest position, and he started the stopwatch on his wrist. "Count aloud," he ordered as he dropped into a front leaning rest beside her.

As she popped out the first twenty push-ups quickly, he matched her in silence. But as she started to slow down, he ragged on her. Hard.

"What's the matter? Arms tired? Or are you just weak, Tate? C'mon. Don't wimp out on me, now. Surely you've got more than this. We're not even to the pre-BUD/S minimum yet."

She finished another twenty push-ups—as did he—and paused in a front leaning rest to catch her breath.

He, however, lay down on the ground beside Sherri so he could talk right up into her red face. "You can always quit, Tate. There's no shame in not being able to hack this. Go back to your nice clean comfortable life where no one yells at you and you don't have to be in pain. You know you want to."

She made it halfway up through a push-up, and her arms trembled, protesting against finishing the movement. Just to make his point, he paused halfway up through his matching push-up as well. He waited patiently while she gathered the strength to finish. She threw him a baleful look, obviously not appreciative of his demonstration of casual strength.

He smirked back at her. "You're not to the minimum yet, Tate."

She took a deep breath, exhaled hard and finished the push-up. Reluctantly, he was impressed. Too bad she wasn't cheating on the push-ups, or he could've yelled at her about that, too.

Watching out of the corner of his eye as her chest brushed the ground, he almost wanted to be that strip of gravel beneath her, getting caressed by those lush globes.

"Forty-three!" she grunted in triumph as she finished one more push-up. She collapsed on the ground, breathing hard, with about twenty seconds to go in the timed rotation.

Clearly, she knew forty-two was the minimum number of push-ups required of a BUD/S candidate in two minutes. Parked in a plank beside her to press home his point, he demanded, "You think you can make it in BUD/S if all you do is reach the minimums? You think just surviving is enough? SEALs don't survive, Tate. They win. If you're going make it through BUD/s you have to strive to win every single training evolution. Where's your desire? Show me some goddamned guts!"

Clenching her teeth, she resumed doing push-ups, straining through a half dozen more before he called, "Time. Two minutes. Get off my road, Tate. Move, move, move!"

She crawled to her feet and stumbled off toward Trevor at the pull-up bars. Truth be told, he was stunned that she'd found the will to do more push-ups after she'd clearly exhausted herself. It was the sort of thing a SEAL might do—

No. No! *Cancel that thought*.

Grinder PT was not for the weak of heart even if a person had all the fitness in the world. The mental challenge of being surrounded by screaming instructors watching a person's every move, and pushing for more no matter how much a soul did, was one of the more daunting training evolutions in the first few weeks of BUD/S.

He and the guys chewed on the girls for nearly an hour before Kettering called for everyone to get in the Jeeps. Two more of the open-topped vehicles had been delivered from Camp Lejeune overnight, and Grif swung into the back of one driven by Sam—a street racer in his free time—landing on the seat plastered from hip to knee against Sherri.

She was breathing hard, and beads of sweat made her skin glisten. An urge to lean over and lick the perspiration off her neck shocked him into staring down at his clenched hands, sandwiched tightly between his knees. The vehicles lurched into motion, and Sherri's shoulder bumped against his.

He restrained a flinch. Dammit, if they were going to be swim buddies, he was going to put his hands all over her before this was said and done. He had to get used to touching her, or at least learn not to get a gigantic hard-on every time he did.

"Having fun yet?" he asked her as conversationally as he could manage. Part of the game was to give trainees mental whiplash by switching in and out of screaming asshole mode.

"Hooyah," she replied sardonically.

He grinned at her, genuinely enjoying himself. He loved being a SEAL, and he loved training like a SEAL. Besides, he knew what came next. She was about to learn the true meaning of being cold. And he got to sit back and enjoy this particular little show.

The Jeeps wound through the town of Holly Ridge and crossed the North Topsail Bridge onto Topsail Island, a narrow barrier island fronting the Atlantic Ocean. Sherri leaned her head back, eyes closed, the slender column of her throat exposed and tempting as hell. Everything about the woman was attractive. He had yet to see her from an angle that was anything but camera-ready. Or bedroom-ready.

His dick stirred, and he frantically turned his thoughts to paperwork. Desk jobs. Regular Navy uniforms. Office politics. He couldn't come up with any bigger turnoffs on short notice, but thankfully, those did the trick.

They drove a few more minutes and parked at a government-owned stretch of beach not open to the public.

Piling out of the Jeeps, they headed down to the water in the predawn darkness. The surf was quiet this morning, the waves no more than knee-high. But it was late October. The Atlantic Ocean would be chilly—around sixty degrees Fahrenheit—cold enough to cause hypothermia in just a few minutes.

"Shoulder to shoulder, ladies," Kettering ordered. "Forward march."

Grif traded grins with the other guys as Sherri, Anna, and Lily marched out into the edge of the surf, turned around when ordered to face the beach, linked arms, and lay down. A wave lapped over them gently.

Ahh, surf immersion. It used to be called surf torture before use of the word *torture* became politically charged. The first time he'd endured it in his BUD/S training, the guys on each side of him had rung out of the course on their very first dunking.

Griffin strolled over to Kettering, who was staring down at a tablet computer. “Did you give them thermo pills last night?” he asked his boss. The SEALs had used swallowable temperature sensors for some years. It made this kind of training safer, but also guaranteed maximum suffering. A win all the way around. If you weren’t the poor slob dunked in frigid water.

Cal nodded. “The sensors are reporting their core body temperatures like a charm.”

“How low are you gonna go with them?” Grif asked.

His boss shrugged. “Same as BUD/S. Ninety-one degrees.”

That was class II hypothermia, and Grif knew from experience that it was excruciating. The entire body cramped as muscles tried desperately to create heat and move blood to the core to preserve vital body functions. Shivering became violent, speech became slurred, and brain function became impaired.

He heard noise over the crash and swish of the surf and moved closer to the water’s edge to hear what Sherri was shouting.

She was *singing*. Every time her face emerged from a wave breaking over her, she belted out a line from a classic song about love being like a heat wave. Anna and Lily joined her. They moved on to a song about sweat. Then to the classic Pointer Sisters song about being so excited.

As the minutes passed and the women’s shivering turned into near-convulsions, their words became unintelligible, tuneless noise. But still the women sang. Their brains too Popsicled to think of complex song lyrics, they resorted to “Twinkle, Twinkle, Little Star.”

Reluctantly, Grif had to give them credit for sticking out the cold as their core body temperatures ticked down on Kettering's tablet.

Ninety-four.

Ninety-three.

Ninety-two.

"That's it. Ninety-one degrees," Kettering announced. "Come ashore, my little singing minnows."

Grif actually felt a stab of compassion for Sherri as she crawled out of the water, sodden fatigues sagging, on her hands and knees, too hypothermic for her leg muscles to function. She collapsed in the sand, shivering and twitching as heat slowly returned to her body.

He squatted in the sand beside her. "While you're down there, roll around a bit. We like powdered doughnuts on the teams."

One blue eye opened to peer up at him, clearly gauging whether or not he was serious. And whether or not she should attempt to kill him.

"You do want to be a SEAL, don't you?" he asked lightly.

She rolled onto her back. Onto her far side. Back to her belly. Caked in white sand, stuck to every bit of exposed skin and wet clothing, she painfully pushed to her feet.

"I'm feeling like a jog to stretch my legs this morning," Cal announced. "How about you, gentlemen?"

Grinning, the other men agreed, and they took off down the beach with the women. They all had to slog through the soft sand, which was work for Griffin, too. But he hadn't pulled a grinder or gone for a dip in the winter ocean this morning. Of course, a run would have the side benefit of bringing the women's core body temperatures back up into the normal range.

Kettering took pity on the women and only ran them two miles—slowly—down the beach before turning them around to head back toward the Jeeps.

They drove back to Camp Jarvis, and the women headed for the showers. While they cleaned up and finished warming up, Cal took the men into the cinder-block building that housed weapons and munitions to pull equipment for the next training evolution.

Cal explained, "Not only do we have to get the ladies physically and mentally toughened up for Phase I of BUD/S, but we need to teach them the swimming and diving skills they'll need for Phase II, and the land warfare skills they'll need for Phase III."

"It takes six months to run all three phases of BUD/S!" Grif protested. "Are you seriously going to sideline all of us for that long to train these wannabes?"

Kettering rounded on him sharply. "I'm under orders to create a female SEAL, come hell or high water. Do you want her to be a liability to a team and get her fellow SEALs killed, or do you want her to pull her weight and be, if not an asset, at least not a liability?"

"Jeebus Crispy," Axel muttered. "Orders? For real?"

Kettering glared at all of them. "For real. Straight from SECDEF."

Trevor whistled under his breath and traded alarmed looks with Griffin. The Secretary of Defense herself was behind this little fiasco? There went any quiet washing out of the female candidates.

Grif argued, "But if the first woman SEAL is only going to be window dressing, who cares if she can hack the job?"

Cal started to roll his eyes but stopped himself. "She'll undoubtedly be sent out on a mission or two with a gaggle of reporters in tow. She has to at least put on a show of being SEAL material."

Griffin suddenly shared Kettering's urge to roll his eyes.

Cal sighed. "We can train these women up to some sort of decent standard, or we can throw one of them onto the teams unprepared and untrained with the knowledge that she'll be a danger to her teammates. Either way, a woman's going to be wearing a Budweiser by this time next year."

"Fuck that shit," Grif exploded. Their gold pins, nicknamed Budweisers for their resemblance to the beer brand's logo, were sacred. They were badges of honor earned through literal blood, sweat, and tears. They signified membership in the most exclusive brotherhood on the planet.

Kettering met his glare of disgust and stared him down so coldly that Griffin fell silent. He didn't often see the boss man go ice cold like that, but when he did, someone was about to die.

Grif's stare faltered. Fell away.

Well, go suck a duck. Kettering wasn't going to be talked out of this madness.

Sherri's words from last night reverberated through his brain. *Where will that leave you? Will you be in or out?*

He exhaled very carefully. Then he said with equal care, "Message received, sir." When Kettering did not rip his head off with his bare hands, Grif risked adding, "I gather you have a training plan laid out that covers all the skills they'll need?"

Kettering's voice was still stern but had lost that brittle, deadly edge. "I do."

Griffin finished exhaling the rest of the breath he'd been holding.

Cal said calmly, "Speaking of which, let's get a feel for how well the ladies shoot and start teaching them how to handle a weapon properly."

Chapter 4

Sherri had never been so exhausted in her life. And they'd been training for one day. *One. Flipping. Day*. She'd been to the Olympic Training Center at six-thousand-foot altitude and never gotten put through the wringer like that.

She fell into bed the minute she finished eating supper, as did Anna and Lily. Sherri murmured, "Is it just me, or do you feel like you've been ground into sausage?"

"Worse," Lily responded wearily. "I feel like a bunch of Navy SEALs worked me over with baseball bats."

Anna moaned, "How on earth are we supposed to do this for six months?"

Sherri answered grimly, "One day at a time. That's how. We survived today. When tomorrow comes, we'll survive it, too."

"I don't know about that," Anna confessed. "If you hadn't started singing when we were lying in the ocean, I might have thrown in the towel right then."

"It's all a big head game," Sherri responded. "The three of us already meet the minimum physical standards to start BUD/S. And if my guess is correct, we're going to be significantly more fit before these yahoos are done with us. The challenge, then, is the mental aspect. Can we take being screamed at and hazed all the time? Can we endure what seems unendurable? Can we fail, and then pick ourselves up and start over again?"

"You make it sound so easy," Anna replied.

Sherri laughed. "Oh, it'll be the hardest thing any one of us ever does. But we just have to decide that, no matter what they throw at us, we'll die before we give up."

Anna said with a little laugh, "Good thing my father always called me the most stubborn female he ever met."

Lily added, "When my gymnastic coaches told me to attempt high-level skills for the first time that would get me killed if I screwed them up, I had to take a leap of faith and trust them to know I was ready. This feels a lot like that. We have to trust our instructors. They know how to build a SEAL. We just have to let the process happen and go with the flow."

Sherri liked that perspective. But she wasn't at all sure she could trust Griffin. He seemed dead set against the idea of any woman becoming a SEAL. What if his end goal was to break them, make them all fail? Was she willing to go with that flow…until it killed her?

She'd learned early in life that getting along with people was a whole lot more productive than clashing with them. Could she find a way to work *with* Griffin and not against him?

An image flashed through her mind of him shouting at her while she lay on the ground, her arms as limp as noodles and burning with exhaustion. He'd been pressuring her to win, not just to survive.

Now that she thought about it, he'd actually imparted an important piece of advice to her. Had he actually been trying to teach her the proper mindset for success? Maybe he wasn't one hundred percent out to see her fail after all.

Or maybe in her pain and exhaustion she was just

hallucinating that he wasn't a mean-hearted son of a bitch.

Well, hell. Now she had no idea what to make of him. She knew he was hotter than should be legal and kissed like nobody's business. And that he could be a gigantic asshole when he chose to be. But which one was the real man? Or hadn't she seen that person at all yet?

The next morning, well before dawn, they went for a long, way-too-fast-for-comfort run and ground out more push-ups, sit-ups, and pull-ups than she'd believed herself capable of two days ago.

They spent the rest of the morning lying on their bellies in the sand of a firing range, shooting at human-shaped targets mounted in front of a tall dirt berm. Lily was an outstanding shot as it turned out, and Anna was steady as a rock, calm and focused, as Trevor taught her how to shoot some of the larger weapons she'd never handled before.

Griffin picked at the most nitnoid details of Sherri's technique, criticizing everything from how she inhaled to where her pinkie finger rested on the gun stock. They started with handguns and worked their way up to M4 carbines.

With the larger weapon, they started shooting at a range of twenty-five yards and gradually extended their range to a hundred yards. Sherri was delighted to hit her target eight out of ten times at that range.

"You have to be ten for ten, all in the kill zone, to secure this evolution," Griffin said shortly.

Securing an evolution was SEAL talk for passing a training requirement. Heaven forbid that they speak plain English. "Buzzkill," she muttered.

He ignored her comment, continuing implacably, "You also have to be effective with this weapon at up to five hundred yards. If you can't pull your weight in a firefight, you and your teammates will die. When it's ten of you against a hundred—or several hundred—tangos, and you're low on ammo, every single shot has to hit."

He had a point.

She lowered her eye to the sight again, and when Commander Kettering cleared the firing line and gave the order to shoot, she imagined herself aiming at enemies trying to run over her SEAL team's position. It lent a grim seriousness to the training that she'd failed to grasp before.

She shot eight out of ten again.

That was when Griffin lay down beside her, his body spooning against her side, big and hard and hot.

"What are you doing?" she squeaked.

"Teaching you how not to shoot like a girl," he ground out. He sounded nearly as uncomfortable as she felt. His arm came across her back and tucked under her right arm, draped across the rifle stock.

"You're not settling the rifle against your shoulder closely enough. It has to feel like an extension of your body."

Right. Kind of like he felt at the moment.

"Wiggle it tight against you. Like this. See how snug it feels now?"

Okay. Was she the only one hearing the double entendre in his words?

Trevor coughed from her other side, where he stood behind Anna. Nope. Not just her.

"Shut up, Fog Breather," Griffin growled.

Trevor chuckled, apparently enjoying Griffin's discomfort.

"You were saying?" she asked blandly. "Tuck it in tight. Nice and snug. Then what?"

His lips moved against her ear. "Smart-ass."

She smirked, her cheek rubbing against the trigger housing.

He muttered, "Exhale long and slow as you acquire your target in the sight."

"My target's definitely acquired," she purred.

"Stop it."

She pulled her eye away from the rubber cup of the gunsight. "Stop what?" she asked innocently.

"You're playing with fire, little girl."

"Go ahead. Burn me up," she whispered.

"Jeez," he breathed. He shifted uncomfortably against her back.

She turned back to her gunsight, delighted at having made the big bad SEAL squirm. "I exhale and acquire the target. Then what?"

She felt his rib cage expand with a long breath in, which he held for several seconds and then let out. His voice was calm, devoid of emotion, when he said, "Draw your trigger finger toward you slowly. Your goal is to touch the trigger guard, not to actually pull the trigger. You want to exert as little pressure on the trigger as you can and still have it shoot. That way you won't dislodge your aim."

She murmured, "I'd hate to dislodge anything, particularly when I already have it lined up right where I want it."

"Shoot the damned target already."

Laughing a little, she lowered her eye to the sight, breathed out the way he'd shown her, and pulled gently through the target.

"Bull's-eye," Trevor announced, peering downrange through binoculars.

"See?" Griffin muttered in her ear. "Just do what I tell you, and we'll both get through this." He stood abruptly.

She eyed him, looming above. "I can't wait to see what else you teach me."

"You're killing me, Tate."

"That's the idea, Caldwell." Yes, indeed. That was the idea. She sensed that any show of weakness from her would bring out the predator in him, resulting in her being eaten alive. And not in a good way.

When her shoulder ached from recoils and her toes were cramping from dehydration, Kettering called an end to the morning's shooting. They went back after lunch, and Sherri didn't think they were ever going to leave the firing range by the time they were finally released.

Anna and Lily headed straight for the showers, but Sherri made her way to the gym, where foam rollers were stored. She wanted to roll out some of the kinks in her shoulder before calling it a day. Assuming the sadists training them didn't have some dastardly night evolution up their sleeves.

The hard foam rolled across the kinks in her upper back, and it hurt so good. She groaned in pain and relief as the knots worked out.

"You gotta quit making noises like that around us guys," a voice said from just behind her. Griffin.

She lurched and slid off the roller, her rear end

thumping unceremoniously on the concrete floor. "You startled me," she mumbled.

"A SEAL should never be startled. You should scan your surroundings continuously, know where everyone in the room is at all times. You should spot every entrance and possible egress point, identify where an attacker would ambush you, and know what your first couple of moves will be in response to any attack."

She pulled a face. "You're singing to the choir."

"How's that?"

"I'm a woman. Worse, I'm a decent-looking woman working in a largely male world. I already do most of what you described in self-defense."

Griffin grabbed a roller and lay down beside her, rolling his hamstrings across the foam cylinder. "I thought sexual harassment has been addressed pretty aggressively in the military."

"It has. But too many men seem to think I'm an exception to the rules."

"Is that why you want to be a SEAL? So you can kick their asses?"

She shrugged as she shifted the roller to her other deltoid muscle. "It wouldn't suck as a side benefit."

"Speaking of which, I apologize for kissing you. That was out of line."

"No worries. The way I remember it, there were two voluntary participants." Besides, it had been more of a mutual collision than a boy-kissed-the-girl moment.

He nodded and turned on his side to roll out his right quad.

"Tell me something, Griffin. What hangs you up so badly about the idea of women as SEALs?"

"It'll change the team dynamics, that's for sure."

"You mean like sex and attraction and flirting?"

He shrugged, declining to answer. But clearly she'd hit the nail on the head.

She responded, "Women have worked in various professions with men upwards of forever, and everyone has managed to get their work done. More to the point, women do all sorts of military jobs side by side with men, and have for decades. But for the most part, everyone manages to keep their libido in check. Give me a better reason than that."

He was silent a long time and then blurted out all at once, "I don't think a woman can have the guts of a SEAL."

"What does that mean?" she challenged.

"I don't know how to describe it. SEALs have...courage beyond the ordinary. They'll sacrifice themselves for the right cause. It sounds lame to call it heroism, but that's basically what it is."

"And you don't think women have that?"

"Not the same way a SEAL does."

How the heck was she supposed to prove that she could be a hero? Nobody could really know how they would react in one of those split-second life-or-death moments until one presented itself.

Taking advantage of Griffin's rare talkative mood, she changed subjects and asked him something else that had been bugging her.

"So how is this training going to work?" she asked. "Are you guys going to yell at us every day and then be civil with us every night?"

He stopped rolling and sat up, stretching one arm

across his body and pulling on it with the other. She was a little surprised at how flexible he was. She'd heard rumors that SEALs practiced yoga and even took the occasional ballet lesson. Maybe those rumors were true.

Griffin finished stretching the first shoulder and went to work on the second one before he answered, "We're in a weird position of having to simulate BUD/S for you three and also teach you how to get through it."

"I get that," she replied. "It just gives me mental whiplash sometimes."

"The BUD/S instructors will do that, too. Particularly in Phases Two and Three. If you survive the first phase, they'll want to get to know you. See if you're the kind of guy—or gal—they'd want to work with. How you react to ribbing or to friction inside a team. Every now and then someone washes out in Phase Two or Three just because they're assholes nobody wants to work with."

"So even if I pass the physical requirements, the boys' club can toss me out simply because they don't like me?"

He met her stare reluctantly. "It'll be different in your case."

"Why?" she demanded.

"Because you're a woman. And we're under orders to graduate one."

"What if I want to get through all three phases on my own merits?"

Griffin started to snort but cut the noise off quickly.

Not quickly enough. She still heard his skepticism.

"Indulge me for a minute, Griffin. Let's play a what-if game. What if I do make it through the physical conditioning phase for real? Then what? Do you think the instructors will give me a fair shot at the swimming and land phases of training?"

He looked her square in the eye. "It'll depend on who they bring in to instruct you. Most of the instructors are older guys. They've been on the teams a while and have aged out or been injured out of the field. They're not going to be fans of a female SEAL."

"What if I can do the job as well as the guys? Then would they accept me?"

Griffin's eyebrows drew together. "I honestly don't know."

"What about you? If you were my instructor, and I could actually pull my weight on a team, would you let me work with you and your guys?"

"It's not as if I have a choice in the matter. This shit's rolling downhill from the Secretary of Defense herself."

"We're playing what-if. What if I make it all the way through BUD/S because I deserve to be there fair and square. Would you work with me then?"

"I suppose so."

He didn't sound the least bit pleased about his answer, but warmth pulsed through her all the same. He'd said yes. He would work with her if she made it through training. It was a hell of a goal to shoot for.

"Maybe you're not as giant a jerk as I thought you were, Caldwell."

He aimed a disgusted look at her but didn't deign to answer. She would take that as a score for the female half of the human race.

Griffin started rolling his head around and rubbing at the back of his neck.

"Turn around," she ordered.

"I beg your pardon?"

She climbed to her knees. "Turn around. I can fix your neck."

"Huh. Break it, more like."

She grinned. "Don't tempt me. But seriously, I can help."

He turned around, sitting cross-legged in front of her. She put her hands on the slabs of his deltoid muscles, and they tensed, hard as rocks. Lord, the heat of that man. It rolled off him in waves, just like the potent sex appeal that poured off him every time he looked at her.

In any other situation, she'd have been all over flirting with this man. Getting him into her bed ASAP. As it was, she was still half-tempted to go for the gusto with him, instructor or not. He was everything she'd ever wanted in a man—smart, funny, handsome, and sexy as hell. He was even kind and decent, if reluctantly so. The man had an ironclad sense of honor, and she suspected that he wasn't the kind to lie to her. In fact, he would be pretty darned near perfect if he weren't so damned determined to destroy her dream.

She probed the muscles across the back of his neck lightly until she found a giant knot in one of them.

"This is old scar tissue," she commented. "How long have you been running around with this knot? It must give you constant pain."

"Pain is optional. I choose not to notice it," he muttered as she dug her thumb into the mass of scarred fascia to start breaking it up. "Ouch!" he yelped.

"Hang in there, Mr. Optional Pain. Just a few more seconds."

The scar tissue started to release. It felt like a zipper unzipping, and she smoothed the pad of her thumb down its length more gently. "Try that," she murmured.

Tentatively, he rolled his head. "Whoa. That *is* better."

He rose to his knees and turned around to stare at her. What was that expression in his eyes? Gratitude? Confusion?

Huh. What did he have to be confused about? Although, Lord knew, he confused the hell out of her. One second she wanted to strangle him, and the next she wanted to have hot monkey sex with the man.

"Where did you learn how to do that?" he asked.

Hot monkey sex? Oh. Wait. He was talking about fixing his neck.

"A fantastic soft-tissue chiropractor at the Olympic Training Center showed me how to do it." The words came out more breathless than she wanted them to, and darned if her cheeks weren't heating up.

"That would be a handy skill in the field. Can you teach me how to do it?" he asked.

If she wasn't mistaken, his voice was huskier than usual, and his breath was coming faster and lighter than before.

"Sure. It takes a little practice, but it's not hard."

"I have a staff meeting with Cal in"—he glanced down at his watch—"two minutes ago. Shit. Show me later?" he called over his shoulder, already sprinting for the gym's door.

"Yes!" she called back.

~

The next day, they got to play with grenades. Well, training grenades that made a lot of noise and threw bits of paper all over the place. The three women and each of their swim buddies stood inside a concrete box about neck high and eight feet square. It was the far-left hand of five safety pits in front of a pockmarked strip of dirt about fifty meters, a little over one hundred fifty feet, long.

Griffin put the first training grenade in Sherri's hand and then stepped behind her, his front plastered against her back. Heat and muscle surrounded her, and all of a sudden she wasn't breathing quite right.

Was it normal for SEAL instructors to get so up close and personal with the trainees, or was he coming up with excuses to snuggle up to her? Were she not so wildly attracted to him, she might just be bothered by how... physically...he was teaching her. But as it was, her pulse leaped erratically every time he touched her.

She murmured, "We have to stop meeting like this, Mr. Caldwell."

"Cut it out."

"Cut out what? Can't a girl enjoy a big strong man's arms around her?"

He huffed in her ear, but didn't sound as convincingly irritated as he should have. She smiled to herself.

Griffin instructed, "Put your left arm straight out and up in front of you like this." He reached around her with his left hand and guided her left arm into the correct position. His forearm rubbed against her ribs, perilously close to her breast. *Yowza.*

"Draw your right arm back by your ear like Jojo demonstrated before."

She turned her head to answer and froze. Her mouth was about three inches from his. *Double yowza*. She managed to choke out, "The motion Jojo showed us is just like throwing a shot put. Which is one of the heptathlon events I've competed in for years."

"Perfect. You don't want to throw a grenade like a baseball, or it will roll after it hits the ground, and who knows where it will end up. You want to lob it in a high arc so it'll drop to the ground and stick where it lands."

She probably knew more about the math of the perfect trajectory for maximizing travel of a heavy spherical object than he did, but she let him adjust her arms and explain what a good grenade throw looked like because it felt so blessedly fantastic to have his hands on her like this.

He stepped back from her, and she actually felt a little…bereft.

"Okay. Give it a try," Griffin directed. "Pull the pin, assume the position I showed you, and let 'er rip."

She went through her highly practiced shot-put motion and heaved as hard as she could. The grenade, substantially lighter than an 8.8 pound shot, sailed downrange.

Bang! A puff of white smoke marked where her grenade had fallen. Griffin stared at the smoke, his jaw as hard as the concrete safety pit around them. She would take that as approval.

Jojo was the first to speak. "Dang, Tate. That's a solid thirty meters out. Good arm you've got there. Not like mine, of course, but not half bad." The guy said that as if she, Anna, and Lily weren't all outstanding athletes. Sherri bit back a sarcastic comeback.

She glanced sidelong at Griffin, trying to not look too smug. But she probably failed.

He simply turned and climbed out of the pit, heading for the parked Jeeps. She scrambled to catch up and tagged along beside him. After all, they were swim buddies and required to go everywhere together. As he reached into the back of the Jeep for a wooden box, she couldn't resist poking. "Aww, c'mon. That was a decent throw. Admit it."

He hefted the crate onto his shoulder and headed for the safety pit at the right end of the line, farthest from everyone else. His jaw muscles had yet to relax after her throw.

"What's in the box, Santa Claus?"

"Inert grenades weighted to feel exactly like live ones," Griffin answered shortly. Poor man hated it when she succeeded at anything.

"Get used to it, big guy. Girls are coming soon to a team near you."

He set the box down outside the safety pit, and she stepped inside ahead of him. Her foot kicked what felt like a rock, and she glanced down. "Oh, look. There's a grenade on the ground in here."

She bent down to pick it up, and out of nowhere, Griffin grabbed her T-shirt and yanked her backward, propelling her clear of the pit. He threw her so hard she flew a good ten feet through the air, landing flat on her back. Then his entire body weight smashed down on top of her. The impact drove all the air from her lungs. She tried to inhale, but nothing happened. *Crap.*

As panic slammed into her, a tremendous explosion deafened her.

Kaboom!

Griffin grunted on top of her.

She stared up at him at a range measured in inches, and he stared back.

"Y'okay?" he bit out.

At last, she was able to suck in a meaningful lungful of air. "Uh-huh," she gasped. "You?"

"I'm good."

Their bodies were mashed together in a blatantly sexual fashion, his thighs between hers, his junk pressed against her lady parts. She knew the exact moment when her body and their position registered on him, because his eyes widened abruptly. Just as suddenly, his expression took on a hooded intensity that made her breath come unevenly.

"What was that?" she managed to choke out. "The explosion, I mean."

"Live grenade. You activated it when you kicked it."

"Oops." She added lamely, "Sorry."

"Not your fault. You didn't leave live ordnance behind. Whoever used this facility last is going to hear about leaving a dud grenade lying around, however."

He rolled off her, leaving her feeling needy and wanting. Why oh why did he have to feel so good? With a quick bunch and flex of muscles, he pressed to his feet. She followed suit.

Oh. My. God.

Where she'd been standing an instant before, an actual crater now gaped.

"That thing could have blown me to bits," she said breathlessly. "You saved my life."

He turned to face her, glaring at her nose-to-nose, and

Chapter 5

Griffin alternated between pleasant dreams of a lithe female smelling of soap and sunshine pressed against him, and nightmares of not reaching Sherri in time to knock her away from the unexploded grenade. He woke up groaning with lust from the first and sweating in fear from the second, his heart racing in something suspiciously akin to panic. Either way, it sucked.

He'd had plenty of close calls over the years, plenty of *oh shit* moments, but glancing down to see Sherri reaching for that grenade had literally made his heart miss a beat.

He had to get over this concern for her. Find a way to think of her as just another one of the guys. Except she wasn't a guy. Hell, she wasn't even one of his teammates for whom he would lay his life down without a second thought. Why then had he jumped for her in that damned fool move and nearly gotten himself killed, too? He could've just yelled at her to back away.

The answer was staring him in the face. But that didn't mean he had to like it. He was attracted to her. *Hell.* He might even be a little obsessed with her at this point. Worse than that, he actually would've liked her under any other circumstances. She had a dry sense of humor that emerged at stressful moments and would serve her well as a SEAL, not to mention she was smart and kind and generous. *Dammit.*

ground out, "*That's* what it means to be a SEAL. And that's why you'll never be a real one. You don't have the heart of a SEAL."

He whirled and stomped away as the other men and women came running. Then the guys chased her and the other women away from the row of pits to perform a safety check of the whole area.

Shaking, Sherri had only one thought running through her mind over and over.

Griffin Caldwell doesn't know the first thing about my heart.

If only she'd been dumb as a post or just plain mean. Then he would have had a decent reason to hate her guts. But as it was, he was finding it harder and harder to work up a righteous froth of indignation at her being here, invading his world. It didn't help matters one bit that she was showing signs of fitting in seamlessly.

"Rise and shine, buttercups!" Cal called as he strolled through the instructors' Quonset hut entrance.

Griffin groaned. He couldn't have gotten more than an hour or two of sleep altogether last night.

"Rough night?" Trevor asked as they bent down to lace up their boots, their heads close.

"I'll live."

"You sure about that?"

"Mind your own business, Crumpet Stuffer."

"I know whose crumpet I'd like to stuff," the Brit retorted.

"Don't even think about it," Griffin growled.

Trevor grinned. "If it had been me getting cozy with Tate like that yesterday, I wouldn't have slept well, either."

Griffin scowled at his teammate. "Fine. She's hot. I admit it. But she's still a woman, and I still don't want her here."

"Yes, but you do want her. And that's the hell of it," Trevor responded heavily.

The guy said that as if he understood what Griffin was going through. Was Trevor getting closer to Anna than he was letting on? More often than not, the two of them did end up paired together for training evolutions. And they were swim buddies, after all. Griffin wasn't sure whether to be relieved or alarmed that he wasn't the only man out here struggling against attraction to one of the ladies.

He stood up and strode over to Cal. "What's on the agenda for today, boss?"

"I thought we'd take the ladies for a swim. See how they feel about drowning."

From across the hut, Axel hooted. "Right on! This is gonna be fun."

Learning how to swim with feet tied together and hands tied behind the back was one of the trippier evolutions in BUD/S, and one that all SEAL candidates dreaded.

Dammit, he ought to be pleased at the prospect of terrifying Sherri out of the program or, failing that, drowning her out. Instead, Griffin's gut was unnaturally tight. What did he have to be nervous about? He could swim all day tied up. Swearing some more, he stomped out into the early-morning light.

Sherri was just stepping out of the girls' hut, rubbing the sleep from her eyes, when he caught sight of her wearing combat boots, fatigue pants, and an olive-drab T-shirt. Her hair was messy, with bits of it wisping around her face. It formed a nimbus backlit by the rising sun that made her look downright angelic. Her cheeks were rosy, a perfect match to the pink hues of the sunrise. Yup. An angel. Whom he desperately wanted to get naked with. Which surely made him not only a sinner but also a sicko.

She stretched her slender arms overhead and leaned first to the left and then the right, working out yesterday's kinks. Man, she was flexible. The things he could do with her... *Stop. That.*

Turning his gaze away, he decided he was not going to fantasize about having sex with his swim buddy just before he climbed into a pool with her and put his hands all over her. Not while he wore a bathing suit that could no way no how disguise his woody.

Thankfully, Kettering had sent them for a run around the long loop this morning. The 15K run gave him time to clear his mind and dissipate the hard-on making his whities too damned tighty. Afterward, they ate breakfast and did a classroom session on calculating windage and elevation adjustments for various weapons.

They did a short training session on how to make a proper fist and punch a person correctly, and then Cal gave the order Griffin had been dreading. "Everybody, go put on bathing suits and meet me at the swimming pool."

Griffin got there first and dipped a toe in the six-lane-wide, twenty-five-yard-long pool. It was freezing cold. For once in his life he was grateful for the coming misery. He jumped in, and the cold clenched him violently. He ached from head to foot instantly and had to forcibly ignore an urge to leap out of the water.

He surfaced, treading water easily as he watched the women approach the pool.

Trev groaned under his breath beside Griffin. The guy sounded like he was in physical pain. Yep. Griffin totally related.

Truth be told, the women all had great bodies. But Sherri… Sweet baby Jesus.

Those legs, good grief. Surely, they weren't legal. He wasn't even particularly a leg man, but hers were so smooth, so slender and muscular, that he couldn't look away if he tried. The pageant girl definitely knew how to work a bathing suit, and was doing so. She walked all slinky and sexy, like a goddamned cat. It was enough to make a man have trouble swallowing.

Eventually, he managed to lift his gaze to the rest of her. Words failed him as he stared at the perfection of her body, swathed in baby-blue spandex. The one-piece racing swimsuit shouldn't be particularly sexy, but on her, it was eye-poppingly hot. How she managed to be both strong and feminine at the same time, he couldn't fathom. But she did it. With cleavage to spare.

Mind effing blown.

She dived into the pool, knifing cleanly through the water and surfacing a few yards away from him, laughing. Droplets of water sparkled like tiny diamonds on her skin, and with her hair slicked back, the raw beauty of her face was revealed. No mermaid princess had ever been more gorgeous or had better cheekbones.

He scowled in her general direction. "SEALs generally jump feet first into water in case it turns out to be shallower than it looks. That way you won't break your neck on a shallow bottom."

She sighed. "It's always a lesson with you. Can't you ever let down your hair for one second and savor the moment? You're such a killjoy."

"I'll have you know I've worked long and hard to become this curmudgeonly," he declared.

She laughed again, a musical tinkling across the water, as he'd secretly hoped she would.

Anna did a cannonball into the water, landing only a few feet from Trevor, splashing him hard. The Brit responded by ducking under the water, grabbing her ankle and yanking her down to the bottom of the pool.

Lily, watching that exchange, slipped into the water more sedately, sitting on the edge of the pool and then merely pushing off the side into the shallow end and waiting quietly for the training evolution to begin.

Griffin swam over to where the three women had gathered, standing in chest-deep water, and announced, "SEALs wouldn't be SEALs if we weren't outstanding swimmers. The first thing you women have to learn is the combat swim stroke. It's a combination of the freestyle and a sidestroke. It's highly efficient and maximizes distance, speed, and endurance."

Here goes nothing.

"Sherri, I'll need you to help demonstrate the stroke."

She swam over to him, and he put his hands on her narrow waist, marveling at the inward curve of her sides and at how deceptively muscular her stomach actually was. Supporting her body horizontal on the surface of the water, he talked her and the others through the mechanics of the stroke.

Trevor helped Anna practice the stroke, and Axel got to Lily first to help her.

Sherri was awkward at first, but quickly got the hang of the movements. He turned her loose to swim to the far end of the pool while he swam beside her, watching and making corrections. Her outstretched hand bumped into his chest, and her head jerked up.

"Oh! Sorry."

"Situational awareness, Tate. How many times do I have to repeat myself?"

"I was concentrating on getting my movements right."

"You have to stay aware of your surroundings at all times," he snapped.

She sighed as if she was sick of hearing him say those words. Tough. He would keep saying them until it became second nature for her.

"I know, I know," she groused. "I'll get kicked out of BUD/S if I don't learn this and every other lesson to perfection."

"If it'll get you kicked out of BUD/S, it's because it will get you killed someday. We keep all the guys who won't die like damned fools and get rid of the ones who will."

She retorted sarcastically, "Got it. Don't be a damned fool. Check."

He closed in on her as she treaded water. Their legs bumped against each other as they kicked, and their arms brushed just below the surface. Interestingly enough, she didn't back away from the contact with him. In fact, her pupils widened and her cheeks flushed a brighter shade of pink.

Maybe that wasn't attraction to him. Maybe she was just out of breath from laboring with the new stroke. He prayed it was the latter. Honestly, he was starting to worry he wouldn't find anything that would exclude Sherri from the SEALs. But being a lousy swimmer was a one-way express ticket out the door.

"Out of the pool, everybody," Cal called from the deck.

As the women squeezed water from their hair, Kettering passed out zip ties to the men. Griffin took two and moved to stand behind Sherri at the edge of the pool.

"Why are you smirking back there, Caldwell?" she muttered suspiciously, throwing him a stink eye over her shoulder.

Smart girl.

"Hands behind your backs, ladies," Cal ordered.

Griffin reached out with a zip tie for her wrists. She blurted out, "What do you think you're doing?"

"This evolution is called 'Drowning.' You're gonna love it," he muttered.

When he squatted down to secure her ankles together, she squawked, "Are you freaking kidding me?"

He grinned up at her, testing the snugness with his finger. "Like I said. Fun times."

For the first time since he'd arrived in North Carolina, he saw fear in Sherri Tate's eyes. So. He'd finally found her Achilles' heel. She was afraid of drowning.

"Into the pool, ladies," Calvin ordered.

Anna and Lily jumped right into the ten-foot deep end of the pool, but Sherri hesitated. Griffin leaned forward and placed his mouth practically on her ear. "Don't make me push you, Blondie."

She threw him a defiant look over her shoulder and jumped into the pool. He watched impassively as she submerged and started dolphin kicking frantically toward the surface. If she didn't relax, she wasn't going to make it back up to air. He started counting in his head.

For the next thirty seconds she kicked for all she was worth but, because she failed to relax, all her vigorous flopping didn't propel her upward sufficiently to break the surface. Athletes with low-enough body fat tended to sink naturally, and these women were no exception.

As Sherri's swim buddy, his job was to make sure she didn't drown. He kept his gaze fastened on her every movement, carefully gauging how well, or how poorly, she was doing. At the moment, she was burning a crap-ton of oxygen flailing around like that. She would run out of air sooner rather than later.

He gave her thirty more seconds. Her movements were jerky now, definitely panicked. With a sigh, he jumped into the pool beside her. He planted his feet on the bottom and parked his shoulder beneath her tush. With easy strength, he shoved her up to the surface.

He let her breathe for a few seconds and then slipped out from underneath her, letting her sink again. Once more, she commenced flopping ineffectively.

Shaking his head, he surfaced behind her, grabbed her by the armpits, and hauled her over to the edge of the pool. She continued to struggle most of the way. If he had to guess, she was out of her mind with terror.

He heaved her onto the deck and hoisted himself out of the pool beside her. "You can relax now. You're not going to die." He added direly, "Yet."

She lay there, gasping for air, her respiration taking way too long to return to normal for an athlete of her caliber. Well, well, well. Miss Sherri Tate, Perfectionist Incarnate, was terrified of water. Or at least of dying in it. That was going to be a hell of a problem for her if she planned to become a SEAL.

"You can quit right now," he murmured persuasively. "I'll cut you loose and never throw you back in the pool. Just ring out, and it'll all go away."

"No. No bell," she panted.

"You know you want to."

That made her open her eyes. Glare up at him. "I'm. Not. Quitting."

"Won't matter if you can't swim. You'll get washed

out for failing the evolution. We're *Sea*, Air, Land operators, not Air Land operators."

"Again," she gritted out from behind clenched teeth.

He had to give her credit for guts. She'd been scared to death and half-drowned a minute ago, but she was demanding to try again.

"You have to relax and keep your upper body still," he lectured. "Pretend you're a mermaid, and let your legs do all the work."

She stared up at him balefully as she lay on her side. She might look like a drowned rat, but she was still a hot drowned rat. "Ready to die?" he asked.

"You're hilarious."

"You have to pass this evolution to pass BUD/S."

"I got that memo. Thanks," she replied dryly.

"Again, then."

He reached out to squeeze her shoulder reassuringly. Pleasure exploded through his brain at merely touching her like this. Her gaze snapped up to his in surprise, and a surge of possessiveness coursed through him—which did a whole lot more than merely surprise him. It shocked him to his core. What was wrong with him? Women didn't affect him like this. But then, he'd never been around a woman training to be a SEAL, either.

He jumped up and helped her as she climbed awkwardly to her feet, her hands and feet still zip-tied.

Appalled at his reaction to touching her, he unceremoniously tossed her in the pool. It probably wasn't the most chivalrous thing he'd ever done. *Stop being a shithead, and do your job*. He followed her back into the water.

No matter how many times he pushed her up to the surface to catch her breath, she just didn't get the hang of relaxing and working with the water instead of against it. Kettering called time on the evolution without her succeeding at swimming while tied up.

One last time, Griffin grabbed her under her arms and hauled her over to the edge. But instead of lifting her onto the deck this time, he pulled a knife out of his calf sheath and quickly slashed her zip ties. Sherri instantly flung her arms wide and kicked her legs hard, propelling herself out of the pool.

Speculatively, he watched her practically run away. *Huh*. Was it the water that had freaked her out, or had being tied up done her in? He boosted himself out of the water and followed her more slowly toward the locker room.

Sherri stood under the hot water, scrubbing her hair furiously. *Damn, damn, damn*. She hated failing, and she hated looking weak, especially in front of Griffin. She didn't know what had happened out there, but when she went under the water and couldn't move her limbs, she'd panicked every freaking time.

She didn't have much time to fret about it though, because, like every day, the training continued at a frenetic pace. Kettering hustled them out of the shower and into another session at the shooting range. At least she was reasonably good at this.

Today, five-foot-long, bull-barrel sniper rifles mounted on tripods were waiting for them when they arrived. Griffin gestured for her to lie down on the ground beside the weapon. Again, he stretched out beside her to demonstrate using the weapon.

Thing was, she liked being close to him like this.

What did that say about her?

Cut yourself a break. All it said about her was that she happened to be attracted to an extremely attractive man. It didn't make her a weirdo or a villain—just a girl who liked a boy.

She glanced to her right and saw that Trevor was similarly plastered against Anna's side. And her teammate didn't look like she minded being cozy with the hot Brit one little bit.

"The key to being an effective sniper is breath control," Griffin murmured from so close behind her that his breath stirred the short hairs curling around her ear.

"Careful," she muttered for his ears only. "I could get used to all this cuddling."

He exhaled in a gust of what felt like humor. But his words, spoken at a volume Kettering could hear as the commander strolled up behind them were, "The other key to becoming a decent shooter is focus. You have to erase everything else from your mind."

Right. Erase the feel of his muscular body unyielding against hers, ignore his heat, ignore all that simmering charm of his—

Not happening. Not with him spooning against her like they were lovers. Aaaand, there went the rest of her breath control. *Rats*.

"I'll act as your spotter. I'll call out windage corrections, and you'll input them into the scope the way Cal taught you in class. Ready?"

Sherri usually liked the single-minded concentration that shooting required. She enjoyed settling into the Zen state where there was nothing but her and the weapon.

But today it was her and the gun...and the man. Which, as it turned out, wreaked havoc on her accuracy.

"What's wrong with you today, Sherri?" Griffin asked after her third shot went well wide of the bull's-eye.

"You."

"Come again?"

"You're distracting me," she confessed.

He snorted. "How are you going to hit your target when there are rockets exploding around you and hostiles shooting back at you?"

"That won't bother me," she retorted.

"But I do."

She lifted her eye away from the rubber cup of the sight to glare at him. "Well...yes."

"You and me. We're having a conversation about this—" Kettering strolled down the firing line just then, coming to a stop behind them. "Later," Griffin added under his breath.

Louder, he said, "Tracers are screaming overhead. The ground is shaking beneath you. Bullets and shrapnel are flying all over the place. Your team is pinned down a few hundred yards below you, and you're on overwatch to save their asses. You spot the sniper trying to take them out, and he's"—Griffin paused to check out the paper target through his spotter's scope—"four-hundred yards downrange. Windage is two clicks left. Now, blow his fucking head off."

She could picture what Griffin described, could smell and taste the metallic tang of the dust. Stress tightened across the back of her neck, and she took the slow, calming breaths he'd taught her.

Her heartbeat steadied. Slowed.

Another breath.

She eased her eye to the sight and slipped her finger through the trigger guard. She reached up with her left hand to insert the wind adjustment. Everything else fell away from her, leaving her in a bubble of silence and stillness. It was just her and the target, linked by her weapon and its hair-thin crosshairs.

She squeezed gently.

The weapon bucked on its tripod.

"Dead center," Kettering announced, peering through binoculars. "Nice shot, Tate. Keep it up." Kettering strolled away to stand behind Lily at the other end of the firing line.

"Hark. Was that praise from the block of ice?" she muttered.

"Aww, Cal's not that bad. Wait till you meet the instructors at BUD/S."

"You always assume I'm going to be the one who gets sacrificed to BUD/S." She propped herself up on an elbow to stare at him. "Why is that?"

He shrugged. "You would be the worst-case scenario for the teams."

She spied Kettering heading back in their direction and flopped back down beside her rifle, muttering. "Add that to the agenda for our conversation later."

What did he mean by that? Worst case? Her? Was she that hopelessly not cut out to be a SEAL?

Chapter 6

LATER CAME WELL AFTER DARK THAT NIGHT WHEN Kettering finally declared them done for the day. Griffin and the other guys had just spent hours chasing the women around in the dark, using NODs—night optical devices—and teaching them how to erase their own tracks. They were at least a mile from camp in a thick stand of brush and towering pine forest.

The women had caught on fast to stealthy movement. Really fast. As if it came naturally to women in a way it didn't with men. It almost made a guy wonder if there were certain skills and tasks women were more suited for than men.

Nah. Men were better than women at all things physical.

Except even as he had the thought, he knew deep down in his gut it wasn't true.

It was an unsettling revelation.

As the others tromped loudly back toward beers or beds, Griffin touched Sherri's arm and gestured for her to stay behind with him. They sank down slowly into the bushes until the others had moved out of sight.

When silence had fallen around them and the night creatures were starting to chirp tentatively once more, he said quietly, "We need to talk."

"Duh, Einstein," she retorted.

He laughed under his breath in spite of himself. He did enjoy her sense of humor when she cut it loose. Most of the time she was too polite to say what was really on her mind. Pulling the NODs up on top of his head, he stood up. She did the same.

"You go first," she surprised him by saying.

Crap. He hated having to talk about touchy-feely stuff in general, and having to talk about it with the source of the problem was worse. But it had to be done. One of the cardinal rules on the teams was never to let tension between yourself and a teammate fester until it rotted team morale.

He took a deep breath and said bluntly, "Am I wrong in sensing that there's something between the two of us? As in attraction?"

Sherri went perfectly still. "Is this a trap?"

"No. It's an honest question."

"Is this part of my training?"

"No, dammit!" he burst out. "You're messing with my head like nobody's business, and I'm trying to confront the problem and deal with it before it gets both of us in trouble."

"For real?"

"Yes. For real!" He exhaled in frustration. "What does it take for you to believe a guy?"

Her shoulders slumped. "It's not you. It's me. I get defensive when men compliment me or try to talk earnestly with me. I always assume they're putting a move on me."

"Why?" He sensed she might just have revealed more about herself than she'd intended to.

"Because they usually are?" she retorted.

She rustled in the darkness. He was tempted to pull his NODs back over his eyes to get a better look at her.

She mumbled, "Let's just say that spending a lifetime having men hit on me has made me a bit cynical."

"Yeah, I get that."

"Really? Do men hit on you all the time, too, Griffin?"

A burst of laughter escaped him. "You never fail to surprise me."

"Is that a good thing or a bad thing?"

He considered her question. "Mostly good. You women are performing better physically than I would have ever guessed women could."

"But…" she prompted.

He shrugged. "I'll admit I was surprised when you freaked out in the pool."

"I don't know what happened. I swim all the time."

"You don't like loss of control," he observed. "The drowning evolution forces you to deal with not being in full control of your body."

Sherri was silent. Thoughtful. Then, "You may have a point."

"Ya think? I've only been doing this for most of my adult life. Perhaps I might know what I'm talking about."

"I wasn't trying to insult you," she said mildly. "I was just thinking out loud."

He subsided. "Fair enough."

Silence fell between them. How the hell was he supposed to circle the conversation back around to his original question…which she had yet to answer?

Sherri leaned back against the trunk of a huge pine tree. He did the opposite, stepping toward the tree until he was well inside her personal space. He didn't touch her, though. If she wanted to pivot to either side to escape him, she was free to do so.

Except she didn't. Instead, she gazed up at him as if she was trying to read his mind. If he wasn't mistaken, her breathing accelerated.

She was totally as into him as he was into her.

But how to get her to admit it?

Using the tip of his index finger, he traced the curve of her cheek. Then trailed it down the column of her neck. Across one collarbone, outlined by the soft cotton of her T-shirt. Then he dragged his fingers down her arm, noting with amusement when goose bumps lifted on her skin in the wake of his touch.

"Admit it, Sherri. You like me."

"I do, actually. I find you smart and your store of knowledge endlessly interesting."

He smiled a little. "Chicken."

"Who are you calling a chicken?" she flared.

"You. You're a big ol' chicken, Sherri Tate."

"Have you noticed what course I'm currently training for?" she replied tartly.

"You're afraid of men. So why do you want to surround yourself with the biggest, scariest ones you can find? Are you pulling some deep psychological junk where you force yourself to face your greatest fear?"

Sherri stared up at him in what he could only interpret as shock.

Holy crap. Was that it? Had he accidentally hit the nail on the head? He'd just been talking out of his ass, trying to get a rise out of her.

Very quietly, he asked, "Why are you afraid of men, Sherri?"

"Does it matter?"

"Yes. I think maybe it does."

She exhaled hard. "I don't like men crawling all over me all the time."

He frowned. "Does it bother you when I touch you?"

"No."

"Why not?"

She glared up at him. "I have no idea, and that bugs me most of all."

Ahh. He smiled a little and ducked his head to capture her gaze, which was currently pointed at his combat boots. Reluctantly, she lifted her gaze to meet his.

"Is it possible that you're attracted to me in spite of me being a man?" he tried.

"Yes, dammit," she spat out in exasperation.

"What's wrong with that?"

"I don't want to like you!"

That made him laugh aloud. "If it makes you feel any better, I don't want to like you, either. But there it is. The heart wants what it wants."

"Since when are you a romantic?" she demanded.

"Aww, honey. Just because I run around in the woods killing stuff for a living doesn't mean I don't like the feel of a woman in my arms, or that I don't want to share my bed with one from time to time."

"From time to time?" Sherri snorted. "You sure know how to woo a lady there, Sparky."

"Hey. My life doesn't allow for long-term relationships. I'm just trying to keep it real."

"Why not? Lots of SEALs are married."

"Huh. Have you seen the divorce rate? Or heard the arguments? Don't kid yourself. It's hell being married to one of us."

"Why's that?"

"We come out of the field wired too damned tight for the civilian world, we expect our families to follow orders like our men, and I'm told we're shut down emotionally."

"You don't seem shut down to me."

"You're seeing me in my native environment. Apparently, in the civilian world, men like me tend not to engage emotionally with others."

She lifted one foot and placed it flat against the tree trunk behind her. "So, if I saw you in, say, a restaurant or a bar, I'd think you were a gigantic jerk?"

"Oh, no. You'd think I was handsome and suave and sophisticated. You'd want to go home with me, get me naked, and take me to bed."

Sherri's laugh was music across his skin. No matter what else she might be, she was attracted to him like a moth to a goddamned flame.

He leaned in closer, planting his right hand on the rough tree bark beside her head. She shocked him by settling her hands on his waist, and he stopped breathing. Literally.

"We shouldn't do this," she said. "It's against the rules."

He exhaled. "SEALs live to break rules."

"It's dangerous."

"Danger is our middle name."

"But—"

He closed the remaining distance between them, pausing only long enough to whisper, "SEALs don't get caught. It's what we're trained to do."

He felt her hesitation as her breath feathered lightly across his lips.

"Do you have the daring to be a SEAL, Sherri?"

His dare hung between them, in that inch-wide gap between their mouths. Would she seize the moment or not? They both knew she wanted to kiss him again.

Without warning, she surged forward, pushing off the tree and flinging her arms around his neck. Her mouth closed on his, and suddenly they were kissing wildly. They went from zero to sixty in way under a second.

His arms wrapped around her, dragging her higher against him, fitting their bodies together. She kissed him with all of herself, moving sinuously against him, her belly rubbing his, her pelvis pressing deliciously against the hard bulge behind his zipper. Great ghosts almighty, he wanted this woman bad.

The scent of her filled his head until he was drunk with it. He plunged his tongue into her mouth, trying to capture the taste of her. Her tongue spiraled sexily around his, and his knees damn near buckled out from underneath him.

"You're so effing hot," he ground out.

"Have you looked in the mirror?" she panted back.

He tugged her T-shirt out of her pants and slipped his hand underneath the soft fabric to touch the even softer flesh beneath. Her back was slender but ridged in muscle, her skin like velvet beneath his hard, callused palms. He pushed the fabric up, out of the way, desperate to get naked with her. To hold the wonder of her. To lose himself in her glorious body.

She arched into his arms, groaning in the back of her throat. She *did* want him as bad as he wanted her. He was pretty sure he'd never experienced a sexier kiss than this. He swirled his tongue even deeper into her mouth, and she returned the favor eagerly. Passionately. Openly.

For a woman who was wary of men in general, she kissed like she couldn't get enough of him. Which made it all the hotter. Knowing that she reserved this reaction for him…

Violent possessiveness flared low in his gut, rocking him to his core. He didn't *get* possessive of women. He enjoyed a little time in their bed. Had a little fun. Hell, a lot of fun. And in the morning, he was gone.

But this woman was a fiery addiction in his blood. All he could think of was getting more, and yet more, of her. He felt himself falling into an unfamiliar pit of need and longing. This might just be the one who did in Griffin Caldwell, bachelor extraordinaire—

"Grif! Tate!"

God *damn* it. Kettering had come back looking for them.

Griffin jerked back, panting, and Sherri brushed a frantic hand across her mouth. Urgently, she stuffed her T-shirt back into her pants.

"Yo! We're over here. In your two o'clock!" Griffin called back, yanking the NODs back over his eyes quickly. Sherri did the same.

"You two okay?"

"Yep. Just having a little conversation. Clearing the air."

Kettering jogged up to them and looked back and forth between them. Thank goodness the NODs covered their eyes, and the boss man couldn't see the lust that still had to be flaring in both of their stares. "Glad to hear you're working things out. You two have been out of sync. I need you to get it together and work as a team."

"Yes, sir," Sherri said contritely. "That's what we're trying to do."

"Fall in behind me, Tate. You can bring up the rear, Grif. Let's see how quietly you can make your way back to base camp."

Kettering turned around to head home, and Griffin waited for Sherri to move off in front of him. Which was for the best. Maybe by the time they got back to the compound, his massive hard-on would have subsided enough for him to walk normally. In the meantime, he would enjoy the sight of Sherri's juicy derriere as she practiced the silent, heel-to-toe stride of the Special Forces. Lit up in bright lime-green, her heart-shaped tush was a sight for sore eyes. Too bad it couldn't do anything for his painfully throbbing crotch.

As he murmured the occasional instruction on how to signal to the person behind her to watch out for a log or a low-hanging branch, the majority of his thoughts focused on that incendiary kiss.

He and Sherri still hadn't figured out what the hell they were going to do about the smoking-hot attraction between them. Unfortunately, he probably wasn't going to sleep properly again until he scratched that particular itch.

By night, Sherri lost herself in erotic dreams of Griffin. Many of them completed the tryst in the woods that would have happened had Cal Kettering not interrupted them. Sometimes in her dreams, Griffin laid her down on a soft bed of pine needles and made long, slow love to her. In others, he backed her up against that tree and pounded into her until she woke, gasping with pleasure.

But by day, Sherri existed in a miasma of pain and sweat interspersed with freezing cold, wet, and sand. Griffin seemed to have redoubled his efforts to be a jerk while teaching her.

She hoped it was because Kettering seemed to be keeping an eagle eye on the two of them, and Griffin was protecting both of their careers from the boss. For which—if that was Grif's motive—she was grateful.

But it was also entirely possible that he was mad at her for luring a moment of weakness out of him. In the mind of a man like Griffin Caldwell, any lust between them would undoubtedly be her fault. Heaven forbid that a man should be expected to control his own libido.

Or maybe he was right. Maybe she was unfairly projecting her general dislike of men onto Griffin.

Her desperately erotic dreams continued unabated, and she found herself sleeping less and less. Better, though, to stagger through each day too exhausted to think than to lose her rested mind in daydreams of hot sex with her oh-so-sexy instructor.

In a way, she was grateful to Griffin for his renewed assholery. It made keeping up the charade of distant professionalism a tiny bit easier to maintain.

But in odd moments, when he caught her by surprise or when she turned suddenly and caught him by surprise, their gazes met for brief instants of naked honesty. The attraction between them was still there, still as strong as ever. It pulsed and throbbed relentlessly between them, a magnetic pull that never wavered. Never weakened. It was maddening.

But there wasn't a damned thing they could do about it. Not with Cal Kettering watching every move they made with the predatory alertness of a hawk.

Her life settled into a weird dichotomy of desperate desire for Griffin at night and deeply despising him during the day. The only reason she didn't lose her mind completely was that love and hate were ultimately the two sides of the same passionate coin, and one was not far from the other.

As the intensity of the training increased, Griffin was always there, right in her face, telling her she wasn't good enough, whispering in her ear that she should just quit now and save them all the hassle. That she was arrogant and stupid for thinking she could be more than just a pretty ornament in this man's Navy.

Problem was, she'd grown up with that crap. Her father had been a Vietnam veteran and a total SOB. Looking back as an adult, she could see how broken he'd been. PTSD didn't have a name back then, and admitting to "combat fatigue" had been a sign of weakness. Sherri's mother had mostly checked out of dealing with her father by tranquilizing herself into a stupor and moving through life on autopilot.

But young Sherri, desperate for Daddy's approval, had kept trying to make him happy. Kept trying to make him proud of her. No matter how much she accomplished, though, it was never enough. Perhaps that was why she'd become such an outrageous overachiever. When one sport didn't please Daddy, try another. When straight A's didn't make him proud, go for A+'s. When being pretty wasn't enough, start winning beauty pageants.

Was that the source of her deep distrust of men, which Griffin had been at pains to point out to her? She shied away from the answer, unwilling to think about the more unpleasant aspects of her past that involved the painful education of a beautiful and naive girl.

Was she pushing for more, and yet more, out of herself because Griffin was never satisfied with her?

Why did she even really care what he thought, anyway?

Of course, she knew the answer to that. And it went beyond the fact that he kissed so well she forgot her own name or that she wanted inside his pants so bad she could hardly stand it. No matter how much he infuriated her, she secretly admired him.

Griffin ran every step beside her, did every push-up with her, powered through every pull-up that she did, swam every lap that she did. It was damned hard to argue that his demands were unreasonable when he was capable of doing all of the things he asked of her and more.

In their instructional sessions, covering anything from breaking down an assault rifle blindfolded to extreme survival techniques, he was forever popping out with some tidbit that made the job easier or more effective. How was she ever going to absorb everything she needed to know to keep up with a man like him?

She had to admit she was glad that she and the other women were getting this private pre-BUD/S training. No way would she have survived the onslaught of physical demands, mental challenges, and emotional abuse if she'd gone into it cold.

As it was, she worried that Griffin and the other men were still taking it too easy on her and the girls. If she was going to survive BUD/S for real, she needed to be pushed hard enough to simulate that grueling course in every way.

As weeks passed, she realized her muscles and mind were gradually adapting to the stress. She had to hand it to these guys. They knew how to train a SEAL. Now, if they would only give the women a chance to succeed at being real SEALs in the field...

November passed, and it was a week into December when Sherri found herself lying face-first in the freezing cold surf, unable to do one more push-up.

This morning's PT had involved doing four-count lunges while holding a giant log over their collective heads. Kenny, Jojo, and Sam had joined the women in the endeavor since whichever lucky girl went to BUD/S would be part of a similar boat team and do group exercises. The SEALs were all about teamwork, after all. If one person couldn't push back up off their bent knee, the other five people ended up taking the extra weight of the log, which made their lunge recoveries all that much harder. It was a diabolical demonstration of all for one and one for all.

When all three women had collapsed, unable to do another lunge, Kettering—whom she'd privately begun to call the Antichrist in her head—dropped them into planks and started calling out push-up sequences.

"Down!" A long pause. "Up! Down!" Another longer pause that made Sherri's arms, already exhausted from that blasted log, tremble. "Up!"

Every now and then, an incoming wave swooshed

over her face while they were waiting in the down position. Because it was important *not* to breathe while doing maximum physical exertion, apparently.

She gave the push-ups everything she had. When she didn't think she could do one more, she found a way. The pain, as familiar to her now as an old friend, rolled through her, building until it was unbelievable. She'd learned over the past few weeks that she was capable of sustaining agony she'd heretofore thought unbearable. Griffin had taught her that pain was optional. The trick was to lock it away in a distant corner of her mind. To ignore it and not even register its existence.

At last, her arms simply gave out. No matter how hard she willed them to push her back up out of the water, she had nothing left.

Was this it? Was this the moment when Kettering declared her a failure and washed her out of Operation Valkyrie? She couldn't summon the energy to care. She was done. Tank empty. Nothing left.

A callused hand appeared in front of Sherri's face. "Need a hand up?" Griffin murmured from above her.

What is this? Human decency from Griffin? In public, no less?

"Since when are you a real person?" she mumbled in the general direction of Griffin's combat boot.

"Always was. Still am," he muttered.

Hah. Griffin had given her father a run for his money in the asshole department for *weeks*, now.

She was inclined to refuse the hand, but she knew without a shadow of a doubt that she could not climb to her feet unaided. And besides, he'd offered nicely.

She rolled onto her side and pressed her hand into his. He pulled her to a standing position.

She stood there, bent over, hands on her thighs, chest heaving, her T-shirt and pants weighted down with seawater and sand, her waterlogged boots too heavy to lift. "Thanks," she managed to wheeze.

"You're welcome. When we get back to base camp, get a shower and then meet me in the mess hall. Eat supper with me tonight."

Her gaze lifted sharply. As usual, his sapphire eyes were unreadable. "Why?" she blurted out. "Is that an order?"

"No. It's a request. And an offer."

An offer of what?

She watched speculatively as Griffin's muscular, dry back retreated from her. She could see the definition of his back muscles, even through his black T-shirt. Was that kind of fitness even legal?

Well, okay then. Supper with Griffin it was. Color her surprised.

When they got back to Camp Jarvis, Kettering surprised her again by announcing, "You ladies can have the shower to yourselves today. Crank the heat up, and do what you can to work out the kinks. Tomorrow will be a hard day."

They were all hard days. But just maybe, if Griffin was willing to treat her like a human being for a change, it meant she might make it through another one.

Chapter 7

An hour later, warmed up and cleaned up, Sherri stood over her footlocker, glaring at its meager contents. It wasn't as if a sexy little black dress had been on Kettering's packing list.

Which was a crying shame. She would have loved to shake up Griffin Caldwell. The man totally deserved it.

She had one nonsports bra in her possession that she'd worn under the summer whites she'd arrived here wearing, and she dug that out. Might as well give the man a little cleavage to contemplate over supper. After all, Kettering had lectured the women that very morning on how SEALs should use every weapon at their disposal to defeat the enemy.

So be it.

She settled on a pair of clean khaki cargo pants that fit her more snugly than her other pairs and a white tank top with a low scoop neck. It left her arms bare, and if she wasn't mistaken, the definition in her shoulder muscles was sharper these days. She threw a zippered hoodie over it for warmth, but left the jacket open to show off her cleavage. It was getting cold in the evenings as Christmas approached.

Funny how the concept of holidays, or of time passing, evaporated in this place. How long had they even been here? She frowned, trying to count the weeks. More measurable were the changes in herself. New personal bests in timed runs and counted exercises. She was generally quieter these days, biting back the sarcastic comments that sprang to mind when Griffin and the others were being particularly nasty. And she felt a new self-confidence from learning a host of survival and combat skills.

Honestly, she hadn't stopped long enough to really look at herself in a mirror for a while. Had she changed outside, too? Her hair was longer now, past her shoulder blades, bleached almost platinum blond by long hours in the sun and surf. The angles of her face were sharper, her cheekbones more defined, her jawline leaner. Her face had lost any hint of roundness, taking on more of a heart shape, and her eyes looked even bigger and bluer against the deep tan she'd developed.

If only she had her full makeup kit here and could hit Griffin with a full beauty-queen broadside.

Still, she did have a tube of mascara and some tinted lip balm with her, plus a blow dryer and a round brush. She did the best she could with the tools at hand, and took a critical look at herself. She wasn't pageant-ready, but she looked decent relative to being covered in mud or sand, with no makeup, hair straggling, and bags of exhaustion under her eyes.

"What's the occasion?" Anna exclaimed as she and Lily came back from the showers.

"Damn, girl. You look hot," Lily added.

"Griffin asked me to have dinner with him tonight."

"Holy shit. As in a date?" Anna yelped.

"No idea. But I thought I'd take the opportunity to rattle his cage a little."

"You're gonna blow the door right off his cage looking like that," Anna declared.

Lily dug around in her footlocker and emerged with a flat metal box that Sherri recognized as a high-end makeup palette. "Would this help?"

Sherri didn't quite dive on the makeup, but she came close. "Ohmigod, Lily. You're a lifesaver. Where did you get that?"

"What's a little contraband between friends?" Lily murmured, flashing her dimples in a mischievous smile.

Since when was Miss Prim and Proper willing to smuggle anything? Would wonders never cease? Maybe Lily wasn't quite as, well, pure as she came across.

Anna held a hand mirror, and Lily held a flashlight on her as Sherri did her makeup with quick efficiency. She gave herself a smoky eye that wasn't too dark for her fair coloring and used liquid eyeliner to give her eyes an exotic cat slant. Thankfully, her skin didn't need much coverage to be smooth and even. She added a bit of blush, a glow powder, and a rose-gold lipstick that didn't draw attention away from her dramatic eyes.

It was a look worthy of a pageant. *Now* she felt fully weaponized.

"Umm. Just wow," Lily murmured. "I knew you were pretty, but I had no idea you cleaned up like that."

Anna also was hushed, maybe a bit awed. "How come you're not a model or an actress?"

Sherri shrugged. "I've been offered both. But I want to be more than a pretty face. I want to do something important with my life."

Still eyeing her, Anna and Lily both nodded in mild understanding.

"All right. Get out of here," Anna told Sherri, breaking the spell. "Captain Hottie Pants is waiting for you."

Lily called after her as she hurried out the door. "We want a full report when you get back. All the juicy deets!"

As if.

"Don't wait up!" Sherri called back over her shoulder.

When she stepped into the mess hall, she was startled to see it deserted except for Griffin. Alarm coursed through her. "What is this?" she asked. "The 'Thanks for playing but you don't have what it takes' speech?"

For his part, he stared at her as if he'd seen a ghost. His jaw actually hung open a little.

Yes. Score! For once, she relished the effect her looks had on a man. "You okay there, Sparky?"

"Umm. Yes. Fine." He seemed to shake himself. "Get some food."

Griffin was wearing a black Reapers T-shirt tonight, and it hugged his body like skin. He, too, had pulled out the big guns for this little rendezvous of theirs.

She ladled a helping of Sue's outrageously tasty gumbo over a scoop of dirty rice, poured herself a glass of an electrolyte drink, and carried both over to the table where Griffin sat. One advantage of this intensive training was she could eat whatever she wanted, and as much of it as she wanted, without gaining an ounce.

Griffin shocked her by standing up and pulling out her chair for her as she approached the table. The poor man looked like he wasn't quite sure which end was up. *Dang*. If she'd known glamming up would have this dramatic an effect on him, she would've done it a *lot* sooner.

She sat down cautiously, watching him. He had yet to give her any indication of why he'd asked her to this private meal. He'd obviously told the other guys to stay away tonight, which meant they'd ribbed him about a date the same way the girls had ribbed her. What was so important that he would take that kind of heat to eat alone with her?

The last weeks had taught her to be wary of head games, which she'd learned came in many forms. What was his angle tonight? Lure her into relaxing, maybe into revealing something personal about herself that he could use to torture her with later?

"Is tonight special, or are you demonstrating that SEALs are going to hold my chair for me in the field all the time?" she tossed out in an effort to loosen the tension suddenly coiling in her belly.

He snorted. "Not bloody likely."

"Then why would you do it here and now?"

"Because my mama taught me to act like a gentleman around ladies?"

A lady, huh? She chose to take that as a compliment. "Where are you from originally?" she asked curiously. She associated old-school manners with the South, but she could be wrong.

"All over. My old man was a Marine."

She leaned back, studying him. Good Lord, he looked amazing, freshly showered and shaved. He'd always been deeply tanned, but his skin had lost that parched quality of having been out in a harsh desert climate for long months that it had had when she first met him. His eyes were deep, deep blue tonight. Ocean blue. *Be still my beating heart*.

Aloud, she commented, "Ahh. So you come by it honestly, then."

"Come by what?"

"Being an asshole, of course."

Griffin grinned and merely shook his head at her.

"You know what your problem is?" she responded. "You keep thinking of me as a woman. The thing is, I'm both a woman and a soldier. Although on second thought, maybe you'd do better just thinking of me as a soldier."

"Honey, I ain't never seen another soldier who looks like you."

She planted her elbows on the table. "You've *got* to get over how I look, Griffin. We've been together day and night for weeks. Surely you're used to my appearance by now."

He shrugged. "There's no getting used to you. I turn around and catch sight of you when I'm not thinking about it, and it smacks me in the face. Your beauty is like a physical blow."

She smirked. "Do I have permission to actually smack you in the face going forward?" Goodness knew, she would like to punch him about a hundred times per day, every time he taunted her for being weak or unworthy, in fact.

He arched one brow at her as if to dare her to try hitting him. She knew better—they'd started a training evolution in unarmed combat a few days back. She had yet to lay a finger on him. She'd had martial arts training, but none of it had prepared her for the vicious, hybrid street-fighting style the SEALs practiced. It was all about the brutal, silent takedown.

She sighed. "Can you at least try to see beyond how I look?"

He laid down his spoon and leaned back, crossing his arms over his chest. His biceps bulged in a display that had her gulping gumbo and burning her mouth in the process.

"Oh, I see past the looks, all right," Griffin said quietly. "So does Cal. That's why you're here."

"Do tell."

He shrugged. "I can only speak for myself."

"Please do."

Another shrug, accompanied by a display of clenched and relaxed muscles across his shoulders that had her gulping gumbo too fast again. Tight T-shirts ought to be outlawed on men built the way he was. At least when she was trying to concentrate on the conversation at hand.

He spoke slowly, choosing his words carefully. "I'll admit, you ladies have surprised me."

Really? Awesome.

Griffin continued, "We're in a weird conundrum here. This isn't the BUD/S course, and our only orders are to prepare you women however we see fit to survive BUD/S. So far we've simulated the way the instructors there will act to the best of our ability. I'm not overtly trying to be an asshole."

"You're doing a magnificent job of being one anyway."

One corner of his mouth turned up in what might be a smile. "The boys at BUD/S will make me look like a pussycat."

"I have to be honest: that's a little scary."

"And therein lies my dilemma. I have to be both BUD/S instructor-jerk and a teaching mentor to you. The two are diametrically opposed."

"Whoa, Caldwell. That was a big word you just used there."

He rolled his eyes at her. "I do have a master's degree in military history."

"From where?"

"Harvard."

Her jaw sagged. "Get out. For real?"

"Yes," he answered impatiently. "I broke my back a few years ago, and while it healed, I went back to school."

"Did you learn anything useful?" she asked with interest.

"Yeah. Politicians and soldiers don't mix."

"Do I detect a hint of bitterness?"

He shook his head. "If you actually become a SEAL, you'll learn fast to be real damned cynical of missions that come down from on high with dozens of noses already poked into them. You'll learn to ask what they're *not* telling you, and you'll realize how politicians' ridiculous notions of what SEALs can do are likely to get you killed."

"Ridiculous as in overinflated?"

He nodded, stirring his gumbo aimlessly. "They think we're bloody supermen. But we're not, as you well know."

"Tonight is the first time you've intimated that I might actually make it all the way to the teams," she said softly.

Chagrin gleamed in his gaze for a moment. "It's not as if I have any choice in the matter. Our esteemed Secretary of Defense has decided there will be a female SEAL. End of discussion."

Since he seemed to be in a mellow mood, Sherri

risked confessing, "*A* female SEAL. If it makes you feel any better, I wasn't especially happy to hear that, either."

His gaze snapped up to hers. "How's that?"

"Even if I legitimately make it through BUD/S on my own merits, I'll still be the girl SEAL the system was rigged for."

His eyebrows arched as if he was surprised to hear her admit that.

She leaned forward. "Do you know what my job was in Washington DC before I came here? I gave press conferences. I dressed pretty and wore makeup, went to cocktail parties, and did interviews with news outlets on behalf of the Navy. Assuming I'm the one who gets thrown to the wolves in BUD/S, what do you want to bet that's exactly what the brass will expect me to do after I graduate from SEAL training?"

He pulled a face. "That's not a bet I would take."

"Nobody wants me to be a real SEAL." She looked at him bleakly. "Including you."

He said nothing.

"I'm the one Kettering is planning to put into BUD/S, aren't I?"

"What makes you say that? You're performing at the same level the other women are. Honestly, all three of you are performing more or less identically. You each have your own strengths and weaknesses, but they're about a wash, overall."

"I'm the only one of the three women with experience being a public figure. I'm the obvious choice to play poster child. Anna and Lily will get to finish training here and go out and do real missions. But I'm so blasted hard to miss that I'd make a terrible field operator."

He shrugged. “I can’t deny that you’re hard to miss. Especially the way you look tonight. But if SEALs are doing their jobs right, no one sees them at all. In those circumstances, your looks shouldn’t be a factor. And you can always cover your face.”

Huh. *That* actually hadn’t occurred to her.

She took another bite of gumbo and, since talking seemed to be the purpose of this little tête-à-tête, decided to go for the gusto and share her greatest fear with him. “I’m going to end up being trotted out, wearing perfectly pressed and starched uniforms, looking like a recruiting poster and acting like a trained monkey, sporting a gold trident I won’t have earned and won’t deserve. You’ll know it, and I’ll know it. And every man who’s ever been a SEAL will know it. That offends me.”

Griffin was silent for a long time. His face passed through several expressions, settling on something very close to reluctant respect. Then he said very quietly, “What are you planning to do about it?”

“I have an idea. But I’m going to need your help.”

Chapter 8

Griffin stared at Sherri. Yet again, she'd shocked the living bejeebers out of him. Never in a million years would he have guessed that she would see through to the heart of the matter like this.

Profound relief flowed through him that she at least understood now what a Budweiser stood for. If the past two months had accomplished nothing else, at least he'd done that.

Of course, she was dead right in her prediction. The brass would make a performing monkey out of her. They might send her on the occasional tightly controlled mission—with a cadre of embedded journalists and cameramen in tow to record it—but nobody was going to let the first female SEAL come anywhere near harm's way, let alone die in the field.

"What's your idea?" He was interested to hear what she'd cooked up. She knew how the Navy senior leadership rolled better than most and would know how to get around them if anyone could.

She leaned forward. "I want to—"

The door behind them burst open, and Grif was out of his seat, facing the threat and reaching for the Ka-Bar knife strapped to his right ankle before the door hit the wall.

He noted in a detached corner of his mind that Sherri had come out of her seat almost as fast as he had. In her case, though, she held her hands in front of her in a classic martial arts stance. Not accustomed to being armed, yet. The detached instructor part of his mind made a mental note to fix that deficiency at the earliest possible time.

It was Ken Singleton who raced through the open door. Griffin stood down.

Kenny blurted out, "Cal's office, stat. Both of you."

Griffin swore under his breath. Surely Cal wasn't busting up a simple supper between him and Sherri. He knew his boss was deeply suspicious of Griffin's feelings for Sherri. But he was allowed to talk with his trainee from time to time, wasn't he?

Griffin hurried for the door with Sherri on his heels. He asked Ken tersely, "What's up?"

"I don't know. Boss told Jojo and Trevor to head down to the airstrip and put out flares. And then he called for an emergency briefing. Apparently, there's a plane arriving in the next hour or so."

Disgust exploded in Griffin's gut. "Please God, tell me it's not some congressional delegation coming to check out the progress of the golden girls."

Kenny answered as the three of them sprinted for Kettering's office. "Nah. Something's happened downrange. Cal's laptop exploded with message traffic when I was having a drink with him. He took one look and started spouting orders."

Normally, SEAL platoons were texted several hours before the show time for a mission brief. Not only the operators but also the full support team that would be sent out with them were all briefed at once.

What could be so important that he and the other

Reapers were being brought into the loop so urgently? They might be training future women SEALs, but the operative word there was *training*. Their whole platoon was down for a training rotation. For the next three months, it was not their turn at bat to deploy.

Kenny and Sherri entered the conference room attached to Kettering's office ahead of him. Cal was already seated at the table, looking even grimmer than usual. Not good. Actual alarm started to buzz in Griffin's gut. Something bad was afoot. Something Cal didn't like. And that man's instincts were never wrong.

Over the next few minutes, Sam, Axel, and the other women joined them. Pregnant silence settled. No one engaged in the usual chatter as they waited to find out what crisis had exploded and where.

Jojo and Trevor burst into the room, and Kettering ordered tersely, "Close the door, gentlemen." Cal stood up and said without preamble, "A few hours ago, Abu Haddad was sighted by an American drone in the Kirdu province of Pakistan."

Abu Haddad? Griffin swore silently and violently. Haddad was only the most wanted terrorist on the whole planet.

"Is he dead yet?" Griffin asked tightly. Haddad, a tribal terrorist leader who'd risen to power at the highest levels of the Taliban, had been a pain in the U.S. military's ass for the past decade. The bastard was responsible for the deaths of hundreds, possibly thousands of Americans, soldiers and contractors, good men and women all. He'd been at the top of the SEAL hit list for a while.

Irritation passed across Cal's face. "It was a

surveillance-only drone. By the time armed assets could be brought to bear, Haddad had retreated into a mountain cave complex."

"But we have a rough location, right?" Axel asked eagerly. "Can we encircle the SOB and nail his ass?"

"That's the idea," Kettering replied.

Griffin's pulse leaped. *Finally*. He and every other operator he knew had wanted a piece of Haddad for pretty much forever.

Kettering interrupted Griffin's racing thoughts. "The Reapers have been called in as SMEs—that's subject matter experts, ladies—to accompany the kill team. Our platoon has logged more time in pursuit of this particular target than any other active SEAL unit."

"When do we leave?" Griffin asked eagerly. He would, with great pleasure, come off a stateside rotation months early if it meant a shot at Abu Haddad.

"Support team's due here"—Kettering glanced down at his watch—"in about twenty minutes. Kenny, Jojo, Sam. You'll be going with them. It'll be a direct flight, air refueling en route, to Bagram Air Base. You'll deploy by chopper to a forward location, where you'll receive a final briefing and then head out on the hunt with members of SEAL Team 8. You'll be guided by a squad of DEVGRU guys who've been doing reconnaissance in the region."

DEVGRU was a highly classified SEAL group within the general SEAL population. Griffin had served a tour with them until he broke his back a few years ago. They specialized in counterterrorist operations and were generally a badass bunch of guys. Topnotch operators. Best of the best. Fun to work with.

Grif leaned forward. "What about me? I've been hunting Haddad for the past half-dozen years. I know the bastard cold. No offense to Jojo, Sam, and Ken, but I know the target better than they do. I should be on that plane."

Kettering looked down the table in his direction but didn't quite meet Griffin's gaze. "We all want in on this one, Grif. But you have your orders. I need you here to see Operation Valkyrie through. I'm keeping you, Trevor, and Axel here for now to continue working with the ladies."

Griffin surged up out of his seat, swearing luridly.

Kettering cut across his epithets sharply. "Sit down."

Damn it! Griffin knew a direct order when he heard one, and he dropped back into his chair, furious. It didn't help one little bit that Sherri was gazing at him sympathetically. She had no idea what it meant to him to get left out of this absolutely critical mission.

Because of *her*.

Because he was being forced to babysit a woman who wanted to play at being a SEAL.

Bile burned like acid in his throat, and it took every ounce of his self-discipline to remain seated, to hold his tongue and not rage against the unfairness of it. One of the first lessons he'd learned as a SEAL was that life wasn't fair. But this one stung. Bad.

He'd dreamed for *years* of bringing in, or bringing down, Abu Haddad. The smug son of a bitch needed his face blown off in the worst way. The Reapers had tracked Haddad to hell and back over there. They'd had too many near-misses to count with the slippery bastard. He and his guys had earned the right to be the ones to capture or kill Haddad.

"You three, go pack," Kettering ordered briskly. "Your kits will be on the C-130. Raid the armory here as needed to supplement your gear."

Kenny had the decency to meet Griffin's despairing stare across the table and murmur, "Sorry, man. I'll put an extra bullet in him for you."

"You do that," Griffin replied bitterly. Then, with slightly better grace, he added, "Good hunting, brother."

"Will do." Then Kenny was gone in a rush of pre-mission adrenaline. The guy's thoughts would already be turning to which weapons he wanted to carry. How much ammo to pack. It would be high-altitude terrain. Rough, rocky, and cold as a witch's tit. Extra thermal underwear. A second balaclava to protect his face from frostbite. Altitude sickness pills. Sleeping pills for when the oxygen deprivation made sleep come hard—

Damn it all! Griffin wanted to be there in the thick of the action. Instead, he was stuck here with a pack of damned minnows who thought they could grow up into sharks.

"Grif."

He looked up bleakly at Kettering. "Yes, sir?"

"If you can think of any intel that would help with this mission, go share it with the boys, eh?"

"Yeah. Sure."

He pushed up from the table, irritated all to hell, and stomped across the street to the barracks, where Jojo, Sam, and Ken were already almost finished packing their shit.

Of the three stooges, Kenny had been on the teams the longest. Kenny had been fresh out of BUD/S, and Griffin had been coming off the layoff for his back when they both joined the Reapers. They'd been deployed together in Afghanistan and Pakistan at least a half-dozen times.

Truth be told, Kenny knew as much about Haddad as anyone. The guy didn't need any tips from Griffin on catching the bastard. Kettering had said what he had about sharing intel to get Griffin out of the room. The boss didn't want to listen to any more whining about being left behind and had given him something to do rather than sit around bitching about it.

Grif couldn't blame Cal. But he didn't like this. Not one damned bit.

"You got this, Kenny?" he asked his longtime brother.

"Yup."

"Look out for Sam. He's the least experienced in that theater."

"Hey, man. I'm right here," Sam griped.

Griffin grimaced at their youngest team member. "Just be careful, and don't underestimate Haddad. He's a sly bastard. Trained by ex-Russian Spetsnaz dudes. He's smart and a total slimeball. Won't hesitate to throw women and children, or even his own men, under a bus to save his own ass."

"I know, Grif," Sam answered quietly. "I've read the reports on him. I hate it that we're not all going on this one together. But I promise, we'll get our man. And all of the Reapers will share credit for it."

That was big of the kid to say. A kill was a personal thing. Not something men like them shared easily or often.

Kenny added, "We'll all share a bottle of whiskey to toast the kill."

A faint buzz of noise became audible. An airplane

was approaching Camp Jarvis. Griffin tried to smile and failed. "Ride's here. Time to rock and roll."

Sam flashed his boyish grin. "Let's go kick some ass!"

Everyone let out a hooyah, but their overall enthusiasm was dampened by the splitting up of their squad. They'd lived, worked, and played together practically nonstop for the past two years.

Grif picked up a couple of bags and humped them out to the Jeep Sherri had waiting out front. He swung into the front seat, and Sam and Jojo jumped in the back. Cal drove the second Jeep, and Kenny rode with him. No doubt getting a few last-minute instructions as the most senior member of the three-man team.

The trip to the airfield didn't take nearly long enough for Griffin to come up with a reason to get on that plane. Sherri parked at one end of the runway, and they all piled out to await the aircraft.

He stood there, agonized, listening to the roar of the C-130 landing. He couldn't be left behind. He *couldn't*. But neither could he find a way to buck Kettering's direct orders.

The plane came to a stop in front of them. The rear ramp dropped down, and a familiar face jogged out of the plane.

"Leo?" Griffin blurted. "What the hell are you doing here? Shouldn't you be home with Janine?"

Lipinski grinned. "I pulled some strings and got put on the op. Janine's fit to be tied, but no way was I missing out on this one."

"Lucky bastard."

"You're not coming?" Leo asked, surprised.

"Nah. Working on something classified here."

Lipinski eyed Sherri appreciatively. "Classified, huh? Looks like a *miserable* assignment." The guy waggled his eyebrows in Sherri's direction, and Griffin felt her tense beside him.

"You still Smurf blue under that uniform, Lipinski?" Griffin asked.

Leo exploded with "You cock-swinging motherfucker piece of shit. Was that your idea? I'll kill you, man."

"It's a good look on you…Smurfy."

"I swear to God, if you guys start calling me that, heads are gonna roll—"

Kenny strolled past Griffin, bags in each hand. "What's that, Smurfy? You think you can take me and the boys?"

Trading insults, Leo and Kenny strode up the ramp and disappeared into the belly of the cargo plane.

Jojo and Sam paused for a moment beside Griffin, and Jojo murmured, "Don't worry about us. We'll get our man."

"We always do," Griffin replied bleakly. "You got all the gear and intel you need?"

"Yuppers. We'll bag the tango and be back here to give the minnows hell before Christmas."

"You do that. And keep an eye on Lipinski. Janine will kill us all if something happens to him."

Jojo shook his head. "There's a reason I never put a move on her. That woman's scary as hell when she's pissed off."

Sam grinned. "Smurfy's welcome to her, man."

"Be careful, kid," Griffin tossed at Sam.

The team's baby member told him in no uncertain terms what he could do with himself while they were gone, and Griffin was still smiling as Sam and Jojo disappeared inside the C-130, too.

In a matter of seconds, the plane was buttoned up and taxiing away, sending a wash of hot engine exhaust at him.

Griffin turned his back to the force of the blast and let it blow him over to the Jeeps. He climbed into the one Sherri was driving.

Jet engines screamed to full power, turbo props cut into the air with a deep, rhythmic thrumming that went right through him, and the red and white lights of the military transport lifted away into the night.

That was it. His teammates were gone, and he was stuck here. Left out of the most important mission of his whole freaking career.

They sat at the end of the runway, watching until the plane became just another speck among the stars. Silence fell around them as Kettering's Jeep headed back to the compound, leaving him and Sherri alone.

Gradually, the crickets and frogs resumed their nightly chorus, but subdued at this time of year. Or maybe they sensed how colossally, royally pissed off he was at being here to hear them.

Sherri murmured, "I'm sorry. I know how much that meant to you."

He whirled to face her, enraged. "No. You fucking don't know. You have no possible way of knowing."

Sherri looked stricken. Which was weird, considering all of the insulting, degrading, awful things he'd hurled at her the past few weeks. Of course, the difference was none of that had been personal. And this was.

She knew it, and he knew it.

He sighed hard. "I'm sorry. That was out of line."

"Apology accepted."

He stared at her, and she stared back. Oddly enough, she did seem to get how frustrated he was to be stuck here when his brothers were winging off toward a dangerous mission.

"You won't be sidelined with us women forever," she ventured.

"Seems like I will."

"Go for a ride with me?" she murmured.

Why not? It wasn't as if he could sit still right now, anyway. Not with how jacked up his adrenaline and irritation both were. He nodded tersely, and Sherri started the engine. He leaned his head back and closed his eyes, fighting down the fury as she headed down a dirt track toward the back end of Camp Jarvis.

Tall, kudzu-draped trees closed in around them, and a little of his fury subsided. It was damp tonight. The air felt heavy. Like it wanted to storm. Perfect. Stormy weather to match his black mood.

A chill hung in the air, and he tugged the hood of his sweatshirt up around his ears. It would be a hell of a lot colder than this in Pakistan.

Sherri zipped the flexible plastic windows closed on her side of the vehicle, and he did the same. She turned up the heater, and it gradually beat back the cold.

They drove for a while in silence. Sherri seemed to understand that he was too mad to talk about it, and even if he could, he didn't want to talk about his damned feelings.

She surprised him, however, by veering down a side road paved with broken, crumbling concrete. Weeds grew up between the cracks, and she slowed the Jeep to a crawl, bumping along slowly. The road was only traversable because they were in a sturdy utility vehicle.

"Where does this go?" he asked.

"To the old base hospital and building complex around it."

"I thought all that stuff was torn down when Camp Jarvis was decommissioned."

Sherri replied, "The wooden buildings were taken down. But several dozen concrete block buildings still stand. The girls and I explored them before you guys arrived. We figured you would use them for urban assault training at some point, and we wanted to get the jump on knowing our way around."

He flashed her a grin. "You know what they say. Cheat, but don't get caught. You definitely shouldn't confess to having cheated."

"It's not cheating to have a look around the place where we live and work," she retorted. "Aren't SEALs supposed to become familiar with any environment they find themselves in?"

"It's good to know you're paying attention to my words of wisdom." He added wryly, "I'll make sure to compensate for your knowledge of the layout of this place when we bring you over here to play Cowboys and Indians."

She stopped the Jeep and turned to look at him. "It's not politically correct to call Native Americans that anymore."

"Black Hats and White Hats?" he replied.

"Better. But it seems to me that, at best, we're gray hats."

"SEALs are the last resort in bad situations. Never

doubt that we're the good guys at the end of the day. We just use more…pragmatic…means than other people to achieve the good end. Leave the political nuances for the folks back home."

"I'd like to know why I'm being asked to kill someone," she responded.

"You won't always be told," he said solemnly. "But you'll be expected to pull the trigger anyway. Ours not to reason why. Ours but to do and die," he paraphrased.

"Tennyson?" she asked in surprise.

"You know it?" he asked in equal surprise.

"'Charge of the Light Brigade,'" she said softly. "They all died in the end."

"Another piece of sage advice, grasshopper: don't think about death. It has a way of coming for those who do."

She peered at him in the dark. "Is that Tennyson, too?"

"No. That's Griffin Caldwell."

"I hear he's a smart man."

Silence fell between them. He stared over at her. If possible, the shadows and darkness made her appear even more otherworldly and beautiful than usual. He reached out and pushed a strand of her hair back, tucking it behind her ear. The shell of her ear was soft and smooth, and she shivered lightly under his touch.

"How is it possible that you keep getting more beautiful?" he murmured.

"You're fatigued and deprived of the sight of any other women," she replied practically.

He chuckled. "You're starting to sound like a SEAL."

"How so?"

"You're losing all that diplomatic doublespeak you used to do all the time."

"Is that good?" she murmured.

"Yes." He leaned in a little closer to her. "That's good."

A patter on the plastic shell of the Jeep made him look up. "Here comes the rain."

"You wanna ride it out in here or find shelter?" Sherri asked.

He wanted her in his arms, and not jackknifed into the back seat of a car like a couple of guilty teenagers. "Do any of those buildings have intact roofs?"

"Yes. There's one. A side wall is gone, but it ought to be dry. It's over there. I don't think we can drive to it, though."

"Let's make a run for it."

Except, instead of running directly after Sherri, he paused long enough to scoop up a big armload of fallen branches and a couple of small logs. By the time he joined her in the partial shell of a one-story cinder-block building, it was starting to rain in earnest.

She helped him break up the branches and build a fire. In a few minutes, a blaze crackled merrily. They sat side by side on an overturned filing cabinet and took turns feeding wood into the fire. When a decent bed of coals had formed and they'd laid some of the thicker pieces of wood on the blaze, he leaned back against the block wall behind him and closed his eyes.

"Tell me about Abu Haddad," Sherri said.

"He's one of the youngest tribal leaders in the whole Taliban. In his midthirties as far as we can tell. Lacks the wisdom of age and thinks he's immortal."

"Sounds like a SEAL."

"Speak for yourself. I'm fully aware of just how mortal I am, thank you very much."

"You've also spent a decade in the field and had some close calls."

"Hence my concern about the youngsters being sent over to deal with Haddad."

"Have a little faith in them. They've been exhaustively trained by you and guys like you."

But was it enough? Were the boys really ready to face a foe like Haddad? Had he just sent his brothers off to die? Griffin fell silent, brooding at the fire.

Sherri prompted, "You were telling me about Haddad."

"Right." It was an effort, but he picked up the thread of conversation. "He's smart, mean, and ambitious. Has taken out most of his rivals and is fond of genocide. When he takes over a village, he wipes out everyone. Including women, kids, even the damned goats. The locals are terrified of him."

"That must make getting intel on him hard."

"Makes it damned near impossible. That's why this sighting of him is such a big deal."

"What are the odds it's a trap?" Sherri asked. "He doesn't sound like the kind of man who allows himself to be seen by surveillance drones unless he wants to be seen."

"It's always possible that any mission we're sent on is an ambush. We train for that eventuality."

"You don't sound entirely convinced," Sherri replied.

"I wish I was there to look out for my guys." He squeezed his eyes shut in frustration.

A crack of thunder made him jump, and they both laughed. He counted in his head between the next flash of lightning and its accompanying rumble of thunder. The night was dark, the rain a steady drumming of sound on the leaves. The trees beyond the building were black and slick. The clean smell of wet grass calmed him deep down in his soul.

Tomorrow would bring another battle, but for tonight, his soul could rest.

"Storm's a mile or more away," he observed.

"It's nice, sitting here, listening to the rain like this. It's cold, though."

She was not wrong. An odd need for human contact swept over him. He opened his arms in an invitation to share body heat—and comfort. She came willingly, snuggling against him and laying her head on his shoulder. Her arms crept around his waist, and she hugged him back.

It was nice. Too nice. Hell, it would've been damned near perfect if the boys weren't on their way downrange without him. He had no business sitting here enjoying a fire on a rainy night with a beautiful woman while his teammates were winging their way toward danger.

He argued with himself that the decision was out of his hands and there wasn't anything he could do about it. But being left behind still rankled.

They sat twined together staring into the fire, lost in their own thoughts for a long time while his frustration rolled through him. Sherri's slender arms were strong around him. Comforting. She understood his pain. She got it. She got him. How many women could he say that of in his life? That would be…zero.

But this woman—she shared a part of his life no woman had ever seen before. She had an inkling of just how tightly bonded he and his SEAL brothers were.

He turned his head and buried his face against her satin

hair. Cripes, she smelled good. Like soft, pretty things with just a hint of spice. The fragrance fit her perfectly.

He couldn't help himself. He kissed the warm spot just below her earlobe.

And damned if she didn't tilt her head to give him better access. He kissed the spot again. And this time, he laved it gently with his tongue. She groaned a little and moved restlessly in his arms.

Lust exploded behind his eyes and behind his zipper simultaneously. Man, he needed this distraction.

Sherri threw her leg across his hips, straddling his lap, and kissed him. Passionately. As if she'd held all this pent-up need inside her for way too long. He *completely* knew the feeling.

She might as well have been a waterfall, unleashing a torrent of desire in him, and nothing he did could stem the flow. Helpless in its grip, he could only kiss her back. He let his hands wander over her, untucking, unbuckling, and unzipping any obstacle in his path.

She was every bit as eager as he to get rid of their clothes, and he stood up, setting her on her feet long enough to finish stripping off the last of her clothes and his. And then she stood before him naked and so beautiful it hurt to look at her. She stepped forward, looping her arms around his neck.

"I've wanted you ever since I first met you in that stupid blue tuxedo," she muttered against his mouth.

"And I've wanted you ever since you laughed at me, stumbling off that jet."

"You guys looked like bums," she responded between kisses.

"I felt like a bum that morning. Man, the hangover I

had. And you set a killer pace on that run and wouldn't shut up. You just kept chatting away while my head tried to pound its way off my neck."

"I knew you were hurting bad," she admitted.

He drew back to stare down at her. "You did that on purpose?"

She grinned up at him. "It wasn't like I was going to get many opportunities to get the best of a bunch of SEALs. I took the opening when it presented itself."

He pulled her close and laughed into her hair. "I can't even be mad at you. I'd have done the same thing."

She laughed against his chest, her body vibrating with humor and life. He couldn't get enough of her. He kissed his way across her temple, along the line of her jaw, under her chin, and back up to her mouth. He cupped her face in his hands and savored her, so relieved finally to have arrived at this moment he could hardly breathe, let alone form coherent thoughts.

Never in his life had he wanted a woman without having her as long as he'd wanted this one. She arched into him eagerly as well, kissing him back with enough enthusiasm to drive him nearly to his knees.

He picked her up and then knelt beside the fire, spreading out the clothes in a makeshift bed. He was more used to sleeping on the hard, cold ground, so he stretched out on his back, drawing her down on top of him.

Her legs tangled with his, and he reveled in their smooth, sleek strength against his. She pressed up on his chest to stare down at him, her hair falling in a curtain of gold around them. The firelight flickered through it, kissing her face with otherworldly beauty.

"I don't care if it bugs you or not, I can't get enough of looking at you, Sherri. You're...perfect."

"For once, I'm not bothered to hear that from a man," she confessed.

"How long can you hold that plank?" he asked playfully.

"Long enough to drive you crazy," she shot back.

"Who knew that all this time I was conditioning you to torture me?" he responded. He wrapped his arms around her and urged her to sprawl on top of him. He murmured, "I'm a big guy. You won't crush me. Use my body heat to stay warm."

"How about I just use your body?"

Not in a million years had he ever dreamed he would hear those words from this woman. "Be my guest, darlin'. I'm yours to plunder."

She purred. Honest to goodness *purred* in response. And then, sweet Mother of God, she crawled *all* over him. She kissed and tickled and massaged her way across his entire body, until he was wound so tightly he could hardly breathe for fear of exploding. When he couldn't stand one more second of the sweet torture, he grasped her waist and lifted her off him. She stared down at him, her eyes huge and black with need.

"My turn," he growled.

Rolling over swiftly, he returned the favor, kissing and nipping and tasting every last spot he'd fantasized over for the past two months. Day and night. Wet. Dry. In the pool. In the mud. Hell, in the shower.

"Let me know if you get cold," he muttered.

"Griffin, my problem at the moment is that I'm burning up. I need you inside me in the very near future."

He nearly lost it then and there. But he managed to pull back from the brink by dint of sheer, stubborn will. Jaw clenched against the agony of holding back the lust pounding through him like a jackhammer, he managed to dig a condom out of his wallet and get it rolled on without coming like an overeager schoolboy. But it was a close thing.

Finally, at long last, after an eternity of wanting this, he positioned himself between her silken thighs and planted an elbow on either side of her head. He stared down at her, memorizing the moment for all time. He never, ever wanted to forget this feeling. Whatever the future might bring, they had this moment together. And he damned well wanted to make it perfect.

"We're good?" he asked.

"If that's SEAL speak for confirming consent, birth control, and freedom from STDs, yes. We're very, very good." She looped her legs around his hips and gave a muscular squeeze.

He laughed under his breath. "I don't think there's any official protocol for asking a fellow SEAL for consent to have sex."

She smiled up at him, and he pressed into the tight, slick heat of her body ever so slowly. As he stared down at her, her smile faded, replaced by dawning wonder. Awe. Blinding joy.

If he thought she was beautiful before, it was nothing compared to her now, lost in the throes of pleasure, her internal muscles clenching and unclenching around him, sending ripples of such sweet agony through him that he could hardly stand it.

Finally he paused, seated to the hilt within her.

She smiled, and her eyes drifted closed as if the pleasure was too much for her to bear, too.

He moved his hips a little, pulling back slightly. She made a sound of protest in the back of her throat, and then he drove forward gently.

"Oh my. Do that again," she sighed.

"Like that?"

"Yes. Definitely yes. Again."

Chuckling, he complied.

That drew a full-throated groan from her this time.

"SEALs know how to do everything in silence, you know," he teased.

Her eyes flashed open. "I dare you to make love to me and not make a single sound," she retorted.

Grinning from ear to ear, he nodded. "Challenge accepted. First person to make noise loses."

And with that, he set out to win. She surged up against him in time with his thrusts, and they established a rhythm that all but made his eyes fall out of their sockets. She was strong and met his power with equal enthusiasm. The sweet friction of body on body, sweaty skin on sweaty skin, hot flesh sliding on hot flesh was mind-blowing.

She bit her lip and then clapped a hand over her mouth as the pleasure built between them. He pressed his lips together so hard he tasted blood, but he didn't care at all. Pain blended with pleasure until it was all one big pool of exquisite ecstasy. Electric shocks zinged through his body, over and over, higher and higher.

Sherri's face and then her entire body flushed pink, and she began to shudder around his shaft, convulsing as orgasms began to roll through her. He couldn't stand it any longer. His control shattered all at once and he pounded into her mindlessly, letting the sexual storm between them rage wildly.

He buried his face in her hair, and she buried her face in his neck as they reached a fever pitch, driving each other completely out of their minds.

All at once, his entire being coiled. For an endless, perfect instant he teetered on the edge of bursting. And then, with a mighty explosion, pleasure totally consumed him.

A hoarse cry ripped from his throat. And he didn't care at all. What a magnificent way to lose a bet.

It registered on him belatedly that Sherri was crying out too against his chest, in every bit as much abandon as he was.

She fell back to the wadded clothes, and he gathered her closer, rolling over onto his back. She sprawled bonelessly across him, breathing as hard as he was.

He stroked her hair lazily as his heartbeat gradually slowed and awareness slowly returned to his body.

For her part, Sherri seemed content to rest on top of him, her ear plastered to his chest over his heart.

Eventually, she murmured, "Who won the bet? I was a little too distracted to notice."

He chuckled, relishing the feel of his chest rumbling against hers. It felt so natural to be lying here with her like this. Like they'd always been the two halves of a whole.

"Hell if I know," he confessed. "I couldn't have told you my own name, let alone who yelled first."

"Hmm. I guess we'll have to do it again, then, and pay more attention next time."

"I like the way you think," he drawled.

"When at first you don't succeed, try, try again."

"A SEAL mindset all the way," he quipped.

Except neither of them could remember who shouted first the second time, either.

They ran out of firewood and the fire burned low at about the same time the rain let up. Its drumming noise faded to a light patter, and Sherri finally rolled off him and sat up, looking around for her clothes. He lifted his hips and pulled her pants out from underneath him.

"Looking for these?" he asked lazily.

"Pants thief," she teased.

"Honey, I'd take away all your clothes and make you run around naked all the time if I could."

"Right back atcha. But the scratches and bug bites…" She shuddered. "No thank you."

"You're going to get plenty banged up in the field. You should get used to it."

"That's work. It's different."

He knew what she meant. In mission mode, he shut down physical sensation. Turned off things like pain and feelings. But here with her, like this, alone with the night stretching out forever around them, he could afford to let all that stuff in.

Huh. Did that mean he trusted her?

"Pass me my hoodie, will you?" she asked. "And here's your T-shirt. I don't know how it ended up all the way over here." She picked up the black garment across the room and carried it back to him.

"You threw it in an excess of eagerness to get me naked," he teased.

She smiled back. "Guilty as charged."

"I'll drive," he offered.

She nodded and passed him the Jeep keys. They ran for it through the last of the rain, and he expertly guided the vehicle around potholes and cracks in the ruined road.

When they reached the main road back to the compound, he stopped the Jeep, turning off the headlights.

"What's up?" she asked quickly, alert for danger.

In a corner of his mind, he took pride in the reflexes he'd helped her develop. "We're about to return to the real world. Well, the training world, at any rate. Tomorrow morning, I'm going to have to go back to being my usual asshole self. I didn't want you to think that this evening didn't mean a hell of a lot to me or that I think any less of you."

She nodded soberly. "I understand. Nothing has changed between us."

He frowned and restarted the Jeep, pointing it at the cluster of buildings lit up against the night. Except something had changed. Everything had changed between them, in fact.

Problem was, he didn't have a single solitary clue what to do about it.

Chapter 9

On its surface, the next morning was just like every other morning for Sherri. Up too early. Exercise too hard while being harassed nonstop. Achieve utter exhaustion. Realize it wasn't even 8:00 a.m. yet.

Today's late-morning training evolution involved being dropped over the edge of a motorized rubber dinghy into the ocean to tread water indefinitely. Which wouldn't have been too bad except for the fifty-five degree water—approximately the same temperature as a glass of ice water—and her combat boots and fatigues weighing her down, impeding her swimming motions.

The combination of cold and exertion took a toll on the mind, interfering with focus. And then there was the fear—a take-your-pick smorgasbord of what to be afraid of. Fear of drowning. Fear of freezing. Fear of sharks. Fear of being lost in this vast, featureless ocean.

Truth be told, Sherri was getting used to being scared to death. It was as if she was becoming numb to it. When a stressful event presented itself to her these days, she found herself coldly assessing the risks and challenges, assuming it would hurt like hell, and then diving in.

Huh. Maybe this training stuff was starting to work after all.

Or maybe she was simply too damned cold, tired, and half-drowned to care if she lived or died anymore.

A motorized growl approached from behind her, and

she turned around to face the dinghy as it came back to pick her up. Praise the Lord and pass the potatoes.

There were two kinds of pickups: the relatively civilized one where a boat pulled up beside her and someone reached down to haul her over the big side-roll of the dinghy. And then there was the running pickup.

In that one, she stuck her arm up in the air, and the dinghy motored past at high speed. Someone in the vessel snagged her arm on the fly, jerked her violently out of the water, and tossed her into the dinghy at upwards of twenty miles per hour. It made her arm feel like it was being torn out of the socket, and all she could think of was that if they missed plucking her out of the water, that huge outboard motor would run right over her and chop her body into tiny pieces of chum for the sharks.

They'd already practiced static and slow-speed pickups today. Which meant this time the instructors would be gunning the dinghy right at her head. She waited till the vessel was about a hundred feet away from her and bearing down on her fast to stick her arm up. She angled her body the way Griffin had taught her and waited for the impact.

Griffin's forearm slammed against hers, and then she was flying up and out of the water like a fish on a hook, twisting midair. She slammed into the rubber bottom of the dinghy, knocking what little air she had in her lungs clean out of them.

Griffin grunted under his breath, "You good?"

She managed an affirmative and rolled to the side just in time to miss being flattened by Anna sailing over the side roll and smashing onto the deck.

For her part, Anna swore colorfully as she quickly rolled aside to avoid being Lily's landing pad.

"All aboard!" Griffin shouted over the roar of the engine.

Sherri sat up, leaning back against the inflated side of the craft. Griffin plunked down beside her, plastering his entire right side against her left side. He was blessedly warm, and she caught herself curling into him to absorb every bit of heat she could suck from him.

Oops. She hoped Kettering hadn't seen that momentary lapse on her part. She pulled back from Griffin belatedly, plastering her shoulder blades against the rubber at her back, forcing herself not to crawl into Griffin's lap. But boy oh boy, it was tempting.

Cal yanked on the tiller, and the dinghy's prow caught a wave and leaped out of the water. As they slammed back down to the ocean surface, Sherri scrambled to hook her fingers under the safety rope lashed down around the bottom edge of the dinghy's deck. She barely managed to hook it before the boat went airborne and slammed down again, all but tossing her out.

Griffin stretched his arms out at shoulder height, hooking his hands under the rope lashed atop the inflated rubber rib. The move had the effect of looping his arm around her shoulders, both holding her down and drawing her more tightly against his side.

She risked a glance up at him and caught his brief, sidelong glance at her.

Everything is going to be the same between us in training after last night, huh? She smiled a little to herself and scooted her hip tighter against his.

She closed her eyes, grabbing every nanosecond of

rest she could, and let her mind drift back to last night in Griffin's arms. He'd been strong and gentle, wild and finessed. He'd made her feel valued and lusted after, treasured and plundered.

If she'd had the slightest idea sex could be like that, she'd have been bedding SEALs a long, *long* time ago. Although she suspected what she and Griffin shared might not be typical of most SEAL sex.

One thing she knew for sure. She wanted more of that. A whole *lot* more.

How they were going to manage to sneak away without being discovered, she had no idea. But Griffin did swear SEALs were good at cheating and not getting caught. Surely between the two of them, they could finagle some time for themselves without anyone else knowing—

Except being with him was wrong.

It would put both of their careers at risk.

But with a fever of need burning her up like this, she couldn't muster any will to care about her career. At all.

Am I really willing to sacrifice everything for this man?

The question exploded across her brain like a heat-seeking missile.

Stunned, she searched her heart for an answer, but found none as they raced ashore like bats out of hell.

Cal ran the dinghy right up onto the beach, executing a nifty maneuver to lift the propeller out of the water at the last second before it ran aground, and Sherri had no more time to think.

Griffin, Trevor, Axel, and the three women leaped out of the skidding vessel in a coordinated egress, using the vessel's momentum to help them drag the dinghy all the way up the sandy beach to the weeds at the edge of the dunes a hundred feet back from the beach.

In combat conditions, they would hide the dinghy with a camo net and vegetation. They'd practiced doing that many times already, however, and today were allowed to skip that step.

Still seated in the rubber inflatable, Cal announced, "Take me to the Jeeps."

Sherri groaned as the women and instructors hoisted the dinghy over their heads with Cal seated in it like a conquering hero. They jogged through the dunes, slogging through ankle-deep sand. Today, the vehicles were parked a quarter mile back from the beach.

It might not seem far, but carrying a boat, motor, man, and whatever water had accumulated in the dinghy in the course of their training evolution, over their heads no less, made that quarter mile suck rocks.

Anna muttered, "Cripes. What does Cal weigh, anyway?"

Axel replied, "I don't know what you're complaining for. Us guys already did our time in BUD/S hauling Zodiacs around over our heads. And here we are, having to do it again, like a bunch of raw recruits."

Griffin retorted, "Aww, you know you love having all these pretty girls see how big and strong and manly you are, Axe. Or should I say Teddy Bear."

Sherri took her cue along with the other women and commenced oohing and aahing.

Axel scowled. "If I didn't think Cal would kick my butt for dropping him, I'd come over there right now and go homicidal teddy bear on your ass."

Trevor commented wistfully, "Where's Kenny when

you need him? Surely a song about homicidal teddy bears would be a number one hit."

Sherri hated to even think about the kind of lyrics Kenny would have come up with about that topic.

Everyone was laughing by the time they got to the parking lot and lowered Cal and the boat to the gravel so the boss could climb out.

Today, Sherri was in the back seat for the ride back to base. How Griffin managed to end up beside her without it looking contrived, she wasn't quite sure. But again, she found herself plastered up against him. The now intimately familiar contours of his body pressed against her side, and she imagined how they looked backlit by firelight against the night.

"Thinking about last night?" he breathed in her ear.

"Mmm-hmm. How'd you know?" she murmured back.

"That look in your eyes. All soft and sexy and wistful." He added, "You'd better cut it out, or someone's going to ask what you're thinking about."

"What are you two whispering about back there?" Kettering demanded from the front passenger seat.

"I was just asking Tate if she was enjoying her training."

"What'd she say?" Cal called back.

Sherri answered before Griffin could. "I told him I can't remember the last time I've had such a great time and how I hope there's more where that came from." She met Griffin's gaze and lifted a suggestive eyebrow.

He smirked back at her.

"Guess we'll just have to make your training harder," Cal responded.

Sherri smiled widely, her gaze never leaving Griffin's. "I'd love it harder. Bring it on."

Griffin closed his eyes briefly as if her oblique dare brought him physical pain.

"You asked. The SEALs will deliver," Cal commented, turning back around to face front.

"Gotta love the way those SEALs deliver," she breathed.

A blunt object poked her in the side. Hard. She couldn't resist muttering out of the side of her mouth, "Too bad that's your finger."

"Keep it up, and it won't be," Griffin muttered back.

"Promises, promises."

Griffin's only response was a low laugh that shivered down her spine and reverberated so pleasurably in her nether regions that she was forced to press her thighs tightly together to stop her entire body from undulating against his. Her breath caught, and her limbs felt even more heavy and boneless than they already had.

"Cut it out," Griffin breathed.

She noticed he was balancing a clipboard in his lap and leaning his elbow into it. Hard.

Thank goodness she wasn't the only one too turned on for words. Although she felt a certain sympathy for him as a man. She was able to hide her predicament better than he was. Taking pity on him, she did her best to hold herself perfectly still for the rest of the ride back to camp.

As the Quonset huts came into sight, Cal declared, "Showers then lunch, or lunch then showers. I don't care which. We reconvene in an hour for advanced escape and evasion."

Griffin had to do a little maneuvering, but he managed to convince Trevor and Kenny to shower first, along with

Anna and Lily. He caught Sherri's eye as she walked toward the showers to join the other women and jerked his head subtly toward the chow hall.

She veered inside. "What's up?" she asked him.

"If you could be persuaded to eat now, the showers will be all ours in about twenty minutes."

Her eyes went wide and then darkened with sharp desire. "Dang, you're good."

He honestly couldn't remember what he ate. But he gulped it down in a haze of desire, vividly aware that Sherri was doing the same at the table in the corner that the girls had staked out for themselves.

Axel and Trevor came into the mess hall, and Griffin slipped out after flashing Sherri a hand signal to give him five minutes. She nodded back infinitesimally.

This was insane. They were acting like a couple of kids cutting class and sneaking out behind the school to make out. But he couldn't find the resolve to stop. Sherri was a fire in his blood, flat out. She was the kind of woman he could almost see himself giving up the teams for someday—a thought so shocking he stumbled jogging down the steps of the chow hall.

Crap on a cracker. Had he found the one? Surely not. She was too stubborn, too independent, too prone to not doing what she was told to do. Life with her would be a challenge at best and frustrating as hell at worst.

He couldn't get her out of his mind. Yes, she was mesmerizing to look at. But she was so much more than that. He found her endlessly fascinating—a mystery he might never solve, but one he would never tire of trying to unravel.

Locking the locker room door behind him, he stripped

quickly and headed for the showers. Blow dryers were going in the women's locker room, and thankfully, they cut off quickly. He heard Anna and Lily talking and laughing as they packed up their gear, and then silence fell. He waited in an agony of anticipation for Sherri to join him and prayed fervently that Kettering wouldn't catch them.

It was a hell of a risk to try this right underneath everyone's noses. But that was why it would work. Nobody would think that he and Sherri would dare fool around right here in the middle of camp.

He heard movement in the women's locker room. And then smooth, soft hands went around his waist and a naked, sleek, female form pressed against him from behind.

"Did you lock the door?" he managed to ask before Sherri completely stole his breath away.

"I did."

Her hand slipped through the suds on his chest and slid lower, across his abs, which contracted so hard they hurt, and lower still. Her hand gripped his erection, and his knees all but buckled.

Her fist slid up and down his shaft, warm and slippery, and just about did him in then and there. He turned around in her arms, and his hands roved up and down the length of her back.

"You need soap," he announced. He reached for the bar of soap and lathered her up until the two of them were sliding silkily against each other. It was so sensuous he forgot to breathe.

Sherri groaned against him, and her right leg rose to wrap around his hips in her hunger for more. He knew the feeling.

He grabbed her buttocks and lifted her up against the wall. She reached between them to guide him home, and he thrust forward eagerly. Her body was a hot glove, as slippery and sexy inside as out.

Her arms went around his neck, and she hung on for dear life as he pounded home again and again, seating himself deep and then deeper still within her. She started to shudder and her internal muscles gripped him, milking his shaft, begging him to join her in release.

Gritting his teeth, he held out. It took every ounce of self-discipline he possessed to let her come around him without joining her. But as her first wave of pleasure passed, he resumed moving in and out of the tight sheath of her body.

The water pounded down on his back, drenching them both in a shower of heat and steam that added to the overall luxuriousness of possessing Sherri and giving himself to her.

Finally, the lust took over and he lost control, matching her surging hips with thrusts of his own. Their bodies slapped together wetly, carnal and raw. Sherri threw her head back and cried out, and he clapped a hand over her mouth as his own strangled shout escaped. He clenched his jaw with all his might, and then his entire body exploded up and into Sherri, deep inside.

She went limp against him, panting. Her forehead fell to his shoulder. And his nose landed in her shampoo-sweet-smelling hair.

He wasn't sure he had any intact bones left. She'd shattered him completely. He let her slide down his body, relishing the feel of her breasts against his chest, the muscles of her thighs against his, the softness of her relaxed belly pressing into his.

He took a step back, drawing her under the spray of water. Eyes closed, head tilted back, she rinsed out her hair. It was a simple act, but there was something so sensual about the way her fingers slid through the wet golden strands, the way her palms smoothed the water back from her face, the way the suds coursed down the slender column of her neck, that he felt his cock stirring again already.

Sherri felt it, too. She opened her eyes, gazing up at him in invitation so ageless, mysterious, and feminine that he could hardly breathe.

"What's your pleasure?" he murmured against her lips.

A smile curved her mouth against his and she surprised him by turning around in his arms. She glanced over her shoulder at him, throwing him a come-hither look that had his cock springing to full attention.

She planted her palms on the wall of the shower, and the look in her eyes dared him to take her this way.

Oh, he needed no second invitation at all. He stepped up and entered her from behind, loving the way she groaned in pleasure as he impaled her. Grabbing her hips, he pulled her back against him in time with his thrusts, watching where their bodies joined until it was too much for him to bear without exploding.

Her ass was juicy and firm as it slammed into him. Her back, the inward curve of her waist, the slender length of her spine—they were so damned perfect he didn't think he would ever tire of the sight of them. The thought that they were his made him so horny he completely lost control of his desire again and slammed into her mindlessly, faster and faster, harder and harder, holding her still and open to take all of him as he rammed into her, balls deep.

Sherri buried her face against her upper arm, biting her biceps to keep from screaming as he made her his.

She came so hard her legs buckled, and he held her up by her hips as he slammed home. The orgasm that ripped through him was so powerful he actually blacked out for a moment. It was as if a giant electrical shock had passed through his entire being, pleasure so intense it bordered on painful.

Gradually, awareness of water running over his body returned. Of shower walls. Of holding Sherri's hips in his hands. Of the aftershocks zinging through him, one after another.

He helped Sherri straighten and soaped up her body for her again. It was as much a massage as a bath, and she stood quietly under his ministrations, utterly relaxed. He knew the feeling.

Unfortunately, the real world called. They both had places to go and things to do.

Man, what he wouldn't give to spend about a month with her, stranded in the middle of nowhere with nothing else to do but explore the myriad ways he could possess her body, mind, and heart.

Whoa. Heart and mind? What was up with that?

"You get out first," she murmured lazily. "Us girls always take longer in the showers than you guys."

"Why is that?" he asked, quickly rinsing off the last of the soap and Sherri.

"More hair to wash and a higher percentage of our

bodies to shave if we're going to be all smooth and sexy for the boys."

"Honey, you could come to me covered in mud without having seen a razor in weeks, and I'd still want you like crazy."

He dropped a quick kiss on her mouth and forced himself to leave the shower before he had to have her again. Nope, she wasn't a fire in his blood. She was a full-on addiction.

He was in *huge* trouble.

Chapter 10

Sherri fell asleep fast that night, not troubled by horny dreams of the man she couldn't have. Instead, her dreams were populated by images of her and Griffin in her favorite settings—lying on a beach, hiking in mountains, making slow, lazy love on a gently rocking sailboat—

A hard hand pressed over her mouth, and she jerked awake.

A combat wake-up. Which meant hostiles were nearby and silence was imperative.

Griffin bent over her cot. He murmured, "We've had word from downrange. The attack on Haddad is going down. Cal wants you to watch and learn from the live feed of the Reapers' body cameras."

Sherri nodded and threw back the blanket, climbing out of bed quickly. Griffin didn't step back quite quickly enough, and she brushed against him as she stood up.

Their gazes met in a brief, private smile, and then he stepped away to wake up Anna and Lily.

The women dressed quickly and followed him outside into the chilly night. Sherri's breath hung in the air as she hurried after Griffin, appreciating his muscular shoulders. God, she loved hanging onto those shoulders while he took her to the moon and back.

Kettering and the other men were waiting in the conference room, and all three video monitors on the wall were lit up in lime green. They showed a barren landscape below. The Reapers must be lying on top of some sort of ridge, looking down into a valley. None of the images were moving at the moment.

"Where are they?" Griffin asked tersely.

"Hunkered down, waiting for the air assets to come on location," Cal answered. "I'm gonna pull up the audio feed from Ops. You ladies will hear everything the SEALs hear in real time."

The way Sherri understood it, the SEALs themselves would say basically nothing from the time the op started until it concluded. Silence was the world of the SEAL in action.

Over the next few minutes, a steady stream of information flowed into the SEALs' earpieces, however. Estimates of how long it would take for the surveillance and attack drones to come into place overhead. Reports of sentry activity outside the farm compound in which Haddad was sleeping and which the attack team planned to take down.

A final readiness check was called for, and the various groups of operators verbally checked in with brief mutters or replied with single clicks over their microphones to indicate their readiness to roll.

The DEVGRU guys were going to attack the cave complex on the other side of the valley, a hairy and incredibly dangerous mission inside tunnels and caves likely to be inhabited by hostiles and booby-trapped up the wazoo. The three Reapers and two other strike teams from SEAL Team 8 were apparently going to sweep down out of the hills from both sides and take the cluster of mud-walled buildings.

A force of a hundred Marines was perched at the

far end of the valley, about a mile away, guarding its entrance against any Taliban reinforcements who might try to come to Haddad's aid. The narrow valley itself made for a steep, rocky natural barrier that would prevent all but the most agile and well-equipped warriors from entering the area. Fortunately, the SEALs were both.

The main purpose of the entire support team—Marines, photo analysts, intel specialists, translators, and air support—was to make sure the SEALs weren't surprised by anything. It allowed the operators to worry only about what was ahead of them and not what was behind.

Sherri felt her pulse leap as the go order was given. The images on the video monitors began to move as the Reapers started creeping down the hillside into the valley below.

Griffin muttered to Kettering, "How do you stand the suspense of sitting in an ops center, watching missions go down like this? I swear, my heart rate's double what it would be if I were out there myself."

Cal grimaced. "It's no fun. I try to watch for any detail you guys miss, any hint of something going off plan that might get you in trouble. I console myself with being an extra pair of eyes for the team."

Sherri caught Anna's infinitesimal shift in her chair to lean closer to Trevor. Interesting. Had that been a conscious move on Anna's part or not? Even more interesting was the fact that Trevor didn't pull away from the contact. He seemed prepared to let the gorgeous brunette lean surreptitiously against his right arm.

Beside her, tension vibrated off Griffin. He really was suffering, being left behind like this. An impulse to reach over and offer him comfort nearly got the best of her. She settled for throwing him a sympathetic look when he happened to glance over at her. He quickly looked away.

Kenny, Sam, and Jojo formed one of three three-man strike teams approaching the compound from different directions. The idea was for at least one team to get inside, and they all would create diversions for one another.

Occasional faint sounds of gravel rolling underfoot were all Sherri heard for the next several minutes as the Reapers crept down the difficult terrain.

Without warning, an explosion and then a huge puff of smoke, dust, and fire erupted from the cave opening across the valley. Tracer rounds burst out of the compound below, and a second huge explosion shook the hillside mere yards in front of the cameras.

Griffin swore at the same time Kettering bit out, "Mortar. Big one."

Griffin leaned forward. "That mortar came from the target compound! This is an ambush!"

It was Kettering's turn to swear.

Tension in the conference room was so thick Sherri struggled to breathe against it. Griffin was rigid in his seat, his knuckles white on his armrests. Trevor and Axel looked about to explode as well.

For the next minute or so, the camera images jiggled wildly as the Reapers beat feet down the mountainside. Now that stealth was blown, it was all about speed. This was why SEALs trained so obsessively. They could run faster, farther, and for longer than anyone could possibly anticipate, thereby gaining a tactical advantage in combat situations.

Kenny, Sam, and Jojo slipped and slid in the loose scree as they raced for the compound. Sherri heard heavy breathing on the audio feed. No doubt about it: they were going balls to the wall.

One of the cameras suddenly sailed up in the air and then crashed to the ground.

"Dammit!" Kettering exclaimed. "One of our guys is down!"

"Which one?" Sherri cried.

Lily asked quickly, "Did he fall down, or was he knocked down?"

Nobody answered either question.

The downed Reaper didn't get back to his feet immediately. The camera view lay still and unmoving, pointed at a clump of dead grass.

Sherri felt bile rise to the back of her throat. That SEAL was hurt. Maybe unconscious. Possibly worse.

Even while barreling down into the Kirdu Valley, even with one of their men down, the Reapers maintained complete radio silence. The other two video feeds showed their owners proceeding forward more slowly now. The tips of the men's assault weapons came into sight now and then as the men swept them back and forth in tightly controlled arcs.

The downed camera moved.

"Yes!" Griffin cried at the monitor on the wall. "Get up!"

The video image slowly righted itself. A long pause and then a wobble as the Reaper climbed to his feet rather slowly and clumsily for a SEAL. Sherri winced. The guy *had* to be hurt.

Who was it? Clever Kenny with a dopey song lyric

or a quick comeback always on the tip of his tongue? Friendly Jojo who struggled to be an asshole when it was time to yell at the female trainees, and who let them cut off a few pull-ups or push-ups at his station when they were exhausted? Or young, sweet Sam, the baby of the bunch and still finding his place on the Reapers?

The injured Reaper moved forward, his pace closer to shambling than sprinting. The tip of his assault weapon wavered and then steadied. Wavered again.

"Isn't he hurt?" Anna asked no one in particular. "Shouldn't he pull back?"

Kettering shrugged. "Half a SEAL is still more capable than most armed soldiers. Whoever's hurt knows he can't operate at full speed with the other guys, but he can still provide covering fire or watch their backs. Maybe hold a doorway, or clear an egress route."

Griffin added, "If nothing else, seeing a third fully armed SEAL approaching adds that much more intimidation factor when the team encounters hostiles."

Which he seemed certain the Reapers would do.

Sherri gulped. It was one thing to train hypothetically for this stuff. It was another altogether to actually see what she was getting herself into. On one hand, it scared her silly. On the other hand, a burst of adrenaline in her gut shouted nothing but excitement at the prospect of being out there in the dark and danger, saving the world.

All of a sudden, the entire valley erupted with movement.

Voices from the support team monitoring the overhead drone cameras shouted, and a deafening cacophony of gunfire erupted.

"What the hell?" the men at the conference table muttered in unison.

Sherri leaned forward, staring in disbelief at the video images. Taliban fighters were standing up, lining the entire rim of the valley. Hundreds of them. Rifles in hand, they started charging like bats out of hell down the mountains at the SEALs now crouched beside the compound.

"Where in the hell did *they* come from?" one of the operators on the ground broke silence to demand over the cacophony of gunfire.

Ops answered tautly, "We had no heat signatures. They either came out of undiscovered tunnels, or they were hiding under some sort of heat-shielding material."

"Head count?" the same operator demanded roughly.

"At least a hundred."

Griffin shoved a hand through his hair in what looked close to despair. "Our guys have to fall back until the Marines arrive. Engage the hostiles in a front-and-back firefight. And Ops needs to call in gunships ASAP."

Cal replied grimly, "It'll take the Marines a solid ten minutes at top speed to join our guys. As for gunships, that valley is narrow and steep. It'll be a bitch to run a ship down in there and not crash."

"Attack drones, then," Griffin responded desperately. "Something! They need support, or they're all going to be slaughtered!"

It was a hell of an ugly ambush. Whoever had planned it had done his work well.

The three Reaper camera views dropped close to the ground. The guys were no doubt taking cover behind whatever they could find at the edge of a broad expanse of dirt.

The Reaper belonging to monitor one held up a fist in camera range and signaled his teammates to prepare to move out.

Anna asked, "Doesn't he know he's got a hurt man with him?"

Trevor answered her gently, "Until that hurt man tells the team leader he can't continue, the team leader will assume the hurt guy can function and not hinder the team."

Griffin muttered, his gaze never leaving the monitors, "We fight wounded and shot up all the time."

Cripes. This was that heart-of-a-SEAL stuff Griffin kept talking about.

The three camera images took off at a run across open terrain. Spits of dirt around their feet indicated that they'd drawn incoming fire. Sherri counted several grunts across the audio feed. Did those translate to bullet hits on their Kevlar vests, or were one or more of the guys shot now, too?

A wooden gate with huge iron hinges came into sight. All three camera feeds halted and then pointed out at the valley.

Streaks of tracer fire, muzzle blasts, and small explosions lit up the entire mountain in front of the Reapers. It had a certain macabre beauty that reminded Sherri of fields of fireflies in the summer up at the lake house when she'd been a kid. Except these fireflies were lethal, each one holding a promise of death. She shuddered in spite of herself.

The disembodied operations voice announced, "Scotty, Sulu, and Bones are in place."

Those were the code names for the three strike

teams set to enter the compound in search of Haddad. Bones was the three Reaper operators. Spock was the DEVGRU team, and Kirk was the Marine contingent.

"They can't seriously be sending those men in anyway, knowing it's a death trap!" Sherri exclaimed.

Griffin glanced over at her. "We'll never get another shot like this at Haddad. We *know* he's in there. Even if all we do is kill the bastard and lose our own men, it'll be deemed a worthy trade."

She flopped back in her chair, aghast. The military was willing to sacrifice so many highly trained Special Forces operators to kill one terrorist?

Ops was speaking again. "Go on my count. Three. Two. One. Go, go, go!"

All three cameras were moving again. Fast.

Camera one went through a recently blown hole in the wall and peeled left. Its wearer scanned the courtyard for movement and hostiles.

Camera three showed a SEAL in full night-combat gear jumping through the hole.

Griffin muttered, "That's Jojo going in. Which means Sam was probably the one who went down before."

The agony in Griffin's voice was palpable. It was clearly killing him to be sitting here and not running this critical mission.

The audio feed went silent as the three Reapers moved swiftly between buildings toward their assigned targets. It was as if the support team knew to shut up and let the SEALs do their jobs now without distracting them.

Kenny paused beside the doorway into a simple two-story structure with perhaps four rooms on each floor, trying the doorknob stealthily. The knob turned a bit under his hand. Kenny waited for his buddies to get into position on the other side of the door. Then he threw the door open while Jojo lobbed in two grenades, one with each hand, then threw in two more for good measure.

A noisy explosion erupted beyond the sight line of the cameras.

"Concussion grenades followed by flash-bangs," Griffin bit out.

Concussion grenades would knock people off their feet, and the flash-bangs would blind and deafen anyone inside for several minutes. The Reapers swung through the door in a tightly choreographed move. Some of Haddad's men sprawled on the floor, incapacitated.

The Reapers swung left into the first room, forward into the back left room, through to the right rear room, and back around to the right front room without encountering any resistance from the half-dozen men incapacitated by the grenades.

Sherri winced a little as the SEALs put bullets into the heads of the downed hostiles. It was brutal, but she understood the necessity. This was a kill-or-be-killed deal. Any one of Haddad's men would happily stand up and kill the Reapers if he could. And intel reported that everyone here was an active terrorist.

The team started up the stairs. They'd nearly reached the top when a huge explosion whited out the cameras and knocked out the audio feed altogether. The camera feeds tumbled wildly as if their wearers were falling—or flying through the air.

Griffin leaped out of his chair as the dust settled. Camera one, Kenny's feed, pointed at a massive pile of concrete slabs, wood, splintered furniture, and debris compound from an ant's eye view. The entire house had blown up.

Camera Two was buried, tucked into a crevice formed by two concrete slabs leaning toward each other in a crude teepee.

Camera Three pointed up at the sky. It was a beautiful, black expanse, dotted by thousands of stars and the misty belt of the Milky Way. In any other circumstances, it would have been breathtaking.

Kettering swore in a low, steady stream. "C'mon. Get up, you motherfuckers. Run for cover. Move, dammit! Be alive!"

The radios were chaotic with SEALs reporting in that the whole compound had been booby-trapped. Reports of fleeing figures on foot out the back of the compound toward the hills started to flow. Overwatch snipers shouted about their positions being overrun, and everybody was shouting for air support and wondering where the hell the Marines were.

It was, in a word, a clusterfuck.

Chapter 11

Sitting there watching a mission going to hell around his brothers was perhaps the hardest thing Griffin had ever done. It was excruciating knowing that he might be watching their deaths in real time. He vaguely registered Sherri's hand gripping his painfully tightly.

Gradually, the dust of the daisy-chained explosions began to settle. At the far edge of Kenny's camera range, Griffin spotted movement. He leaned forward, squinting at the form, trying to make out if it was friend or foe.

"Get up, get up, get up," Cal was chanting under his breath.

Very slowly, Kenny's camera moved to a seated position.

Thank the Lord.

The form moving toward Kenny wore native garb—a knee-length white shirt with a dark vest over it, and the round cap of the locals. The bastard was pointing an AK-47 at Kenny.

"Kill him!" Griffin ground out.

Kenny was obviously dazed, because his own weapon came up far too slowly. Wobbled. Steadied. Wavered again. Finally, Kenny fired. The kick of his assault weapon knocked Kenny onto his back, for his camera saw sky as well.

Kenny rolled to his side. The hostile was lying on the ground in a lump, unmoving.

"Good shot," Griffin gasped. He felt like he was Ken on the ground, trying desperately to regain his bearings, to gather his wits and get his head back in the game.

Jojo's camera, the buried one, moved a little. A shower of dust fell in front of that feed, and then the video shook as if Jojo was coughing, perhaps. Very slowly, inch by agonizing inch, Jojo's camera began the long crawl toward open air at the far end of the concrete tunnel.

Kenny's camera moved at hands-and-knees height toward a dark lump on his right.

Cal was first to identify it and started moaning, "Nonononononono," under his breath.

And then Griffin saw what it was.

Sam.

Down. Crumpled in an unnatural heap that the human body wasn't meant to lie in.

"He's not moving, Cal," Griffin groaned.

Sherri started to cry quietly beside Griffin.

Aww, noo. Please God, no. Not goofy baby Sam. The kid was an overgrown puppy, sweet, loyal, and eager to please. Everyone loved Sam. He had the makings of a great SEAL.

And just as certainly, he lay in the dirt of an Afghani valley dead, all that potential, all that life, wiped out. Ended. Gone.

Trevor's head bowed beside Griffin, the Brit's lips moving in a silent prayer. The finality of sending up a prayer for Sam's soul was a spike straight through Griffin's heart.

He'd seen death before. He'd lost teammates before.

But never like this, up close and personal, sharing a live feed of a brother's death.

He spun his chair around fast, grabbed the trash can in the corner behind him, and heaved into it.

Grimly, he turned back around and resumed watching the nightmare unfold.

The operations folks were shouting about the compound being overrun by hostiles. They ordered teams Sulu and Scotty to pull back. The other two strike teams radioed back, asking to go in and find the Reapers, but they were ordered again to retreat. Team Bones was a loss.

But Kenny and Jojo were still alive!

Cal grabbed the phone and shouted into it, demanding and then pleading for a rescue of his guys.

Teams Sulu and Scotty were grudgingly told that if they happened to see the Reapers on the way out, they were green-lighted to grab Team Bones.

Trevor said grimly, "Ten to one, those teams have turned around and gone back into the compound to 'happen to see' our boys."

All of a sudden, gunfire erupted around Kenny. Dirt flew up and the *rat-a-tat* of gunfire was deafeningly close. Hands grabbed at Kenny and Sam's cameras, and not in a helpful way. Kenny's Ka-Bar knife flashed, and Griffin swore. The hostiles were on Kenny, and he was fighting hand-to-hand, now, trying to hold them off.

Sam's camera lifted up in the air and smashed down to the ground. The video feed went dead.

It was Griffin's turn to moan. He had never in his life felt this helpless.

And then something smashed into Kenny's camera—a rifle butt, perhaps. That feed went dead, too.

Griffin's stare riveted on Jojo's feed, still inching toward the gap at the end of the crevice in the rubble pile.

Finally, Jojo reached the end of the long tunnel. Hands abruptly reached into the opening. Grabbed Jojo roughly. Dragged him out.

A silhouette flashed on Jojo's helmet camera.

"That's a SEAL!" Griffin cried.

Jojo's camera tilted, then righted. Someone had just slipped under Jojo's shoulder and was half carrying, half dragging him away from the disastrous ambush.

The camera bounced violently as the men hauling Jojo broke into a heavy-footed run.

Griffin had done it before. A fast combat carry to clear an injured man from the field. It was massively hard work, but all SEALs were glad to do it for their teammates.

More flashes exploded on Jojo's camera feed, but the men carrying him plowed onward.

Jojo was laid down on his back. The guys had put him on a stretcher. Now at least four men would be humping him out, which would let them move faster.

Grass and dust suddenly swirled above Jojo.

"Helo. It's dropping in to pick up Jojo!" Griffin exclaimed. God bless whatever pilot was crazy enough or had a big enough death wish to brave the heavy firefight to get to a hurt SEAL. The interior of a helicopter came into sight in Jojo's camera feed. A face leaned over Jojo. The guy wore a helmet marked with a white cross. *Medic.*

Jojo's helmet was removed, and the camera pointed at a wall of padded vinyl insulation.

"Where's Kenny?" Griffin asked raggedly. "What happened to him?"

Cal put his hand over the mouthpiece of the phone. “Unknown. Drone surveillance operators are looking for him. They’re going back through the footage of the past two minutes or so to track him. They’ll give us a situation report when they know more.”

Griffin waited as long as his raging need to know could stand and then asked again, “Anything?”

“No,” Cal answered grimly. “Nothing.”

“Are they lying to you?” Griffin shot back.

“Maybe.”

Griffin couldn’t sit one more second. He pushed to his feet and paced back and forth in the tight confines of the conference room, down the length of the table and back.

“Sitrep?” he bit out.

“Not good,” Cal answered reluctantly. “Marines got ambushed in the pass. Multiple casualties. Tangos seem to be trying to take prisoners.” A pause, then, “No word from DEVGRU. They’re still unaccounted for in the tunnels. One confirmed dead on Team Sulu. One confirmed dead on Team Bones. One overwatch sniper confirmed dead, two more sniper casualties possible. Their positions were overrun and now have negative radio contact.”

“Kenny?”

“Missing. Presumed dead.”

“Now what?” Sherri asked in a hush.

Good fucking question. Griffin squeezed his eyes shut against the burning grief.

Cal answered grimly, “Army’s sending in a battalion at first light to clean up.”

Which was military speak for recovering the bodies.

Griffin spun and slammed his fist against the wood-paneled wall, which turned out to have concrete behind it. Otherwise, he'd have put his fist right through the wood. He swore violently.

Trevor leaned over Sherri, muttering into her ear. She nodded and her gaze swiveled to Griffin. The sympathy in her eyes was more than he could stand.

Griffin barged outside into the cold, crisp twilight. Stars were starting to shine overhead as if not a bloody thing had just happened, as if nothing was wrong. As if one of his brothers hadn't just *died*.

Griffin felt a quiet presence fall in beside him as he strode down the road, heading for the woods. *Sherri*. She didn't say anything, just kept pace beside him as his stride lengthened into a run.

He ran—hard—for perhaps twenty minutes. Finally, when he was winded and the worst of his agony had condensed into a diamond kernel of vengeance tucked away deep in his heart, he stopped.

"Thank goodness," Sherri gasped. "I didn't know how much longer I could keep up with you."

He looked around. They were at the far turn of the long course, miles from the camp. And then he looked at Sherri.

Mistake.

Her eyes were infinitely sad. Understanding. She'd known loss this deep before.

And that was what broke him. A single, hoarse sob escaped his throat.

Sherri rushed forward, gathering him in her arms. As his legs gave out and he sank to his knees, she went with him, pulling his head against her chest, cradling him tightly.

He wrapped his arms around her, holding on for dear life. Images of Sam flashed through his head. The kid sneaking off to fish, even if all he had was a stick, some fishing line, and a makeshift hook. Sam, listening to music so loud through his earbuds it kept the other guys awake and made them complain. His boyish smile that made him look even younger than he was. His laughter. Oh, man. His laughter. Sam had loved life.

Griffin couldn't hold back the grief as it tore through him in racking sobs.

And all the while, Sherri held him tight, absorbing his pain into herself. She didn't speak. Didn't try to push any thoughts-and-prayers platitudes on him. She just shared his pain and silently offered her strength and support.

Eventually, the worst of the initial grief passed, leaving him drained. He felt wrung out like a cheap washcloth. Griffin raised his head and pressed the heels of his hands into his eye sockets.

"I'm sorry—" he started.

"Stop." Sherri cut him off sharply. "Don't you *ever* apologize for loving your brothers and feeling the loss of one keenly."

One corner of his mouth momentarily quirked up. "Yes, ma'am." He rose to his feet and drew Sherri into a hard, long hug. "Thanks for being here."

"Any time."

"For real."

"I meant what I said, Griffin. Any time. Any place. You call, and I'll be there for you."

Huh. She really was starting to sound like a SEAL.

He looked around, identifying the forest in minor shock. "Well, hell. I really ran us out to the back forty, didn't I?" He didn't relish the long run back. Not feeling this soul-weary.

Sherri wriggled in his arms and dug a cell phone out of the back pocket of her cargo pants. She hit a button and plastered it to her ear.

"Hey, Anna, it's me."

Sherri listened for a minute. Then, "I don't blame them. If I lost you or Lily, I'd react about the same way. Hey, could I ask a big favor of you? Griffin went for a run around the long loop, and we're at the back end of nowhere out here. Any chance you could hop in a Jeep and come pick us up? Neither one of us feels like hiking all the way back. Thanks, girlfriend. You're the best."

Sherri pocketed her phone. "She'll be here in a few minutes."

"What's up with the guys?"

"They're locked in Cal's office with a whole lot of booze."

Griffin nodded. If he hadn't taken off like he had, that was exactly what he would be doing right now.

The sound of a Jeep engine broke the silence before long, and Anna pulled up beside them. Sherri climbed in the back, and Griffin swung into the passenger seat. Nobody spoke. Words weren't adequate to express how any of them were feeling right now.

They arrived back at the compound, and Anna paused in the act of getting out of the Jeep to make eye contact with Griffin and nod soberly. No doubt about it. She'd lost someone close to her, too. Knowing shone in the dark sadness of her brown eyes. It was a terrible club to belong to.

Anna tossed him the car keys and disappeared into the women's barracks, leaving him and Sherri alone.

"Wanna blow this Popsicle stand?" he asked her, shifting into the driver's seat.

"As in leave base?"

"Yeah."

"Won't we be going AWOL?"

"I think Cal will understand, given the circumstances. We've all earned a night off."

Sherri hopped into the front seat.

Thank goodness. He really did need to get out of here, and he didn't trust himself alone tonight. No telling what foolish, self-destructive idiocy he would engage in.

He frowned as he guided the Jeep toward town. Honestly, he would rather wake up beside Sherri in the morning and not feel like shit for being with her.

Son of a bitch. That could not possibly bode well for either one of them. Sex was one thing. He could justify that as mutual scratching of an itch. But feelings? Those threw what was going on between them into another league altogether. They were talking an actual relationship when feelings got involved.

He drove in silence, wrestling with the emotions roiling way too close to the surface. He was too raw, too hurt, to hold them back, though.

Contemplating the choices, he surprised himself by driving past exactly the kind of bar he would've chosen had he been alone. It looked trashy, the parking lot was full of pickup trucks, and classic rock blared through the cheap plywood front door.

Instead, he shocked himself by pulling into a high-end resort down by the beach. It looked classy, with beautiful tropical foliage and a wide veranda bar with umbrellas and a stone railing facing the beach. It was the kind of place a person went to sip a nice cocktail after supper. The clientele wore preppie clothes—attorneys and accountants. No rednecks here.

The other place—the crappy dive—fit him. This posh place fit Sherri.

"Interesting choice of venue," Sherri commented as he turned off the ignition.

She reached for the door, and he touched her elbow. "Stay there. I'll come around and get the door for you." Why he wanted to treat her like a lady and observe the niceties of the real world, he couldn't say and didn't feel like psychoanalyzing tonight.

He opened the door for her and even held out his arm. She looped her hand around his forearm and leaned in close as they strolled out to the beachside bar. He led her to a table facing the beach, away from where most of the people were clustered. A hostess asked for their order, and Sherri surprised him by asking for a large order of french fries, an expensive bottle of scotch, a pitcher of water, and two glasses.

When the single-malt scotch came, Sherri poured generous splashes in both glasses. Thankfully, she wasn't planning to water it down. She picked up her whiskey. "To Sam."

To Sam, indeed. Griffin tossed back his scotch, sucking in a sharp breath as the alcohol hit the back of his throat. "Are we getting wasted tonight?" he asked.

"I don't know. You tell me. What do you need?"

He stared out at the black sheet of the ocean as it whispered to the stars. Eventually, he turned his gaze on Sherri. "I need you not to go to war and die like Sam."

Sherri poured them each a glass of water and slugged hers. Then she lifted the scotch bottle and waited expectantly for him to throw back his water. Ahh. Hangover prevention protocol—carbs and hydration.

He downed the water and watched her refill their glasses with amber liquid in silence. She picked up hers and sipped it this time, while he threw his back and then commenced snacking on the fries.

Only then did she respond to his earlier comment. "I need *you* not to go to war and die like Sam, either."

"I'm serious, Sherri. I don't want you in harm's way. It scares the hell out of me to think about you out there in a mess like we witnessed tonight."

"It scares the hell out of me, too. But it should scare you to think of yourself getting caught in a mess like that."

He shrugged. "Shit happens."

"Why are you allowed to take that attitude about life and death, but I'm not allowed to feel the same way?"

"You're beautiful. Smart. Talented. You can do anything you want. The world is at your feet. Go do something awesome with your life. But don't come crawling into the mud and filth that I live in. Being a SEAL is dirty, hard work. You should do something glamorous with your life."

"I think being a female SEAL is plenty glamorous. And besides, I've had all the glamour I can stand for one lifetime. I want something of substance to hang onto in my life. Someone—" She broke off.

So. She wanted someone to come home to someday, too, did she? Good to know.

She continued, "When I'm old and worn out, looking back on my life, I want to know I've done something important."

"Then raise money for starving kids in Africa. Save the whales, for crying out loud."

Sherri put down her glass and leaned forward, staring hard at him. "Why are you so dead set on me not being a SEAL? You've seen enough of me in training to know that I can hack it. I meet all the physical standards. I'm good at shooting and stealth. I have nerves of steel. What else do you want from me?"

He ground out, "I want you to live."

She ground back, "Then train me to be the very best SEAL you can. Teach me the skills I'll need to stay alive." She calmly filled their glasses with scotch.

They both grabbed their glasses and tossed back the contents. Without comment, she refilled them again. Not with water.

They were at an impasse. He'd just realized he had feelings for her strong enough to panic at the idea of her getting killed in combat. No way could he survive watching her die in real time on a helmet cam. It would kill him. Problem was she'd finally seen what SEALs really did…and she still wanted in on it. *Damn, damn, damn.*

She poured another round, and he tossed his back in frustration. The scotch was starting to hit him, and his head felt light.

She asked, "So what's the plan, Sparky? Are we going to agree to disagree? Then maybe sit here watching the waves and get wasted?"

This was too important for him to give up on and merely agree to disagree. "What's it going to take to convince you to give up on this insanity and live a normal life?"

"I don't know. Are you willing to walk away from the teams just because I'm worried about your safety?" she retorted.

Damn it!

His frustration spilled over, and he blurted out, "Marry me. Stay home. Make a life for yourself. Be there when I come home from downrange. I'll give you whatever you want. The white picket fence and a porch swing. Or a mansion if you'd like. Hell, kids."

Horror tore through him. What in the *ever-loving hell* had he just done? He realized a part of him meant the proposal, and that horrified him even more.

Sherri smiled gently. "Thanks. Really. That's a sweet offer. I understand it's the whiskey talking. But how about you stay home and raise the kids while I go downrange?"

He slammed his glass down on the table, and heads turned at the sharp noise. He took a deep breath and lowered his voice. "You'll *die* if you go out there."

Sherri leaned back, smiling. "Hey, we've made progress. At least you now acknowledge that I could actually make it out into the field as a SEAL."

He stared at her. Her face swam slightly, and he squinted to make the two images of her come back into one.

She'd changed since she'd come to training. She was more confident now. Moved with a hint of cool swagger. He and the boys were succeeding at turning the women into no-kidding SEAL material. She was more stubborn than she'd been a few months ago, too. He knew in his gut that nothing he said was going to talk her out of this crazy determination of hers to be one of the big boys.

He grabbed the neck of the whiskey bottle and stood up abruptly. "Let's get out of here."

"And go where? Neither one of us is safe to drive. And no matter how messed up you are by Sam's death, I'm not passing out on a beach with you in the middle of winter."

He snorted. "Have a little faith in me, grasshopper."

He concentrated on walking straight, without any hint of a wobble, back into the hotel. Made his careful way to the front counter. "I need a room for the night, please." *Hah. Not even the slightest slur.*

He plunked down a credit card on the counter as Sherri caught up with him. She'd taken care of the bar tab. *Oops.* He'd forgotten about that. Must be drunker than he'd realized.

A key card was handed to him, and he escorted Sherri across the elegant lobby to the elevators. Somewhere along the way, she'd kicked off her sandals, and they dangled in her left hand. Barefoot, a little drunk, with her hair tousled by the night breeze, she was turning every head in the lobby.

Look all you want, gentlemen. She was going upstairs with him. He joined her at the brass elevator doors and looped a possessive arm over her shoulders. His pulse leaped as she leaned her head on his shoulder. He would never get tired of holding this woman close.

The hotel room was nicer than any place he'd stayed in a very long time. He'd lived in plywood hooches and slept on the ground for so long he'd almost forgotten places like this existed. It even smelled good in here, like some fancy air freshener.

Sherri flopped across the high, king-size bed piled with pillows and bolsters. "I do believe I'm a bit drunk," she announced.

"I should hope so. You've had nearly as much scotch as me, and I'm definitely drunk." He added, "And I've got eighty pounds on you. Get up so I can pull the covers down. Then you can crawl into bed and pass out."

Except when she stood up, Sherri started shedding clothes. The tank top came over her head, exposing a white lace bra that was sexy as hell against her tanned skin. She dropped her pants next.

Holy centerfold model! That thong ought to be registered as a lethal weapon. Griffin gulped. Apparently, he wasn't so drunk that his body didn't leap to instant, painfully hard attention at the sight of her.

She glanced up at him, and her mouth curved into one of those infinitely mysterious female smiles that Mona Lisa had perfected. Sherri reached behind her back and unhooked her bra. The skimpy lace fell away from the globes of her breasts, and Griffin stopped breathing.

"Like what you see?" she murmured.

"Uh-huh," he managed to choke out. He cleared his throat. "I'm mesmerized by you."

She slipped into bed and pulled the snowy-white sheet up to her waist, leaving her magnificent chest and those rosy peaks uncovered, tempting him to lose his mind in her.

"Why don't you get naked and bring your mesmerized self on over here, sailor?" she said in a husky tone that tightened his groin even harder.

He fumbled at his belt. Yanked his T-shirt over his head. Dropped his pants.

Sherri leaned over and turned off the bedside lamp, plunging the room into darkness. The quiet, rhythmic crash and swish of waves was faintly audible outside. Better.

He padded across the thick plush carpet and slipped under the covers and into Sherri's arms.

She was warm and sleek and welcoming. Damned if she didn't feel like coming home. Maybe that marriage proposal hadn't been so crazy after all—

Whoa. Hard stop.

He was not a marrying kind of man. Not while he was still an active operator. And not when he could pull a Sam and die at any time.

"Why did you leave your trunks on?" Sherri muttered into his ear.

"Because I don't do drunk sex with women. Nothing good ever comes of it."

"Sounds like there's a story behind that," she commented.

He snorted. "Leo Lipinski. He hooked up with Janine and was too drunk to remember to use a freaking condom. Now she's pregnant, and he's married. And mark my words, she's gonna be no picnic to live with."

Humor laced Sherri's voice as she responded, "Why do you say that?"

"She doesn't know squat about the SEALs or what it takes to be married to one. Hell, I don't think she could even hack being a regular Navy wife."

Sherri shrugged in his arms. "It takes a special spouse to handle the long absences of their partner at sea."

"Well, Janine ain't it. And now Leo's saddled with her."

He felt Sherri's silent chuckle. "Who knew you guys think so deeply about these things?"

He pulled back to stare down at her. "Don't women think about it?"

"About making bad life choices under the influence of alcohol? All the time. Of course, we tend to be worried about roofies in our alcohol more than guys."

He drew her into a hug. Man, he felt comfortable with her like this. "Are you telling me you roofied my scotch? Are you trying to take advantage of me?"

"You're the one who left your undies on. I got the message loud and clear."

Silence fell between them, and he listened lazily to the surf.

"Thanks for tonight," he said quietly.

"You're welcome. It's what friends are for."

But what if he wanted more than friendship with her? Where did that leave them? *Hell*. What if his half-drunken proposal hadn't entirely been the alcohol talking?

Chapter 12

SHERRI WOKE UP LAZILY TO ROSY LIGHT STREAMING THROUGH white gauze curtains. She was cocooned in down comfort. The ocean crashed and retreated nearby, and warm, muscular flesh was cozy under her ear.

She opened one eye. A stubble-covered jaw filled her field of vision. A hard, lean jaw. *Griffin*.

Right. Sam's death. Griffin's grief. A bottle of scotch and the beach.

She rolled onto her back, enjoying the elegant appointments in this upscale room. Her movement woke up Griffin. One second he was relaxed and quiet beside her, and the next his formidable presence filled the room.

"Good morning," she murmured.

"Good morning to you." His voice was sandpaper rough.

"How are you feeling?" she asked.

"Better than I have a right to, given how much scotch I drank. You?"

She took inventory. "I'm good. But then, high-quality liquor doesn't leave as much of a hangover as the cheap stuff."

Strong arms gathered her close and he rolled over, looming above her. "Dammit, Tate. You're even more gorgeous first thing in the morning all sleepy and messy."

She grinned up at him. "Thank you."

"Toothbrush," he declared. "My mouth tastes like a sewer."

Laughing, she followed him to the bathroom and they used the complimentary toothbrushes and toothpaste together. She threw the balcony door wide open and relished the chill on her bare skin. The sun was just peeking over the horizon, a strip of liquid fire streaking across the surface of the ocean.

She felt Griffin move to stand behind her. His arms came around her waist, and his chin came to rest on her shoulder. They watched the sunrise together. It was a quiet, intimate moment between them. Something more than casual friendship was definitely happening here.

"Don't ever take a sunrise for granted," he surprised her by murmuring.

It made sense. In his line of work—in *their* line of work—each day was a precious gift. Goodness knew, losing Sam had only reinforced that fact.

Griffin's lips touched the column of her neck. His mouth was warm and felt good as he kissed his way across her shoulder. His tongue swirled in her ear, and a jolt of desire ripped through her. Who knew her ear was such an erogenous zone?

She turned in Griffin's arms, and his mouth closed on hers. She surged into the kiss, pressing her body hungrily against his.

She sensed that his need for this morning was as great as hers. After last night's devastating loss, she wanted—no, needed—the affirmation that she and Griffin were alive and well. She needed his vital energy. Craved the raw desire between them.

His hands gripped her head gently, and he pulled her

even closer, his tongue plunging wildly into her mouth. She sucked on it hard, pulling him to her desperately.

He backed up toward the bed, and she followed eagerly. He fell backward across the bed, pulling her down with him.

She practically purred in her eagerness to get him inside her. She threw her leg across his hips and pushed up to straddle him. He stared up at her, his eyes black with desire.

She reached between their bodies, gripping his erection in her fist. His hips bucked. His hot flesh felt like velvet over steel, and she passed her hand up his shaft and back down, relishing his power and hunger. She loved that she did this to him.

Taking her time, she guided him inside, loving every single hot, hard inch of him filling her. Griffin watched her like a hawk, his gaze never leaving her face.

It was erotic as heck being in control of their lovemaking like this. She had no doubt he could seize control any time he wanted, but he seemed to enjoy letting her take the lead this morning. When he was buried to the hilt, she rocked her hips a little.

"Mmm. Nice," she murmured.

"Uh-huh," he agreed.

If she wasn't mistaken, the big bad SEAL sounded a little breathless. She did that to him? *Sweet*.

She moved again. A little more forcefully. Oh. That was very nice, indeed. She lifted herself half off his shaft and then plunged down. Her body shuddered as waves of pleasure smashed through her. Ooh. She had to do that again!

She matched the rhythm of the waves outside. Up.

Pause. *Down*. Shudder. Her internal muscles gripped Griffin's flesh convulsively, pulling him even deeper inside her. It was possibly the most erotic experience she'd ever had.

Again and again she repeated the maneuver, and each time the pleasure ripping through her was almost too much.

She slammed down again, but this time she couldn't contain the pleasure any longer. It exploded into an orgasm, tearing her apart from head to toe and fingertip to fingertip. She cried out and fell forward, bracing her palms on Griffin's solid chest.

His arms swept around her and he rolled quickly, reversing their positions. His forearms landed on either side of her head, and he stared down at her, his eyes glazed with desire.

"Hang on, baby."

She wrapped her arms around his broad chest, and her legs around his narrow hips. She stared up at him, drinking in the sight of his facial muscles contorted with the intensity of the pleasure pounding through him. His eyes were black, the deep blue of his irises completely subsumed by the lust raging between them.

He withdrew a little way and then slammed home.

"Oh God. Yes," she groaned. "Again."

He obliged and started to withdraw again, but she was having none of that and her hips surged up against his as she gripped him more tightly with her legs.

Griffin laughed a little. "I'm not going anywhere. Trust me. I'm right where I want to be."

"Show me," she demanded.

His grin widened. It was his turn to pick up the

rhythm of the ocean outside and slam home again and again. He was so strong that he inched her across the big bed, but she loved it. She let go of all control, matching his thrusts with thrusts of her own hips. Their bodies slapped together, sweaty and slick, over and over until she couldn't think. Heck. She could barely see.

His body was big. Hard. Muscular, flexing against hers. He smelled like mint toothpaste and clean, male musk. Like the forests he ran around in.

She relished how safe and protected he made her feel. He was her bulwark against the world. Nothing could hurt her if he was here with her like this. One with her.

She cried out, arching up off the mattress, hanging on to Griffin's broad shoulders for all she was worth as pleasure ripped through her.

With a shout, Griffin surged one last time inside her, and the last of his control was torn away.

Where she ended and Griffin began, she had no idea. He completely drained her at the same time he completely filled her soul.

Gradually, by slow degrees, she regained awareness of her fingers and toes. She wiggled them experimentally. *Yep. Still there.*

She registered the way his chest pressed against hers. The way his breath stirred strands of her hair against her cheek. The way her body cushioned his.

They fit.

Not just physically, although they were a crazy perfect match for each other in that way.

It felt right to be here with him like this. It felt like…home.

Griffin swore quietly and rolled off her, dragging her

with him to sprawl half across his chest. "Sorry. I was too, umm, lost in enjoyment to realize I was crushing you. You should have said something," he muttered.

"It was nice."

"You're too polite."

"I'm not being polite. It *was* nice."

He dropped a lazy kiss on the top of her head. "Are you okay? I didn't hurt you, did I? I might have been a little too…enthusiastic…there at the end."

"Do you hear me complaining? That was amazing, and I feel fantastic."

"Well, okay then. I guess I won't wallow in any more performance anxiety."

She laughed a little. "Trust me. You've got nothing to worry about in that department."

"Man, you're good for my ego."

She punched his arm lightly, and he chuckled.

Silence fell between them. She was shocked at how comfortable it was just to lie here with him like this. No words were necessary. It was enough to be lazy together in the aftermath of their lovemaking.

She might have dozed a little, even. It was the best rest she'd had in ages. For the first time in months, she was completely relaxed. She'd had no idea how badly she needed this. Honestly, she felt like a new person.

Griffin stirred beneath her ear. "Hungry?" he asked.

"Ravenous."

Without moving her off his chest, he reached for the phone on the nightstand. "What do you want for breakfast?" he murmured.

"Pancakes," she answered promptly. "A big stack of them dripping in butter and maple syrup."

"Coming up, Princess."

While they waited for breakfast to be delivered, they showered in the oversize stall with its double heads.

"Scrub your back?" Griffin offered.

She turned and presented her back to him. He washed her gently with the scratchy sponge.

"My turn." Taking the loofah from him, she commenced scrubbing her way across his muscular back. "Every single time I've been naked in those showers with you and that stupid wall was between us, I've wanted nothing more than to be all soapy and slippery and naked in your arms."

"Wish granted," he declared, drawing her against his body.

Thankfully, room service was slow, and they had time to make lazy, slippery love in the shower, and for her to wash and rinse her hair, blow-dry it, and don one of the hotel's fluffy bathrobes before she heard a knock on the hotel-room door.

She waited until the door closed and then stepped out of the bathroom.

Griffin was barefoot, his jeans slung low on his hips, and hadn't bothered to don his T-shirt. She gulped at the sight of his perfect physique, wreathed in muscle.

He held a chair for her at the little table over by the balcony door, and she slipped into it, shy all of a sudden.

Ever perceptive, he asked as he sat down in his own chair, "What's up?"

"You can be a bit intimidating, you know."

"Me? How?"

"Have you looked at yourself in a mirror?"

"I might say the same for you, Miss Beauty Queen."

She blew a stray strand of hair out of her face. "I joined this operation to leave all that behind."

He snorted. "Meanwhile, I'm a grizzled old wreck."

She picked up her knife and fork and risked a glance up at him. "You're a warrior. Not too many men in this day and age can say that."

He shrugged, setting off a display of rippling muscles that had her thinking about another round in the sack with him sooner rather than later. *Food first*. Then sex.

She dug into the fluffy pancakes with gusto, while Griffin made short work of steak and eggs.

Eventually, he pushed his plate back and propped his elbows on the table. "Thanks for this. I didn't realize how much I needed it."

"Funny, but I was about to say the same thing to you." Their gazes met in a moment of naked intimacy that rocked her more than she dared to let on. He looked away first, staring out at the ocean glittering in the morning light.

"There's something I'd like to talk to you about," she ventured.

He glanced back at her, then frowned faintly as if he sensed her hesitation. "Surely after everything we've shared, you know you can talk to me about anything."

"I hope so."

Now she had his undivided attention. His gaze was laser-sharp, taking in every nuance of her body language and expression all of a sudden. *Gulp*.

She said firmly, "When we get back to Camp Jarvis, I'm going to tell Commander Kettering I'm volunteering to be the one to go to BUD/S."

Griffin's eyes popped wide with surprise. "Why?"

"Because it's not fair to ask you to stay here training me any longer. You need to get overseas and be with your team. They've just suffered a devastating loss. And besides, if I know you and your guys, all of you will be out for revenge. The Reapers could use your help to nail Haddad."

"As true as all of that may be, why would you throw away your shot at being a real SEAL? You're every bit as good as Anna and Lily."

She shrugged. "It's the right thing to do."

"But is it what you want?" he persisted.

"Hey, aren't you the guy who told me last night you didn't want me anywhere near real operations? That you were terrified I would die if I went out in the field?"

He scowled. "That's not the point. The point is you're good enough to have a shot at it for real. Why would you throw that away? You're not the kind of person to settle for second best. I *know* you."

She supposed he did. The stress of the training he'd put her through had a way of stripping away all the artifice and revealing a person's essential being. But that sword swung both ways. She knew him, too.

Which was why, as sure as she was sitting here, she knew he would start to resent her going forward, for keeping him away from his brothers-in-arms.

She pushed her own plate back, planting her elbows on the table and matching his stare head on. "I want you to teach me how to survive BUD/S. I'm not talking about more screaming and logs and freezing in the ocean. I've got all that stuff wired. I need you to tear apart the mental aspects for me and talk me through the ultimate lessons I'm supposed to draw from it all."

"That would be cheating," he replied shortly. "BUD/S is not only a rite of passage, but also carefully designed to weed out those who can't cut it as SEALs."

"Yes. But it would get me out of your hair fast so you can get back to your team."

He frowned.

She drove the point home. "We all know I'm not going to end up being a real SEAL anyway. So what does it matter if I cheat? Besides, you said all SEALs cheat. They just don't get caught."

"Are you so eager to get rid of me?" he asked lightly.

"Don't try to change the subject."

"Can't blame a guy for trying."

"I've given a lot of thought to this. It's not a spur-of-the-moment decision. I'm the right woman to do BUD/S. I have the publicity experience, and I can handle the spotlight better than Anna or Lily could."

Griffin sighed heavily, as if he saw the logic of her argument but didn't like it.

She continued. "It's not as if the Navy is going to let me have a fair shot at the course, anyway. The fix is on, and everyone knows it. So let's get this thing done as quickly and easily for all of us as we possibly can."

"You do have a point," he said slowly.

"Perfect!" she said brightly. "Let's get back to camp and let Kettering know what I've decided. Then you and I can sit down and get to work. The sooner the better."

"Don't try to bulldoze me," he warned. "I want to talk with Cal about this before I agree to your plan."

"Fair enough." It wasn't a win, but it wasn't a defeat for her, either.

At least he was willing to consider her proposal. That

was miles beyond where he'd started this whole process of training women SEALs a few months ago.

Now to convince Cal Kettering.

Chapter 13

Cal turned out to be an easier sell on the idea than Griffin had expected he would be. The guy seemed relieved not to have to choose between the women candidates, and he agreed with Sherri that she was the best choice to handle the media coverage and fame that would come with being the first woman SEAL.

Griffin couldn't believe he was doing it, but he found himself arguing against the whole idea to the two of them. "I never thought I'd hear myself say this, but Sherri would make a decent SEAL. Are we throwing away a potentially useful asset in order to hurry her through the program?"

Cal leaned back in his desk chair, his eyes bloodshot. The guy obviously was sporting one hell of a hangover today. Thanks to Sherri's water and french fries last night, Griffin had avoided the same fate.

"Are you sure about this, Sherri?" Cal asked. "Once I pull the trigger, there will be no turning back."

"I'm sure."

"Why?"

"Come on. We all know I'm the media-ready one of the three of us women. Don't get me wrong, Anna and Lily will make great special operators, but neither one of them would know how to be a poster child. And we all know that's precisely what the Navy wants."

Cal looked back and forth between Griffin and Sherri

long enough that Griffin actually started to feel fidgety. Cal asked him without warning, "How long will it take you to make Sherri ready for BUD/S?"

Griffin frowned. "She hasn't done the obstacle course yet, and she hasn't passed the drowning evolution. Beyond that, I think she could be ready in a matter of days."

Cal looked at the calendar that was his desk pad. "There's a BUD/S class starting INDOC in two weeks. I'll make the call."

The reality of the end of his time with Sherri hit him with the weight of a sledgehammer. He was going to leave her behind to suffer through BUD/S alone while he flew halfway around the world to catch a terrorist. Which was as it should be. But damn it all, he was going to miss her.

She would move on. Become a celebrity. Forget about him. Find herself some pretty-boy movie star or up-and-coming politician to hook up with.

Griffin rose to his feet. There had to be at least a little whiskey left over somewhere in the instructors' barracks from last night. He suddenly felt a burning need to tie one on. Hard. And without a pitcher of water and carbs to dull the effects of it.

Sherri rose as well, thanking Cal quietly.

Griffin reached for the office door to open it for her.

"Oh, and Griffin?" Cal said casually.

No, no, no. He knew that tone of voice out of his boss. Bracing himself for a direct hit, he turned to face Cal. "Yes, sir?"

"You'll be going with Sherri to Coronado. I'll see to it you're assigned as an adjunct instructor for the duration of her BUD/S course."

"What?" he and Sherri exclaimed in unison.

"You didn't think I was going to throw her to the sharks without any kind of backup, did you?"

"But Haddad—"

"That SOB will wait. Right now, I need you to finish Operation Valkyrie. Get Sherri through BUD/S. Then we all can go back to our regularly scheduled lives. Trust me, the Reapers will get their pound of flesh out of Abu Haddad. But we'll do it together. All of us. As a team."

Griffin was startled by the fury vibrating in Cal's voice. The man rarely showed emotion, and when he did, it was cold and tightly disciplined. He'd honestly never seen Cal like this. The man had a serious hard-on for killing Haddad.

Griffin knew how his boss felt. They were on *exactly* the same page.

He nodded tersely. "I'll have her ready."

"See to it she makes it through BUD/S. Do whatever you have to, Grif."

"Roger that, sir."

Which was why that afternoon found him at the swimming pool with Sherri and a handful of zip ties. She threw skeptical looks back and forth between him and the pool.

"We're going to start in the shallow end today," he explained. "I'm going to break down how to swim while tied up, and you're going to practice it without the zip ties until you master it."

It felt weird to spoon-feed her the trade secrets to

passing a training evolution like this, but so be it. If the Navy wanted a woman SEAL, then a woman SEAL he would give them.

"The trick is to accept that you're going to spend most of this type of swimming underwater. You'll only surface to breathe. Where people mess it up is by trying to get their faces above water and keep them there."

"You could've told me that the last time you nearly drowned me," Sherri replied tartly.

"One of the big objects of BUD/S is to mess with your mind and see how you handle it. How mentally tough are you? Since we're not worried about that with you anymore, I can tell you all the tricks."

She scowled and slid into the pool, standing chest deep in the water.

"Clasp your hands behind your back and hold your feet together like they're zip-tied. I'll move you into the deeper water, and I'll be right there with you this time. Any time you feel like you can't get to the surface to breathe, let go of your hands and kick yourself up to the surface."

When the screaming and harassment and abject terror were stripped out of the drowning evolution, Sherri picked up fast on how to swim like a dolphin, relaxing and letting herself sink gently between breaths, and then kicking up to the surface just long enough to breathe.

"Good. Now, let's put you in clothing. It's heavier, and you'll sink faster and deeper. It's the same motion, though. You'll just have to work at it a little harder."

It took her a few tries to overcome momentary panic attacks, but she got the hang of it soon enough.

"Ready to try it with zip ties?" he asked.

She nodded, looking more determined than scared. Good. That was the right mindset for this evolution.

He stepped up behind her at the edge of the pool and ran his palms down her arms, drawing them behind her back. He took a quick look around to make sure they were alone and leaned forward to place a quick kiss on the side of her neck.

Sherri laughed under her breath. "Is this some new version of the drowning evolution? Distract the trainee so bad they can't concentrate enough to pass the test?"

"Something like that." He put on the zip ties and pulled them as tight as they would be in the real BUD/S course. "Ready?" he asked her.

"Yes," she answered firmly.

He placed his hands on her waist and tossed her out into the swimming pool. He was considerably gentler than her BUD/S instructors would be. But today was about teaching her how to do the swimming, not terrifying her.

Griffin watched her carefully as she sank into the water, counting in his head. After about fifteen seconds, she dolphin kicked several times and her face briefly broke the surface. She took a deep breath and then sank again. In about fifteen more seconds, she repeated the maneuver. Perfect. He nodded in approval the next time she surfaced. She smiled briefly and then sank again.

He jumped in beside her and pulled her into water she could stand in. He said, "Now see if you can travel with it. You'll have to swim a few lengths of a pool like this," he called.

She added forward motion to the maneuver easily.

After she'd swum to the far end and back to him, he cut her loose.

Immediately, she threw her arms around his neck and kissed him soundly. "I did it!"

He grinned back at her. How in the hell had he gone from determined to wash her out of the program to taking almost parental pride in her success? It was crazy.

They climbed out of the pool, and while she toweled off, he reached into his duffel bag. "I have something for you." He handed her a piece of rough hemp rope about two feet long and the thickness of his wrist. She turned it over curiously in her hands.

"What's it for?" she asked.

"Calluses. You're going to do a whole lot of rope climbing, tug-of-wars, swinging on ropes, and the like. I noticed last night that your hands are too soft."

Her gaze snapped up to his, and instant heat flared between them. He continued doggedly, "Whenever you're sitting around doing nothing over the next few weeks, you need to rub that piece of rope across your palms. Don't make them bleed or tear the calluses you do have. But you need to toughen up your hands."

She smiled at him. "You think of everything."

"Hardly. I'm just trying to think of anything that could trip you up so we can prepare you for it."

"I really appreciate what you're doing for me, Griffin."

He met her gaze head on. "I appreciate what you're doing for me."

She blinked, and that looked like moisture accumulating in her eyes.

"Don't you dare cry on me, Tate. And definitely don't cry at BUD/S."

She stood up a little straighter and squared her shoulders. "Big girls don't cry, Caldwell."

Truth be told, he didn't think he would mind all that much if she cried on his shoulder sometimes. *Hell*. He'd cried on hers last night, and the world hadn't ended. But first, he had to get her through BUD/S. And the guys there would eat her alive if she dared to show any kind of vulnerability.

He sent her to the showers alone. He didn't think he had the will to resist her, and Cal was in the gym working out, which meant he would shower soon. Instead, Griffin made his way back to the instructors' barracks.

Trevor lay in his bed, in significantly worse shape than Cal. Griffin jogged over to the mess hall and grabbed a loaf of bread, some crackers, an armful of water bottles, and a roll of antacid out of a first aid kit. He took his haul back to the hut.

"Where'd you disappear to last night?" Trevor asked, enunciating carefully.

"I had to get out of here for a while. Went down to the beach. Had a few drinks. Slept it off."

"With Sherri?"

Rule number one of being on a SEAL team was never to lie to your brothers. It made for some uncomfortable conversations and some painful confessions. But absolute trust was, bar none, the most important aspect of the work they did.

He sighed heavily and sat down on the edge of his bed. He looked Trev dead in the eye and said, "Yeah. With Sherri."

The Brit nodded. "She's been good for you."

Startled, Griffin blurted out, "How's that?"

"She's mellowed you." As Griffin scowled in displeasure, Trevor added quickly, "In a good way. She makes you laugh. She has taken a few of the rough edges off you."

Griffin shrugged. "That's because she's a woman. I'm not gonna treat her like I would one of you Neanderthals."

Trevor spoke slowly. "I'm not so sure the influence of women on a team would be a bad thing."

Whoa. Never in a million years would he have expected the Brit to take that stance. "Do the ladies know how you feel?" Griffin asked.

"Good Lord, no. I would never hand them such a powerful weapon to wield against me."

Griffin traded rueful smiles with Trevor, silently acknowledging that the battle of the sexes was alive and well.

"But I'm told that expressing our feelings is good for us," the Brit said seriously.

"Speak for yourself," Griffin retorted. "The only reason you're thinking about your feelings is because we took a terrible hit last night."

"That's precisely what I'm talking about," Trevor replied. "When we've lost a brother in the past, we've all gotten stinking drunk, acted macho, and never acknowledged how bad it hurt. But last night, Cal actually cried. I didn't know the man even had tear ducts."

Griffin stared. "For real?"

"Yes. For real."

Finally, the moment broke and they grinned at each other. He muttered, "You're so full of shit."

Griffin noticed that Trevor pointedly didn't ask him if he'd slept with Sherri. But then, he didn't volunteer the information, either. “In other news,” Griffin said as he stretched out on his own cot, “Sherri’s going to BUD/S in two weeks.”

“No kidding?” Trevor exclaimed, sitting bolt upright and clutching at his skull. “I’m surprised Cal didn’t hold her back to be a functional operator.”

“She volunteered.”

“Did she, now?” The Brit stared thoughtfully at Griffin. “Why do you suppose she did that?”

He shrugged. “She said something about being best suited to deal with the media attention the first woman SEAL will have to endure.”

“So she sacrificed herself for the others,” Trevor said soberly. “That was noble of her.”

Noble, huh? Griffin hadn’t thought of it in that light, but he supposed it was. Funny. He’d never thought in terms of any woman as noble before. But it wasn’t a bad way to describe what Sherri had done.

“We’ll miss her around here,” Trevor commented. He added what sounded like an afterthought: “We’ll miss you, too.”

Griffin grinned. “You’ll be so busy trying to get into Anna’s pants, you won’t notice I’m gone.”

Trevor’s cheeks turned bright red, and Griffin started. He’d meant that as a joke. But was there something going on between the Brit and the brunette that he’d missed? Apparently, yes. Reserved, classy Trevor and fiery Anna with the big mouth and fast wit?

Did Sherri know? Was that part of why she’d volunteered to leave? So Trevor and Anna could have a shot at finding happiness? The phrase *noble sacrifice* floated through his head.

And he hadn't even thanked her for giving up her dreams and ambitions for the greater good, which was exactly the sort of sacrifice a SEAL might make.

Well, hell. He'd been outSEALed by a woman.

Chapter 14

Two weeks later

SHERRI WAS MET AT SAN DIEGO INTERNATIONAL AIRPORT by a public affairs officer who looked about twelve years old and whose name tag said *Schneider*.

Griffin was on the same flight, but they'd agreed to pretend not to know each other when they arrived in California. He would make his own way to the naval base. Griffin gave her a single terse nod as she followed Schneider outside, and she flashed him a quick thumbs-up. She felt completely naked without him at her side. Now that she was here in California, hours from beginning the toughest training of her life, she was secretly and selfishly glad that Kettering had sent Griffin with her to face this beast.

Naval Base Coronado was comprised of eight separate military installations, and Schneider took her to a large building in the North Island portion of the base.

No surprise, a dozen news vans from various national outlets were already clustered out front, their mobile satellites pointing at the sky.

And the circus begins.

Schneider directed the driver of their staff car to pull around back. The public affairs officer hustled her inside through a loading dock and tucked her in some poor schmuck's office that had been appropriated for this fiasco.

"Why all the secrecy, Ensign?" she asked her handler.

"The Pentagon wants a big reveal of you, so that's what they'll get." The kid passed her a garment bag and a roll-aboard suitcase.

"What are these?"

"We had your roommate in Washington, DC send this stuff for you."

Sherri unzipped the garment bag, not surprised to see several of her uniforms inside. She opened the suitcase and stared down in dismay at her entire pageant tool kit. It included hot rollers, makeup bags, a lighted mirror, hair spray, deodorant, even double-sided carpet tape.

"What's the tape for?" Schneider asked over her shoulder.

"It holds down a bikini bottom or holds up a dress. Or if you're wearing something with a super-plunging neckline, the tape will keep you from accidentally flashing the audience."

"Huh. Live and learn," the guy mumbled.

"A girl's got to suffer for beauty," she commented sarcastically.

"You women can have all that primping and hard work."

Lucky bastard. "Why is all this stuff here?" she asked him.

"They want you to look your best for the cameras."

"Of course they do." Even knowing what she was in for, it irritated her to no end. She'd just spent months busting her butt to be ready for BUD/S. Never mind that she was in the best shape of her life, mentally girded for a trip to hell and back, and carrying in her noggin every trick and hint that Griffin could think of to share with her.

Nope. All that mattered to the powers that be was that she look hot on camera. Fine. They wanted the pageant queen? Then the pageant queen they would get. She sat down at the desk, plugged in her lighted mirror, and went to work.

An hour later, she was polished and lacquered to within an inch of her life. Her hair was swept up in a sophisticated French twist, and her makeup was flawless. She'd even taken time to shape and polish her nails.

She had to admit, it felt weird to put on pantyhose and high heels after months of running around in fatigues and combat boots.

Schneider insisted she wear a skirt. Orders from above and all. Must show a little leg for the boys. The higher-ups had also insisted on her wearing service dress whites. No surprise there. Might as well go full recruiting poster with this appearance.

As she slipped into her uniform, it dawned on her why SEALs were forever tugging at their dress uniforms. The heavily starched collar rubbed at her neck horribly after the soft, floppy collars of tactical combat shirts.

She paused in front of the full-length mirror mounted on the back of the office door to give herself a critical once-over. Only thing that would make her look more girlie would be a sparkly evening gown.

Ugh. The press was going to love her. And the SEALs were going to hate her with a fiery passion. She didn't even want to think about how her BUD/S instructors would retaliate against her for dressing up like this and prancing around in front of a bunch of reporters.

She took a deep breath. Here went nothing. She followed Schneider, her heels clicking loudly, and she caught herself wincing at the noise. She had become adept at the silent heel-to-toe walk of special operators, but it was impossible to do in three-inch stilettos. Mincing along on her stupid heels, she followed Schneider into what looked like the wings of a stage.

"Is this the base theater?" she whispered.

"Yes."

"How many reporters are out there?" The buzz of voices from around the corner was shockingly loud.

"Theater holds 550. Every seat's full."

"Bloody hell," she muttered.

"You'll walk across the stage to the podium in the middle. There's a prepared statement waiting for you. I would have run it past you, but I was told you were incommunicado on some secret assignment."

Yeah. Pretraining to be a SEAL.

Schneider continued, "You'll take questions for about ten minutes, and then there will be a photo op with you and the Naval Surface Warfare Commander, Rear Admiral Duquesne. That's pronounced 'doo-cane.' Don't mess it up, or he'll tear your head off. Got all that?"

She threw the guy a withering look. "I've been doing press conferences at the Pentagon longer than you've been legal to drink."

The kid warned, "Heads will roll, starting with mine, if you flub this thing."

"I got that memo, thanks."

"All right, Lieutenant Tate. Are you ready?"

She smiled a little. "No. But let's do it anyway."

The podium loomed a mile away from her in the

middle of the stage. Schneider went out and did lighting and sound checks, and then the lights went on for real. The kid made a short statement officially announcing that the Navy had selected the first female candidate for BUD/S training.

Eyeing that long walk, she threw caution to the wind. Might as well give them her best runway walk. Using her long legs to full advantage, she stalked boldly across the stage.

She glanced down at the prepared remarks and stifled a snort. *I'm so grateful to have this opportunity and will do my best to make all women in the armed forces proud…*

Blah. Blah. Blah. She could practically recite what the statement said without having seen it. Goodness knew, she'd written enough of these milquetoast statements in her career.

She would dress up for the Navy. She would play along with the whole poster-child thing. But if she had to actually speak to the press, she was not going to be their bubbleheaded mouthpiece. She drew the line at that. Nope, she was going to do this statement her way. She looked up from the notes and smiled at the banks of blinding lights.

She held the smile a moment extra so they could all get their recruiting-poster shots of her.

Then she said into the microphones, "I'm not sure what all the fuss is about, folks, but thanks for this big welcome to my SEAL training. I had no idea you did this for all the trainees who come through here. It's mighty patriotic of you."

The press corps chuckled.

From the wings off to her right, Schneider pointed

frantically at imaginary notes on an imaginary podium in front of him. *Sorry, kid. No can do.*

She and Griffin had talked about this, and they both agreed she would be better served not letting the Navy dictate entirely how this whole rigged training gig would play out. Whatever the brass at the Pentagon had planned, it would likely come across as contrived and obviously a setup.

If this was going to appear real, she had to take control of her image and story. It was her only chance not to get eaten alive by the BUD/S instructors, fix or no fix on her passing the course.

To that end, she said briskly and completely off script, "Let's get a few questions and answers out of way right up front. Am I honored to be here? Absolutely. The finest warriors on earth come out of this place. Am I scared? Of course. Any sane person would be, going into this kind of a test. How long have I trained for this? My whole life. Do I think I'll make it through the training? I hope I will if I'm worthy. But that will be up to the instructors I work with."

She glanced over the heads of the rows of reporters at the line of BUD/S instructors who had filed into the hall quietly when the bright lights went on, and who stood still and silent across the back of the theater. Thought she wouldn't notice them, did they? *Hah.* She was getting darned good at situational awareness these days.

Their expressions were unanimously stony, their crossed arms shouting their disapproval of her.

Someone called out from the audience, "When does your training begin?"

"As soon as I can get out of these blasted pantyhose and high heels."

Another laugh. Then the next question, "Are you worried the instructors won't give you a fair shot?"

She speared the row of silent warriors in the back with a stare. "BUD/S instructors are in the business of identifying operators they would trust with their lives and whom they'd like to work with. My job here will be to prove I'm one of those people."

She caught the snorts and rolled eyes from the men in the back. Whatever. She'd made a believer of Griffin, and he'd been dead set against her initially.

She lifted her chin faintly to the boys in the club, positive they would know the gesture for the challenge it was. And then she threw down the gauntlet. "After all, BUD/S instructors are bright guys. Only someone stuck firmly in the past would fail to see the potential benefit of women in today's Special Forces."

As a group, the line of instructors froze. What? They didn't expect the girl to have any guts? Surprise, boys.

Someone shouted a question about what BUD/S training entailed, and Schneider hurried out to field that one, walking the press corps through a PowerPoint presentation that would be made available after the press conference. It broke down BUD/S into its pretraining pipeline, called INDOC, and three actual BUD/S phases—Physical Training, Sea Warfare, and Land Warfare.

She used the time to observe the guys in the back. God bless Cal Kettering for exposing her to a bunch of SEALs before she got here. Otherwise, all that menace rolling off them might have actually made her nervous.

Another instructor slipped into the auditorium, joining the line of men. He wore camo pants and a navy-blue T-shirt with the yellow UDT/SEAL INSTRUCTOR logo over his heart. *Griffin*. She would know that silhouette, that set of shoulders, the quiet, contained movement anywhere.

So. He was going to infiltrate her instructors? Good to know. She yanked her attention to the question being directed at her. "...how far through the program do you think you can go before you wash out?"

There it was. The subtly dismissive, misogynistic dig she'd one hundred percent expected before this circus concluded.

She stepped out around from behind the podium, planted her left elbow on the lectern, and stared down coldly at the impudent reporter. The room fell silent. Tense, dead silent.

When she could have heard a pin drop, she gave up all pretense of pleasantness and said tersely, "Just what do you think I'm doing here? Playing dress up with the boys? I came here to be a SEAL, and that's what I intend to do. This isn't a game."

If the instructors across the back of room had been dogs, they would all have been tilting their heads at her quizzically. She felt their confusion, even from the other side of a large theater. Poor dudes had no idea what to make of her.

Mission accomplished. Griffin had told her to take the fight to the SEALs and not wait passively for them to bring the fight to her. They would still do everything in their power to break her, but at least this way they might respect her a little while they did it.

She nodded crisply. "If you ladies and gentlemen have no more questions, I'd like to get on with my training."

She didn't wait for the rear admiral to join her on

stage. She was frankly too ticked off at the moment to deal with pressing the flesh and pasting on pageant smiles. As she stalked off stage right, Schneider scurried out to the podium to thank everyone for coming and to give out the schedule for future press conferences to update them on her progress through the course.

Seriously? The media was going to get report cards on her? No wonder the guys in the back were scowling like they'd been force-fed battery acid.

"Lieutenant Tate!" Schneider whispered loudly from the stage. She glanced back, and he was waving frantically at her to join the admiral, who'd come out from the wings on the other side of the stage and was fielding a few questions.

She deliberately misunderstood him and waved back, then all but ran back to the office, where she quickly changed into a utility uniform and combat boots. She slapped her baseball cap on, pulled it down low, and rushed from the building before Schneider could corner her.

She burst out into the warm California sun, duffel bag over her shoulder, pageant tool kit abandoned in the office. Spotting an enlisted man about to climb into a big green utility truck across the street, she jogged over to him.

"Hey, I'm lost. Any chance you could give me a ride over to the Center?"

"You mean the BUD/S school?" the guy blurted out.

"Yes, please."

"Climb in." She clambered into the cab, and the driver threw the big vehicle into gear, asking, "You gonna be working admin over there or something?"

"Something like that."

"Cool."

Yeah. Something like that.

Chapter 15

THEY GAVE HER AN ENTIRE DORMITORY TO HERSELF. IT privately irritated the living crap out of her and meant she had a significantly longer run to fall into formation in the mornings, but the admiral wouldn't budge, apparently. She did not get to live with her classmates.

She didn't waste her breath asking if, when she was out on SEAL missions, she would get her own tent and toilet. There would be time enough to cross that bridge later.

INDOC Day One dawned at 4:00 a.m. sharp with Grinder PT in a giant concrete parking lot. As she gutted through round after round of now-familiar calisthenics while being screamed at, the only thought in her mind, running over and over on a loop, was *God Bless Cal Kettering and the Reapers for preparing me for this*.

The instructors didn't for a second give away any hint of surprise that she could keep up and pump out the required repetitions. Not so with her fellow trainees, who jeered and hassled her almost more than the instructors. But they gradually fell into silence as she matched them rep for rep.

When an end was called to the grinder and they were sent over to a water buffalo—a large tank of water on wheels—to get drinks, a big, beefy dude named Grundy sneered at her back, "Gee. I didn't know the Navy gave us whores to fuck in training whenever we feel like it."

Sherri whirled and strode right up to the bully. She was vividly aware of the sharp interest of all the instructors to see how she handled the moment.

Chest to chest with the slightly taller guy, she ground out, "Grundy, I'm not gonna pull rank on you, and I'm not gonna tell you that was inappropriate. I'm not even gonna tell you this course will be hard enough without us trainees being at each other's throats, or that we should freaking work together. But I am gonna tell you this. You better sleep very, very lightly if you ever say anything like that to me again."

"Are you threatening me, Tate?" Grundy sputtered.

"Not at all," she replied coolly. "Just a friendly reminder that SEALs tend to close ranks when one of their own gets messed with."

"Yeah, but you'll never be one of them."

She smiled knowingly. "Neither will you with a non-team-player attitude like that."

She turned and took the cup of water an instructor held out silently to her from a range of about two feet. The guy had to have heard every word she said to Grundy. Which was no skin off her nose.

Surf immersion was as miserable as she remembered, and dang, the Pacific Ocean was cold. Honestly, she thought it was worse than the Atlantic. But the stars were beautiful, and she distracted herself by enjoying the way dawn overtook night as she lay there shivering.

The guy on her right stood up, swearing, and waded ashore a mere three minutes into the eight-minute immersion session. A minute or so later, she heard the loud triple clang of a brass bell ringing across the training facility.

"The exodus begins!" one of the instructors shouted in glee. "Who'll be next? How about you, Tate? Are you having fun yet?"

"Sir! Yes, sir!" she shouted back enthusiastically. "I'm having a fine morning, sir! Glad to be here, sir!"

Thankfully, nobody called on her again, because her teeth started to chatter so badly she didn't think she could talk. But she knew the drill. They'd drop the trainees' core temperatures to a safe but unholy, awful 91 degrees, pull them out, and run them to a sand dune to warm them up, roll them in the sand like powdered donuts, then run them back to the surf to rinse, lather, and repeat.

While she waited for the cramps and convulsions to set in, she contemplated how interesting it was to know what was coming next. She certainly didn't relish the coming pain, but thanks to Griffin and the Reapers, she knew she could handle it. And that made all the difference.

The bell rang two more times before they finally staggered out of the surf for the last time.

"Where's the lipstick now, Tate?" someone hollered about six inches from her face.

"Don't n-need it, sir!" she shouted back, shivering from head to toe. "I look f-fabulous with b-blue lips!"

The instructor started to grin, but stopped himself at the last moment. Griffin had assured her the instructors cracked themselves up all the time, and that she should look for moments of humor to break up the continuous psychological assault that was BUD/S. Plus, the instructors liked the students who were cheeky enough to make them laugh now and then.

Three more guys DOR'ed—dropped on request—before the run was over. Six down, and it wasn't even lunchtime. Hooyah.

She'd learned at Camp Jarvis to take one day at a time, and the next week passed in a blur. She was by no means the top physical performer in the class, but she wasn't the last, either. She fell slightly below the middle if she had to guess. Griffin had commented that often the most physical guys with the best times didn't have the mental toughness to hack the course. She held on to that thought.

But she was competitive. She set a private goal to make it into the top half of the class before the three weeks of INDOC ended.

Sadly, Grundy didn't drop out. He was forever making snide comments and agitating for the instructors to kick her out, but he didn't call her a whore again. It was a small victory, but she would take it.

For the most part, the other trainees were too wrapped up in their own misery to give a damn about her one way or the other. She suspected they counted on her washing out when they hit the actual BUD/S course anyway.

The instructors said little about her performance, merely writing down her times with silent disapproval. Of course, they disapproved of everything. They were like a bunch of grumpy toddlers who hated *everyone*. The notion privately amused her when one of them would really wind up into a tirade in her face.

She got up one morning, a year into the three-week indoctrination course, and jogged out to join the remaining trainees. They were down thirty-one guys out of two hundred so far.

"Today, lady and gentlemen, I give you the Playground!" the instructor in front of the formation bellowed.

Griffin had told her the obstacle course was sometimes called that. While they went for a warm-up run down the beach, she mentally reviewed the various obstacles the Reapers had built for her and the best ways to get through them.

The replica o-course at Camp Jarvis was as close to exact as the Reapers had been able to build. She had run it dozens of times and knew how completely wiped out her arms would be by the end of the thing.

Today, they walked through the course once while instructors demonstrated each obstacle. Then it was the trainees' turn. She waited in line quietly, resting and breathing deeply.

"Tate, you're up. And…go!"

Hand over hand across the parallel bars. Arms behind her neck to run through the tires. Jump onto the upended logs and then the hard leap up to catch the top of the wall in front of her. Big pull, legs up and over. Slide down the back of the wall, jog to the rope-climb wall.

The guy beside her, one of Grundy's buddies, was going out way too fast and pulled ahead of her. From the top of the rope-climb wall, which she was just starting, he taunted, "What's the matter, Tate? Girls can't hack it?"

"I'll see you at the finish line," she grunted.

She ignored him, pacing herself steadily, taking advantage of her slender body to wiggle fast through the low crawl on her belly under logs and barbed wire. She moved all the way to the left side of the fifty-foot-tall net climb, right next to the frame where Griffin had shown her the cross ropes were most taut, and used her legs primarily to make the climb, giving her arms as much rest as possible.

On she went, obstacle by obstacle, like Griffin had taught her, pacing herself and resting her upper body whenever she could. About halfway through the course, at the rope bridge, she passed the loudmouth, who was sucking wind now. Her balance was excellent, and she moved quickly across the single walking rope, using the two handhold ropes for balance.

Time for the tower of terror. To climb its four platforms each stacked about seven feet apart, a person turned with their back to the platform overhead, reached up and grabbed the edge, and then kicked their feet up hard, doing a 270-degree flip and landing on their stomach flat on the floor of the next level.

Lily, a gymnast, had gone up this thing like a monkey. She'd worked with Sherri to teach her how to throw her hips out and then up, making the maneuver more about momentum and less about brute strength.

Reach. Pull. Kick. Flop.

Reach. Pull. Kick. Flop.

One more time, and she was some thirty feet up on the top level. Time to shimmy down the long rope slanting away from the tower. She lay on top of it on her belly, letting her right knee hang down but hooking her right foot over the rope behind her for balance. She started pulling herself hand over hand down the long slope, letting gravity do much of the work. She was dismayed to see Grundy leering up at her from the bottom of her rope. He reached out, grabbed it, and gave it a hard shake.

Sure enough, she flipped underneath the damned rope, hanging by her ankles and hands.

Jerk.

She let go with her feet, swung her feet up and over the rope again, and laboriously reset herself on her belly on top of the rope before continuing down. It cost her a lot of time, but this way her arms would get the absolutely necessary break they needed.

"You're slowing down my course!" an instructor yelled up at her. No way had the guy missed Grundy's stunt.

She saved her breath and merely continued downward doggedly. She finished the rest of the course without incident and slogged through the sand to cross the finish line in just under nine minutes. Off her best time by nearly a minute. But nine minutes was the cutoff to pass the evaluation today.

As the other guys got more familiar with the course, their times would come down, and she would fall out of the middle of the pack into the bottom quarter with a time like today's.

"Problem out there, Tate?" one of the senior instructors strolled over to ask her as she caught her breath.

"No, Chief."

The guy looked surprised. He must've expected her to whine about Grundy shaking her off the rope. If Griffin had told her once, he'd told her a hundred times, SEAL training wasn't fair.

The guy stared at her a few seconds more, clearly giving her a chance to narc on her classmate, but she just stared back at him implacably. They both knew what had happened out there. She didn't need to say anything.

Reluctantly, a spark of respect lit in the guy's eyes just before he spun away from her, shouting at someone else to get his pansy ass in gear.

She caught glimpses of Griffin from time to time, but he stayed away from her, merely observing. He'd told her she would have no trouble with the INDOC training and that he wouldn't be interacting with her there, since he was going to be working the actual BUD/S course with her.

The three interminable weeks of INDOC passed without any more incidents from Grundy. Whether the instructors had a talk with him, or he feared getting kicked out if he was too big an asshole, Sherri had no idea. She was just grateful for the break from the constant harassment.

They had one whopping day off between INDOC and BUD/S, and she planned to spend every minute of it sleeping.

Except at 9:00 a.m. sharp, a knock on her door woke her up. What the heck? She got out of bed and opened it.

Griffin. Wearing his full service dress blues.

Wow, wow, and triple wow. It was the first time she'd ever seen him in a formal uniform, and man, did he clean up well. The double-breasted black blazer was perfectly tailored to his broad-shouldered, narrow-hipped physique. She couldn't help but stare at the gold trident pin prominent above a ridiculously impressive rack of ribbons.

"To what do I owe the honor?" she murmured, cautious of what the uniform might signify or that he might not be alone.

"May I come in?"

"Of course." She stepped back. He passed her by, and she shut the door behind him. He turned and swept her up in his arms in a tight hug, fraught with...something.

"Everything okay?" she murmured.

He lifted his head from where he'd buried it against her neck. The expression in his eyes was bleak. *Oh, crap*. Was he here to wash her out? Had she failed before she'd even made it to BUD/S?

"I have a favor to ask of you," he said heavily.

"Anything." Goodness knew, she owed him huge for all he'd done for her. She was just now coming to understand how amazingly well he'd prepared her for BUD/S.

"Sam's funeral is today. Since you happen to have the day off, I was wondering if you would go with me."

"Oh," she said softly. "I'd be honored to go with you. But if the press is there, and anyone spots me, it'll turn into a circus."

"I already thought of that. I had that Schneider kid from Public Affairs acquire civilian clothing for you. I figure if you're not in uniform, the odds of you being recognized go way down."

"I'm willing to try if you are," she responded quietly.

"Please."

The poor man sounded like the weight of the world was parked squarely on his shoulders. No way would she let him face Sam's funeral alone. Not if she had a chance to stand by his side and lend him strength or emotional support. Frankly, she was impressed that he'd asked for support of any kind. He must be even more torn up over Sam's death than she'd realized.

"I'll be back in a sec," he murmured.

He swept out of her room, and she used the moment to hit the restroom and brush her teeth. Then Griffin was back with a paper bag and a familiar suitcase.

"Where did you get my pageant kit? I was hoping Schneider would throw it out after that stupid press conference."

Griffin handed her the bag, and she pulled out a conservative dark-blue dress that was perfect for a funeral. Schneider had even gotten her size right. She made a mental note to thank him the next time she saw him. She already owed him an apology for blowing up his press event.

While she dressed and did understated makeup that would be a fitting tribute to Sam and not cry off her face, Griffin perched a hip on the windowsill.

He commented, "Your performance at that press conference made quite a stink. Cal caught holy hell for you going off script until it became clear the press loved you."

She glanced at his reflection in her mirror, shrugging as they made eye contact. "I read the room and took a chance."

"You were lucky."

"I'm also good at my job. Well, my former job."

She pulled her hair back into a low bun and secured it with bobby pins.

"What did your instructor buddies think of the press conference?" she asked curiously as she covered her bun with a tasteful black lace net.

Griffin scowled. "They couldn't shut up about how hot you were."

She laughed a little. "Well, it was the Navy that insisted I get all prettied up. That wasn't my idea."

"Honey, there's no disguising your beauty. I expect if you put a paper bag over your head, you'd still find a way to look great wearing it."

She stood up and turned around to face him. "This isn't a paper bag, but do I look okay?"

He pushed off the sill to come stand in front of her. He rested his hands lightly on her shoulders. "Sherri, I'm not kidding. You're going to be turning heads when you're ninety. You're stunning. It'll be an honor to have you on my arm."

She laid her palm on his smooth-shaven cheek. "I'm sorry it has to be in these circumstances."

They traded looks of deep understanding. They'd shared the trauma of Sam's death, and both felt his loss keenly. Today was going to be hard, but it would be a little less awful because they would get through it together.

She picked up the black leather clutch Schneider had been kind enough to include with the dress and nodded at Griffin.

"Could you keep something in your purse for me?" he asked grimly.

"It's a clutch, but of course."

He held out his hand, and a shiny, gold trident pin lay in it. She stared down at it doubtfully, not understanding what he was doing.

"It's a tradition at SEAL funerals," he said in response to her unspoken question. "You'll see."

She tucked the Budweiser in her clutch and followed Griffin out to a big silver pickup truck. He helped her climb inside and then moved around to the driver's seat.

"Is this yours?" she asked as he guided the vehicle off base.

"Yep."

"So you're stationed here?"

"The Reapers are part of Team Seven."

All the East Coast teams were even numbered, and the West Coast teams odd numbered.

"So you're going home at night, propping your feet up on a coffee table, sipping a cold one, and watching cooking shows while I work my tail off, huh?"

He smiled briefly. "I'm staying on base for the duration of your training. I have a room in the visiting instructors' quarters. Helps me blend in with them. Also, I'm close by in case you need me."

"You guys have thought of everything. I'm fairly certain I don't deserve all the fussing you're doing over me."

"I have a job to do—get you through the program. And I'm a SEAL."

His implication was clear. SEALs didn't fail at their assignments.

They drove north of San Diego to Miramar National Cemetery, and Sherri was relieved to see security was heavy getting to the memorial service. She supposed any large concentration of SEALs in one place was a potentially juicy target for bad guys.

Griffin flashed his military ID out the window and was waved onto the cemetery grounds. They parked and followed the line of people walking toward a stone pavilion at the top of a long hill.

Sherri walked beside him up to the open-walled structure filled with big, silent, hard-looking men. Some wore uniforms with Budweisers glinting on their chests; some wore civilian clothing. But they were all SEALs or retired SEALs. Of that, Sherri had no doubt. By the way their eyes were never still, scanning their environment constantly, by their hard physiques, by posture alone, she recognized them.

A uniformed naval officer peeled away from the cluster of civilians wearing black that had to be Sam's family and strode toward her and Griffin.

"Commander Kettering," she said formally.

He shocked her by stepping forward and giving her a brief, warm hug. "Thanks for coming with Grif. He needed you today," he said quietly.

She froze in shock. Just how much did Cal know about her and Griffin's secret relationship? Crud. Maybe it wasn't so secret after all.

"...holding up, Sherri? Did we prepare you enough?" Cal was asking.

She answered, "INDOC wasn't bad. I'll let you know how BUD/S goes."

"Any problems with the instructors?" he asked.

"Not that I'm aware of. A few students have hassled me, but I've handled them."

"So I hear," Kettering replied.

Her gaze snapped to his. "Do tell."

He smiled. "I get twice-weekly reports on your progress."

"From whom?"

"I have my sources."

She would have pushed for a name, but the funeral was getting ready to start. They took their places in the standing-room-only service. It was a sad affair. The death of a bright, talented man taken far too young and far too soon couldn't be anything but tragic.

Griffin radiated pain beside her, and she reached out

to hold his hand as the service continued. He stood perfectly still, his face a stony mask.

A lone bugler stepped forward to play "Taps." The somber notes rolled across the rows of white marble headstones stretching away in all directions, sweet and plaintive, calling a fallen warrior home to rest for the last time.

Sherri felt tears rolling down her cheeks and didn't bother to reach up to wipe them away. She wasn't ashamed to cry for Sam. She also cried for the pain of his brothers, all these strong, stern men suffering in silence.

The United States flag was lifted from Sam's casket, folded into a triangle, and solemnly presented to Sam's mother, who bowed her head over it and cried quietly. Sherri's heart broke for her, especially.

And then Griffin leaned close to whisper, "I need that trident now."

She handed it to him and watched him step away, joining a line of men forming near Sam's casket. Cal Kettering, as Sam's commanding officer, went first. He stepped up to the casket, bowed his head for a moment of silent farewell, and then slapped his hand down hard on the wooden top of the casket. The accompanying crack of noise made Sherri jump. It echoed out across the hillside and fell away into silence. Kettering lifted his hand away, and a trident was embedded in the wooden lid of the casket.

The next man stepped up and did the same. One by one, the SEALs paid tribute to their fallen brother. Rows of golden tridents covered the top of the casket before they finished, dozens of them, final farewells to one of their own.

The funeral ended, and Griffin came back to her side, tear tracks evident on his face. He didn't wipe them away, either.

Trevor emerged from the crowd of men as Griffin walked her back toward his truck.

"Hey, Blondie!" Trevor swept her off her feet in a big bear hug.

She smiled warmly at the Brit who had always been kind and respectful to her and the other women. "It's good to see you. Just not under these circumstances."

Trevor nodded, his gaze somber. "This won't be the last funeral you attend."

"How are Anna and Lily?" she asked.

"Progressing well. Anna's here somewhere. I think she went to pay her respects to Sam's family."

Sherri scanned the crowd eagerly for Anna's lean build and lush brunette hair. No surprise, she spied a crowd of SEALs around Anna, talking with her. Even from this distance, it was obvious that several were hitting on her.

"Oh, for the love of Mike," Trevor muttered. He must have spotted Anna and her retinue of would-be suitors.

"She could probably use a rescue," Sherri suggested to Trev.

He flashed her a supremely irritated look. "I'm not her knight in shining armor."

"You sure about that?" Sherri shot back.

For an instant, something raw and painful flashed in Trevor's green eyes. "It's not that simple," he mumbled.

She glanced briefly at Griffin. "It never is, Trev. But the good ones are worth fighting for."

Changing subjects, Trevor asked, "How are you faring among the wolves?"

"I finished INDOC yesterday. It was a squeaker, but I made the top half of my class."

"Well done. Brilliant!" Trevor exclaimed warmly.

She shrugged. "We'll see how BUD/S goes. I have a feeling the instructors are really going to be looking for ways to break me."

Trevor smiled. "You know what they say. Never quit. Never consider it."

"I'm not planning on doing either."

"Make us proud, Minnow," Trevor murmured as several more SEALs strolled up.

"Hey, aren't you that girl trying to be a SEAL?" one of the men blurted out.

Sherri froze. *Crap*. Nobody was supposed to know that she'd had months of pretraining with a bunch of SEALs. Operation Valkyrie was *highly* classified. "I am that girl, but I'd appreciate it if you didn't make a fuss about it. Today is Sam's day."

"You knew him?" another guy asked.

"I *am* in the Navy," she retorted. "I know quite a few naval personnel. Like these gentlemen, for example."

Cal Kettering materialized beside Griffin, commenting blandly, "She's done some public affairs work for the Reapers in the past. She's family."

The defensive posture of the other SEALs melted immediately. Family to one SEAL was family to all.

Griffin leaned close to mutter in her ear, "Let's get out of here."

She was all over that.

But when they drove away from the cemetery, Griffin didn't head back toward Coronado. Six months ago, she would have asked where they were going. Now, she just leaned back to see where they ended up. She definitely took life more as it came, after the past several months of training. Not to mention, she trusted him.

Griffin turned off the highway and followed a narrow tarmac road to a high, white gate. He punched a number into a keypad and drove through when the gate opened.

It turned out to be a marina.

He led her down a long dock to a large motor yacht in pristine condition. It was named *Easy Day*.

She grinned. One of the SEALs' unofficial mottos was "The only easy day was yesterday."

"What's this?" she asked.

"Home sweet home."

"You live on a boat?"

"I don't really live anywhere. I'm deployed a whole lot more than I'm stateside. But this is where I hang my hat when I'm not overseas somewhere, going balls to the wall—" He broke off. "Sorry."

She laughed. "I live and work with a bunch of sailors. Trust me, I've heard a *lot* worse."

He handed her aboard. The interior was as tidy as the exterior, cozy and comfortable. However, her heels and formal dress were wildly out of place.

"Do you have some sweatpants and a T-shirt I could borrow?" she asked him.

He jogged down a short stairway to what was undoubtedly his bedroom, stripping off his uniform jacket as he went. He emerged in a minute, wearing jeans and a Reaper T-shirt and carrying another Reaper T-shirt and a pair of gym shorts.

Sherri went belowdecks to the stateroom she found there and changed. She emerged into the living room barefoot and wearing his clothes, which were baggy on her, but blessedly comfortable. A rumble started beneath her feet, and the dock started to retreat. He was taking the boat out!

She went upstairs to the bridge and stood beside him as he expertly steered the vessel out of the marina and into open water. The Pacific Ocean stretched away in a dark sheet of glittering sunshine. The skyline of San Diego retreated behind them as they cruised north along the shore.

The boat picked up speed, and she raised her face to the warmth of the sun and the cool caress of the salt spray. Man, she needed this.

They cruised in companionable silence for perhaps an hour. Then Griffin cut the engines and steered the *Easy Day* into an inlet tucked in among the rocky hills of the California coast.

"Can I interest you in a picnic?" he asked.

"You're a god." She sighed.

He grinned. "I am, but give me a little time to prove it."

"Can I help with lunch?" she offered.

They maneuvered around the tiny galley, bumping into each other constantly. The good news was each time they did, Griffin paused to kiss her. He fed her bites of the cold shrimp salad he made while two spectacular T-bone steaks marinated.

Then he carried the steaks out to the aft deck, lit a hibachi grill, and laid the steaks on it when the coals were hot. The steaks sizzled merrily, giving off an aroma so fantastic that saliva puddled in Sherri's mouth.

"Wine?" he asked her, holding up a bottle.

"Of course." She took a sip of the rich, dark vintage and sighed in appreciation. She finished the first glass, and he refilled her goblet again. "Are you trying to get me drunk, Mr. Caldwell?"

"What if I am, Miss Tate?"

"I sincerely hope your dastardly plan includes taking advantage of me."

A broad grin split his face, his teeth white against his dark tan. "I think that could be arranged. Food first, though. You're going to need your strength."

"Hah! We'll see who needs their strength. I've been in hard-core training, in case you haven't noticed."

He flipped the steaks and sprawled on the chaise longue next to hers. "Oh, I've noticed. So have all the guys. They're scared shitless at how well you're doing."

"Poor little boys, about to have a girl invade their sandbox."

He took an appreciative sip of the wine. "I gotta say, I'm actually getting used to the idea."

"You don't have to sound so shocked," she teased.

"I guess it boils down to whether or not you can pull your weight and do the job. If you can, why not let you play with the boys?"

"Well, praise be. The Neanderthal is reformed."

"I wasn't that bad, was I?"

She laughed at him. "You were a total jerk."

"Sorry."

Her smile widened. "I'll allow you to make it up to me later."

They spent the afternoon lounging on deck, enjoying the cool Pacific breezes and the warm California sun. Sherri dozed on and off, soaking up the quiet and relaxation. Sometimes her training had gotten so intense that she forgot anything else existed. Her whole world narrowed down to pain, exhaustion, and instructors in her face.

As sunset bled across the open water in shades of crimson, Griffin disappeared inside. He emerged with a giant bowl of chopped salad filled with all kinds of goodies—ham, carrot bits, hard-boiled egg, a couple kinds of cheese, spinach, and even kale.

"I had no idea you were such a health nut," she commented, digging into the salad enthusiastically.

"A finely honed body requires excellent fuel."

"You're talking to a pageant girl. I know full well how important it is to eat properly."

"Did you like doing beauty pageants?" Griffin asked curiously.

"I liked the scholarship money, and the contests I entered typically included talent or a social platform the contestants endorsed and worked to improve."

"What was your talent?"

"Violin."

"Of course it was," he replied dryly.

"Why do you say it like that?"

He shrugged. "Because you're perfect. Of course you're a concert violinist on top of everything else."

"I'll let you in on a secret. I'm actually a pretty mediocre violinist. I practiced three difficult pieces for about five years until I could play them flawlessly, then I rotated them at the various competitions I entered."

Griffin grinned at her. "So your skill at cheating the system started early."

She grinned back. "I'm born SEAL material."

"What was your social platform?"

Her smiled faded. "Domestic violence prevention."

He studied her intently enough that she felt an urge to squirm. Then he said quietly, "Well, shit. I'm sorry." Then more quietly, "How bad was it?"

"He never hit me. But I watched him beat up my mom more times than I can count." Images crowded forward in her mind of her mother, bruised and broken. Of her own helpless rage. Of grief and fury, and vowing never, ever to be that vulnerable or weak. She pushed her past back and said aloud, "I got out when I was sixteen—graduated early from high school and went to college on the scholarship money from the pageants. When that ran out, I joined ROTC to pay for the rest of my school. That's how I ended up in the Navy. But I got out of that house, and I owe him nothing."

"Father or stepfather?" Griffin asked.

"Father."

"Damn. That's even worse. At least if you're not their blood, you can hold on to that."

Sherri shrugged. "He gave me DNA, but I choose what to make of it. And I choose to be nothing like him."

"Good for you."

She smiled ruefully. "Oh, I'm undoubtedly messed up twenty ways from my childhood. But I've done my best to move on and become my own person."

"I'd say you've done a pretty spectacular job of it," Griffin commented.

"My dad is ex-military. He fought in some seriously messed-up places and saw some terrible things. War broke him. My mom swore he was different before he went off to fight."

"Don't kid yourself. War breaks everyone to some degree. What matters is how you handle the shit in your head when you get home. Warriors like us are just trained to handle it better than the average grunt."

Sherri went dead still. He included her in the ranks of elite warriors? Really? Did he even realize what he'd just said?

A Navy SEAL perceived her as capable of becoming his equal in war. She *could* do this. It wasn't until this exact moment she realized that she'd harbored doubt over whether what she was striving to achieve was actually possible. But Griffin thought she could do it. She let the knowing of that sink in as deep and warm as the sunlight soaking through her.

Griffin stood. As she gazed up at him from her chaise, he opened his arms in invitation. She rose and went to him gladly. Openly. Trustingly. She stepped into the circle of his acceptance and protection, confident for the first time that she truly belonged there beside him. She laid her head on his chest and listened to his heart beating slowly and steadily.

"You make me feel safe," she murmured.

"You are safe with me. Not only would I never, ever raise a hand to anyone I love in anger, but I'll kick the ass of anyone who tries it with you. Including your old man."

Sherri snuggled a little closer to his warmth as Griffin's arms tightened around her. She responded, "I can kick butts for myself now."

"That you can. He'll never hurt you again."

Griffin's quiet observation rang with truth. She let that sink all the way down into her soul as well. She'd done it. She'd once and for all gotten clear of the miasma of fear, guilt, and desperation to please that had defined her life up till now.

Huh.

And she had Griffin to thank for it.

"How am I ever going to pay you back for everything you've done for me?" she asked.

His chest vibrated with a silent chuckle. "I can think of a few ways."

She lifted her head to mock-scowl up at him. "You men. Always thinking with your crotch."

Griffin speared his hands into her long hair, cupping her head and tilting her face up to his. "Don't underestimate me, Sherri. I think about you with a hell of a lot more than my crotch. You fascinate me. Make me feel things..."

His voice trailed off, leaving them staring at each other. His emotions appeared to be as raw as hers. Normally buried feelings were sitting right on the surface today, out in the open for both of them to see.

"I want you, Sherri."

Take that, for example. He clearly wasn't talking about sex. She stared back at him, shocked at the intensity of feelings welling up in her chest. "I want you, too," she heard herself whispering back.

Griffin nodded slowly, accepting everything she was offering in her whispered words. He said merely, "So be it."

And then he bent down, swept her off her feet, and carried her inside. He laid her on his bed and followed her down to the mattress.

She welcomed him with open arms and an open heart. He kissed her gently, and she kissed him back leisurely, reveling in this new intimacy between them. He kissed her from head to foot, and then she did the same with him.

Even though they'd done this before, today felt different. It was as if she learned him all over again. Where she'd seen lust and strength and raw sex appeal before, now she saw the man beneath the soldier. The heart beneath the man. And the feelings closely held within the scarred and battered heart.

Their lovemaking was slow, careful even. As if each of them wanted to protect these new and fragile pieces of themselves they'd shared with each other.

When Griffin finally entered her, they found an easy rhythm, their bodies moving in sweet harmony, caressing each other, encompassing each other. Giving and receiving.

And there was joy.

Oh sure, she'd enjoyed sex before. But this was different. Pure happiness infused every slide of flesh on flesh. Every surge and thrust was an expression of acceptance. Every moan a sound of welcome. It made her feel…whole.

And she sensed that it was the same for Griffin.

They spoke with their bodies, saying to each other what they could not say with words, sharing the deepest needs of their hearts, taking each other's hurts and pains into themselves, healing them, and giving them back as something wonderful. Love, even.

For surely this unbearable lightness, this utterly ecstatic belonging, this completeness of finding home, could be nothing less than love.

As they strained toward each other, she stared into his

eyes, reveling in the myriad feelings flowing through his gaze, happily letting everything she was feeling show as well. He smiled down at her, and she smiled in return. And together, they found heaven.

They fell asleep to the lazy rocking of the ocean and the cries of seagulls. She woke up as the first light of the moon streamed in the porthole. She reached out, but the pillow beside her was unoccupied.

She pulled on Griffin's borrowed T-shirt and padded upstairs in search of him. She found him on the foredeck, leaning back in a deck chair, feet propped on the rail, sipping a beer and watching the stars.

She moved to stand beside him, and he looped an arm around her waist, drawing her to his side.

"It sure is peaceful out here," she declared.

"Enjoy it. Your life on the teams will be anything but."

"So I hear."

"The day will come when you crave all the normalcy you're trying so hard to leave behind," he observed.

She found that hard to believe. But she also trusted him to know what he was talking about. She only hoped when that day came he would still be around to enjoy normal with her.

In the meantime, she relished the quiet of this moment with him. She wasn't sure what they were forging between them, but it was good and strong and wonderful. It might not be enough to survive in the long term, but it was enough for now.

Chapter 16

ONE HUNDRED SIXTY TWO OF THE ORIGINAL TWO HUNDRED in her INDOC class made it through the course and commenced BUD/S. They were introduced briefly to their new training cadre, and Sherri's pulse leaped when Griffin stepped forward out of the line of grim-faced men.

The first day of training bore a striking resemblance to INDOC. Too much PT, too cold water, sand everywhere, constant screaming, and running, running, running.

That night, she crawled into bed immediately after supper. The sun had barely gone down outside. But then, it wouldn't be even close to up when she rolled out of bed in the morning.

The door to her room opened silently, and she froze. Stealthily, she slipped her hand under her pillow for the air horn Griffin had insisted she hide there. He didn't say it out loud, but he worried that someone would try to mess with her, isolated in this dorm by herself, far away from her fellow trainees. He'd assured her he would always be nearby. If she blew the horn, he would come.

A big black silhouette loomed in the doorway.

She tensed.

A low voice murmured, "It's me."

Griffin. She sagged in relief. She really didn't need to be attacked in her room on the first night of BUD/S. He closed and locked the door, then slipped under the covers, drawing her into his arms. It had only been one day, but it felt like a lifetime since he'd held her like this. She sighed in contentment and buried her face in the delicious smell of him.

"Enjoying the big show?" he whispered.

She snorted. "Not exactly."

"How do you think you're doing?"

"I don't know. You tell me."

"The instructors are blown away by your physical performance. They'll never admit it, of course, but you're the talk of the chow hall."

"What about my mental performance?"

"They don't know what to make of you yet. Since the other trainees are mostly refusing to interact with you, they're not getting a read on what kind of team player you are. They're interested to see how you do on a boat crew."

So was she, truth be told.

"You'll be on Smurf crew," Griffin said. The trainees were divided by height into teams for group calisthenics to include log PT, boat carries, and the like, where having everyone be of similar height mattered. The shortest boat crew by height was traditionally nicknamed the Smurfs. Not only was it a reference to their lack of height, but it might also have something to do with coming out of the ocean blue with cold all the darned time.

"Of course I'll be stuck with the Smurfs." She sighed.

"Don't knock it. Small crews tend to be fast and wiry. What they lack in size and brute strength, they make up for in speed, feistiness, and will to survive."

"At least I won't be with Grundy," she commented.

"He's a putz. He won't make it onto the teams. It hasn't gone unnoticed that he has gone out of his way to sabotage you. He was warned about it by the INDOC instructors. If he tries that in BUD/S proper, we'll chew him up and spit him out."

"I look forward to it."

"Don't be too smug when it happens," Griffin warned.

"Got it. Poker face all the way for me."

His arms tightened around her. "You're doing great. I'm so damned proud of you."

"I've still got a long way to go."

"One day at a time, babe. One day at a time."

He held her until she fell asleep, which took about two nanoseconds. She didn't wake up when he slipped out from under her. But when she woke up at the ass crack of not even close to dawn the next morning, she felt emotionally refreshed and ready to roll.

Which was a good thing. BUD/S was in a whole 'nother class above INDOC in overall suckage.

Four guys rang out in the first hour of Grinder PT on the big concrete pad beside the beach, and three more didn't make it through immersion. Today, instead of running to the dunes and back to warm up, the trainees were given minimal recovery time and sent right back out into the ocean for a timed swim.

It was brutal. Had she not already known the combat swim stroke the SEALs used, Sherri seriously doubted she'd have made it through the swim. Whether they would have left her out there to drown or someone would have come along to fish her out of the water was anyone's guess. Either way, she felt like a drowned rat when she finally staggered ashore, completely gassed.

Griffin stood over her as she lay on the wet sand, gasping for air. "You good?" he asked shortly.

"That sucked," she managed to get out.

"Worst evolution of the day," he muttered under his breath. "It's all downhill from here." And then he strode away to get in some other unlucky sod's face as the guy crawled ashore.

After the swim from hell, *then* the instructors took them running. The mere announcement that they were going for a scenic tour down the beach was enough to make another guy ring out.

Sherri didn't give even the slightest thought to dropping out. She was in this to finish. Period. Nothing they could do to her would make her quit. They might wash her out involuntarily, but she would never, ever go of her own free will.

The days settled into a routine. Up early, exercise like mad, go until the exhaustion was beyond bearing, then go some more. Into bed the moment the last training evolution ended. Regain semiconsciousness as Griffin slipped into her room if he was able to sneak away from his instructor duties.

He didn't even hint at sex, which was kind of him. Although she would've fallen asleep in the middle of it even if she had wanted to give it a go. He merely held her, or sometimes gave her a massage to work out a particularly sore muscle. But the strength she derived from his visits was immeasurable.

She occasionally felt a stab of guilt at getting a nightly heads-up of what the next day's training would entail and how to pace herself to get through it. But then, this whole BUD/S experience was fixed, anyway. They wouldn't flunk her out no matter how she performed. Often, Griffin shared tips and tricks that turned out to be worth their weight in gold for surviving various evolutions with a minimum of suffering.

About two weeks into the seven-week physical training phase, he brought her a bottle of liquid electrolytes and minerals that she slugged from every night. It tasted like salted metal, but he assured her it would help immensely with her recovery times. Apparently, operational SEALs took supplements like it all the time to stay in fighting trim.

The Smurf crew groaned initially at being stuck with the girl, but when they figured out she could pull her weight—literally—and that she was unfailingly positive and encouraging to her teammates, the complaining subsided.

In fact, at the mess hall one evening about three weeks in, when Grundy made a point of spilling an entire tray of spaghetti on her, the guys of Smurf crew jumped out of their seats and surrounded her, ready to do battle on her behalf.

She merely laughed it off, commenting to Grundy, "Remind me never to let you handle grenades in my platoon."

Not only was it a direct insult, it was a subtle reminder that she was an officer and could conceivably end up leading a team where he would work for her.

Grundy scowled, his jaw hanging open, while she did her best badass catwalk over to the trash can to pick strands of spaghetti off herself.

If nothing else, she felt inordinately grateful that her team had backed her up.

The next day was their first attempt at a fun little evolution call surf passage. It started with getting softened up by an hour or so of four-count lunges while holding an inflatable rubber raft over her boat team's heads, plus push-ups, flutter kicks, and a lot of screaming in her face.

Then she and her teammates ran out into the surf, jumped in their boat, and commenced trying to paddle it out past the surf line where tall waves broke over them, knocked guys out of boats, and overturned boats outright.

Sherri took a critical look at her crew. All the strong guys were on the port side of the boat. Not good. She shouted, "Smitty, trade places with me."

She knew from playing this game in the Atlantic Ocean at Camp Jarvis that the strength of the paddlers had to be evenly distributed, or the boat would get slightly sideways of a wave and tip over. She jumped to her new side of the boat in the nick of time.

She timed the approaching wave and shouted, "Dig in with your paddles...*now*!"

They made it over the wave, but the guy in the very front of the boat, Jabrowski, got flipped out and sailed overhead to land in the surf beside her. Sherri thrust her paddle at him. "Grab on!"

Fortunately, he was one of the strongest guys on the crew, and he managed to snag her paddle as the surf pulled at him. With the help of two other guys, she hauled him over to the raft. Instructors yelled at them from shore to quit fucking around and paddle.

Sherri helped grab Jabrowski's belt and pull him back into the boat. Another wave broke over the boat, inundating them all. She coughed up seawater with the rest of her boatmates.

She commenced singing a song Griffin had called a sea shanty. Its rhythm helped all the guys paddle in unison. They picked up the chant and roared the song as another wave smashed into them, sending their boat's prow vertical. They all leaned forward, digging in with their paddles, smashing through another wave face and slamming down on the back of it. Boat upright, everyone inside.

"A win for the Smurfs!" she crowed. Her teammates cheered as the instructors waved them back in to shore. They were spared remedial physical training as a result of their performance and were released to head up to the chow hall for lunch ahead of the other hapless teams, most of whom were floating in the surf, tossed out of their overturned boats.

Sherri piled her tray high with food and sat down to eat as much of it as she could before they were called to form up for the next evolution.

Smitty and Jabrowski plunked their trays down at her table, and she looked up in surprise as all the Smurfs sat down with her. Son of a gun. She actually had to surreptitiously wipe away definitely not tears of gratitude as they talked and laughed, casually including her as if she was one of them.

"Where did you learn how to pass surf like that, Tate?" Smitty asked her.

She shrugged. "I've done something similar before. It's physics, really. Boat's got to be perfectly perpendicular to the wave to go over it and not get flipped."

"What about when to paddle?" Jabrowski piped up.

"Paddles digging into the wave help the boat stick to the wave face and not flip," she replied.

Jabrowski nodded. "Makes sense." A pause. "I'm Mike."

"Sherri. Although I also answer to Barbie." The guys at the table laughed at the nickname the instructors favored for her.

"What the hell made you want to do something like this?" Smitty asked around a mouthful of meat loaf and mashed potatoes.

"It's like climbing a mountain. It was there." She added, "And I happen to like shooting things and blowing shit up."

"Fucking A!" her teammates shouted.

She looked up to see Griffin and about six other instructors had just stepped into the dining hall. As one, they stopped and stared at the scene before them. Every jaw but Griffin's tightened. He met her gaze and nodded infinitesimally in approval before turning away to sit with the other instructors.

Things got easier for her after that. She and the other Smurfs joked around and cheered each other on when the going got tough.

But as the days passed, the max run and swim times continued to come down, and Sherri watched nervously as those times crept steadily closer to her personal bests. She got more opportunity to swim here than she had in North Carolina, and she did improve her two-mile ocean swim times quite a bit. But still she worried.

The one thing the Reapers had not been able to simulate adequately at Camp Jarvis was the long-term toll this kind of training intensity took on a body. Her right shoulder ached most of the time. It felt like she'd irritated the rotator cuff. Nothing but rest would heal it, and that was the one thing she got none of around here.

Then when she tweaked a muscle in her back, Griffin insisted she go to one of the medical trainers, who performed a borderline miraculous deep tissue massage on it. While she slept that night, Griffin stayed up for hours, icing her back on and off.

By morning, most of the inflammation was gone and she felt human again. God bless Griffin.

Grundy continued to ride the fine line of getting kicked out for his ongoing harassment of her. She let it roll off her back for the most part. She had no time to deal with his issues, and frankly, as long as he didn't mess with her again like he had on the obstacle course, she didn't care what he said or did.

Four weeks through the seven weeks of Phase I, she walked into a buzz of voices murmuring in the morning mess hall.

"What's up?" she asked her Smurf buddies softly.

"Ray Peevy is joining our instructor cadre," Smitty muttered.

"Who's he?" she asked.

Smitty stared at her incredulously. "Only the most famous DEVGRU operator in the past twenty years. Guy's a legend."

She frowned, smelling a rat. "Why's he coming here? Isn't training BUD/S candidates a little below his exalted status?"

Jabrowski leaned across the table to mumble, "Way I hear it, he's been sent here to get rid of you.

Everyone thought you'd be gone by now, but you're hanging in there."

She shrugged. "My times aren't going to hold up much longer if they keep bringing the max times down."

Smitty grinned. "I overheard a couple of the instructors talking about how we're at the final training times now. You're good to go, kid."

"Maybe. But we head into the heavy water evolutions over the next few weeks. And swimming isn't my greatest strength. They'll find a way to get rid of me if they really want to. I suppose they can always drown me."

The guys laughed and went back to eating and chatting around her. Why had Peevy really been brought here? She was certain it had to do with her. But what did it mean? Was he here to assess the girl SEAL, or was he indeed here to bust her out?

After lunch, Peevy was introduced. The guy was short, stocky, swarthy of complexion, and had a vertical scar that ran from the middle of his forehead, across his left eye, and down his left cheek. Sherri also noted the guy was missing his right index finger. He looked like he chewed nails for breakfast.

They were told to gear up for water retrieval training. She ran back to her room, put on fatigues, grabbed her orange life vest, and ran back to the formation, last to arrive as usual.

"Kind of you to join us, Miss Tate," Peevy growled.

She was used to being last because of the longer trip she had to make to her room, and used to being harassed for it. She said nothing in response. Peevy stepped close to her, tucking the brim of his baseball cap literally underneath hers. His breath reeked of garlic.

"You got anything to say for yourself?" he snarled low.

She murmured back for his ears only, "I happen to like garlic. Next time try kimchi. I can't stand the smell of that."

He stepped back and shocked her by bellowing with laughter. Everyone stared at her. She stared straight ahead, stone-faced. She knew better than to celebrate her victory openly. To do so was to invite the kind of attention from her instructors that no trainee wanted.

They loaded up in Zodiacs, which were rigid inflatable rafts equipped with monster outboard engines that could flat-out fly across the water. The trainees were dropped one by one in the ocean and then left to float around for a while.

After a chilly half hour, Sherri heard an engine gun in the distance. The pickups had begun. The Zodiacs were moving slowly past each swimmer without stopping. Apparently, this was their chance to practice running pickups before they tried it at bat-outta-hell speed.

She spotted a Zodiac bearing down on her and put her arm up, angling her body properly. She recognized the face of the pickup partner peering down at her as the vessel approached. *Oh, no. Grundy.*

He leaned down, and as the Zodiac got nearly on top of her, instead of reaching for her arm, he slammed his open hand down on top of her head and shoved her under the boat. She scrambled frantically to back away from the propellers and to get out from underneath the rubber ceiling holding her down.

She opened her eyes and the salt water burned them

like mad, but she spied light off to her left and kicked in that direction.

Except whoever was driving the boat cut the motor just then, which made it drift toward shore—to the left, right back over the top of her.

Crap! If she didn't surface soon, she was going to be in real trouble. Anyone leaning over the edge to fish her out wouldn't be able to see or reach her under here. She did her best to remember her training and relax, not burning up all her air at once, but the panic won.

I am going to die.

Chapter 17

Something big splashed into the water beside her. Rough hands grabbed her shirt collar and hauled her violently onto her back. And then she was out from under the Zodiac. Her face popped up above the water, and she dragged in a frantic breath.

Hands unceremoniously grabbed her rear end and shoved, and more hands grabbed her from above and pulled her into the Zodiac. A wet instructor flopped onto the deck beside her. *Peevy*.

Well, shit.

"Make me go into the water again after you, girlie, and that'll be the end of you," he growled.

She didn't have the air or energy to do more than nod.

Smitty appeared above, leaning over her. "What the hell happened? You're a better swimmer than that."

"Grundy," she grunted. Her teammate turned to glare at her would-be drowner now sitting innocently on the other side of the boat.

She noticed Peevy watching her closely, and she pressed her lips shut. She wasn't about to accuse a classmate of trying to kill her. Not until she talked with Griffin. He'd never briefed her on how to handle attempted homicide, for crying out loud.

Jabrowski growled from beside her, "Sounds like somebody could use a blanket party."

"No!" she replied sharply. "Don't any of you guys

jeopardize your place on the SEALs for that asshole. I'll handle him."

"How?" Smitty asked.

"The powers that be will figure out he's not a team player. He'll get his comeuppance sooner or later. But I don't want any of you guys throwing yourselves on your swords over him. Promise me."

"Fine," the Smurfs grumbled.

"I'm serious." She glared at each one of them in turn until their gazes fell away from hers. Thank God. Point made.

She coughed up about a gallon of seawater and was excused from the final training evolution of the afternoon, a visit to the shooting range that she would have enjoyed, frankly. It reminded her of the range at Camp Jarvis and spooning with Griffin.

She waited for Griffin to show up at her room after supper, but darkness fell and there was no sign of him. *Drat*. She really needed to talk to him about what had happened and what to do about it.

Did she dare try to go see him?

She was supposed to be a future SEAL, after all. She could get into one man's room unseen.

The base was quiet tonight. Still, she stuck to the shadows and cut through a parking lot by ducking low between cars.

She made it about five feet inside the front door of the instructors' quarters before one of the instructors, Chief Vidmeyer, stepped out into the hallway, intercepting her. "Bell's the other way, Tate, if you're here to ring out."

She ignored the jibe. "I need to speak with Master Chief Caldwell. It's an emergency."

"What kind of emergency?"

"A classified one."

Vidmeyer stared skeptically at her, but her own stare back didn't waver. After a few seconds, he said shortly, "Room 204."

"Thanks." She strode past the guy and jogged upstairs.

Griffin answered her knock quickly and looked up and down the hall in alarm as he gestured her into the room.

She said, "I'm actually here on official business. I talked to an instructor downstairs, already. Chief Vidmeyer."

"Well, hell," Griffin muttered. "He's anal enough to put a stopwatch on your visit."

She smirked at Griffin. "No hanky-panky for you, big guy, unless you're up for a quickie."

"I'd rather wait and take my time with you, thanks."

His scowl deepened considerably, which sent warm fuzzies through her. It was awesome that he craved her fully as much as she craved him. He threw his arms around her, drawing her into his lap as he sat on the sofa. "I can still steal a fast snuggle while we talk, though."

With Vidmeyer's stopwatch in mind, she got right to business. "I have a small problem I need your advice on. Grundy tried to kill me today."

"What the hell?" Griffin exclaimed, staring at her in disbelief. "How?" Thunder was gathering rapidly on his brow, and a cold calculation entered his gaze that didn't bode well for Grundy's long-term health. His arms tightened around her protectively.

"During the water retrieval evolution, he didn't grab my arm. Instead, he shoved my head under the boat. I barely got clear of the propeller. Ended up getting stuck under the boat and couldn't surface."

"Any witnesses?"

"I have no idea. I didn't want to talk to anyone until I ran it past you. It's a serious accusation to make of a fellow trainee."

"Hell, yeah, it is. I expected someone to take a pot-shot at you during the course, but I didn't think anyone would try to kill you outright." He shoved one of his hands through his hair, a sure sign he was worried. "Who was driving the boat?"

"I don't know. Peevy jumped in after me and fished me out, though."

Griffin frowned thoughtfully.

"What's the deal with him, anyway?" she asked.

"Cal asked him to come here, observe you, and give him feedback on whether or not you'll make a decent SEAL. Peevy's as well known as any operator ever was or will be. Cal figures if he gives you the nod, just about every other SEAL on the teams will give you a chance. Peevy will be your toughest critic, but he can also be your greatest ally."

Made sense. "Do I tell anyone about Grundy trying to drown me? Surely attempting to kill a classmate crosses some sort of line."

"Ya think?" Griffin snorted. "I'd take Grundy out myself if it wouldn't get me tossed off the teams."

Griffin stared off into space, clearly thinking through options. Finally, he said heavily, "Lemme have a chat with Ray. Find out if he saw anything on the boat today.

He doesn't miss much. Legit, he's one of the smartest operators I've ever run with."

"You worked with Ray Peevy? I hear he's, like, legendary."

Griffin shrugged modestly. "We worked in DEVGRU together until I broke my back."

She already knew Griffin had the full respect of his Reaper teammates…and now she knew why. "DEVGRU, huh? Badass, Caldwell."

He rolled his eyes at her. "You keep doing your BUD/S thing. I'll find out what Ray saw. Then we'll figure out how to proceed."

At least he wasn't blowing her off. Thank goodness. She stood up. "I'd better get going if you don't want Vidmeyer to spread all sorts of rumors that might damage your lily-pure reputation."

He gifted her with another eye roll. "By the way. Practice tying knots before you go to bed tonight. Tomorrow is the underwater knot-tying evolution."

"The—" She broke off. "Are you kidding me?"

"Nope. You'll have to swim a length of the pool underwater, pausing to tie five knots along the way. The secret is nimble fingers and keeping your cool."

"Got it. Sounds like fun."

"It's a pain in the ass. Get fast with the knots before you go to sleep. It's worth the lost rest to get through this evolution in one pass."

He hugged her tightly and gave her a quick, hard kiss before walking her to the door. "I probably won't be able to come tuck you in tonight. I gotta go find Ray, and that may involve a bottle of whiskey and some war stories."

She kissed him quickly, one last time. "Good luck with that."

"Go get 'em, Blondie."

"Right back atcha, Hot Stuff."

His laughter floated out the door behind her.

No surprise, Vidmeyer's door was open and he was seated in such a way as to see her on the way out. She couldn't resist stopping in front of his doorway and saying casually, "He was magnificent…even if he was a two-minute wonder."

A crack of laughter escaped Vidmeyer before he pulled himself together to growl, "Get out of here, Tate."

The next morning, she noted that both Griffin and Peevy were sporting dark wraparound sunglasses. It must have been a late night with that bottle of whiskey.

The last evolution before supper was the underwater knot-tying exercise. She made it through four knots the first time through before she ran out of breath and had to surface.

"Tate!" Peevy shouted. "There are two ways to do things around here—the right way and again!"

She grimaced, panting as she was ordered out of the pool and had to endure several rounds of screamingly awful calisthenics before she was ordered back into the pool.

This time, she worked more quickly and managed to finish the last knot just as her lungs felt as if they were going to explode out of her chest. A hard kick and a glide, and she touched the end wall of the pool.

An instructor sitting on the bottom of the pool in a scuba tank jerked a thumb up toward the surface.

With pleasure. She kicked up to the edge of the pool and rested there for a moment, gasping.

"Quit making out with the edge of my pool, Tate," Vidmeyer growled. She thought he sounded a shade less irascible today.

They went for a night run after supper, and she enjoyed the cool air and stars over the Pacific. The moon rose while they were returning to base, and its silver light bathed the beach in wonder.

"Zoning out on me, are you, Tate?" a voice growled beside her.

She glanced over to see Peevy jogging along beside her. "Just enjoying being a SEAL, Master Chief," she replied.

"You aren't one yet," he snapped.

"Only way to become a SEAL is to *be* one," she replied.

Peevy harrumphed and ran on ahead of the formation without comment. Nothing like shutting down a legend. Not sure if she'd helped her cause or harmed it, she continued on toward base. And her bed.

Chapter 18

Griffin waited in Sherri's darkened room for her to get back from the night run. He stretched out on her bed, relishing the scent of her shampoo rising from her pillow. Man, he was completely besotted if even the smell of her made him happy.

But he couldn't help it. Just thinking about her made everything seem better. No wonder the married guys said having a wife to come home to made crap out in the field not seem so bad. It had to be this feeling.

Not that he was considering proposing to Sherri, he told himself hastily. No, sir. None of that.

Hell, she was just getting started with her career. The last thing she needed was him expecting a permanent relationship from her. Even if that was exactly what he wanted with her.

When had *that* happened?

He thought back, and as far as he could tell, it had come on slowly. Granted, to look at her was to want to sleep with her. But the rest of it—the genuine liking, respect, and trust—that had crept up on him, inch by inch. He even thought now that she would make a decent SEAL, and he'd said so last night to Ray Peevy.

Ray had been surprised, to say the least. But near the bottom of that bottle of whiskey, Griffin had extracted a promise from his old teammate to give her a fair shot to prove herself.

Ray had accused him of having a thing for her, which, thankfully, Griffin hadn't been too wasted to remember to deny. It had been on the tip of his tongue, though, to confess to Ray that she was his girl. *Damn*. He would have to watch that. It was such an ingrained habit to be totally honest with Ray that he could land himself in serious trouble if he wasn't careful. No more binges with the Peeve until Sherri was through training and the two of them could come out in the open with their relationship.

But man, that was a long way away. She still had months of BUD/S training to get through, and then a year or more of training with her permanent SEAL team before she would go active. The idea of waiting that long to claim her as his made him want to put his fist through a wall.

The door opened and Sherri entered, screeching to a halt just inside the door and dropping into a defensive stance.

"Good instincts," he commented without moving from her bed. He knew as well as anyone that any move toward her would have earned him a kick in the groin or a well-placed punch in the face. Both of which he would have deserved for sneaking up on a SEAL—even if she was still a baby SEAL.

She straightened and reached for the light switch.

"Leave the lights off," he said quickly. "The blinds are open."

"Oops. Sorry."

"Situational awareness, Tate," he half teased, half admonished.

"Yeah, yeah, I know. But I lose my mind when you're around. You distract the heck out of me."

"I can live with that," he replied, gathering her into his arms.

"I'm all sweaty and covered in sand," she protested.

He chuckled. "As if either of those things would bother me."

"Good point. Still. Let me go catch a quick shower, and I'll be right out. Unless you'd like to join me and make it a long, leisurely shower."

She did not have to ask him twice. They emerged from the shower with her considerably cleaner and him considerably more relaxed. He dressed before slipping into bed with her to do his second favorite thing in the whole world—hold her in his arms until she fell asleep.

"How'd your talk with Ray go last night?" she asked in the soft darkness.

"Good and bad. The good news: Cal judged him correctly. He's not opposed to women operators if they can pull their weight on a team and not be a liability. Ray's first impression is that you're plenty smart enough and seem physical enough. But he's waiting to see if you're mentally tough enough. He wants to see how you deal with Hell Week."

"And the bad news?"

"He didn't see anything between you and Grundy on the boat. He did say your boatmates were mad enough at Grundy for him to believe the guy tried to drown you. He's gonna keep an eye on Grundy, though. Bastard won't get another chance to hurt you on Ray's watch. Ray was offended at the mere idea of one SEAL trying to screw over another."

"Good. So am I," she mumbled, sounding sleepy.

He didn't take offense at her drifting off

midconversation like this. He remembered all too well the continuous, dragging exhaustion of BUD/S. He'd certainly had missions that were worse, but those had come later, when he was tougher and more used to feeling like shit on a shingle. Those missions also didn't last for months on end. A few days, maybe a few weeks, without proper sleep or meals, and then they were over and he and his team got a break to recharge.

"Sweet dreams," he murmured, kissing her temple gently.

"Love you," she sighed as she slipped into unconsciousness.

He froze, not moving a muscle. She *what*?

Holy shit. What was he supposed to do with that? Pretend he hadn't heard her say it? Say it back? Respond with something lame like *thank you*? Panic ripped through him.

But then something even more alarming occurred to him. He wasn't panicked because a woman had told him she loved him. He was panicked because he didn't want to screw up responding to it.

What the hell did that say about him? About them?

As always, when Sherri's alarm went off at 4:00 a.m., she woke up alone. She rolled out of bed, yanking on clothes by rote, stomping into her boots, and French braiding her hair as she jogged down the stairs.

Griffin was in charge of log PT this morning, and he worked out her class ferociously. If she didn't know better, she would think he had it in for her. He seemed to choose every exercise she was the worst at to run the crews through. Did the mental whiplash of their double life get to him, too?

Smurf crew was only down one guy—Brewster had medically washed back with a knee injury. He would be given time to recover from surgery to repair it, and then he would have an opportunity to start the training pipeline again. She hoped he tried. He was a good guy. His departure left six of them hoisting, hugging, and lugging the log.

Some of the other crews were down to as few as four guys, and they struggled mightily to get through log PT sessions. The lesson was clear to everyone. Survive as a team. Die as a team.

Friday of that week, they spent much of the day alternating between relay races in the infamous mud flats and paddling for their lives in the boats to avoid getting slammed into rocks on shore by particularly brutal surf. She muttered a warning to her buddies to memorize the coastline in as much detail as they could during daylight, because Hell Week was likely to include doing these dangerous rock portages at night.

Also at her suggestion, Smitty, the strongest Smurf, was made their permanent coxswain. His job was to keep their boat from broaching—turning sideways to waves—and flipping over. Jabrowski, the nimblest Smurf, was elected to sit in the bow and leap ashore onto the rocks. His job was to hold the boat's line tight and keep it from floating back out to sea on the waves as his teammates jumped ashore. She sincerely hoped Smitty and Jab made it all the way through Hell Week. Otherwise, their boat was screwed.

They'd just finished a round of relay races, taking

turns carrying their teammates on their backs through pools of slippery, smelly muck when Chief Vidmeyer yelled, “Tate! Front and center!”

Wiping mud out of her eyes, one of which was swelling shut as a result of catching an accidental elbow on the cheekbone from Smitty, she ran over to the cluster of instructors and drew herself up to attention.

Vidmeyer sneered. “Your Highness’s presence is requested at a press conference in an hour. Head on back to your room and get cleaned up. A staff car will drive you over to the base theater…Princess.”

Damn. And she’d finally been making headway with the guy. Now he was back to despising her. And who could blame him?

While she didn’t object to a rest break in theory, her team was now going to be down a person and take the hit in her absence. She was shocked to realize she would rather be here, floundering facedown in mud, than getting all gussied up and talking to the press. “Do I have to leave my teammates?” she asked Vidmeyer.

He blinked, momentarily looking startled. For an equally fleeting moment, respect passed through his hard gaze. “Yes. That’s an order. Oh, and speaking of orders, the admiral says not to fuck this up.”

She saluted smartly, snapping her hand up to her brow and back down. Sarcasm dripping in her voice, she responded, “Yes, Chief. No fucking, Chief.”

Openly smirking, Vidmeyer lifted his chin. Without ire this time, he said, “Best get going, Lieutenant Tate.”

Whoa. That was the first time he’d broken his asshole persona with her, and the first time any of the instructors had referred to her rank since she’d started BUD/S.

Thoughtfully, she walked back to her room. By the time she got there, the mud had mostly dried and was caking off her clothing. She knocked the worst of it off and gave her hair a good scrub with her hands. She worked on it until she could run her fingers through it. She'd learned the hard way that too much dirt clogged up her shower drain, and then she had to go without showers for several days until the BUD/S instructors got around to asking someone to come unclog it for her.

She went into her bathroom and looked at herself in the mirror. Beneath the dried mud, she was sunburned, and her left cheekbone had a lump on it that gave her eye a distinct squint. Her lips were cracked. Her clothes were filthy. And with bits of mud still clinging in her hair, she looked like a crazy homeless lady. In point of fact, she suspected most homeless people were significantly cleaner than she was now. How in the heck she was going to cover up the toll of BUD/S and make herself over into the recruiting poster in an hour, she didn't know.

She eyed her shower, then looked back at her reflection. Looked back at the shower.

If she was ever going to be accepted by the SEALs as one of them, she was going to have to start acting like one of them. And that did not include dressing up, primping, and prancing around like the Barbie doll they so loved to accuse her of being.

Without even passing a washcloth over her face, she marched out of her room and went downstairs to wait for the staff car, mud and all.

The driver's eyebrows shot straight up to his hairline when she climbed in beside him, but the guy said nothing as he delivered her to the back door of the base theater.

Schneider, the public affairs officer, was not so restrained. "I told them to let you have a shower and get cleaned up before you came over here! I have your makeup kit and clean uniforms for you. Crap, crap, crap. Now we're going to be late. The admiral's going to be pissed. He has another meeting after—"

"Schneider. Stop."

He stared at her, not comprehending. She explained. "My instructors did give me time to clean up. I chose not to."

"You… What?" he sputtered.

"I'm doing the press conference like this."

"Are you crazy? I can't put you in front of cameras looking like that!"

"Why not? I'm in the middle of a training day, and this is what I look like in the middle of a training day."

"No, no, no. This isn't what the Navy Public Affairs Office has in mind at all. I got explicit instructions from headquarters—"

"It's not open for discussion," she interrupted gently. "I do the press conference like this or not at all."

She didn't give Schneider time to consider that choice, but instead walked past him. She knew where the stage was and headed directly for it with him running along in her wake, panicking. He actually wrung his hands as he ran backwards beside her, arguing every step of the way.

Ignoring him, she strode right out onto the stage.

The journalists were talking among themselves, checking sound, and talking with their cameramen, since the press conference wasn't due to start for another fifteen minutes.

But as members of the press corps spotted her, silence spread quickly across the large space. Shocked stillness settled over them all. She stared at them and they stared back, taking in her rather dramatic appearance. Personally, she relished her all-over shade of beige, caused by the thin layer of mud residue.

She spoke into the microphone. "If you all can start early, I have places to go and things to do."

It took a minute or so of scrambling, but the lights went on, and when she got thumbs-ups from the camera crews, she spoke into the microphone. At least this time Schneider hadn't bothered writing down prepared remarks for her.

"Greetings, ladies and gentlemen. Thanks for coming out today to check in on me. As you can see, I'm still standing. In an effort to keep this short so I can get back to my teammates, I'm going to make a quick statement and try to anticipate most of your questions."

She noted movement in the back of the theater as a silent row of SEAL instructors filed in, much like last time. Except this time she could put names with the faces. She knew who the jerks were, who the decent guys were, who the skeptics were, and who her silent supporters were.

Dryly, she said, "Yes. BUD/S is hard. No, I don't like it. Nobody does. Yes, I get along fine with my teammates. No, I don't get along with my instructors. Nobody does." That got a laugh out of the reporters.

She continued, "I've had a few minor injuries along the way, which is perfectly normal. No, I don't feel particularly discriminated against, nor do I feel singled out or favored. I'm just another trainee, which is a tribute to the professionalism of my instructors and fellow trainees. The hardest part is always the next training evolution, and as SEALs are fond of saying, the only easy day was yesterday."

There. Griffin had just slipped into the back of the auditorium. She didn't even have to look up from the reporters to feel his presence.

She finished up with, "I have every reason to believe I'll make it through the remainder of Phase I. Particularly since I would rather die than quit. Let's see. What else? I don't know where I fall in class ranking. I don't care. I'm giving it my all, and that's what matters to me. That and doing my best to see my teammates make it through, too. That's all I've got for you today."

"Why are you covered in dirt?" someone shouted out.

"Because I left my teammates running relay races through mud flats, and I plan to rejoin them as soon as we're finished here." She caught movement in the wings stage left, and out of the corner of her eye spotted an admiral's gold sleeve stripes.

For Admiral Duquesne's benefit, she added, "You guys didn't seriously expect me to get up every morning, put on makeup and do my hair to go play BUD/S, did you?"

That got a laugh out of the press, and she leaned toward the mic. "I have to confess, though, that the instructors do call me Barbie from time to time."

The reporters loved that. On that high note, she said, "If you'll excuse me, I really don't want to miss any more training. My team needs me."

Admiral Duquesne started out onto the stage, and she flat-out fled. Not only did she not want to have to pose for pictures with him, but she also didn't want to get stuck here any longer than absolutely necessary.

Poor Schneider couldn't chase after her because he had to introduce the admiral.

She burst out of the theater and looked left and right. There. Her instructors were just leaving the building. She ran over to them. "Any chance I can catch a ride back to my team?"

Peevy moved over in the back seat of a Hummer. "Hop in."

Frankly, she was surprised they hadn't forced her to run all the way back to the beach. Relieved, she tried to be invisible on the ride back while the instructors chatted and joked. With a nod of thanks at them, she jogged down the beach to her team. The Smurf raft had capsized, and her buddies bobbed in the water, helpless against the power of the surf. Waves slammed them against the rocks and then swept them back out to sea over and over.

Jab had made it ashore, and she helped him snag Smurfs one by one as they washed back in over the next few minutes. The bottom had partially torn out of their boat, but that didn't prevent them all from being sent back out into the water for one more surf passage and rock portage in the ruined raft.

Smitty shouted as they simultaneously hung on to the side of the raft and paddled for all they were worth, trying to get a wave to pick them up and carry them shoreward, "Never thought I'd say this, but I'm glad you're back, Tate!"

"I missed you guys, too!" she shouted back.

They had no more breath to speak as they were unceremoniously dumped out of their raft and slammed into the rocks like the flotsam they were.

By the time Jab and another guy finally snagged her and dragged her ashore, she was more drowned than not. Thankfully, the evolution was secured, and they stumbled back to the chow hall to shove down as many calories as they could before they fell asleep in their food.

"How was the press conference?" Smitty asked.

"As short as I could make it. They loved my attire. Haute mud-mask couture."

"You didn't."

She grinned back at her teammate. "I did. Admiral Duquesne looked none too happy about it, either. But he can suck my"—she finished lamely—"toes."

Jab shook his head, tsking. "If you're gonna be a SEAL, you've got to get better at swearing, kid."

The remainder of the dinner conversation devolved into swearing lessons for her. She laughed hard at the Smurfs' creativity, and a good time was had by all. Mostly, though, she was relieved they didn't hold it against her that she'd been pulled out for a stupid press conference.

The next night, Vidmeyer announced the trainees would have all day Sunday off to rest…because Hell Week started Monday morning.

This was it. The ultimate test of whether or not she would make it as a SEAL. The fix could be in to graduate her as much as anyone wanted, but if she couldn't hack Hell Week, the SEALs would know it and she would never be considered a legitimate member of the brotherhood.

It was a sacred rite of passage. Period.

But that didn't mean she couldn't stack the deck in her favor a little.

Late Sunday morning, she gathered the Smurfs in her room for an unofficial team meeting. Afterward, grinning from ear to ear, they dispersed to do various errands. Two guys went into San Diego to obtain a tank of helium and hide it near the beach. When the instructors weren't looking, they would fill the Smurf boat with it to make it lighter to carry.

Two more guys went shopping off base where they wouldn't be spotted, and everyone helped them hide boxes of chocolate and bottles of brandy for several miles in each direction up and down the beach.

Sherri bought and handed out jars of the thick petroleum paste used by triathletes and ultra-marathoners to prevent chafing. Even though she embarrassed the men by saying so, she told them succinctly where to smear the stuff. She also warned them to wear bathing suits under their clothes and hide the suits during their forced showers to prevent their confiscation. Griffin had assured her that chafing and raw tender bits would be one of the worst agonies of the week.

Over supper that night, she gave the guys one last pep talk, sharing every hint she dared from Griffin without giving away that she'd been coached to death on how to survive Hell Week.

She encouraged them to save ten percent of their energy for helping each other. She told them that when they decided to quit, they should give it five more minutes before taking action. She warned them that the instructors would likely force them into survival situations that required them to attack each other and even beat the hell out of each other. She told the guys not to hold back because she was a girl, and she would do the same for them. She even told them she expected to share body heat with them, to sleep spooning with them, and to end up mostly naked with them a time or two.

And last of all, she exhorted them not to even think about quitting. To get it in their minds that they would die before giving up. They made a group pledge to stick it out as a team, come hell or high water. Pun intended.

On that pledge, they dispersed to get one last night's sleep before the next five days and nights of no sleep, demolition pits, obstacle courses, night drowning evolutions, surf passage, mud flats, two hundred miles of running, and whatever else the instructors could throw at them to break the will of any normal mortal.

Griffin came to her as soon as she turned her lights out.

As she settled in his arms, she murmured, "Any last advice?"

"Yes. When you think you can't make it one more second, remember I'll be waiting for you when it's over. We'll go hang out on my boat, and you can sleep about eighteen hours straight. I'll have all the food you want, and I'll have ice packs and massages waiting for you. All you have to do is keep going until you get there."

She nodded, grateful for the mental image to hang onto.

Griffin's last words, whispered to her just as she fell asleep, were "I believe in you."

Chapter 19

Hell Week was...hell. If she took every miserable moment she'd experienced over the entire course of her training, magnified each one by ten, crammed them all together, and added sleep deprivation, mental torture, and completely inhuman pain to the mix, it still wouldn't come close to the agony of it.

Griffin had told her if she could make it to Wednesday night, she could surely make it the rest of the week, for it would just be more of the same. She randomly remembered his observation while falling into a pile with her boatmates on the beach. They'd actually won a surf passage race, compliments of excellent teamwork, and had earned a five-minute nap. Which was manna from heaven.

Someone shook her awake, screaming in her face, and she stumbled to her feet, shivering violently. She was never going to be warm or dry again. *Oh, wait. Griffin*. Fuzzily, she tried to remember making love with him that magical day on his boat a lifetime ago.

They were off and running again, this time to the chow hall. She added butter to her coffee, gulped it down too hot and burned her mouth, and shoveled in as many calories as she could as fast as she could in the few minutes they were given to eat.

Jab fell asleep in his plate, and she poked him hard. "Wake up. Eat."

"Right. Food," he mumbled.

She actually picked up his coffee cup and poured it down his throat. Then the instructors slammed through the doors, yelling, and they were back outside, picking up their boat, hoisting it overhead, and running down the beach.

Griffin is waiting at the end of this.

Whether or not the helium they'd smuggled in and filled their boat with actually made it significantly lighter, the morale boost was considerable. The Smurfs grinned at each other every time they picked up the raft.

Same with their hidden snacks. Yes, the sugar of the chocolate bars helped, and a swig of brandy was bracing and warmed a soul from the inside out. But the psychological boost of getting away with something was substantially more important.

She glimpsed Griffin now and then and got the impression he was subtly keeping an eye on her. But he couldn't help her this time. She had to do this on her own. She was grateful he understood and stayed away from her, merely supporting her from afar with his presence.

He made the suffering worth it, somehow. Oh, she knew that this was all a test of character at the end of the day; no matter how hard Hell Week was, she would encounter missions harder in the field. But seeing Griffin's tall frame out of the corner of her eye, catching sight of his handsome face, reminded her what it meant to be a SEAL and what she was striving toward.

Whenever she was dead sure she couldn't take another step, she thought of him. And it never failed to help her take that next step.

Wednesday night, Jabrowski missed the shore when

jumping out of their boat and went down headfirst onto the rocks. He slipped under the surf, and Griffin and another instructor dived in after him to pull him out of the water, unconscious.

By the time she and the other Smurfs clambered ashore, Griffin was out of the water, his clothes clinging wetly to him, outlining every contour of his spectacular body in wet cotton. Even in her advanced state of exhaustion, she couldn't help but appreciate the sight. Two more days. And then she could have that body all to herself. Minus the clothing.

The instructors wanted to load Jabrowski into one of the ambulances standing by, but the Smurfs argued passionately as a group for him to get a chance to wake up and continue on.

Jab regained consciousness, and a medic declared him to have a mild concussion, recommending that he stop training. But Jab and the Smurfs made such a stink that he was given another shot at finishing Hell Week. Unfortunately, by midday Thursday, to the Smurfs' dismay, he was hallucinating and had to be taken to the hospital. Griffin sidled over to her to mutter out of the side of his mouth that Jab would be rolled back a class and given another shot.

When she relayed that to her fellow Smurfs, they nodded and passed out, spooning together in the blessedly warm and dry sand of a dune near the beach. But then, so did she. She was so numb with exhaustion, cold, and physical agony, she had not one brain cell left to worry about anyone else except herself and her remaining teammates.

She honestly didn't remember much of Thursday. She

didn't think she was delirious, but it passed in a strange fog of mental detachment. She watched her body being bruised and abused as she pushed it far, far beyond its limits. Pain still registered, but it didn't even matter any more. She would keep doing the things the instructors told her to, stumbling forward from one evolution to the next until it either ended or she died. And at this point, she didn't care which.

They lost two more Smurfs, one to a broken wrist, and one to voluntary withdrawal. Of one-hundred-sixty-two initial trainees, they were down to forty-four guys and a girl.

Then came the final run. An all-night sprint to the finish carrying a rucksack. It was a race through the desert, running from point to point to check in before being sent on. She was so stupid with fatigue she didn't know where she was half the time. She just followed the guys in front of her and prayed they knew where the hell they were going.

It was a moonless night and so cold she couldn't feel her fingers or toes. Which was maybe a blessing. What she couldn't feel couldn't hurt. She was at the point of trying to catalog what didn't hurt instead of what did.

One step at a time. One foot in front of the other.

Griffin. Think of Griffin.

As always, he was her touchstone through this nightmare. She would never be able to repay him for the gift of giving her *him* to aim for. Without knowing that he would be waiting at the end of this horror, she seriously didn't know if she would have had the will to continue on. At some point, she feared she would have just lain down and died.

But this week, she'd discovered that even dying was a choice. And because of Griffin, she chose to live.

She staggered up to yet another checkpoint and gulped down the bottle of water someone shoved at her.

"Head due west for two clicks, then angle southwest at the orange pylon for three clicks to the next checkpoint. Get out of here, Tate."

West. Right. Wherever the hell west was. She spotted the guy coming up behind her—crap, Grundy—and took off, hoping to get a little ahead of her personal harasser-in-chief.

As far as she could tell, they must be past the halfway point of the run, because now they were heading back toward the west, after spending several hours slogging east through the sand and rocks.

The rocks were the worst of it, always waiting to roll underfoot and turn an ankle or send a girl tumbling to the ground in her exhaustion and inability to catch herself anymore. She lost count of how many times she'd fallen tonight.

She dared not hope this was the end, or that when she got back to base this nightmare would be over. The disappointment if she were wrong would be too much to bear.

Instead, she concentrated on thinking about nothing at all. She put her body on autopilot and zoned out as hard as she possibly could. No pain. No cold. No fatigue. No fear. Just determination. *To. Keep. Moving.*

The orange cone came into sight, and the path turned slightly left, angling southwest between two tall walls of rock. A narrow canyon wound away in the darkness. She stumbled down it, relieved to be almost halfway through this leg of the night's interminable run.

All of a sudden, a black gap loomed in front of her, some sort of deep pit in the ground. Jerking out of her half-conscious state, she just barely managed to stop her forward momentum and not pitch into the hole.

Momentarily alert, she peered down into it. It had to be at least ten feet deep, with vertical sides. It was about a dozen feet to the other side. Too far to jump in her current state and with the heavy ruck on her back. She looked left and right. The gap stretched all the way across the narrow gully.

Truth be told, it was mostly luck that she'd even spotted the pit. A sliver of moon had come out from behind a cloud just then, illuminating the shadows in just the right way for her to see the lack of stones littering the path.

Was she supposed to climb down in the hole and back out the other side? She didn't see anything even resembling handholds in the smooth wall across from her. Maybe she was supposed to go up and around the pit.

She took a minute to examine the cliff walls on each side of the pit. Both were tall, nearly vertical, and looked dangerously unstable.

C'mon, brain. Kick in. There had to be a trick to this. She looked around on the ground for a rope or a ladder or something that would make an obvious tool for crossing the chasm.

She had to backtrack a way, but she spied a stout, long tree branch of some kind tucked along the base of the cliff on her left, barely visible.

It was too narrow to walk across if she laid it across the pit. Was she supposed to go hand-over-hand underneath the pole? It looked strong enough to hold her weight, but she dreaded the idea of trusting her arms to support her weight and that of the rucksack at this juncture.

She picked the pole up and planted one end on the ground, then hung from the other end. It bent a little, but would hold her weight.

She eyed the pit. Eyed the pole, which was a good twelve feet long and relatively straight, almost the diameter of her wrist.

If she planted it in the bottom of the pit, the top five feet or so of it would stick up out of the pit. She'd pole-vaulted in college and understood the physics of it. Instead of using the pole's bend-and-snap to go up vertically, she could use it to fling herself forward horizontally.

Oh yeah. She could do this. And vaulting would be a whole lot easier than asking her exhausted arms to hold her body weight for several minutes.

Grabbing the pole, she backed up thirty feet or so. Gathering what little energy she had left, she held the pole out in front of her and took off running with all the speed she could muster.

It felt exceedingly weird to plant the pole in the bottom of the pit against the base of the far wall, but the principal was the same. Instead of sailing high up into the air, she sailed forward, flinging her legs out in front of her and riding the flex and snap of the pole across the chasm to the far side.

She landed on her knees and pitched forward onto her belly, grunting as the weight of the rucksack squashed her. She had the presence of mind to hang on to the pole and dragged it out of the pit beside her while she lay there for a minute, catching her breath.

"Pass me the pole!" someone called out from behind her.

Grundy. She was half-tempted not to. After all the crap he'd given her these past few months, it would be sweet revenge to leave him stranded and force him to take a long, strenuous detour up the steep gully walls to get around the pit.

Laboriously, she pushed up to her hands and knees. She didn't have the strength to climb to her feet just yet. Man, she was tired. Simple kneeling made her light-headed.

"Throw that over here!"

"You know you're an asshole, right?" she called, reaching for the pole.

"Don't you dare," he snarled.

"Thing is, I'm a team player at the end of the day, Grundy. And I have a modicum of human decency that you lack. You're never going to be a SEAL because you only think of yourself, and everyone knows it."

"I take care of my team."

"You only take care of them so they'll take care of you. You're selfish. The instructors know it. And you'll ultimately fail."

"Shut the fuck up, and hand me the damned pole."

"You're missing the point, Grundy."

"Which is?"

"Now would be an excellent time to apologize for all the garbage you've pulled on me since INDOC."

He stared at her across the gap, and she stared back, pointedly not passing him the end of the pole. He looked away first.

So. He did have a soul. And he did know he'd been a shithead to her. That was something, at least.

"Why are you doing this?" he finally asked.

"Consider it one last chance to get your act together before you wash out of BUD/S," she said firmly.

"Fine. I'm sorry. Now give me the pole."

He didn't mean it for a second, but an insincere apology was better than nothing. And just because he was a jerk didn't mean she ought to be one, too. She passed the long pole over the pit, and he grabbed the end of it.

"This is too flimsy to hold me and my pack," he complained.

"Fine. Climb the arroyo walls. It's no skin off my nose," she retorted.

Mostly because her hamstrings were cramping like big dogs after her sprint to vault the pit, she leaned forward and planted her hands on the ground to stretch while he made his way across the obstacle.

Hanging underneath the pole by his hands and feet, Grundy crossed the pit. He flopped to the ground beside her and rested for a few seconds before pushing up to his knees. They knelt side-by-side, panting for a minute, at the edge of the pit.

"Tate?"

"Yes?"

"You'll never be a fucking SEAL." He gave her a hard shove, and she toppled over the edge of the pit, screaming.

Thankfully, the weight of her ruck made her do a half somersault on the way down, and she landed on her back, the ruck cushioning her fall. Still, it hurt like hell. Laughter drifted down to her as she passed out from a combination of exhaustion and impact. And then there was only blackness and silence.

Chapter 20

Griffin's earpiece crackled, and Vidmeyer's voice transmitted into it, "Grif, you on freq?"

He keyed his microphone. "I'm on. What's up?"

"Tate has missed the check-in at checkpoint six."

"By how much?"

"She's about fifteen minutes overdue. It was a short leg. She could've crawled it by now and been here. We tried to ping her GPS locator, but the signal's not working."

Worried, but trying to keep it out of his voice, Griffin radioed back, "On my way." As he drove from the finish line out to the far point of the land course, he had to ask himself an equally disturbing question. Why had Vidmeyer felt obliged to let him personally know that Tate was in trouble?

Had he sucked that bad at hiding his feelings for her these past weeks? Goodness knew, it was hard to keep his eyes off her. But then, all the instructors were prone to watching her. Not only was her physical performance fascinating to all of them, but she was stunningly beautiful, even when sunburned, exhausted, and covered in sand or muck.

He jumped out of the Jeep at the checkpoint and jogged over to Vidmeyer as yet another bedraggled trainee staggered across the line, was force-fed a bottle of water, and sent on his miserable way.

Griffin asked tersely, "Any sign of her?"

"Nope. She's almost a half hour late. She's gotten lost or passed out somewhere out there."

Griffin frowned. Neither of those felt right to him. She was smart as hell and had always had an excellent sense of direction at Camp Jarvis. Even in total darkness with no landmarks at all, she'd always known which way was which. As for passing out, it was possible, but not likely. Any trainees who made it to this last challenge had what it took to finish the run and to finish Hell Week.

"She's a strong runner," he commented. In fact, it was her greatest strength, and she'd never struggled to finish run-based evolutions.

"True. She's tough over land," Peevy replied, strolling over and jumping into the conversation. "There are still a number of guys on the course behind her." He glanced at the checkpoint supervisor. "Have any of the trainees reported seeing her down out there?"

"Nope. Nada. No one said a word."

Peevy asked the guy soberly, "What are the odds her classmates saw her down and aren't telling us?"

All the instructors clustered around the checkpoint traded grim looks with each other. Had the instructors' head games pushing the other trainees to turn on Sherri come home to roost in the worst possible way?

Peevy broke the loaded silence. "The Smurfs liked her. And most of the other tadpoles didn't seem to give a crap about her one way or the other as long as she didn't drag them down."

Griffin could only think of one other possibility. "She could've hurt herself."

"The trainees have flare guns in their rucks. She'd have shot hers off by now," Vidmeyer responded.

"If she's conscious," Griffin snapped.

"C'mon," Ray said briskly. "I'll drive. You hunt for her."

Griffin climbed in the passenger seat of the Jeep, a pair of infrared binoculars in hand. Peevy drove along the run route, and Griffin scanned either side of the course for the telltale white blob of a human heat signature.

They made it all the way to the previous checkpoint without any sign of her.

A quick check with the guys there showed she'd checked in over an hour before, and had been coherent and in as good a physical condition as could be expected of anyone in the last few hours of Hell Week. She'd apparently drunk her water and had been last seen headed in the right direction.

"Who went out just behind her?" Griffin asked.

The instructor checked his clipboard. "Grundy."

Even Peevy joined him in groaning aloud. Griffin and Peevy piled back into the Jeep and headed out in search of Grundy and any information Sherri's nemesis might have to add to the mystery of what had happened to her.

They found him two checkpoints ahead, getting ready to head out.

"Grundy! Hold up!" Griffin called out to him.

The guy turned around. His eyes were dull and glazed. Dude was in the final phases of exhaustion. Which was normal a few hours from the end of Hell Week.

Peevy walked up to Grundy and spoke slowly and clearly. "Have you seen Miss Tate tonight?"

"Nuh-uhh," Grundy mumbled.

"Think hard," Peevy said. "You left checkpoint six about thirty seconds behind her. Did you pass her on the trail?"

"Don' know."

Griffin frowned. The guy sounded a little too surly, which sent his internal antennae wiggling wildly. "You're not in trouble, Grundy. We just need to know what happened to her. She disappeared." It was a lie that the guy wasn't in trouble if he'd seen that Sherri was in distress and hadn't reported it. But Griffin was happy to hand the jerk rope to hang himself with.

Grundy frowned back. If Griffin was reading the guy right, he was wavering for some reason. *Bastard definitely knows something.*

He leaned in even closer, lowering his voice to an ice-cold promise of more pain than Grundy could imagine, even in the final throes of Hell Week. "If you know something and don't tell us, and something bad happens to her, I'll personally see you bounced out of BUD/S so fast your head spins. Do you understand me?"

Griffin never broke stares with Grundy, even though he felt Peevy's quizzical gaze on him. *Shit*. Ray knew him too well. He was giving away too much about how he felt about Sherri. But it wasn't like he had any choice. She was *missing*. And there just weren't that many places between checkpoint six and checkpoint seven where she could've gotten lost.

Grundy mumbled, "Last I saw her, she fell in that pit."

Peevy got to the question first. "What pit?"

There was no pit anywhere along the course of the run the trainees made.

"The one in the canyon."

"What the hell are you talking about?" Griffin burst out.

"The pit. You know. With the pole. Had to cross it on that pole..." Grundy looked back and forth between him and Peevy in confusion.

A string of curses erupted inside Griffin's head. He squelched it forcibly. He had to keep his head in the game, panic or no panic eating a hole in his gut. "Where exactly was this pit you're talking about?"

"After checkpoint six. Two clicks west to the orange pylon and then turn southwest for three clicks. The pit was right after the turn at the pylon."

"Describe the pit," Griffin ordered.

"It went from one side of the canyon to the other. Fifteen or twenty feet wide, maybe twelve feet deep. It wasn't marked for squat. Had Tate not been kneeling beside it, I'd have never seen it coming. It was a fricking safety hazard, man."

Griffin frowned. "If she was kneeling beside it, how did she fall into it?"

Grundy's eyes popped open wide. "Uhh, hell if I know. I climbed across it, and when I looked back, she was nowhere to be seen."

Liar.

Peevy said sharply, "And it didn't occur to you to go back and check on your classmate?"

Grundy squirmed a little. Shuffled his feet. "It's a timed evolution. Every man for himself, right?"

"You're a sorry son of a bitch—" Griffin started.

Peevy cut him off. "Later, Grif. Clock's ticking. We have no time for this now."

Griffin pivoted away from the trainee a millisecond before he ripped the guy's face off. Good thing Peevy had distracted him, or there'd have been blood in the dirt. And body parts.

"Get out of here, Grundy," Peevy growled.

It was back to the Jeep for Peevy and Griffin, back to checkpoint six. They traced the route of the course carefully, heading west. The trail the trainees were supposed to follow was clear in the faint moonlight, a white ribbon of dirt among the rocks and brush.

A little shy of two kilometers out, Peevy stopped the Jeep abruptly, practically throwing Griffin against the dashboard. "What the hell, Ray?"

The older man was already out of the Jeep, kneeling a few yards in front of the vehicle and off to the left. "Look at this."

Griffin came around the Jeep and knelt beside Ray, asking, "Whatcha got?"

"Boot prints. Couple sets of 'em. Recent. One big set, one smaller set."

"Tate and Grundy, maybe? Did she go off course? Maybe he followed her by accident?" Griffin asked.

"Let's see where the tracks go. We're almost two klicks from the checkpoint. This pit of Grundy's has to be close." Peevy took off jogging, and Griffin fell in behind him.

The tracks led about two hundred feet off the main trail and into a narrow arroyo. Peevy stopped, looking back. "Somebody cleaned off a trail. Made it look like this was where the tadpoles were supposed to go. See how those rocks are moved back and the gravel's been scraped off the ground?"

Griffin was a decent tracker, but nothing like Ray. However, now that Ray pointed it out, he could see where someone had gone to pains to convince exhausted SEAL trainees this was the direction they were supposed to be running.

Peevy reached for his ankle knife, and Griffin slammed into full combat mode. If Ray thought there was some sort of threat, Griffin believed him without question. The guy's instincts were legendary for a reason. Griffin eased out his own Ka-Bar knife, and they moved forward cautiously. What the hell had Sherri gotten herself tangled up in?

Griffin admonished himself to clear his mind. Be one hundred percent in the present moment. He listened to the night sounds of the desert around him. Felt a light, cool breeze on his skin.

Peevy held up a fist to stop.

Ray eased forward a few more feet and then crouched in the shadow of a tumbleweed. "Perfect spot for an ambush," he breathed into Griffin's ear.

True. But who would spring an ambush out here for a couple of SEAL trainees? It made no sense whatsoever. Peevy hand-signaled for Griffin to swing to the right, climb the canyon face, and parallel the arroyo, while Ray did the same to the left.

It was a classic SEAL tactic. Ambush the ambusher.

Griffin moved off silently to the right. At first glance, the roughly fifty-foot-tall cliff face looked vertical. But on closer inspection, he spied plentiful handholds and toeholds. He climbed to the top of the rock face quickly. Staying low to avoid presenting a profile to anyone else out here, he made his way along the canyon rim.

From this angle, the pit was clearly visible when he drew level with it. What in the *hell* was going on out here? He moved over to the edge of the cliff to climb down and hopefully find Sherri unharmed in the bottom of that black hole, but then he spotted something that made his blood run cold.

A discarded orange pylon.

He tossed it over the edge of the cliff and climbed down after it as fast as he could without breaking his neck. He jumped the last dozen feet or so, panicked for Sherri's safety.

He knelt at the edge of the pit as Ray worked his way down the opposite rock face. "Tate?" Griffin called down into the hole. "Sherri? You down there? It's Griffin Caldwell."

Silence.

Ray pulled out a red-filtered flashlight and shined it down in the pit.

Empty.

But Ray immediately swore. Griffin asked quickly, "What do you see?"

"Ladder marks. Lower me down. I want to take a closer look." Ray moved to one end of the pit for Griffin to stretch out on his belly and let Ray use his arm like a climbing rope to lower himself into the hole.

Ray's voice floated up. "She was down here, all right. Looks like she fell. Landed on her ruck. But someone else was down here with her. Three...maybe four... men."

"Her classmates?"

"These aren't SEAL-issue boots."

"*What?*" Griffin squawked.

"Close your eyes. I'm gonna take some pictures of these tracks," Ray said.

Protecting his night vision, Griffin closed his eyes against the flash of Ray's cell phone camera.

Then Ray said, "Someone came down here and hoisted or carried her out of here. Some of the tracks get deeper like they were carrying a heavy object."

"Like Tate?" Griffin asked, numb with shock.

"Looks that way. You got radio reception?" Ray asked.

His implication was clear. It was time to call out the cavalry. Griffin keyed his mic but got no response. "No reception. We'll have to get out of this canyon."

Griffin held an arm down to Ray. While the guy climbed up to him, Griffin reported, "I found an orange pylon on top of the cliff. Same kind we mark the run course with. What if someone put out a fake pylon when she was coming, turned her into this canyon, and ran her into this pit trap?"

"Why would someone go to all that trouble to kidnap Tate?" Ray asked reasonably. His hand slapped into Griffin's, and Griffin heaved hard. Ray popped out of the hole and onto his belly beside Griffin.

They rolled to their feet. "I have no idea why anyone would snatch Tate," Griffin answered raggedly. "If her classmates wanted to get rid of her, there are a crap-ton of easier ways to do it."

Ray keyed his throat mic. "This is Peevy. Come in."

Nothing. Griffin and Ray took off running at full speed back toward the mouth of the arroyo and radio reception. They popped out of the canyon, and Ray tried again.

A voice answered immediately, "Go ahead, Peevy."

"We've got a problem. Looks like a trainee was lured off the course and kidnapped. We need a search-and-rescue helicopter launched ASAP."

"Say again?" the voice squawked.

"Launch a damned search-and-rescue helicopter right effing now," Peevy snarled.

"Who's lost and say last known location," a deep, stern voice cut into the channel.

Griffin lurched. If he wasn't mistaken, that was Admiral Duquesne's voice. The old man was a SEAL and had a reputation for being a top-notch operator back in the day. He must've been monitoring the wrap-up of Hell Week from his office.

Ray answered, "Missing trainee is Tate. We tracked her to a pit trap two klicks west of checkpoint six. She was taken out of the pit by several men on foot. I'm heading back there now to see if I can find vehicle tracks and give you more to go on."

"I'll make the phone call to launch a chopper," Duquesne said tersely.

Thank goodness nobody was questioning Griffin's and Ray's sanity. About a hundred yards beyond the pit trap, the canyon petered out, its high walls fading back down into the desert floor.

Ray hopped out and swung his flashlight back and forth in front of the Jeep. In a matter of seconds, he muttered, "Gotcha, jerkwads."

In an agony of impatience, Griffin waited while Ray crouched beside whatever track he'd found and took pictures. Then Ray jogged back to the Jeep. "They drove her out of here in a heavy-duty truck. Dual rear wheels."

"Can you tell what color it was?" Griffin asked half in jest.

"Nah, but I can tell you it went north and then peeled back to the east."

Ray swung into the Jeep, and Griffin stared at him. "How the hell do you know that?"

"Look that way. You can see a line of dust hanging in the air from where the truck kicked it up."

Griffin looked to the north and saw nothing but desert and darkness. "I'll take your word for it. I swear, you have bionic eyes."

The moment of levity helped Griffin focus on what had to happen next. "Can you follow the truck's trail?" he asked Ray.

"Head that way. I'll call the turn."

The suspended dust trail ended at a paved highway several miles beyond the pit trap where Sherri had been taken. And even Ray couldn't tell any more about where the truck had gone once it hit dry pavement.

Sherri was gone.

Chapter 21

Sherri woke up slowly, so groggy she could hardly string thoughts together.

Small room. Dark. Only the faint sound of wind rustled around her. She felt alone. Horizontal strips of faint light gave her the vague impression of a decrepit cabin.

No surprise, her ankles were tied to the legs of a chair, and her arms were tied behind her and secured to the chair back. It was uncomfortable, but she was blessed with flexible shoulders and the position wasn't unbearable.

She ached from head to foot. Although calling it an ache didn't quite do justice to the screaming agony shooting through her body. Nonetheless, it felt so damned good just to sit down in this hard, uncomfortable chair and rest that she had no desire to complain.

Whatever kind of head game this was by the BUD/S instructors, she didn't much care. She closed her eyes once more to grab whatever nap she could get before the torture began again.

Sunlight blazing through the window woke her up the next time. That and nigh intolerable heat. She'd gotten accustomed to the pounding sun of the California desert in BUD/S, but being trapped inside a small, enclosed space like this was like sitting in a broiler.

What was this all about? No one had ever mentioned anything about prisoner-of-war training being part of

Hell Week. Surely, Griffin would have told her about it and not thrown her into this cold.

Maybe it was some secret SEAL rite of passage.

She assessed her overall health quickly. Sore as hell from the past five days and nights of hell. Hungry. Thirsty, but not dangerously dehydrated…yet. If she kept sweating at this rate, she was going to need water bad in a few more hours. As it was, she felt the first ticklings of a headache, a sure sign she was dehydrated.

She tested the ropes binding her to what turned out to be a sturdy metal chair. They were solid. She was effectively unable to move for now. Might as well go back to sleep. She had a whole lot of that to make up.

The next time she woke up, the heat of the day felt like it might be starting to break. Red sunlight came in low through cracks in the siding, and she quickly oriented herself. Off to her left was west. Duly noted.

The noise that had woken her up—an approaching vehicle engine—cut off. She listened with interest to the rattling of locks on the door, and then three men stomped into the tiny cabin, filling it with their big bodies. They all had bandannas tied over their faces and were dressed in black cargo pants and T-shirts in shades of brown, gray, and green.

Sherri examined their physiques closely and didn't recognize them as any of her BUD/S instructors. But that made sense if this was some sort of prisoner training. They would be a different cadre of instructors from the regular BUD/S guys.

She waited quietly, interested to see what would

happen next. The good news was she'd had hours' worth of badly needed sleep and felt like a new woman. But a woman who had to pee.

One of the men moved behind her and went to work on the knots holding her wrists behind her back. She tried to envision the knot being untied based on the tugs at her hands. Felt like a handcuff hitch. No way out of that once it was cinched down. *Well, fudge*.

The knot untier moved around in front of her and squatted to untie her feet. He straightened and gestured for her to get up.

She stood and promptly fell to the floor as her legs collapsed out from under her. The combination of Hell Week and lack of circulation from sitting so long had won out over her will to stand.

Rough hands grabbed her upper arms and hoisted her upright. She was shoved into a tiny bathroom that hadn't seen a sponge and scrubbing powder in decades. The sink and toilet were rusted, the bathtub filthy.

One of the instructors parked in front of the bathroom door but did not close it. Grimacing, Sherri used the facilities. At least the guy had turned his back. It could be worse.

She turned on the faucet to wash her hands, and a sluggish stream of rusty water emerged. Nope. She wasn't that desperate to splash her face or rinse her hands.

Feeling a thousand times better, although a dehydration headache throbbed steadily now, she took a quick look around the bathroom. The window was nailed shut, and she suspected an attempt to pull out the nails would result in a god-awful screech that would give away any effort to escape.

Ceiling looked made of solid wooden planks. Floor, the same. No escape was happening from in here without a crow bar or something similar.

She stepped out into the main room. Immediately, two of the masked men—Red Bandanna One and Blue Bandanna—grabbed her by the arms and hauled her back to the chair. Pictures were taken of her with a newspaper held under her chin.

Once she was trussed up again, Blue poured a bottle of water down her throat, which she drank eagerly.

Then, without having uttered a single word, the three men left the cabin. Locks were locked. The engine started, and silence settled around her again.

That was weird. If this was some sort of POW training, wouldn't they have left guards nearby?

Experimentally, she rocked the chair, thumping the chair legs loudly. She waited for a response. Nothing. She was definitely alone.

She leaned forward, balancing awkwardly on her toes and turning to see what was behind her. A rusted-metal cot frame leaned vertically in one corner. An old recliner with a ruined seat filled the other corner.

Sherri searched for any sharp objects she could use to saw through the ropes. Nothing obvious. But maybe if she could get to the bed frame, the rusted metal would be rough enough to act as a file. The ropes were thick, and it would take forever to saw through them. It appeared, though, that she had nothing but time on her hands.

She started the slow process of inching her chair backward toward the corner.

What the hell was going on? Griffin had made it clear that the minute Hell Week ended, he would be waiting for her and take her to his boat.

Was this something else? Some special hazing designed to drive her out of the SEALs? Some breakaway group of instructors who had it in for a woman who dared try for the teams?

Where was she, anyway? She tried to peer through the filthy windows and didn't see much beyond beige smudges. On her painstaking path to the bed, she angled close to a wall and bent at the waist to peer through a crack in the cabin's wrecked siding. She saw the double track of what barely constituted a road snaking away into desert as far as the eye could see. The terrain was flat. Featureless. It looked nothing like Coronado or the surrounding area.

Where the hell *was* she?

Internal alarm bells fired hard. This was *not* ops normal, and whoever those guys in bandannas were, they were not supposed to be holding her prisoner like this.

A moment's terror pierced her train of thought, but she suppressed it fiercely. Fear was not helpful. She was on her way to being a Navy SEAL, dammit. She could bloody well act like one.

Her hands bumped into rough metal, and she angled her wrists painfully to bring her ropes against the bed frame. She started to saw.

Griffin was beyond frantic. The helicopter search turned up nothing. Sherri definitely wasn't wandering around in the desert somewhere off course. Daylight brought an expanded search, NCIS was consulted, a police BOLO issued, and Cal Kettering arrived on a military jet at noon. Grundy was questioned again, but stuck to his story that she'd fallen in a pit trap and he had no idea what happened to her after that.

"Anything?" Cal asked Griffin, who met him at the plane.

"Nothing. A daylight examination of the pit trap confirms what Ray Peevy saw last night. She was lifted out of the pit, put in a truck, and driven away to parts unknown."

"GPS in her ruck?"

"Disabled before she left the pit."

Kettering's gaze snapped to his. "Professionals?" Cal bit out.

"Who else would know to look for a GPS in her gear, let alone take it out?"

Kettering cursed quietly. "Are all SEAL instructors and trainees present and accounted for?"

Griffin swore in a hush. "You don't think our own guys took her out, do you?"

Cal replied grimly, "I don't know what to think at this point."

Griffin drove Kettering over to the SEAL training building and took him into the operations center. As exhausted as the instructors were coming off Hell Week, Griffin was privately gratified to see all of Sherri's BUD/S instructors clustered in the operations center.

Even more gratifying was the fact that they all looked worried. As he listened to muted conversations flowing around him, it was clear to Griffin that they weren't concerned as a function of covering their own asses. They were legitimately worried about Sherri's well-being.

Son of a gun. She had quietly managed to win over these die-hard skeptics.

Someone brought in food, and Griffin ate out of habit and knowledge that bodies need fuel to operate at peak efficiency.

Around midnight, Cal came over to where Griffin stared bleakly into space. "When's the last time you slept, Grif?"

"I don't know. Thursday, maybe."

"You're pushing forty-eight hours on your feet, brother. Go down for a nap. You won't do her any good if you're too whipped to function. I'll wake you up if we hear anything."

Not only was Cal right, but his words had the ring of an order from a superior officer.

Griffin slid down a wall and collapsed in the corner to close his eyes for a few minutes, reluctantly allowing that even he had his limits. If and when they got a lead on Sherri, he needed to be sharp.

In his exhaustion, he started dreaming almost immediately. He wasn't the least bit surprised that he dreamed of her.

Sherri laughing. Sherri cuddling in his arms. Sherri staring up at him in the throes of pleasure. Her courage, her determination, her dry sense of humor—they all swirled around him in a Technicolor montage of joy.

And then the scene shifted. Darkened. He dreamed of her imprisoned in a small, dark space, afraid and alone. Tortured. Brutalized. Convinced he wasn't going to come for her.

He lurched, banging his head against the wall as he jolted awake. Where the hell was he…

Right. Ops center. The FBI and police in California and several nearby states were on high alert for her. As manhunts went, it was turning into a big one.

Griffin closed his eyes, fighting back the agony trying to claw its way out of his chest. *Where are you, Sherri? Who took you, and where did they take you? Talk to me, baby.*

But no matter how hard he mentally tried to communicate with her, all he got back was silence. Frightening, maddening silence.

Sherri had no idea how soon her captors would be back to give her water and let her use the toilet again. As the hours ticked past and darkness fell, she sawed nonstop at her ropes. Fear began to creep in past the pain in her shoulders. She had to hurry. They would come to care for her eventually. Otherwise, they wouldn't have bothered to give her that first bottle of water.

It felt as if her bonds were weakening a little. Pulling hard against her ropes to hold them taut, she sawed even more feverishly against the edge of the bed frame. She felt the bits of rust catching and pulling at the rope's fibers. Was that a little wiggle that hadn't been there before?

All of a sudden, her straining hands popped free. She'd done it.

Bending down, she quickly picked loose the knots holding her ankles to the chair legs. Cautious of landing on her face this time, she stood up carefully, using the back of the chair for support.

Exquisite agony raced through her body as blood returned to limbs, her joints took their first, creaky movements in over a day, and muscles randomly cramped.

She made it over to the front door and gave it a tug. It was solidly locked. Which was kind of ridiculous, given how flimsy the rest of the cabin was. She took quick stock of the supplies at hand.

First, she tore the cloth back off the recliner. It was roughly a three-foot square piece of heavy upholstery fabric. She laid it on the floor and piled on it the pieces of rope that had bound her, several handfuls of stuffing from the chair seat, a couple of the bed springs from the cot, and a piece of flat metal the length of her forearm from the cot that lay on the floor.

Thinking fast, she raced into the bathroom, broke the mirror with her elbow, and scooped up several shards of the broken glass. They would make for good signaling devices or makeshift blades. Using the discarded water bottle from earlier, she drank as much of the nasty sink water as she could and prayed it wasn't laced with deadly bacteria. Then she filled the bottle full and added that to her stash.

She picked up the metal chair she'd been tied to, and tossed it through the bathroom window. Then, working quickly, she tied the cloth into a bundle around her finds, threw it outside, and climbed out after it. Using her bare hands, she paused long enough to rip off a long sliver of the wooden siding. It was just about the right length and heft for a walking stick.

Slipping her arm through the makeshift sling, she headed out in the same direction the sun had set. Her reasoning was that if she walked to the west long enough, she would eventually run into the coastal cities of California. Assuming the kidnappers hadn't been able to drive more than a few hours inland, she was no more than a hundred or so miles from the coast. It was a working theory at least, and better than just wandering aimlessly out here.

She remembered Griffin's survival lectures back at Camp Jarvis. Move at night in hot environments. It saved strength and water and made a person harder to see when they were on the move.

Speaking of which, she gathered a handful of dried grass and used it to brush away her footprints as she moved away from the house. She made a point of hopping from rock to rock for a good hundred feet or so and then resumed sweeping her footsteps. It wasn't the all-out sprint away from her prison that she wanted to do, but Griffin had stressed the importance of hiding one's tracks over speed.

When the shack was no more than a speck behind her, though, she did take off running. Again, she had to restrain her impulse to flee madly, forcing herself into a steady, ground-eating jog she could sustain for hours.

Huh. After that all-night run with a heavy rucksack, jogging out here like this with nothing but a light cloth bundle slung across her body felt pretty darned good. Her muscles were far from recovered from Hell Week, and the enforced stillness of the chair and dehydration hadn't helped with the kinks, but as she moved and her blood flowed more freely, the worst of the discomfort subsided. When she stopped to rest, she would do some yoga stretches to work out the residual stiffness.

She figured she could cover around four miles per

hour jogging and maybe three miles per hour when she had to slow for rough terrain. Give it thirty hours of hard travel to get to civilization. She wouldn't be able to do that continuously because of daylight and daytime heat. Say, four days of travel to be conservative.

She would need to find water and shelter before it got too hot each day. And she had to assume her captors would come after her, so stealth was called for. To that end, as she jogged, she stuck handfuls of dead grass in her hair and waistband.

Near morning, she got lucky and ran right into a small seep, landing on her behind as her boot skidded out from under her in slick mud.

Digging with her hands, she created a little hollow and watched eagerly as it slowly filled with muddy water. If she let it sit in her bottle for a while, the worst of the sediment would settle, and she could drink through a piece of the cloth over the bottle mouth to further filter the water.

She carefully filled her bottle with water and waited impatiently for the water to clear. As soon as she could see through it, she chugged it down and filled the bottle again. She was losing precious travel time, but water was the most critical resource for her survival.

I'm coming home, Griffin. Just be patient. Although knowing him, he would be anything but patient over her disappearance. She doubted Grundy would 'fess up to dumping her in the pit, so until someone got around to coming back to fish her out, nobody would have known she was kidnapped—unless this was, in fact, part of her training. Which she seriously doubted at this point.

She was no expert on geography, but she guessed she was somewhere in the Mojave Desert. And in all the preparation she'd done for BUD/S, all the discussions Griffin had with her, never had she run across a single reference to hauling BUD/S candidates out into this bleak wasteland and dumping them.

When her belly ached from drinking water, she filled the bottle one last time, did her best to obscure her tracks in the mud and continued on. She could only pray her captors underestimated her fitness and stamina. It was one of the SEALs' secrets to success, and she hoped it worked doubly for her as a woman.

The sun rose at her back as she wound through a series of washes and gullies. She tried to keep heading generally west, but the canyons wound all over creation. Eventually, she started the long climb up a rough rock outcropping.

As the morning began to heat up, she considered shelter. About halfway down the west face of the ridge, she spotted what she'd been looking for: a large boulder with a deep hollow carved out of the dirt at its base. Approaching the den with caution, she used her stick to clear the space from any resident snakes before crawling in. She had to evict a couple of scorpions and then built piles of rocks at each end of the opening and draped her piece of cloth over them, covering the opening.

There was just enough room for her to curl up in a loose ball. Using her arm for a pillow, she closed her eyes and dozed lightly. Her sleep was fitful, no doubt because she kept half an ear alert for anyone who might approach her hiding place.

The space heated up until it felt like an oven, and she finally caved in and turned back the corner of the cloth to let in a little fresh air. It was still oven-hot. But at least she was free and enduring this heat on her own terms, not tied to some damned chair, waiting passively like a lamb for the slaughter.

Where are you, Griffin? Are you looking for me?

She had to believe he was searching for her by now. If she heard any aircraft pass over, she had the mirror shard to signal it. Until then, she dared not leave any trail signs for Griffin in case her captors were hunting her.

Surely, they would. If they'd gone to all the trouble of kidnapping her, they must have some definite reason for doing so.

Yet again, she wondered who her kidnappers were and what their beef with her was. But it was a mystery.

Her last thought as she drifted to sleep was *I'm coming, Griffin. I'll run all the way to you if I have to.*

"Phone call just came in to the Training Center main switchboard!" a communications tech called out over the general noise. The ops center went silent instantly.

"Who is it?" Duquesne barked.

"Recorded message. Electronically altered voice."

"Play it on speaker," the admiral ordered.

Griffin listened tensely to the deep, inhuman drone of an electronically generated voice saying, "We have Tate. We want Griffin Caldwell. We'll make a trade."

Every stare in the room snapped to him, and he stared back. What the hell did these jokers want with him?

The voice was still speaking. "…one hour, you will call the following phone number and receive further instructions." A phone number was recited.

The call ended and a dial tone replaced the odd metallic voice.

Duquesne demanded, "Caldwell, who the hell was that, what the hell do they want with you, and how in the *hell* did they know you're here?"

Cal moved to stand beside him in front of the admiral as Griffin answered, "I have *no* idea who that was or what's going on."

"Enemies?" Duquesne asked.

Griffin frowned. "I've been an operator a long time. I can't even begin to list the people I've pissed off."

"Anyone recently?" Duquesne bit out.

Cal interrupted. "Your office, sir?"

Duquesne nodded and headed for an office attached to the communications center. Its owner wasn't present, and Duquesne appropriated the desk, sitting down in its chair. Griffin closed the door behind Cal as Duquesne asked, "What's up?"

Cal said grimly, "Are you positive that this isn't some sort of response by rogue SEALs to the presence of a woman at BUD/S, sir?"

Thunder landed on Duquesne's brow, and he rumbled, "It had better not be. I run a tight ship around here, and my instructors wouldn't dare pull a stunt like that. Consider that line of reasoning off the table."

Griffin had to agree with the admiral. Most of the instructors had adopted a wait-and-see attitude toward Sherri. He spoke up. "It sounds like Lieutenant Tate is merely a means to an end. That end being me."

Cal responded, "Yes, but who knows that you and Sherri Tate are connected?"

All three men stared at each other in silence for a moment.

Duquesne said, "Maybe the kidnappers took whatever trainee they happened to catch. Any warm body they could trade for Caldwell."

Kettering retorted, "Possible, but not probable. I'm inclined to believe her kidnapping was not random."

Griffin pressed his lips together until he felt them forming a thin, white line. Did he dare tell them that he and Sherri were much more than mere instructor and student to each other? It would blow his career to kingdom come. But if it would help save her—

He opened his mouth to speak, but Cal cut him off, saying, "A few months ago, part of Griffin's team was in on the Haddad fiasco."

"The mission that went all to hell in Kirdu province?" Duquesne responded.

Griffin's gut tightened in grief as Cal answered grimly, "Yeah. That one. Any chance this is related to that?"

Griffin thought out loud. "Abu Haddad knows who the Reapers are. After all, we've made the bastard's life miserable for the past decade. We've chased him from one end of Afghanistan to the other end of Pakistan and back. But how would he know who I am specifically? By name? He has no way of knowing I'm the platoon leader, let alone where to find me."

Griffin and Cal stared at each other for a long moment, turning over that puzzle in their noggins. Which was why Griffin saw the exact instant the thought that had just burst into his brain burst into Cal's.

"Kenny," Griffin breathed.

Was it possible? Was Ken Singleton still alive? Had his Reaper brother been captured by Haddad and not killed after all?

"Son of a bitch," Cal muttered.

"Somebody talk to me," Duquesne snapped, looking back and forth between the two of them.

Cal explained quickly, and Duquesne burst out, "So you think Singleton survived and under duress has given up Grif's name as the platoon leader of the Reapers?"

"I sincerely hope so," Cal answered fervently.

Griffin followed the trail of logic. "If Kenny gave up my name, he may also have given up Lieutenant Tate's name. Is it possible Haddad got one of his people close to the BUD/S program?"

Cal frowned. "We would spot one of Haddad's zealots in a thorough background check."

Good point. Griffin thought aloud. "What about a BUD/S instructor or trainee? Could Haddad's people have blackmailed one or somehow compromised one?"

"Like who?" Duquesne demanded.

Griffin hated to name names or point fingers without solid evidence. But the face of Grundy did flash in his mind's eye immediately. The police had already questioned the guy at length, of course, but he wanted to take a run at the guy himself. What were the odds Grundy wasn't working alone? Had Abu Haddad gotten to the guy?

There would be time enough to sort that out after Sherri was found.

To that end, Griffin asked the admiral, "We're making the trade, right? Me for Tate."

"I don't know about that," Duquesne responded skeptically.

Griffin planted both his hands on the desk, not afraid to beg for Sherri's life. "If this is Haddad's people, they'll kill her if they don't get me. I'm a SEAL. I've had *all* the torture and interrogation training. Sher—Tate hasn't had any. She's not prepared to deal with bastards like Haddad."

"She's well on her way to being a SEAL," Duquesne replied. "I think we can expect a certain amount of fortitude out of her. If nothing else, we know she has a strong survival drive."

"That won't be enough against Haddad," Griffin argued. "They won't hesitate to do the worst to Tate. You have to let me take her place."

"They'll have to give us proof of life before I'll even consider it," Duquesne declared. "I'm not losing two SEALs when I may already have to lose one."

He thought of Sherri as a SEAL, huh? Under any other circumstances, Griffin would have been jubilant. But now he was freaking out over the thought of her tortured and dying, alone and terrified.

Griffin fought for control and spoke as evenly as he could. "I get where you're coming from, sir. But I want to do this. I'm volunteering."

"Why?"

He stared at the admiral. What the hell was he supposed to say? *I love her, and I've secretly been in a relationship with her for months?* He couldn't admit that to Cal, let alone to the big boss.

Why Cal chose to dive in at that moment and rescue him, Griffin had no idea, but he was profoundly grateful.

Cal said, "Grif is my lead trainer in Operation Valkyrie. He worked with Tate and the other female trainees for months prior to bringing Tate out here to BUD/S. He knows her very well. We both feel responsible for her being at Coronado and for her being in this predicament. We owe her. She's family."

Duquesne was silenced by the invocation of family. At length, he said heavily, "If we were to make the trade, I would need a full battle plan for how we make the handoff and how we track and rescue both Caldwell and Tate."

"Yes, sir," Cal said briskly. "When we got the call, I asked a few guys to get to work on that very thing."

"Who?" Griffin and Duquesne demanded together.

"Ray Peevy will be coordinating it," Cal answered.

Thank God. With Ray's capable hands on the wheel, he and Sherri might just make it home from this op alive.

Chapter 22

SHERRI EMERGED CAUTIOUSLY FROM HER LITTLE HOLE IN the ground. Twilight made the sky the same dark blue as Griffin's eyes, and she had to force back a sob at the thought.

She could do this. All she had to do was run back to him. If she'd survived Hell Week, she could survive this. Although immediately on the heels of Hell Week, a grueling desert trek without food, adequate water, and fitful dozing at best was a lot to ask of her body and mind.

Not that she had any choice. She sighed, packed up her meager gear, drank her water because she remembered Griffin saying the best place to carry water was inside your body, and headed out. She'd noted a bump on the horizon due west of her this morning, and she aimed for that silhouette now. When the stars came out, she would use the North Star to keep herself pointed west.

She stopped after an hour or so and dropped to one knee to stretch out a nasty Charley horse in her left calf. It felt like a dehydration cramp, but there wasn't much she could do about it except grit her teeth and stretch until it passed.

As she straightened to continue on her way, she noticed a tiny blip in the distance, off to the north, that hadn't been there before she stopped. The blip gradually turned into a tiny tube.

That's the dust trail of a motorized vehicle.

Did she dare try to wave it down, or was it her captors out looking for her? Undecided, she stared at the gray puff as it grew larger. It dawned on her the vehicle was heading toward her.

Crap, crap, crap. She dropped to the ground, searching frantically for a hiding place. A bush, a rock, anything that would give her cover. Nada. She was out in the open and a sitting duck.

It had already been determined that the phone number in the message went to a burner phone, which would no doubt be destroyed the moment the call ended. Griffin's instructions were to loiter on the line as long as he could so the tech guys could locate it. The kidnappers would surely move after the call, but it would give the SEALs a general starting point of where to hunt for Tate.

At a nod from a tech guy, Griffin made the call. The phone rang a half-dozen times, and then a voice, electronically distorted, said, "Griffin Caldwell is to come alone and unarmed to the following coordinates. He will exit the vehicle and head due north on foot until we approach him."

The line went dead.

The people around Griffin swore. No way had that little burst of signal been traceable. Honestly, it was about what he'd expected. If the working theory was right and Haddad's men had Sherri, they were professional Special Forces operators.

A communications guy called out, "We just received an image of Tate with yesterday's newspaper under her chin. We have proof of life."

Griffin darted across the room to look over the guy's shoulder. It was her, all right. She looked haggard, sitting in a metal chair in what looked like a cabin. But she was alive. Profound, knee-weakening relief soared through him.

Duquesne said grimly, "All right, gentlemen. Gear up. Let's bring her home."

If she didn't find cover in the next minute or so, she was *dead*.

Although the ground looked table flat, it was deceptive. The desert was riddled with ripples and gullies left over from the rare rains out here. She spied a shallow gully not too far away and rolled over to it as fast as she could. She frantically dug it wider with her bare hands.

As soon as the crevice was deep and wide enough to hold her entire body, she stretched out in it. She buried her legs with some of the loose dirt, and then she piled the rest of the dirt on top of the upholstery cloth on her lap.

The sound of an engine became audible. They were getting *close*.

Working quickly, she lay down and then eased the cloth and its load of dirt over her torso and face. The weight of it settled heavily upon her, and she turned her head to the side, breathing through a single tiny crack between the fabric and the ground above her.

It felt like being buried alive. Her breathing accelerated in panic, and she frantically did the four-count breathing technique Griffin had taught her to use when shooting a sniper rifle. It supposedly slowed the pulse and respiration.

In. Count to four. Out. Count to four.

Okay, so she was counting to four really fast. But she was doing it. Over the next half-dozen breaths, her counting slowed a tiny bit.

And then a tiny bit more.

Tires crunched through the gravel, and then stopped. Over the noise of the idling engine, she heard male voices calling at each other.

In Russian.

She'd studied it in college and, while not fluent, was reasonably conversational. She strained to hear them. One said something to the effect of whatever Timur had seen moving on the horizon must have been an animal. Another voice speculated that it must be a *volk*—a wolf in Russian.

A third voice corrected him scornfully, saying that out here it would have to be a *kohyut*—a coyote.

The first voice swore angrily and then snarled, "When we find the girl, kill her. We don't need her anymore. Haddad only said he wanted the primary target alive."

Haddad? The terrorist who'd killed Sam was behind her kidnapping? Who *were* these guys?

"The inside man said he was sure Caldwell would make the trade for the woman. We can fake having the woman when the target shows up at the rendezvous point."

Griffin was going to hand himself over to these guys in exchange for her?

No. Flipping. Way. She was *not* letting him sacrifice himself for her.

The first voice snapped at the others to get back in the truck. The engine revved, and tires crunched loudly, spinning and then catching traction in the loose gravel. The vehicle retreated, and silence fell around her.

As much as she hated being buried, she almost hated the idea of sitting up and exposing herself even more. Inch by inch, she eased the cloth shroud down her body. Her face emerged and she pulled in a long breath of blessedly fresh air. The stars in the black sky above were so thick they looked like dust in the heavens. It was stunning. She would love to show Griffin this.

She *had* to get back to him.

The tire tracks of what looked like some sort of truck or SUV started no more than thirty feet from her hiding place and headed off to the west. That had been way too close a call. She'd gotten complacent and almost gotten caught.

At least she'd probably chosen the right direction to travel. Her captors would be worried she was headed for civilization and help, and they would likely head toward the nearest inhabited area.

On the assumption that they could move much faster than she could, she elected to parallel the tracks and continue westward. She stuck to valleys and swales as much as possible, stopping often to listen for engine noise, approaching each ridge on her belly and peering over before proceeding.

Her chapped lips cracked and bled, and a dull headache crushed her head by slow degrees in a painful vise, but she couldn't afford to stop and hunt for water. Not with those Russians out here hunting her.

Griffin swallowed one GPS tracker, another one was sewn into his pants, and a third one was hidden in his collar. Duquesne really, *really* didn't want to lose track of his location.

He was given a belt with a video camera installed in the buckle, a thin, flexible battery lining the entire belt. It would run for at least twenty-four hours of continuous video feed to a satellite. That was all the gear the comm guys were able to plant on him before he had to leave. Cal personally drove him to the coordinates in the Mojave Desert, close to the Nevada border.

The mission would run as a full-blown operation, complete with gunship support on standby, search-and-rescue helicopters ready to launch, intel and attack drones loitering overhead, and sixteen armed-to-the-teeth SEALs following him and Cal at a safe distance in a pair of Hummers.

"Do you think they brought her all the way out here?" Griffin asked Cal.

"It's where I'd come with a hostage if I wanted to be left alone and not be spotted by a living soul."

"Rough terrain," Griffin commented grimly.

"We'll have drones with IR cameras over you at all times. If Sherri's nearby, we'll find her. They'll see her heat signature."

Griffin couldn't even allow himself to think about the possibility that she was dead and had no heat signature.

"You know the drill," Cal said briskly. "Get visual on the kidnappers, then go to ground and don't get caught. Follow on foot if able, or let us take over pursuit from above."

"Got it."

"And Grif?"

"Yeah?"

"Don't be a hero."

He snorted. Too late for that. He was headed out there with one goal, and one goal only. To save Sherri's life. His own safety—his life—was completely irrelevant.

Sherri moved steadily west, paralleling the truck tracks. By her reckoning, it had been dark at least four hours, placing it near midnight when the now-familiar truck tracks abruptly cut across her path, heading due south. Why the change of direction?

She peered ahead and spied the black silhouette of a rocky outcropping thrusting up from the desert floor. The truck must be detouring around that. She debated following the truck or continuing due west.

The least number of steps taken won out, and she pushed on toward the ridge. Rising gradually, it appeared to drop off more steeply on the other side. She climbed it carefully, wary of turning an ankle or otherwise making herself immobile.

As she approached the top of the ridge, she eased down onto her hands and knees, and then down onto her belly, to crawl the last few yards. She peeked beyond the rim and stared.

A heavy-duty pickup truck was parked in the valley below. It had to be her kidnappers. Who else would be out here in the middle of freaking nowhere?

She made out two men sitting in the bed of the truck, each cradling what looked like a modified AK-47 with an extended clip. She could see the black shape of a driver at the wheel, but she couldn't see if there were any more men inside the vehicle. They didn't appear in any hurry to go anywhere.

Should she wait them out here, or go around them and continue west? She much preferred having them in front of her where she could see them if they turned around and came back toward her. The idea of having to keep looking back over her shoulder made her deeply apprehensive.

She was losing the best part of the night for travel, though, when it was cool but not freezing. The lure of pressing on toward Griffin and safety was powerful. Undecided, she studied the terrain in search of a good route around the kidnappers. The slope in front of her was steep but not impassible. It would be a hairy slip-and-slide descent if she chose that route.

The valley itself was funnel-shaped, wide to her left and narrowing to a point at her right. She might be able to follow the ridge around that way.

What was that she saw at the base of the cliff to her right, where the ridge did a sharp one-eighty back to the south?

She squinted at the big black shadow there, perplexed. The topography didn't match the way the shadows lined up down there.

The men in the back of the truck moved abruptly, sitting up, alert.

Her attention swung back to the south. From her high vantage point, looking out over the entire valley, she spied a man moving toward the truck cautiously on foot.

He was decked out in full tactical gear, and she didn't need more than a single glance to know he was a special operator. Her pulse leaped. *Is that Griffin?* Come to find her?

The two men in the back of the truck rolled over

its edge and disappeared into the shadows below her. Someone came out of the passenger side of the truck, and the driver eased out of his side. She lost sight of all four men quickly. They were good. Moving like professionals, they crept away from the truck stealthily.

The soldier drew closer. *No doubt about it. That is Griffin.*

She had to warn him he was walking into an ambush!

But how? She had no radio, no flare gun, no light. She eyed the slope in front of her. Could she create a landslide, maybe? It would give away her position to the men below. Men who'd stated their desire to kill her earlier.

Still, she had to do *something*. No way was she sitting up here and watching Griffin walk into a buzz saw.

An intel specialist reported into Griffin's earbud, "Box canyon. Steep but not sheer cliffs. One pickup truck. Two tangos in the back. Photo analyst thinks she sees weapons. One heat signature on the west rim of the valley."

Griffin snorted. They'd kidnapped a SEAL trainee and demanded that a SEAL meet them out here. They'd better be armed to the teeth if they expected to walk away from this alive. Not to mention, nobody messed with Sherri without answering to him.

Cal said in his ear, "Okay, Grif. Contact's made. Back off, and let the full SEAL team move in."

"Is there any sign of Tate?" he asked on the open frequency that included the intel team.

"Negative."

"If she's not here, I'm going to have to go in there and play this out," he responded.

"Negative, Grif," Cal snapped. "Let us take these guys."

"You know as well as I do they'll never talk. If they don't take me to her, she could be anywhere, dying."

Cal started to argue, and Griffin pulled the earbud out of his ear, letting it hang on its cord down his chest. Nope. Not gonna squabble with the boss about this. If Sherri wasn't in the truck, he was handing himself over to these bastards.

It was entirely possible they would shoot him as he approached. But in that case, Sherri was likely already dead, and he didn't have any great desire to live in a world without her, anyway.

Arms held low and away from his sides, he walked forward toward his fate. If this was how he died, so be it.

Sherri froze in the act of standing up to stomp on a small boulder and send it down the slope as one of the Russians called out of the shadows, "Show your face, Caldwell!"

Her gut leaped at the confirmation that the special operator approaching was indeed Griffin.

Even better, now that the hostile had spoken, Griffin knew there were men hiding out here. In reality, he probably already knew exactly how many there were and where they were, given the technology SEALs could bring to bear on an encounter like this. She sank back down slowly to watch the scenario unfold, her protective instincts on hyperdrive.

Griffin lifted his NODs up on top of his helmet. Her heart jumped with joy at the sight of him, so close.

Now the two of them just had to get out of this confrontation alive.

"Come toward the truck!" the accented voice called out of the darkness.

"Identify yourselves!" Griffin called back. "Show me Tate, or I don't come any closer!"

"You're in our gunsights, Caldwell!"

"Then shoot me now!"

Sherri winced. He was brave to call their bluff like that. She knew Haddad wanted him alive, but he didn't know that.

Silence greeted his challenge.

"That's what I thought," Griffin called back. "Show me Tate!"

"She's nearby!"

Sherri smiled a little. The guy didn't know how right he was. She was by no means as dangerous as a fully trained SEAL, but she wasn't chopped liver, either. She watched for a way to tip this stand-off in Griffin's favor.

"We will take you to her!" the Russian called.

Liar. Don't believe him, Griffin, she thought hard.

Dammit, he continued forward.

She scanned the valley, trying to spot where the Russians were hidden. The voice shouting at Griffin was coming from across the narrow chasm. She spotted a man-sized shadow off to the shouter's left. Which meant there were probably two guys beneath her somewhere. She carefully slid a little further forward, watching for the slightest movement, but nobody even twitched beneath her.

As Griffin approached the truck, Sherri recognized his hair-trigger readiness in the relaxed way he held his body. She also recognized an atypical thickness through his torso. He was wearing some sort of body armor. Thank goodness.

Without taking her gaze off him, she fished in the cloth bundle at her side, finding and gripping the piece of steel she'd taken from the bed frame. It didn't have a sharp edge, but it had a nice heft and made for a decent improvised weapon. She eased it clear of the bundle.

Catlike, she shifted her feet beneath her by slow degrees, rising by inches into a tightly coiled crouch.

And just in time, for all of a sudden below her holy hell broke loose.

Chapter 23

GRIFFIN SAW THE GUY ON HIS LEFT AT THE LAST SECOND before the bastard jumped him, and managed to duck the guy's open arms, slipping under the bear hug. But then another guy was on him from behind, grabbing him around the waist. Griffin threw his elbow back, and the point of it connected hard with something bony on the guy's face.

A grunt, and the arms around his waist loosened. But not before the first attacker got in a wicked throat punch that doubled Griffin over, coughing and gasping for air. Two more men closed on him from his right.

Not good. These guys were fast and knew what they were doing in a fight. He didn't stand a chance four on one. But he fought anyway, kicking, punching, ducking and dodging, doing his level best to avoid being wrapped up in someone's arms.

The last two guys reached him, and it was a free-for-all. The good news was no matter what direction he threw a kick or punch, he struck someone. The bad news was they were landing several blows for every one he delivered. They figured out pretty fast that he had on a Kevlar vest and changed aim, going for his head and limbs.

Sherri's face came to mind, and he took the hits. Ignored the pain. Fought on grimly for her. If he could beat these guys off, maybe he could get one of them to tell him where she was stashed.

He became aware that they were herding him toward the narrow end of the valley, stacking themselves in an arc that forced him to fall back from their flurry of fists. Why weren't they using guns on him? Or at least knives? They must be under orders to grab him and take him alive.

If he could just hold out a few more minutes, Cal and the Hummers full of SEALs would get here and make short work of these jokers.

But then he took a punishing blow to the side of his head and saw stars, dazed.

Shit. He was in trouble now.

Sherri saw the moment Griffin's head snapped to one side, and he staggered, half-conscious.

Worse, as she slid along above the fight as it moved to the right, she spotted a cave entrance, or maybe a tunnel of some kind. As she recalled, there used to be silver mines out here. More recently, some of those complexes had been converted to drug operations, mazelike warrens with multiple ingress and egress points.

If those Russians got Griffin underground, all of his fancy tracking devices and video intel feeds would go dead, just as had happened to that DEVGRU team in the Kirdu ambush. No one had heard from them until they dug out of the tunnels two days after the ambush.

She had to keep Griffin outside that cave! It was now or never to help him.

She took off running down the steep slope. It was more of a controlled fall than actual running, and it took all of her strength to stay upright and keep her feet underneath her.

She hoped they wouldn't notice her coming while they concentrated on Griffin, who was giving them all the fight they could handle. She was all over ambushing these bastards who were beating on her man. Cold fury coursed through her, and she knew without a shadow of a doubt she would have no trouble killing anyone who messed with Griffin. He was more than her lover, more than a mentor and friend. He was her whole blessed world.

She reached the bottom of the slope, letting the momentum carry her forward at full speed. She joined the fracas and slammed the metal bar across the back of the head of the nearest Russian with all her strength.

Griffin glimpsed a fifth shape coming, this one charging down the slope like a bat out of hell. The apparition came silently, and he braced himself for impact. The fight, already going badly against him, was about to tip over into an outright loss.

He roared in his fury and redoubled his efforts, flailing like crazy as his assailants pummeled him.

The silent runner ran up behind Number Four and clocked him over the head. Hard. The Russian dropped like a rock.

Help. It was help!

He spun left, facing the two Russians that way. Griffin felt the third Russian turn away to face this new threat, backing up against Griffin.

Mistake. Griffin flung his right elbow backward as hard as he could, aiming kidney high. Number Three cried out and went down to his knees as Griffin ducked a wild swing from Number Two. Unfortunately, that moved Griffin right into a vicious kick from Number One that glanced off his forearm and caught him on the chin.

Pain exploded in his face, and involuntary tears of stinging pain leaked out of his eyes.

Must stay on his feet. To go down was to die.

From behind him, a female voice grunted, "Four Russians. With orders not to kill you."

Sherri.

Alive.

And here.

Fuckin' A.

He'd already figured out the "four Russians" part. But they couldn't kill him? Sweet. He could go full offensive. He did so, uppercutting the Russian on the right with his fist, while he snapped out a fast, lethal kick at Number One's groin. Both shots connected.

He heard Sherri grunt in pain behind him, and a whole new level of fury flashed through him. He spun, grabbed Number Three by the throat, and whipped him around just in time to catch a vicious chop from Number One.

Sherri leaped to his right, defending his open side, holding off Number Two.

Number Three, struggling in his grasp, mule-kicked backward, and Griffin used the momentum of the guy's one-footedness to kick the standing leg out from under the bastard, who went down hard. Instead of jumping back, Griffin took the aggressive tack and jumped forward over the prone man, who anticipated wrong and rolled toward where Griffin had just been standing.

Griffin stomped down with all his strength on the

prone guy's outstretched hand and felt bones crunch under his boot. He lunged up at Number One, slamming him into Number Three, which threw Number Three to one side.

The third Russian screamed and went down clutching his throat.

Sherri swung toward Number One and slammed whatever she was holding into the guy's temple. He staggered. Griffin clocked him in the junk with the steel-toed tip of his boot, and the bastard went down to the ground in the fetal position.

Number Four was just rousing when Sherri lifted what looked like some sort of makeshift shiv. The guy put his hands behind the back of his head. Good call. She was vicious with that thing.

The sound of engines roared into range. The Hummers.

They screeched to a halt about twenty feet away, and SEALs poured out of both vehicles.

Number Four grunted, "*Ohkonchatelnyui variahnt*."

"No!" Griffin shouted, grabbing at Number One's jaw.

Too late. The guy bit down hard and glared up at him. "*Govnyuk*," the Russian snarled as foam began to emerge from his mouth.

"Same to you," Griffin snapped.

"What did he call you?" Sherri panted from behind him.

"Let's just say I'm not his favorite person."

"What the hell?" she squawked, stepping back and bumping into Griffin.

The other Russians also commenced foaming at the mouth and went still on the ground.

"Cyanide capsules. Standard Spetsnaz Ops. No capture."

"Do SEALs do that?"

"No. We don't get caught. Or if we do, we don't talk."

"Are you okay?" she asked urgently.

"Are *you*?"

She stepped toward him, and he turned toward her, sweeping her off the ground in a mighty hug. She clung to him just as hard, burying her face in his neck.

"I thought you were going to die," she gasped.

"I thought you *had* died. God, I've never been so glad to see anyone charge into battle like that."

"I love you," she whispered.

Fireworks exploded inside his head, and his heart felt like it was going to bust right out of his chest. He opened his mouth to tell her he loved her too, but just then the SEALs swarmed around them, and he set her down quickly, stepping back to a respectable distance.

As the crowd of big bodies surrounded them protectively, Sherri stared at Griffin, trying to make out his expression in the dark. Even though it was only a few feet, the space between them felt huge. She felt the loss of his arms around her like a physical blow. She needed him right now. Needed the reassurance that she was safe. That he would always come for her like this.

She'd just told him she loved him, and he hadn't said a single thing in response. He'd set her away from him, for crying out loud. Even worse, he shook his head at her a little when she started to reach for him again. Her hands fell back to her sides.

Griffin looked away and then stepped away as Ray Peevy approached.

"Are you injured, Tate?" Peevy asked briskly.

"I'm dehydrated. Hungry. Frankly, I hurt all over."

Especially in her heart. She'd just gone through the scare of her life, believing that Griffin was going to die. She'd charged into battle armed with a piece of bed frame against men who'd stated their intent to kill her. And he was looking at her with no more interest than if she'd been a bug crawling across his boot.

Peevy nodded. "It's not often someone gets to do Hell Week twice in a row. Let's get you to the medics, Tate. They'll fix you right up."

She heard Cal order the SEALs to fan out and search for any more hostiles.

Sherri turned and called back to Kettering, "There were just the four Russians. The evolution is secured."

A relieved laugh went up as Peevy led her away from the bodies and away from the man she loved—who didn't love her back.

Ultimately, it was decided to load the Russian corpses into their truck and drive it back to Coronado. A forensics team would try to identify the dead men, and the FBI and CIA would try to track down whoever they worked for. Not that it was any great mystery to Sherri. These had to be Haddad's men.

Kettering didn't seem surprised when she told him she'd heard the men say Haddad wanted Griffin alive. She gathered from the icy cold enveloping him that he and the Reapers had distinct ideas about what should happen to Haddad in the near future. He also didn't act surprised when she relayed hearing the Russians talk about having a man on the inside of BUD/S. His jaw just got a little tighter and a little harder than it already was.

Sherri noted that Griffin ended up riding back to base in the other Hummer. Was that intentional? Had she completely freaked him out with her whispered declaration?

The answer to that was painfully obvious.

Man, she'd been a fool. She'd spent all of Hell Week imagining them together, him making some grand declaration of his feelings, and her reciprocating. She had romanticized him beyond all reasonable expectations. Which was her fault. She'd completely forgotten the kind of man she was dealing with. His love, his life was the SEALs. He had no room in his heart for anything or anyone else.

It was nearly dawn by the time the caravan of vehicles pulled into the SEAL training area. She started to climb out of the Hummer, but uncharacteristically stumbled. And pitched right into Griffin, who had apparently come over to check on her.

How obvious was it to physically throw herself at the poor guy? Her face on fire, she pushed away from him quickly, mumbling an apology.

"Got your balance, now?" he asked lightly.

Sure. She was totally balanced and in control of herself. *Not*. She'd just realized that everything she thought she knew about him had been a lie. Or worse, it had been a fantasy she'd cooked up in her head to deal with the stress of her situation. How lame was that? She was pathetic.

Vidmeyer piled out of the Hummer behind her and commented, "Not bad, Tate. Not bad at all…for a girl."

She retorted, "One of these days, you'll learn to call me a woman. Then maybe you'll have a shot at me liking you."

The instructors milling around her hooted. Ray Peevy clasped her shoulder lightly. "Good to have you back, Tate."

At least some of the SEALs were glad to have her. But she couldn't take any joy in having won over the others when she'd lost Griffin. Mission accomplished, but at what price?

The crowd of SEAL instructors parted in front of her abruptly, and she gulped as Admiral Duquesne strode forward. His expression was unreadable.

"Welcome back, Lieutenant Tate."

"Thank you, sir."

"Later today, at thirteen hundred hours, I'm convening a review board to determine your status going forward."

She frowned, confused. What had she done wrong?

He said briskly, "You didn't complete Hell Week and have missed a number of training days hence. That necessitates a training review."

He turned and strode away, leaving her staring at his back in shock. The men around her went silent. Maybe they were as stunned as she was.

"So that's it," she said heavily. "The Navy has found its loophole to get rid of me after all." She looked around at the suddenly grim-faced SEAL instructors who'd come to her rescue without hesitation when she'd needed them. "Thank you for saving my life, gentlemen. It has been an honor knowing you all."

Griffin was so angry at Admiral Duquesne that he didn't trust himself not to physically harm the man. It was a travesty to subject Sherri to a review board for missing training. It certainly hadn't been her fault she'd missed the last few kilometers of the night run, nor that she'd been running for her life while her teammates did push-ups on the freaking beach.

He gathered himself to follow the admiral and give the old man a serious piece of his mind when a hard hand closed around his arm.

Ray Peevy.

He scowled thunderously at his teammate. "It's crap. She's earned a right to continue her training. Duquesne has no business tossing her—"

"We have something else to take care of first, my brother," Peevy said soberly. "Some*one* else."

Right. The mole inside BUD/S. Back in the valley, Sherri had relayed having heard the Russians talk about their inside man being certain Griffin would trade himself for her.

"Any idea who the inside guy is?" Griffin asked.

"I have my suspicions. How about you?" Ray responded cautiously.

"Same."

"Who are you thinking?" Ray asked.

"Grundy," Griffin muttered under his breath.

"Grundy," Ray confirmed. "Shall we go have a small conversation with him?"

Griffin and Peevy traded dark looks. Neither of them was going to come out and accuse anyone of committing treason without concrete proof, or at least a confession of some kind. But if Grundy was guilty, they would see him taken down if it was the last thing they both did.

Peevy asked one of the milling instructors, "Where are the BUD/S trainees now?"

"Chow," someone replied.

Griffin and Peevy pivoted and fell into step, striding grimly toward the mess hall.

Feeling immeasurably refreshed by a quick shower and drinking about a gallon of water, Sherri stepped inside the cafeteria where her remaining teammates were currently eating breakfast. She had one more piece of business to take care of before she got booted out of here. When she stepped inside, a shout of welcome went up. The Smurfs rushed forward to hug her.

Smitty demanded, "What the hell happened to you, Tate?"

"Long story."

Someone else blurted out, "We heard you were kidnapped and then some bastards tried to trade you for Caldwell."

She smiled ruefully. "There are no secrets among SEALs, are there?"

"Nah."

Therein lay the problem. She and Griffin were never going to be able to keep their relationship secret. It was a foolish pipe dream to think she could both be a SEAL and have him.

Glancing over the heads of her boatmates, she spotted the guy she'd come here to have words with. She marched across the room toward Grundy, sitting at a table with several of his boatmates. He stood up, scowling, as she stalked toward him. “Made it back finally, I see,” he sneered.

“No thanks to you.”

“I don’t know what you’re talking about.”

Nope. Not going to apologize to her. Not going to acknowledge he’d pushed her into that pit, leaving her helpless and alone for the kidnappers to grab. Well, she’d given him a chance. Which meant she didn’t have any compunction about this.

She drew back her right hand, made a proper fist the way Griffin had shown her a thousand years ago, and punched Grundy as hard as she could.

He doubled over, hands over his broken nose, blood pouring from between his fingers. His boatmates surged up out of their chairs, and Sherri’s boatmates surged forward to surround her.

“What the hell, Tate!” Grundy howled.

A half-dozen SEAL instructors leaped forward, separating the bristling groups of trainees. Two more instructors strode forward into the fray. Griffin and Ray Peevy.

“What was that for, Tate?” Ray Peevy growled.

She glared at Grundy. “Are you going to be a man and tell them, or shall I?”

“Fuck off, Tate,” Grundy shouted.

All the instructors turned questioning looks at her. She registered varying degrees of shock in their stares. She wasn’t sure if she should be complimented or insulted by their surprise over her capacity for violence. Did they think she was going to sit around crocheting doilies once she became a SEAL?

She spoke tightly. "The last night of Hell Week on the desert run, there was a pit across the trail. I found a length of wood and pole-vaulted it. Then Grundy ran up behind me. I helped him cross the obstacle." She glared at Grundy, finishing with "Then he *pushed* me in the pit and took off. I was knocked out by the fall to the bottom. And Grundy *left me there* for the kidnappers to find and take."

The instructors all seemed to grow a few inches in stature and breadth as they pivoted to stare expectantly at Grundy. Peevy spoke for all of them. "This true, Grundy?"

"Fuck no."

"You gonna add lying to your long list of character flaws?" Peevy asked quietly.

"It's my word against hers!" Grundy exploded.

Peevy nodded solemnly. "That is true. Thing is, she's the one who was kidnapped, escaped, trekked through the Mojave Desert evading Spetsnaz operators, and capped it off by diving into a fight against said operators to help out Caldwell. That gives her word a certain weight that yours lacks."

Griffin spoke up. His voice was so cold it sent shivers down Sherri's spine. "Lieutenant Tate overheard her kidnappers talking about their inside man here at BUD/S. If we have our research people dig into your life, Grundy, are we gonna find some funny money in a bank account, maybe a gambling problem or some blackmail pictures of you lying around? Are you the one who threw me and Tate under the bus? Did Abu Haddad's guys get to you?"

The bluster went out of Grundy all at once. His

shoulders drooped, and his entire body seemed to fold in on itself.

Ray Peevy stepped forward and wrenched Grundy's arms behind his back. Someone handed Ray a zip tie, which he secured around Grundy's wrists. "You're under arrest, Grundy. Do not say anything until the military police arrive and can properly inform you of your rights."

"What's gonna happen to him?" one of the trainees in the back of the crowd asked.

Peevy replied, "We're going to get a full written confession from him, and there are some intelligence analysts who will want to speak with him before he ships out for Fort Leavenworth."

Sherri winced. Leavenworth was the military's federal prison.

She glanced around and realized that every single man in the mess hall—trainee or SEAL—was staring at Grundy with silently damning eyes.

Peevy took a long look around the assemblage and then locked stares with Grundy. "Look around, my friend. You've been judged and found lacking. You're not one of us."

"This is your fault, Tate—" Grundy started.

Griffin snarled, "Ray told you not to talk. If you value your life, Grundy, take the man's advice."

The SEALs nearest to her subtly shifted positions until they formed a solid wall of protective bodies around her.

A pair of military police came in and took custody of Grundy, reading him his rights as they marched him out of the chow hall. Sherri watched them load Grundy in the back of a squad car and pull away.

In the wake of his exit, Sherri joined in with the collective exhale of relief around her. SEALs were violent people who lived in a violent world, but they were also honorable to the core. A criminal betrayal by someone who had come close to becoming one of them seemed to shake everyone in the room.

Good. She wasn't alone in being appalled.

The Smurfs burst out cheering and pounding Sherri on the back enthusiastically as the wall of SEALs around her broke up and people headed back to their breakfasts.

Grimacing in discomfort, she begged, "Easy, guys. My Hell Week only just ended. I'm gonna need a few days to recover. In the meantime, I'm a wee bit sore."

Her teammates laughed and herded her over to a table, insisting she sit down while they fetched breakfast for her.

She spied a familiar profile heading for the exit beside Ray Peevy. Griffin pointedly didn't look over at her as he passed by her table.

She got the message loud and clear. When push came to shove, and any other SEALs were present, he wasn't about to be caught showing her any feelings. He would step back from her every time, setting her away from him the way he had in that valley.

Right. As long as she was in the SEAL pipeline, her love for him was futile. And doomed.

Chapter 24

BEFORE HER TRAINING REVIEW HEARING, SHERRI CALLED Schneider and asked him to bring her dress uniform and makeup kit to the Training Center. If she was going to be thrown out of the SEALs, she was darned well going to do it on her own terms.

She went full beauty pageant, hair done, makeup flawless, dressed in hose, white skirt, and her perfectly tailored white summer uniform blouse. She knew how intimidating her beauty could be when she put it on full display, and she did so today.

At ten minutes before one o'clock, she stepped into the large classroom where she, her instructors, and the admiral would convene in a mockery of a hearing to determine her future in the SEALs.

Or out of the SEALs, more accurately.

Cal Kettering already sat at a small wooden table facing a larger table at the front of the room. An empty seat waited beside him. For her, obviously. Rows of chairs stood behind the small, forlorn table stuck out there, all by itself, for everyone to stare at. And jeer at, no doubt. The whole setup looked like a miniature courtroom.

Great. The bastards were even going to stage a monkey trial to pretend like this was all fair and above-board. What a travesty.

"You'll sit here beside me," Cal said quietly.

She moved forward and sank onto the front edge

of the hard wooden chair, too tense to lean back. "I'm sorry, sir. I did my best for you. Please don't pull Anna and Lily out of Operation Valkyrie because I failed."

He opened his mouth to speak, but the door opened just then, and Ray Peevy walked into the room in full dress uniform. Whatever Cal had been about to say went unsaid.

Ray surprised her by walking up to the little oak table and stopping in front of it. "Lieutenant Tate," he said formally, "it has been an honor to work with you." He reached up to his chest and put his hand over his gold SEAL insignia in what looked like some sort of informal salute.

Without warning, he slapped his hand down hard on the table with a sharp crack of noise. Sherri jumped about six inches off her chair before landing on the hard seat again.

She stared down at the table where Ray had slapped it. His gold Budweiser was planted in the oak desk-top. The pin swam in her vision as tears of gratitude filled her eyes. The Navy might be evicting her from the boys' club, but this show of respect by one of its legendary heroes meant the world to her. Her struggle and suffering hadn't been entirely in vain. This SEAL had seen her, measured her, and in some small way, judged her worthy.

She could live with that.

Stunned speechless, she looked up at Peevy. She had no words to express the depth of her gratitude and nodded mutely at him in thanks.

He nodded back tersely and stepped around the table to take a seat in the back of the room.

Chief Vidmeyer and two more of the senior instructors strolled into the hearing room. They stopped abruptly as a trio and stared when they saw that trident planted on the table. They looked up at Peevy conspicuously not wearing his SEAL pin, down at the Budweiser, and back up at her.

Vidmeyer nodded very slowly, as if to himself. Then he walked up to the table, solemnly took his SEAL insignia off his chest, and slapped his hand down on the table. She was ready for the crack of noise this time. But the shock of his show of support was no less overwhelming.

He withdrew his hand, and a second pin had joined the first in front of her.

Without speaking, both of the instructors with Vidmeyer did the same. One by one over the next few minutes, every single instructor who had worked with her BUD/S training class walked into the room, spied the table gradually being covered in gold SEAL insignia, and added theirs to the rows of Budweisers.

Only one SEAL was notably absent today. Griffin.

Where was he? Why wasn't he here? Of all people, he was the one she would have expected to come and show his support for her. Unless her kidnapping had convinced him once and for all that he didn't want her on the teams.

Whatever his reasons were, he didn't show up. Didn't add his trident to the rows accumulating on the desk in front of her.

With every slap of another SEAL's hand on her desk, the sound was a sharp reminder of the one SEAL who wasn't here.

She would not cry. She wasn't ashamed to let these

men who could have been her brothers in a different time, a different world, know how much their tribute meant to her, but she would *not* show them weakness. Never that.

And she damned well wouldn't cry for Griffin. She'd really thought they had something. She'd thought he'd made peace with her becoming a SEAL, that she'd finally found a man she thought she could trust. A man she could love. A man who would take care of her. Look out for her. See all of her.

But in the end, he'd left her, too.

In a way, this hearing was her funeral. The end of her long struggle to scale the unscalable mountain peaks—of becoming a SEAL, and of breaking through Griffin's emotional walls. She'd given both everything she had, but it hadn't been enough.

She'd failed as a SEAL.

Even harder to swallow, she'd failed as a woman.

In a way, she was grateful to Griffin for staying away. He'd already humiliated her enough by rejecting her. She didn't need him to witness this final degradation as well.

At precisely one o'clock, Admiral Duquesne, his executive officer, and a stenographer filed into the room. The admiral stopped in his tracks at the sight of the table in front of Sherri peppered with gold SEAL pins. He stared down at it a long time while she stared at him.

If she wasn't mistaken, she thought she saw the tiniest hint of a smile cross his face before he looked up at her sternly. "It appears your instructors have spoken, Lieutenant Tate. Loudly."

She nodded in acknowledgment, too emotional to trust her voice.

Briskly, he took his place at the front table, facing the room, and laid down the training folder he carried. He opened it and, while everyone watched in charged silence, browsed through it.

"It says here your instructors find you to be a consistent performer, determined, positive, and unflaggingly supportive of your teammates. Would you say that's an accurate summary of this trainee in your experience, Commander Kettering?"

"Yes, sir."

"Lieutenant Tate's final Phase One training report is not included in this file," Admiral Duquesne stated. "Chief Vidmeyer, since you are here in person, would you mind giving that report to me now, for the record?"

She heard the faint rustle of Vidmeyer standing up behind her but didn't turn around to look at him. Instead, she stared down at the table and all those beautiful gold eagles clutching tridents and flintlocks.

Vidmeyer's voice rang out behind her. "Trainee Tate has passed all required training evolutions and is recommended for continuation into Phase Two of BUD/S, sir."

What?

She did turn around to stare at Vidmeyer then. He stared back at her, his expression deadpan. Only by a single brief dip of his chin did he acknowledge her.

"Do the rest of you concur with that assessment?" Duquesne asked from behind her.

"Yes sir!"

She jumped at the loud bark from all of the SEALs at once.

She pivoted back to stare at Duquesne. What was he going to do with *that*?

The admiral leaned back in his chair, arms crossed, staring at her and then at the rows of SEALs seated behind her. At length, he said, "We appear to have consensus. I concur that Lieutenant Tate should proceed on time with her classmates to Phase Two of BUD/S."

A cheer went up behind Sherri that was almost as gratifying as the table full of Budweisers in front of her.

Admiral Duquesne stood up, and the executive officer called the room to attention. Sherri and the SEALs stood up quickly.

"Gentlemen, it seems all of you are missing the appropriate insignia on your uniforms. Please remedy that situation immediately. Dismissed."

Duquesne whirled and strode out of the room, and Sherri watched him go in shock. Cal Kettering grabbed her hand and pumped it warmly as he gave her a half hug with his other hand. "You did it, Tate. Congratulations!"

The SEALs swarmed her as a group, pounding her on the back and shaking her hand. It hurt her sore and bruised body, but it was the best possible kind of pain.

The reality of what had just happened broke over her, and she smiled widely. She'd scaled the all-male fortress of the SEALs and cracked it wide open.

"How miserable are you guys going to make Phase Two for me after this?" she asked wryly.

A big laugh went up around her. "Oh, we're going to make your life a living hell," Peevy crowed.

She grinned back at him. "You know, I think I'm okay with that."

She stepped outside into the warm California sunshine and turned her face up, enjoying it on her skin.

"Wait up, Tate!"

She turned to see Chief Vidmeyer jogging up to her. "All trainees get forty-eight hours liberty after Hell Week, and you didn't get yours. Take the rest of today off. Tomorrow, too. I just got the admiral to okay it. We'll see you back here in a couple of days. And be ready to bust your butt."

"You've got it, Chief. I'll be back, and I'll be ready."

Cal Kettering strolled over to her as she looked around, unsure what to do with herself with two whole days of nobody telling her at the top of their lungs what to do or where to go. "Can I give you a ride somewhere?" he offered.

"Yes, you can—if you know where I can find Griffin Caldwell."

"You gonna punch him out, too?" Cal asked wryly.

"No. I need to thank him for everything he did for me." *And make it clear that if he doesn't want to be with me, I will accept that and move on*. No matter that her heart was broken. Or more accurately, shattered. Maybe forever.

"He's probably on his boat. I'll drive you over to the marina if you'd like."

"That's kind of you, sir."

Cal led her to a pickup truck no less tricked out than Griffin's. She was silent as Cal drove the vehicle up the coast. But when he slowed to turn into the marina, she said grimly, "So, are you and the Reapers going after Haddad?"

"Oh, hell yeah."

"I wish I were two years farther down the road so I could go with you. After the past few days, I'd like a piece of that guy myself."

Cal laughed quietly. "You really are turning into a SEAL, aren't you?"

She hopped out of the truck and paused in the act of closing the door. "Why do all of you keep sounding so surprised about that?"

He smiled. "Because you're just so damned much better looking than the rest of us. You want me to swing by here in a while and pick you up?"

"No, thanks. I see Caldwell's truck over there. I'll ask him to give me a ride back to base. And sir?"

Kettering looked over at her.

"Thank you for everything."

"My pleasure. You're going to be a hell of an asset to the teams. All of you women are."

Smiling, she slammed his door and watched him drive away. Then she turned, took a deep breath, and headed for the *Easy Day*. Saying goodbye to Griffin was going to be the hardest thing she'd ever done…Hell Week included.

Taking a page out of the SEAL playbook, she didn't overthink it and just jumped in. Here went nothing.

Chapter 25

STEPPING OUT ON THE *EASY DAY*'S AFT DECK, GRIFFIN plunked down the case of beer he planned to go through this afternoon. It wouldn't erase the pain in his chest, and it wouldn't bring back Sherri, but he was prepared to let it try. He fell into a lounge chair, staring out at the ocean, which glittered back at him damningly.

He was a jackass. And an idiot. He didn't deserve Sherri after chickening out last night and not telling her he loved her, too. But all the guys had been almost within earshot, and habit had taken over. Their relationship was a secret, and revealing it would have destroyed both of their careers.

Although after spending the past twelve hours experiencing what life would be like without Sherri in it, he wasn't sure he cared a hell of a lot about throwing away his career.

Thing was, he couldn't—he wouldn't—throw away her career for her. Not after all she'd been through to get here. She'd earned a shot at the teams, dammit.

Nice try at making excuses, asshole. You chickened out, plain and simple. You choked when the moment was right to tell her how you felt.

If he had it to do all over again, he'd have found a way. Whispered it back to her—

"Permission to come aboard?"

Sherri? What the hell was she doing here? Had

Duquesne thrown her out of the SEALs after all? Righteous anger on her behalf bubbled up in his gut—

"I know you're here, Griffin. Your truck's in the parking lot."

"Oh, umm, yeah. Come aboard. I wasn't avoiding you. I was just surprised you're here. Everything okay?" he asked cautiously, coming forward to lower the short gangplank and help her aboard.

She startled him by saying, "No. Everything's not okay. That's why I'm here."

"Duquesne didn't seriously kick you out, did he? Have you talked to Kettering? I'm sure he'd still take you in Operation Valkyrie back at Camp Jarvis—"

"Duquesne approved me to continue on to Phase Two of BUD/S."

"Oh." He stared at Sherri, who looked like Malibu Navy Barbie today—no, better than that. She looked like a million bucks. "Congratulations," he mumbled belatedly. "That's fantastic. You did it. You must be so proud of yourself."

"I guess so."

"Why aren't you happy? You should be shouting to the heavens with joy! You've just made it through Phase One of BUD/S, and no woman has ever done that before."

"I am happy about that."

Aww, hell. She was here to have it out with him about what a giant jerk he was. He had never for a second doubted that she would catch his failure to reciprocate her declaration of love. He said quickly, "Will you give me a second to explain before you blow your stack at me?"

"Explain what?" she asked innocently. Way too innocently.

He winced and stepped forward to within arm's reach of her. "Go ahead. Slap me. Or slug me. Break my nose like you did Grundy's."

He stared at her, losing himself in the light, bright blue of her gaze, which wasn't giving away a blessed thing.

He braced himself as she took another step toward him. But then she did the darnedest thing. She wrapped her arms around his neck and pressed the entire slim, sexy length of her body against his. He wrapped his arms around her waist out of long habit, reveling in the way her body fit his. Beneath her uniform she felt more muscular than in the past, but still curvy and lithe. She wore being SEAL-fit well indeed.

"What is this?" he mumbled as she tilted her face up to his.

Her mouth captured his in a kiss, and he didn't question it. She was here, and she wanted him. That was plenty for him. More than he deserved. She mumbled, "Does it matter what this is?"

Actually, it did. But he wasn't sure he knew how to explain that to her. "Umm, Tate?"

"Hmm?"

"Uniforms aren't authorized on the *Easy Day*."

"Oh yeah? Whatcha gonna do about it?" she purred in a sultry voice that had his entire body tightening in anticipation.

He combed his fingers through her hair, pulling out the pins holding it up. It spilled over her shoulders like golden sunshine.

He reached for the flat buckle of her belt and snapped it open. "About last night..." he started.

She reached for the buttons on her blouse and popped them free from the top down, revealing a sexy white lace bra with her breasts practically spilling out of it and stealing from his mind whatever he'd been about to say.

"Day-umm," he murmured. "I never had any idea you women officers wore stuff like this under your blouses."

"Wait till you see what's under my skirt."

Under her... huh? He slid his hands around her waist to the skirt's zipper and eased it down. She stared at him in challenge, and he pushed the white fabric down over her hips, which she wiggled a little to help the skirt fall—or maybe to make his eyes roll back in his head, which they nearly did.

A thong. She was wearing nothing more than a tiny scrap of white lace under her sheer pantyhose that did more to reveal than conceal, more to tantalize than hide.

"Holy shit, Sherri."

"You were saying?"

"A thong under your uniform, Lieutenant Tate? Is that regulation Navy attire?"

"SEALs live to break rules," she muttered against his lips.

"Amen." He cupped her tush in his hands, loving the resilient spring of it.

What had he been saying? His mind was quickly turning to mush while his dick turned to stone. She stepped back, and he stepped forward until he'd trapped her against the wall. He kissed her neck, working his way up to her ear, sucking on the lobe and then swirling his tongue inside her ear and sweeping around its rim until she gasped. Whether she knew it or not, her body undulated a little against his.

There was something he had to say to her, had to remember. It was important—

She spoke instead, gratifyingly out of breath. "About what I said last night. I wanted to explain."

He lifted his head to stare down at her, his left hand braced beside her head. "Explain what?"

"You have to understand—"

He cupped her breast in his right hand, running the pad of his thumb across the rosy peak barely concealed by the flimsy lace. She drew in a sharp, quick breath.

But she still managed to say, "I had just spent over a week undergoing the worst sort of misery."

"I remember Hell Week vividly," he murmured, wedging a muscular thigh between hers. Her thighs clasped his convulsively, and her hips tilted as she rubbed her lady parts against his leg. He doubted she knew she was doing it, but it turned him on so hard he about exploded right there.

He fought to concentrate on what she was saying. "...you were my touchstone through the whole ordeal. Whenever I thought I couldn't take one more step or survive one more minute, I thought of you and of being with you when it was all over."

"Like this?" He slid his hand down the smooth, flat warmth of her belly and slipped his hand between her legs. Through nylon and lace, he rolled his fingertips across the swollen bud there, nestled between folds of velvet soft flesh. She inhaled sharply.

"Uhh, yes," she gasped, panting a little as he stroked the sensitive pearl. "During my, uhh, escape through the desert, uhh, when the heat got really bad, and I was, umm, dehydrated…" Her voice trailed off as she arched into his hand and cried out.

"You were saying?" he asked, smiling against the junction of her neck and shoulder.

"Right. There were times when I got kind of delirious. Might even have hallucinated some."

"That's normal under those conditions," he murmured, kissing his way across her jaw to capture her mouth. She kissed him back with abandon, derailed from whatever she'd been trying to say. *Mission accomplished.*

Her hands tugged at the bottom of his T-shirt, pushing it up between them, and he stepped back, grabbed the back of it, and dragged it over his head.

"Better," she declared.

He pulled her into his arms and spun her away from the galley, making it onto the stairs down to his stateroom before he got distracted again and ended up backing her against the wall, kissing both of them into a sexual haze.

Her leg wrapped round his hips, she tried again. "When the fight with the Russians was over and you hugged me, I said I loved you."

"I heard. And I—"

She cut him off before he could tell her he loved her back, pressing her hand over his mouth and speaking quickly. "It was just my exhaustion and relief and everything else I'd been through talking."

He froze. Pulled his head away from her hand to stare down at her in the dim passageway. *So this is breakup sex?*

She was denying that she loved him? Panic ripped through him, and he had to take several deep breaths to banish it. If he was going to make this right, if he was going to have to fight for his woman, he had to keep his wits about him.

"No, it wasn't just your exhaustion or relief talking," he said quietly.

"Of course it was. I was well beyond the limits of my endurance. I wasn't thinking. It just popped out."

"Truth has a way of doing that." His composure was fraying quickly. Must keep his head together and make her see reason. And the only way to do that was to stay calm. Be logical.

"But I wasn't in my right mind," she disagreed. "That's what I'm trying to tell you."

He swept her up in his arms and carried her the rest of the way down the stairs, depositing her on her feet beside his bed. He reached around behind her to pop open her bra hooks. The lace dropped away from her perfectly shaped breasts, which were possibly the most beautiful sight he'd ever seen. Desperation to make up for his colossal screwup coursed through him.

He hooked his index fingers under the bra straps and slipped them down her arms, dropping the garment to the floor. He kissed her deeply, pouring all of his feelings for her into that kiss. Trying to show her how he felt about her by worshipping her mouth, hell, worshipping all of her—body, mind, and soul. He relished the light peppermint taste of her, fresh and sweet. His head spun with the soft scent of her, the feel of her in his hands, the way her body fit against his. God. Now he was the one whose train of thought blew through his fingers and drifted away.

At length, she lifted her mouth away from his. "It didn't mean anything either time," she said woodenly. "It was stress talking—"

He cut across her words. "I'm going to have to call bullshit on that."

"*What?*" She pushed at his chest, and he stepped back from her.

Furious sparks snapped and crackled in her eyes as she glared at him. He shrugged and said, "People under extreme duress have a tendency to tell the truth. I think you *do* love me."

She opened her mouth angrily, the expression on her face hot.

He interrupted smoothly. "Go ahead. Deny it. But we both know the truth."

She let out an angry growl that was half scream.

"Ready to hit me now?" he challenged.

"Don't tempt me," she ground out.

"Why not? I deserve it. You'd make me feel considerably better if you just hauled off and walloped me."

Her anger seemed to stop dead in its tracks as she stared at him in surprise. "Why do you deserve a good wallop?"

He crowded her until she was forced to fall backward onto the mattress. He followed her down, bracing his hands on either side of her head, his knee between hers supporting his weight.

Her hair fanned out in a golden nimbus around her, and she looked like an angel—an angry one, but an angel nonetheless.

He spoke quietly. Honestly. "I panicked last night."

"You don't ever panic," she retorted.

He snorted. "Wanna bet? I lost my mind when we

figured out you were missing. And since *one* of us is being honest here, I'll admit that the idea of you walking away from me panics me. Particularly if I lose you because I lost my nerve."

"Go on." She stared up at him expectantly, waiting.

He sighed. He should've known she would make him spell out every last bit of it. "The SEAL rescue team was closing in on us fast, and I was afraid they were within earshot. If I'd said it back to you and someone heard me, not only my career, but everything *you* had worked and suffered for could have been ruined. I wasn't so much concerned about me as I was about you. In that split second, I took the coward's way out and didn't risk everything to tell you the truth."

"There's no one around to hear you now, Griffin. What *is* the truth?"

"Let me show you?"

She nodded.

Rather than rely on just his words, he quickly kicked off his swim trunks and rolled back to her, gathering her into his arms. Reaching between them to guide himself home, he entered her slowly, taking his sweet time. He savored the heated tightness of her body, the delicious friction of flesh on flesh, the way her eyes widened and darkened as he filled her, inch by mind-blowing inch.

As always, they fit perfectly. Their bodies started to move, finding unison immediately. Her strength called to his strength, his need to her need. It felt like coming home to be with her like this. Only here, with her, was he whole.

He looked down into her eyes, losing himself in their crystalline blue. It was like gazing into tropical waters, deceptively deep in their stunning clarity. She gazed back up at him, uncharacteristically serious.

Maybe she felt it, too. The past several days, frantically worrying that he'd lost her for good, had changed something deep inside him. He'd always known she was precious and special. But now he also knew she held his heart in her hands—and that he would never get it back.

Funny, but he was okay with that.

He murmured, "I already knew I was a goner for you, probably even before we left Camp Jarvis. But I didn't want to distract you from your training. And I wasn't ready to admit that I'd fallen for you. Hard."

She arched up against him, meeting his thrust with one of her own, seating him so deep inside her, he thought he'd touched eternity. He paused there, memorizing the sensation, staring down at the perfection of her in awe.

Then she moved impatiently beneath him, and he grinned, obliging her by setting up a steady, slow rhythm that she matched, thrust for slow, deep thrust.

"When you were missing," he continued, shivering a little as her internal muscles gripped him strongly, demanding more from him, "a piece of me was missing, too." He withdrew partway, and her calves tightened around his glutes, unwilling to let him go. Smiling a little, he gave her what she wanted and drove home.

He confessed, "When I thought I might never see you again, my world...ended."

"Mine, too," she whispered.

Their bodies moved as one in an urgent ride toward oblivion. Her arms were strong around his neck, her legs stronger around his hips. She held him like she never wanted to let him go, and he loved her back like he never wanted her to even think about letting go.

He showed her with his body that she was his whole world and prayed she felt the same. He held nothing back. He put it all on the line. His heart, his soul, his love. If she would have him, he was entirely hers.

Again and again he stroked into her, deeper and deeper until she was stretched as tight as a bow beneath him, waiting for the final arrow of release to fire.

All at once, his entire being exploded into orgasm, ripping him apart as he arched into her one last time, shouting hoarsely. Sherri met him halfway, crying out as she shuddered violently beneath him and around him.

He actually blacked out a little, so powerful were their mutual orgasms.

When he regained awareness of his surroundings, it dawned on him that he was crushing her, and that they were both breathing hard. He rolled onto his back, taking her with him. She sprawled across him bonelessly, her hair spilling across his chest in strands of gold. Lazily, he ran his fingers through its silken softness.

"Huh. You weren't wrong about people speaking the truth under duress," she commented.

"How's that?" He managed to form words to reply.

"Didn't you hear what you shouted just now?"

He frowned, reaching back through the fog of that epic orgasm to replay it in his mind. He started to chuckle. Then to laugh.

"Son of a bitch," he chortled as his laughter finally wound down.

Quickly, he reversed their positions, propping himself up on an elbow to stare down at her. "How about we try this one more time? And this time, when neither one of us is out of our mind with fear, or exhaustion, or orgasmic pleasure?"

"You first, Mr. Caldwell."

"My pleasure, Ms. Tate." He gazed down at her, drinking in her tousled beauty, so much sexier and more natural than her polished pageant self, and deciding he liked her exactly like this best of all.

He smiled, letting all the joy in his heart out and said, "I told you once you didn't have the heart of a SEAL."

"I remember," she murmured.

"I was twice wrong. Not only do *you* have the heart of a SEAL, you have the heart of *this* SEAL. I love you, Sherri. I'm yours. Every last scarred, beat-up, stupid-at-relationships, lousy-at-expressing-feelings bit of me."

Her smile was nothing short of otherworldly. "I love you, too, Griffin."

Sherri sat on deck watching the sun slip into the west, and a deep calm washed over her. This place, this moment, this man—they added up to a sense of happiness, of rightness, she doubted anything else in her life could ever top.

She consciously made a memory of this sunset. In the future, whenever she was far from home in a dangerous place, she would recall this exact moment and know that the world had good in it. Happiness.

Griffin emerged from the galley where he'd been cleaning up after grilling her the best steak she'd ever had. The man did know what a girl needed after Hell Week and a week from hell. He'd pulled on a pair of jeans slung low on his hips the way she liked them best, and his chest was bare. She would never tire of the sight of him like this, barefoot and sexy as hell.

He came to her chaise longue and reached down for her, drawing her to her feet. And then he did an odd thing. He went down on one knee before her. Washed in the crimson light of the setting sun, he looked like some sort of knight of olden times kneeling there.

"I have something for you, Sherri. I ordered it a while back, but I swore the day you went missing that I would give it to you when I found you, alive or dead."

"Well, that's morbid," she teased gently.

He smiled up at her, but his eyes remained serious. "I heard about the guys giving their Budweisers to you in the hearing this afternoon. The entire SEAL community is talking about it, and my phone has been blowing up over it."

She nodded, still humbled by the display. "It was overwhelming."

"It was well deserved," he said firmly.

She smiled down at him. It was nice to hear him say that out loud.

He continued, "I'm sorry I wasn't there to see it. But Cal asked me to stay away from your hearing."

"Why?" she blurted out.

"He knows me too well. And he saw how hard I freaked out when you went missing. He's no dummy, he knows how I feel about you. I think he was worried if the hearing didn't go your way, I would lose my cool and go after Duquesne."

"Would you have?" she asked, curious.

"Oh, hell to the yes. I know better than anyone how

much you deserve to be on the teams. You've earned every bit of it."

Warmth flowed through her at his ringing endorsement. And to think, he'd been the most determined of all to force her out of the SEALs. They'd come a long way, the two of them.

"Why are you down there on the floor?" she asked. "I'd much rather have you up here kissing me."

"Because I still haven't given you this." He held out a small black leather box.

She took it, smiled at him over it, and opened it.

She stared at the piece inside. She'd expected a Budweiser pin. But she was wrong. Oh, it was a SEAL insignia all right, but it was a ring. A bright-gold ring, with a tiny eagle clasping a miniature trident and flintlock in its talons, its delicate wings flying over a spectacular solitaire diamond.

"I know you can't marry me yet," Griffin said. "You have to finish BUD/S, and I have to go to Afghanistan and kill Haddad. But would you keep this with you as a promise ring? One day, I promise I'll come home, put it on your finger, and make you my wife."

She stared down at the ring and back at him. Tears blurred her vision until the man and the ring were one great, shining blob of joy.

"Yes, Griffin. I'll keep it. And I'll come home, too, put it on my finger, and marry you. And I'm holding you to your promise."

"Never fear. I'm all yours, Sherri Tate. Forever."

Laughing, he rose to his feet and gathered her in his arms for a glorious kiss, bathed in the last rays of the sun, to seal the deal.

Acknowledgments

My writing doesn't happen in a vacuum, and in fact, I rely on a number of friends and experts to fuel my work and keep me accurate. Unfortunately, the people I call on when I have a technical question about Special Forces missions or covert operations cannot be named here nor be publicly thanked for their invaluable assistance. Therefore, this will be an un-acknowledgement.

To the outstanding men and women who have patiently answered my questions or demonstrated some operational technique at the drop of a hat…thank you, thank you, thank you. You know who you are, and I'm grateful beyond words for your generosity. I'm also humbled that you trust me not to misuse sensitive information or endanger ongoing operations. I hope both my discretion and my stories live up to your faith in me. It's an honor to be allowed a glimpse into your world and share a bit of it with readers.

Here's a special sneak peek at the next book in Cindy Dees's Valkyrie Ops series

DIVING DEEP

Anna Marlow slipped inside Miss Mabel's Country Saloon and Dancehall, pausing to let her eyes adjust to the dim, neon light while the odors of stale beer and cigarette smoke assaulted her nose. The way she heard it, Miss Mabel was actually a fat, bald guy with roving hands and a taste for blondes. Sometimes, it was good to be dark-haired and caramel complected.

Where are you, Trev? What's got you hiding in a bar you despise?

She checked off faces, looking for the familiar features and tall, elegant physique. Sometimes in her fantasies about her Reaper teammate, Trevor Westbrook was a dashing spy or British nobleman. He certainly looked the part with his whiskey hair and cognac eyes.

Of course, he was significantly less civilized when it came to training with the rest of their U.S. Navy SEAL teammates. When the range went hot, he was a predator through and through.

One of these days, she would get cleared to go into the field for real. And then she could finally prove that SEAL training worked on a woman.

She scanned the line-dancing crowd shuffling back and forth on the wood-plank floor. Absently, she noted exits and obstacles, plotted egress routes, catalogued sight lines, and spotted potential hostiles. *Low threat environment.*

A Marine from nearby Camp Lejeune—if his high-and-tight haircut was any indication—veered away from her, looking vaguely alarmed. Whoops. She must be scowling harder than she'd realized.

Stand down, girlfriend. This isn't a mission. She'd been training non-stop for a solid year, and emerging from the world of hardcore SEAL operations into a real-world environment full of civilians like this was a shock to her system.

Trevor's vintage Dodge Charger was in the parking lot, so he was definitely here, somewhere. Where would a Trevor beast hide?

The telltale cluster of women caught her attention first, circling their target like agitated sharks. *Target acquired.* She headed for the feeding frenzy and spotted their quarry. *Tally ho.* Trevor was hunched over a beer on the last barstool at the end of the bar, scowling murderously. Not that it stopped the ladies from surrounding him in a tight flock. If they had any idea how dangerous he really was, they would be giving him a much wider berth.

She reached the group, a preponderance of blondes. One of them snapped, "Go find your own guy. This one's taken."

"Yeah. I know," she replied flatly. The complete lack of emotion in her voice apparently gave the woman pause. Or maybe the cold promise of bodily harm in Anna's eyes penetrated her alcohol induced fog. Either way, the woman fell back as Anna moved forward. *Splash one*.

The hovering women dispersed for the most part as she scowled her way through them. The next woman who put up resistance—a redhead—required a pretend-accidental hip check to move her aside.

"Hey!" she complained stubbornly.

When Anna gestured with her head for the woman to scram, the redhead grabbed her beer and beat a hasty retreat.

Trevor's head turned slowly, just far enough for one baleful golden eye to glare at her.

Grinning unrepentantly, Anna slid onto the stool next to him, vividly aware of how he towered over her. And she was no delicate flower, herself. "I cleared out the groupies, didn't I?"

"Thanks for nothing."

She waved an airy hand. "No thanks needed. I'm happy to run off the local talent. What are teammates for, after all?"

"You do realize I was going to get laid, tonight."

"Laid? With that bunch, you could've had a full-on Roman orgy."

He groaned. "Even more the opposite of thank you."

"You sound like you've never had an orgy. I thought you Brits were all super repressed in public but completely off the chain in private."

He glared into his beer glass, which was mostly full. Some of the Reapers drank more when they were upset, but Trevor went the other way. He tended to get quiet and withdraw into his own head when he was chewing on a problem.

What on earth was up with him? She'd heard him and Cal Kettering, the Reapers' commander, shouting in Cal's office earlier. What those two peas in a pod could be arguing about, she had no idea. But Trevor was her swim buddy, which, as she saw it, gave her every right to stick her nosy nose into his personal affairs.

"Wanna talk?" she asked over the din of country music twanging across the dance floor.

"About what?" he asked cautiously.

"Hey. It's me you're talking to. No need to be cagey about whatever's got you messed up enough to hang out at Mabel's."

He shrugged. "Can't talk here. Too many wagging ears. And besides, I'd much rather watch the wagging ass—"

Anna slapped a hand over his mouth. "Don't say it. I'd hate to have to kill you on behalf of my #metoo sisters."

"You're a me-too-er? Who was dumb enough to try assaulting *you*?" Trevor blurted.

She lied, "Are you kidding? I'd break any guy in half who messed with me." That might be true now, compliments of him and the other guys who'd trained her in unarmed combat. But it hadn't always been that way. As a girl, she'd gotten pretty before she got tough.

"By the way, you look…like a girl…rather…you look nice. Like, really nice."

He'd noticed? Suddenly, she was glad she'd taken time to put on mascara and a little lip gloss and to wear her hair down for once. Abashed, she mumbled, "Good recovery, there, Slick."

"May I buy you a drink?" he asked gallantly.

There he was. The for-public-consumption version of the urbane, sophisticated, British gentleman who never missed an etiquette beat. She answered politely, "I'll take whatever you're having."

"I'm drinking this piss water you Yanks call beer."

"Don't be dragging American beer, now," she retorted.

He lifted his glass to let the light behind the bar shine through the amber liquid. "It's not even the right color."

"It's better than that sludge you Brits call beer."

He snorted. "Lightweight."

"Call me that on the wrestling mat where you can put your money where your mouth is," she challenged.

His mouth quirked at one corner. "Big words, little girl. You prepared to back those up?"

She wasn't that little. And she was a world-class Crossfit™ athlete who'd spent a year training all day, every day, with Navy SEALs. Not too many women on earth could claim to be stronger than her.

"Any time, big guy," she shot back.

They fell silent while the bartender plunked a foam-topped glass of beer in front of her. She took a sip of the yeasty brew. Personally, she preferred whiskey, but Trev was buying, and she wasn't going to quibble over it.

"So, swim buddy of mine. You wanna tell me what you and Cal were yelling about earlier? He's mighty ticked off about it, whatever it was. He's been stomping around camp, muttering under his breath, ever since you left."

Trevor's entire face went tight and tense, which constituted a violent reaction from Mr. Always-in-Control.

The orange and yellow light from a beer sign overhead flickered across his face, licking his skin with neon flames and painting crimson highlights in his brown hair.

What in the heck had happened between him and Cal?

Both were career spec ops types, both had led their own squads, both were consummate professionals. After Griffin Caldwell had left to instruct out at BUD/S while Sherry Tate attended official SEAL training, Trevor had more or less stepped into the role of Cal's second-in-command...even though the Reapers were pretty casual about command structure in general.

With a definite note of desperation in his voice he pleaded, "Leave it alone. Please."

She snorted. "Have you met me?"

"Unfortunately, yes. I have."

"Ouch." She said it playfully, but his blunt retort hurt more than she wanted to let on.

"It's nothing personal, Anna. But you don't want to know what Cal and I talked about, today."

"You call what you two did talking? I could hear you from the barracks across the street."

He opened his mouth to answer, but a voice boomed behind her, making her jump.

"Yo, Trev!" their huge teammate, Axel "Axe" Adams, bellowed from a range of approximately two feet. Axel sported his usual biker garb—a sleeveless leather vest over a sweat-stained, heavy metal T-shirt, a thick, chrome chain hooked to his belt and disappearing into his front jeans pocket. He continued, bellowing, "Why aren't you out there dancing and scoping out chicks? It's a target rich environment, bro."

From behind Axel, Joaquin "Jojo" Romero piped up. "Cal told us specifically to blow off some steam, tonight. Have some fun. Loosen up a little. Does Trev look loose to you, Axe?"

"Naw, man. He looks some-kind-a tight to me."

"How tight would that be?" Jojo asked drolly.

The big man tilted his head, considering Trevor. "He's so tight I'd need a sledgehammer to drive a toothpick up his ass."

Trevor rolled his eyes as Jojo laughed and waved the bartender over. Leaning across the bar, Jojo shouted over the noise, "Have you got a half-decent single malt scotch back there?"

The bartender nodded.

"We'll need the bottle and a half-dozen shot glasses, then," Jojo shouted back.

A half-dozen? Anna's heart dropped. The whole team must be here. There went her intimate conversation with Trevor to convince him to open up to her. Dammit.

Trevor might be a natural extrovert, but he preferred to have serious conversations one-on-one. If the Reapers started drinking together, she would never get him to tell her what had gone down between him and Cal.

"C'mon, you two," Jojo shouted in her direction. "We've got a booth."

"You all go have fun!" Trevor shouted back. "I'm good here."

Well, hell. Now she would have to choose between hanging out with the team or staying here with Trevor, which would be a blatant invitation for the entire Scooby gang to harass them both about hooking up. And that would be a sure recipe for Trevor never to speak to her alone again.

She stood up reluctantly. To Trevor, she suggested lightly, "Come over and be social with the team. Maybe do like Jojo suggested and let your hair down a little. He is right; you do seem tense."

He opened his mouth, clearly intending to say no. Her heart dropped all the way to her feet in disappointment, and she mentally drop-kicked her stupid feelings as far away as she could punt them.

A little voice in the back of her head whispered that she was an idiot for harboring a secret crush on him. It was hopeless. He would never see her as anything other than one of the guys. At best, he might one day see her as a little sister. But nothing more.

Axel stepped around her and threw one of his massively muscled arms across Trevor's shoulders, dragging him off his bar stool by brute force and rumbling, "Nobody likes a party pooper, man."

Sympathy for Trevor stabbed her. It wasn't like anybody ever successfully said no to Axe. He would just pick you up and make you do what he wanted you to. She followed the two men as Axel cheerfully marched Trevor toward the opposite side of the saloon and the big booth Leo Lipinski and Lily Van Dyke were already sitting in.

Leo was the only married guy on the team, although his wife was still living in California and showed no signs of moving across the country to join him any time soon, here in North Carolina.

Lily was the other woman on the team and a great kid. An ex-gymnast, Lily was the smallest, quickest, and most agile of the three women Cal had chosen to be the first female SEALs. She came across as a sweet little thing, but she had steel in her.

Axel shoved Trevor at one of the bench seats, and the Brit staggered forward before regaining his balance. Anna shook her head. Trevor was six-feet of pure muscle, and Axe tossed him around like a rag doll. That guy was an ox. But he was their ox.

Axel gestured at her to slide into the banquette seat after Trevor, and she gulped.

They were colleagues. Just friends. She could do this. Keep it casual. Professional. Do *not* notice Trevor's muscular thigh only inches from hers or the way heat poured off of him to envelop her in the tight quarters of the booth.

Axel sat down, casually knocking her across the sticky vinyl and mashing her entire left side against the furnace that was Trevor. *Hello, sailor*.

"Sorry," she muttered in his general direction.

"No help for it," he replied dryly. "Axel's a mastiff who thinks he's a Chihuahua."

Jojo barked at Axel in a high-pitched yap from across the table. Axel wadded a napkin and threw it at Jojo, who snagged the paper missile neatly out of mid-air and sent it back at the bigger man.

Lily, wedged between Leo and Jojo, laughed and warned Axel, "Don't try to out-throw the Jo. He wasn't drafted by the NFL for nothing."

Axel snorted. "Puny human. I could crush him."

"Oh yeah, Hulk?" Jojo retorted. "Try me."

Axel half-rose, and Anna took advantage of the moment to claim a little more of the seat and slide a few inches away from Trevor. He threw her a sardonic, sidelong glance, but she studiously ignored it, picking up her shot glass and holding it out to Jojo. While she was at it, she grabbed one of the full shot glasses and slid it in front of Trevor.

He lifted the scotch, sniffed it appreciatively, and then tasted it. His eyes drifted closed in what looked like pure ecstasy. Wowsers. To make him do that in bed…to feel him lose herself in pleasure inside her—

It had been *way* too long since she'd had herself a man.

Jojo picked up his own shot glass. "A toast," he announced. "To Sherry Tate for finishing Phase Two of BUD/S. Here's to her finishing Phase Three."

Anna joined in the enthusiastic chorus of hooyahs. She was so damned proud of her sister-in-arms she could bust.

"Better her than me," Lily commented. "I'll take being trained by you meatheads over going through the formal BUD/S course any time."

Anna chimed in, "I'll drink to that."

Both of them were being trained extremely off the books, in a classified program called Operation Valkyrie, to be Navy SEALs. Meanwhile, their teammate, Sherri Tate, was being extremely publicly trained to be one.

The idea was for Sherri to be a highly visible, non-operational, poster child, and to draw all of the media attention away from Anna and Lily so the two of them could quietly become operational. They would be deployed without America's adversaries being any the wiser to the presence of women in the SEAL community.

But in talking with Sherry when she came up for air in the rare breaks in her rigorous schedule, it sounded like the guys at Coronado were training her for real. Instead of getting two actual women SEALs and a fake cover story, it looked like Cal Kettering was going to get three women SEALs out of the Valkyrie Ops program.

Because of their exceptional professionalism and general maturity, the Reapers had been specifically chosen to train and work with the first women SEALs. Which the guys in the platoon seemed to see as both a blessing and a curse. Women, because of their unique skill sets, would open up operational opportunities for the Reapers that no other SEAL team had. But…working with women.

It had been a big adjustment for all of them.

Trevor had been outspoken in favor of women Special Forces operators, particularly when they'd first arrived and the other guys had been skeptical. He'd argued that women would be a hell of a force multiplier and able to infiltrate areas of operation unavailable to male soldiers. Not to mention nobody, nowhere, knew to look for women operators. The ladies could slip under the radar in ways men couldn't.

Thankfully, Anna and the other women had proven him right so far. As they'd started running full combat simulations, the ladies were surprising everyone.

Jojo refilled everyone's glasses, and Lily lifted hers, saying, "To Sam and Kenny."

Trevor froze beside Anna. A wave of pain rolled off him so hard it slammed into her like a physical blow and was so intense it stole her breath away. Under the table, she touched his leg just above the knee, lightly, silently questioning if he was all right.

Sam Dorsey and Ken Singleton had been lost on a mission in a Pakistani hellhole called the Swat Valley. They'd been set up. Ambushed by a terrorist named Abu Haddad. Sam had died, and Kenny had been injured. When reinforcements arrived, Kenny had disappeared without a trace. Nobody knew what had happened to him. Which was almost worse than knowing he was dead.

Trevor and Kenny had been close friends. The way she heard it, Ken had adopted the British exchange officer when he'd first arrived and shown the new guy the ropes.

Below the table, warm, strong fingers gave her hand a quick, hard squeeze. Trevor's hand withdrew, coming up above the table to reach for his shot glass.

A somber mood enveloped everyone in the booth as they raised their glasses and clinked them together. Anna murmured, "To Sam's puppy dog smile and Ken's terrible country music lyrics."

Trevor added, "As my Irish grannie used to say, 'May they have been an hour in Heaven before the Devil knew they were dead'." The words were spoken lightly, but she heard the underlying grief. It was rare that he let out his real feelings, let alone ones as raw and painful as these. An urge to throw her arms around him and hug him nearly overcame her.

Leo leaned forward, his face grim. "To revenge." He'd also been on the disastrous mission where their brothers had been lost. And, he'd been a changed man since he came home, silent and angry.

Anna echoed Leo's toast along with the others. To revenge, indeed. Every one of them carried a mental bullet with Abu Haddad's name on it.

Trevor tossed back his scotch, and she caught the odd expression that crossed his face. Over the past year, she'd made a private hobby of studying him when he wasn't looking at her, or she probably wouldn't have noticed the faint flicker of…something.

Did it have to do with the shouting match earlier? She hadn't told any of the Reapers about Trevor and Cal's argument. Today was a liberty day, and she'd been the only team member on base this afternoon to hear it. She briefly debated bringing it up now, confident the rest of the team would bully him into fessing up to what had gone on in Cal's office.

But Trevor would not appreciate her airing his personal laundry in front of the others. Even if it was a known fact that SEAL teams had no secrets—both by operational necessity and by the stubborn, unrelenting meddling in one anothers' lives.

As the level in the bottle of scotch dropped, the joviality and insults around the table increased. Trevor faked enjoying himself beside her, laughing at the jokes and throwing out a few token insults of his own. But she definitely sensed his mood darkening as the evening progressed.

Weird. Trevor wasn't a mean drunk. He was the guy who always remained smoothly in control, charming and funny right up until the moment he passed out.

She finally leaned close enough to him to smell the expensive cologne he wore when off duty. His tanned neck was right there, all powerful muscles and tendons, ripe for the nibbling. His hair was short for a field operator at the moment, but still longer than military regulation length. Dark waves of it lay soft on his neck, tempting her to run her fingers through it.

She murmured in his ear, "What are you scowling so hard at your scotch for? What did it ever do to you?"

He jumped like she'd hit him with a taser. "Uhh, nothing," he mumbled. "I'm good."

"Well, I know you're good. But that doesn't answer my question. What's wrong?"

"Really. I'm fine."

"Really. That's bullshit," she retorted.

He exhaled in annoyance. "Fine. It's bullshit. I don't want to talk about it here."

"Fair enough. Let's go somewhere else where we can talk."

"Let's not," he replied sharply.

Dang it. She kept forgetting that the fantasy in her mind where he liked her back wasn't real. What was it going to take for him to trust her enough to open up?

"Let me out, Axe," he snapped.

Great. Now she'd scared him off. Who knew how many months it would be before he got over her practically licking his ear like that?

Axel slid out of the booth and she followed suit, mentally kicking herself every inch of the long slide. The second he had a clear escape route, Trevor bolted, practically running for the exit.

He hadn't handed off his car keys to anyone at the table, and she had a responsibility to make sure he didn't drive after drinking a lot. But, he obviously just wanted to get the hell away from her. Defeat crowded the back of her throat until she felt like she might choke. Or, perish the thought, cry.

Dismayed, she watched him go. To follow or not to follow?

COMING SPRING 2020

About the Author

New York Times and *USA Today* bestselling author of sixty books, two-time RITA award winner and five-time RITA finalist, Cindy Dees writes military romance and romantic suspense. A former U.S. Air Force pilot and part-time spy, she draws upon real-life experience to fuel her stories of love on the edge. When she's not heavily caffeinated and typing like a maniac, she can be found walking her Doberman Pinscher named Waffles, reading, cross-stitching, gardening, doing hot yoga, and traveling. She loves to chat with readers, and all her social media links are on her website cindydees.com.